SIN & ashes

Joseph S. Pulver, Sr.

Hippocampus Press

New York

Acknowledgments

"The Delirium of a Worm-Wizard" in *Nightscapes* No. 12 (December 1999) [online magazine].
"Kynothrabian Dirge" in *The Book of Eibon* (Chaosium, 2002).
"The Exorcism of Iagsat" in *The Book of Eibon* (Chaosium, 2002).
"Engravings" in *Black Wings: New Tales of Lovecraftian Horror* (PS Publishing, 2010).
"Scarlet Obeisance" in *The Tindalos Cycle* (Hippocampus Press, 2010).
"The Last Few Nights in a Life of Frost" in *Weird Fiction Review* (Centipede Press, 2010).

Published by Hippocampus Press
P.O. Box 641, New York, NY 10156.
http://www.hippocampuspress.com

Cover art by J. Karl Bogartte.
Cover design by Barbara Briggs Silbert.
Hippocampus Press logo designed by Anastasia Damianakos.

First Edition
1 3 5 7 9 8 6 4 2
ISBN 978-0-9844802-4-1

Contents

for ST.an Sargent

—my friend! !!, and one of the very BESTest!! !

Death's Head Blues

I was twenty-five when James Ellroy's *L.A. Confidential* did that thing to me Emily Dickinson spoke of—how you recognize poetry as poetry if it takes off the top of your head.

That mind-shearing moment. My head.

Discovering Ellroy was like discovering Philip Dick, Howard Lovecraft, and a gibbering lunatic Joyce, an unholy trinity, fused into one body, one flesh. Madness and horror and diabolism in its panoply of wicked splendor crawled from Ellroy's brain to mine. A man doesn't look upon Ellroy's blackly lustrous sights and walk away unscathed, his perspective unaffected. Such an experience brings on, as the song says, many changes.

Fifteen years later, I'm down at the crossroads gaping at the soul of one Joseph Pulver splashed across the page of this paean to the great human afflictions of love and lust, suffering and loss. Hope and its lack. Cowardice. Doubt. Treachery.

Yeah, I'm gawping in amazement, shaken by Pulver's eviscerating vision. He wields language as a scalpel, a Thompson submachine gun, an axe. *Sin & Ashes* is a wrecking ball. *Sin & Ashes* is also a paradox, a contradiction in terms. The music and the word. A dirge illuminating the monstrous and immense machinery of the underworld that ticks and whirs behind the screen, beneath the floor, inside the warm soft flesh of every lover, every murderer, every grinning scoundrel, every closeted saint. Torture is ecstasy. Insanity is order. Sorrow is the effect and love the cause.

Sin & Ashes. Sin & Ashes. Sin & Ashes. The collection takes off your head, all right. At the neck. Mr. Ellroy, please find your seat.

The maestro, the chronicler of doom and damnation, has a sip of single malt, a long drag from his cigarette. Clicks open the midnight blue violin case. Exhales a mouthful of smoke. He draws the bow, tests the string. His smile is a death's head smile.

There is a hush before the beginning of the dark night of the soul. An inhalation.

And then. It starts with sound, but deeper than sound. It originates in the blood. Resolves . . . to a human frequency. A man in a cheap motel talking in monotone on a black phone. A match head sizzling, a mystery woman's husky contralto whispering through the red-red O of a seductive smile she's practiced since Day One, Year Zero. Click-clack of bourbon and ice in a glass while somewhere ivories tinkle and *Casablanca* filters through velvet. Sam plays it while the lights go down and ghosts bump shoulders. Mystery man talking soft and low, talking, talking; mystery woman whispering, buttons slipping from her blouse. Snick of a revolver chamber dropping open, blunt-nose bullets sliding in; six potential invocations of Mr. Death. The wheel spins, snaps closed. Fizz and crackle of the VACANCY sign. It's murder. And then, and then. The sign flickers, off. Only the cold, dead moon.

It starts with a sound, but not just any sound. This vibration resonates from the deep, the lost places, below and beyond the subterranean, a whine like the first flea God made ever, something on the register where subatomic collisions occur, a feeling within roots and marrow that gradually rises through the scale until it arrives, blasting into your consciousness, lighting up your nerves Roman candle style, flash-pop white heat battery of paparazzi, crime reporters shooting corpses, electric chrysanthemum bulbs overloaded, neon jungle supernova, lonely bluesy wail of fallen angels blowing on their bleeding saxophones, their fiery trombones, leaves your brain circuits shorted, sparking, slagged. You're alone. We're *all* alone. And once again, it's too fucking quiet.

Joe Pulver calls down the fire. Joe Pulver's the Man. He's got the Power.

He summons the ghosts of Jim Thompson & Hunter S.; Bogart & Cagney; Robert Chambers & William Burroughs. The Great Old Ones, dead and dreaming in the Undying City, and their disciples who could have worshipped at the altar of Mammon, of Wall Street, or Las Vegas, just the same—because, don't you know, everybody worships the stars. Inspector Legrasse couldn't save us, so he orders another double on the rocks while a barfly with a bad peroxide job and worse makeup cozies up and slips her hand into his pocket. The blind jazzman grins and says he shot his woman down, shot her down, yes he shot his woman down. The blues go on and on, forever on. The stars go on turning on their axis of dark matter and nothingness.

The skull moon, devil moon, shines down, frigid, pitiless, oblivious to what evil lurks in the hearts of men. The melancholy music of the spheres plays for everyone, for no one, for the cockroaches and the dust.

Pulver walks through haunted valleys, across benighted plains. The badlands of the heart, its ruined boulevards and dark alleys, its decrepit palaces of pleasure gone to ruin, fields and forests laid to waste. The phantom realm filled with the cries of betrayed lovers and butchered swine, the lamentations of gamblers who rolled them bones and watched the eyes of the Ouroboros slowly open. A delirium from which those caught fast never wake.

Desert nights, coyotes on the prowl, streetwalkers on the strut, bag men, con men, grifters, forgotten gods, the damned. Black cars cruise Perdition's highway, or cracked blacktop of no name streets in no name towns, guided by the indifferent stars, dusty headlights, neon grills of a string of backwater bars. Rosy-fingered dawn, or maybe the lake of fire, is the light at the end of the tunnel. The punishment and the reward.

Burnt-out cigarettes and gun smoke. Spilled scotch. Spilled blood. A roll of bills soaked in that scotch, that blood, buys you easy love, simple comfort. But in the dark before the light, nothing is easy, everything's complicated, a cat's cradle on the cosmic scale, and comfort is as cold as a razor at your neck. Regret doesn't come cheap.

Joe Pulver's world is a little bit of heaven, a whole lot of hell. Just like ours.

—LAIRD BARRON

". . . its face was something glimpsed in nightmare. Just a glimpse, before the blinding blur of the knife blade, as it came down, again and again and again—"

—Robert Bloch, "A Toy For Juliette"

SIN & ashes

Love Her Madly

(For a light, Jim Morrison. Gone too soon.)

Each remembered the spot they'd last stood, or sat, or cried, or slept
... or loved ... Jim Morrison remembered idyllic, decadent Paris.
Sort of—*the Louvre, Île-St.-Loius, the Hôtel de Lauzum, La Coupole.*
Paris was the land of the poet. Picasso, Scott & Zelda, Wilde, Baude-
laire, Sartre, Rimbaud, they ate there, they drank and loved, and cried.
He, in his fashion, did no less. But that was then, this is now ...

Janis sat in the corner all beautiful and sad and child soft. The
bottle of Southern Comfort still empty, she'd drained it in life, but
she held on to it anyway. It was her security blanket. Around Pearl's
neck hung a boa, all black like the way she felt. The feathers were
like a million centipede legs walking all over her. Each leaving a stain
of sadness. A slow blues rang eternal in her ears.

And Jimi was there—half there anyway. Still dreamin'. But here
was starless and black as the cover of a bible. There wasn't any crying
wind, and there was no fire. He couldn't see the floor, let alone the
sky. Like Janis he just sat there. Dreamin' of rainbows.

Phil Ochs wasn't marchin' anymore, wasn't singing rebel songs
packed with the news either. He stood alone and mute in his retire-
ment into sorrow. Why sing? No one wanted to hear the news of the
failed Revolution, no one wanted to march toward brighter tomorrows. He shrugged his shoulder, then wiped a tear from his boyish
cheek. All these decades and still the chords of freedom did not ring
in Mississippi, nor—

Gram Parsons and Tim Buckley and Nico were there tucked
away in corners crying. Robert Johnson, Keith Moon, and John Bon-
ham were raising hell someplace else. Terry Kath, Sandy Denny, Len-
non, Felix Pappalardi, Steve Marriot, Rob Tyner, Zappa, Ricky
Nelson, and Jerry had gone on to Rapture.

Of the others left in oblivion's dungeon skirts of blackest, light-less black, nobody was having a hot time, or rockin' or jammin' or rai-sin' the roof or flying high above bass strings. Nobody sang about the body electric, or what they really wanted to do, or their back pages. In fact, nobody sang at all. Drummers didn't keep time, guitarists had lost their lines. Here, there were no seasons turning, or lazy sunny af-ternoons. And certainly no garden parties. It seemed this Forever—Desolation Row if ever there was one—never changed. In this land, Death had no mercy.

Morrison was there among the dead cats lost to their hopeless-ness, he was still waiting. But not stoned, not a rock. He might have had the blues, but he was too restless to just sit here like a ghost. He'd soared, passed The End, beyond the heartache and blue Sundays alone and the forests of night, beyond the perimeter, wanting to know things. He'd always wanted—needed—the answers. The curi-ous always do.

Though Jim couldn't see much in the Forever-gloom, he got up. He wasn't going to just sit here. No way. He wasn't gonna wait until tomorrow no more. So he left. Walked on down oblivion's vast hall. With that swagger—proud, with just a little drunk and a little sexy fire thrown in. Morrison had that mojo workin' in it. Walked passed, the silent winds and the crying beasts, right up to the Doors of Perception.

And there they stood. They were immense—imposing and grand—but then they had to be. Jim ran his hands over them. Never expected pearly, or inlaid with jewels, didn't think they'd be shim-mering fiery gold, or be covered with the symbols of any persuasion. Smooth as polished onyx and just as black, but they didn't open when he pushed on them. Wouldn't budge an inch. No way, no how. So Morrison screamed—"Hello!" Not quiet like no butterfly. No. He opened up. All the way. Like a crow twice the size of the moon he let it rip. Hung it right out there, loud enough to be heard in the broiling torture pits of Hell. But it never got that far. It only echoed in the starless hall like mocking laughter.

"Anybody home? *Awake?* ANYBODY ALIVE IN THERE?"

No sound. Not a rattle or a murmur.

"HEY! You listening?"

Jim had said it before. Years & years & years ago. But there he was just standing there with his petition on his lips.

He waited. Then he waited a bit more.

He ran his hand through his hair and looked around. He scuffed the toe of his boot on the floor before the great doors and looked up at them. Jim shook his head and smiled—a knowing smile. He knocked, knocked firm. And knocked again.

Then he waited.

Jim sang two lines from Smiley Lewis's "I Hear You Knocking." Smiled and laughed. Wasn't gettin' in all right.

Knocked again, a little firmer. Then drummed flat-palmed, just to let 'em know he wasn't going anywhere.

There was no answer. Morrison always suspected there wouldn't be one. Maybe he should knock again? Softer? Maybe no one could hear him? Maybe they were busy, or just gone? Morrison ran his fingers through his hair and looked at the doors. He cocked his head and considered them. Maybe he should start poundin' on 'em like some pissed-off riot cop? Didn't they say there'd be less problems on this side? And no troubles, and no cares? And no bullshit?

It took decades of wandering to get this far—here. Talk about purgatory. If this was infinity he wished he was still back there— back home among the living—back in L.A. At least the people there had something to look forward to.

Morrison sat with his back pressed to the doors. He laughed. If it took decades to get here, how long was he going to have to wait for them to open?

They'd said he was on a death trip. Maybe he was—*then*. But he was a seeker, like the poets of old, vibrant and committed and true, and he understood answers don't just walk up to your front door and ring the bell. No, you've got to stick your hands in right up to the elbows and root around, then you've got to grab it—even if it burns, and really look at it—even if it's blinding, and figure it out. Well, that's just what he was going to do. Figure this whole thing out.

❋

Under a clear blue sky, wide as all the miles of heaven, in the baked tan desert of New Mexico Dig-Her (& her & her & her—) was as unmoving as the two-story cactus just across the hot-as-an-oven macadam. He just stood there soaking up the rays. He was adding swelling water topped with great waves and the smell of salt to the blue warmth. He could smell hot dogs steamin' in beer—good beer, not that cheap over-priced horsepiss. He saw the guy in the bright white coat under the striped three-colored umbrella—"Give me two dogs with the works. Yeah, the works"—and he heard the girls laughing.

Yeah, the beaches. "Very-very-*very* cool," he whispered like a hot slow breeze.

The Beach was the livin'-end. A carnival of skin and colors under bright blue without rain. He reached out to the water. The rolling waves and foam crashing at his feet. Surfin'. That's what he wanted. Not that he knew how to, but he'd learn. Out there all the girls loved surfers. He'd learn, for them he'd learn, and they'd love him for it. For the girls.

Warm California girls. Every single, perfect one with golden hair and adoring perfect smiles. Sexy smiles just for him.

Only for him.

Dig-Her (& her & her & her—) closed his eyes and inhaled. It was all so sweet. So beautiful. He sighed.

He looked at the long road shining in the heat, his bridge to the West. West to freedom West to the Golden State of bounty and en-terprise. Out to where the sea met the land. He was headed out West to meet all the girls.

All his warm, waiting, California Girls.

✳

Twenty-five years—most murderers don't even do twenty-five years—Morrison had been on this mystery walk, not that time mat-tered here.

Morrison was full of anger, and suffering, and pain, and deep longings. But like all the great poets he was full of love; sometimes it touched people like a baby's smile, sometimes like a perfect after-noon. Sometimes it hit 'em like the truth.

That's what he'd always been looking for—the Truth. Wasn't here—least it wasn't answering the door. Jim needed to find the truth.

✳

The underage black girl was dancing—stripping, grinding away against the brass pole—to "The Wasp (Texas Radio and the Big

Beat)." Tommy Carter sat with his back to her. He took no pleasure in her plight. He knew about all the abuses; the fast lies and the dope and the pigbag creeps with their tattooed cocks and their fists. He knew all about the diseases, and the early, violent deaths. He'd seen more than a few. He remembered their bodies, just lying there, finally—sadly—quiet, in cathedrals of booze and needles. He knew all about the girls. Seen 'em with cocks rammed up their asses, or jammed down their throats for a slice of thin green. Knew about the two kids waitin' at home.

Fuckin' L.A. All sunshine, all the time. That's what they said. They had it ass backwards. All pain, all the time. All pain.

Tommy Carter thought this was a strange selection to peel to, but he really, really loved Morrison & the Doors as a kid and took pleasure in hearing one of his old favorites.

"Damn! Morrison could sing." He had the power. Didn't ever hold back. Not one iota. And Manzarek was like the sunshine on the blue surf. He just carried it along. Gave it color and drama. Jim made you stand up and take notice of the surging wave, Ray made you want to dive right in. And Johnny, well, he was the kind of heartbeat every kid had—strong and energetic. Robby was the perfect counterpoint to it all. Subtle. Always so subtle, even with the fuzz and the urgency.

"Damn. They were great. They really had it."

Tommy Carter sipped his draft and waited.

"Midnight Jack" Gaines came in Danny's Glitterdome all the time to scout new talent for his stable. Word had it he was running a new op, and his "oldest" girl was still months away from sixteen, but only days away from her fourth abortion.

Tommy Carter wanted to bust his ass bigtime. Right after he kicked it up and down Sunset for a week or two. But that would have to wait. Carter needed information. Needed it badly. And right now that "halfass-sleaze" "Midnight Jack" was probably the only guy in L.A. who knew where to find Cesar Hidalgo.

"Gang shit. Wastin' each other, and the innocents."

Tommy Carter saw it every day. Too much of it: three-year-old babies ripped up by stray fire; single mothers getting gang-raped on their way home from long hours for horseshit wages; Crackheads figuring what's the difference—at least for a second things were cool; the poor, hopelessly adrift and homeless; twenty-two-year-old women with their heads caved in, the contents of their stomachs, greasy fries and sperm—"Some last supper"; eleven- & twelve-year-old kids thrown out on to the violent streets, out there alone selling their bodies—their souls—to eat scraps, or just to stay alive.

"Dear sweet Jesus, what's it all come to?" *And why? Hey, you listenin'? What about the elderly? They're scared to death. And worse.*

So much worse.

L.A. was a strange world; nowadays more than ever. The vampires and the midnight ghoulies—they shoulda stayed in their coffins. But no. They were out haunting every night; full moon or no moon. & the Skinheads & the Crazies & the Crackheads & the Crips & the Bloods & the Latinos & the Losers—all rubbin' elbows and knuckles up against each other. White Power (White Lies was more like it!) & Black Power & Political Power (oughta call it horrifically deep corruption, theft, and just plain rape) & Law and Order & one con after a stream of bullshit, all sittin' on top of another lie (Shit. They didn't even put a cherry up on top.) . . . Factions, sects, pockets of bottled-up-tight dissention, each with a razzle-dazzle spin and a violent agenda. One gasoline, one fire. All real dynamite.

Violence it was in the air, in the food, in just about every eye. These days Hell opened her doors (or legs if you had the scratch) every night on the streets of L.A.

Shit. Even his brother cops, or some of 'em anyway, were runnin' their games: pushin' blow and crack, musclin' the pimps (and the hookers for freebies and cash), or just scarin' the shit out of anyone and everyone.

L. A. was one big con. One big sprawled-out mess of murder and madness, just waitin' for the trumpet to blow.

'Course they were all living on the fault line, and maybe, just maybe, every once in a while you couldn't blame 'em. They might lose it all, or they might not be here in the morning. So what the hell? Go ahead! Blow off a little steam, but use a little moderation. Just once. Please.

Miss Silicone Superstructures bounced over with her cherry red for-25-I'll-suck-it-clean-collagen lips and asked Tommy if he was ready for his third of the four-drinks-@-750-a-pop-minimum.

"Sure. But try to find one that's cold this time."

"Don't you like it hot, Daddy?" She smiled and licked her lips.

"Used to."

She walked away with a booty-shakin' swing that would have popped tires (& a few other things).

Ain't a day over seventeen. And I ain't been seventeen since Morrison died.

"The Wasp (Texas Radio and the Big Beat)" stopped and the next dancer came on. Tommy looked around for "Midnight Jack," who was still a no-show. The sleazebag better show up soon or he was going to kick his ass up and down the block—twice! Tommy looked at the new stripper for all of two seconds. More of the same; long legs that went right up to her belly button, beefed-ups lips and tits, and a smile that said she was willing to polish your knob or straighten out your kink as long as the price was right.

Tommy thought about retiring. Maybe someplace where they had wild horses and colorful birds (the ones with bright feathered wings and sweet songs), and green forests and chipmunks runnin' around, and only one McDonald's, and where people lived with what God and their parents gave 'em.

Was there such a place outside of his dreams? If he was a betting man, and he wasn't, he was as certain as hell it didn't exist. Especially in California.

Cherry-Red came back with a draft and scooped up a ten. "Thanks for the tip, Daddy." Another weak smile.

$2.50 for half a smile? Christ, she didn't even graze his arm with one of those made-to-order supertits. This whole fuckin' place was a con. Everybody in East Jesus, Kansas, thought it was just Hollywood—the glitter, the stars, the fortunes won or lost on looks or connections, the broken dreams—but it was the whole damn city. You breathed it in just like the smog. Or you died.

Tommy Carter sipped his draft. No wonder Dennis Miller came on every Friday night and went into a rant; he had to or he'd go nuts with all this shit flying around. Tommy lit a Kool and went back to watching the door.

❖

Dig-Her (& her & her & her—) hadn't taken a human life since his waltz across Texas. But he was racking up dead lizards. Figured he was nailing about one a mile. He had a couple of snakes too. They rattled and fell silent. The lizards he took more time with. Some were fast, some slow. He liked the fast ones best. Thought of their speed as fear.

Two hot miles of treading blacktop back he wished he had a gun. The occasional passing bird had caught his eye. Shootin' 'em out of the sky, watching their metal-winged freeflight into hell's pavement, would have been a great pleasure. But he had the rocks, some sharp, some blunt and heavy & sticks & a lighter & his knife. Life was good. And he had his Western Dream: L.A. The place would be bustling with life: girls, and food, and lights, and girls, and fast hot cars, and girls, and ice-cold beer, and girls—

Dig-Her (& her & her & her—) looked down the open road. He heard the singin' call. Heard it loud and clear.

RightLeft. RightLeft. RightLeft—Dig-Her (& her & her & her—) eased on down the road. Off to his right he saw a gila monster, smashed its head in with a rock. He liked the fast lizards best . . .

✴

Each romantic—talented, tragic, burned by the commercial—steps from the living theater and there it is. Morrison had escaped, but to where? This boring black, crowded with excessive fools and frightened children. Christ, they'd all forgotten how to howl, how to tear it up. They'd forgotten the pleas and the rage and every sweet, wanton song of love. How? Morrison hadn't forgotten. Twenty-five years on he remembered every detail, at least the ones he was there for. *The girl in the red dress . . . The day in the desert . . . The sounds . . . Ray's smile . . . Hearing the first single on the radio . . . He remembered the Indian, he remembered what it felt like to touch the Earth, to smell hyacinths and utter curses. He remembered The Whiskey and all the poetry he'd never set down . . . Glory days.*

Jim wasn't sure why he was sittin' here waitin'. For what? Judgment Day? Seemed to him he already had his. His curiosity pushed him on. The way a big old blustery wind filled with scents & sounds & flittin' at the edge of light possibilities pushes on the instincts of a prowling tomcat. It got down in his feet.

He stood, then paced. Looked at the doors. "Aw, Christ." He was a thinker, Nietzsche had taught him that; how to get on with it, move on and beyond it, break on through. "This is a waste."

Time to walk the walk. He had to get back. Tell all the people to straighten it out and live & love & enjoy it while it lasted. Yep. He was going to tell 'em there was no Greener Grass.

Somewhere high over New Mexico and every other place on Earth, Morrison's boots walked the star roads. He wasn't sure, but he thought he was headed west. Home. Right back to that beautiful, bustlin' night-time carnival. L.A.—

✦

Dig-Her (& her & her & her—) left two young women gutted like fish in New Mexico. One, nearly headless, he tried to fuck. Couldn't get it up. "Stupid fuckin' worthless bitch-cunt!" He kicked her in the abdomen and yelled it over and over and over.

The other he'd sodomized after she was dead. He sat her head between her collar bones as he rammed it right in & rammed it right in & rammed it right in & rammed it right in & rammed it right in— right into her deeply tanned ass. The adoration in her unfocused eyes was the most beautiful sight he'd ever seen. God, she was sexy. He wished he could've kept the head and those beautiful, beautiful eyes, but he knew he couldn't, so he kissed her open lips and moved along.

✦

It was funny, just a small-town boy from West Virginia and after four days moving through this desert and he was starting to like it. There was something about the cactus, and the colors of sunset were beautiful. Reds and pinks and purples unlike any others. And when the light had bled away, the night was filled with stars—he couldn't believe how many there were. It was really the wide open spaces and God really did have a way with things. Some things anyway. It was just people that spoiled it. Stupid, tight-assed, greedy people, they wanted and they took and they didn't give a shit about what kind of mess they left behind. He had reason, and purpose, they just had de-sire— They weren't worth shit.

There were six cactus on the hill of spilt rock and sand. Six tall fingers reaching toward heaven. He admired the strange wonderland in moonlight. Nothing here seemed wicked or ugly. It all made sense.

It was easy to be in control here.

But then a car with a girl driving passed and he had a ride and the radio blared and she babbled on and he felt it all rise up inside and he gave it its freedom and watched her surrender. Bloodwork was like painting; inspiration followed by realization. He wondered if anyone ever got the chance to admire his art, decided he didn't really care. He parked the car behind the hill of spilt rock and sand. He wiped his hands and the blade of the knife on her print skirt and slept in the back seat. Dig-Her (& her & her & her—) dreamed of California and warm beautiful girls smiling.

In the morning he put her ring—his sixth memento—in his watch pocket and buried her in the sand. Not deep. If the animals got her, well they had to eat too . . . Then he walked back to the road. Two miles and a snake later he saw the beer bottles and the cigarette butts. "Stupid, dirty, lazy-ass people. Ain't worth shit." He marched west. The sky was picture-perfect blue with white puffy clouds. He began to add water and rushing salt foam and the sound of laughing, adoring girls—

❋

Clare looked out at the waves topped with surfers. Today was a perfect day. Nothin' on her card but the next wave and the rest of the day's sunshine. She thought about getting a hot dog and a Coke— "Maybe later." She went back to watching the tall brunette with the skull & roses tattoo and the fluorescent green board. He moved like liquid lightning.

Maybe this one her Dad wouldn't mind, Dad liked the Dead, played their CDs all the time. Drove Mom right outta her skull. Mom had moved beyond the Dead and the Beach Boys and the '60s. Once Dad's jacket & tie came off he hot-footed in right back to Dreamland—he talked about the concerts (and sometimes the rallies turned riots) and meeting Mom in college and singing "Hello, I Love You" to her one night in a bar, and wishing he'd been at Woodstock—not that he did drugs anymore, but he still loved the music. That's how Clare had picked up on the Doors. Dad loved the Doors; had every CD, and still refused to part with his old LPs. He loved to tell her about when he saw the Doors in concert. And slowly Clare succumbed to Jim & Ray & Robby & John. Dad was so overjoyed he popped in Tower and bought her her own copies of every disc, and a poster he really liked, which Mom had—in her gently authoritative Mom-way—told him not to buy.

Jen in her cheap white sunglasses and near-perfect figure plopped down on the towel. "Which specimen do you like?"

Clare smiled. Jen was always shopping; clothes, boys. Jen had it all and wasn't shy. Clare would trade two years growth or 10 IQ points not to be shy. She pointed at the surfer boy she'd been observing.

"Nice pick," Jen said.

"I try."

They both laughed.

"Your dad's going to love the tattoos."

"At least they could talk about the Dead. After Jeff, I think he'll go for almost anybody that looks like they wouldn't burst into flames if they stepped into the sunlight."

"Coffin-Boy, pleeeease."

Another round of laughter.

"I seem to recall you picking a winner or two."

"Blame it on my youth, or rebellion."

Clare wondered what either of them had to rebel against. At seventeen they had clothes, and cars, and nice homes, and good skin, and Thank God, parents you could talk to. They both got good grades without much effort, and didn't get dragged down into a lot of social BS. Life was pretty good. Sometimes boring, but pretty good.

The gulls made slow, bored circles . . .

❀

All the needles and the crack and they were fuckin' with this new plague, straight up, no condoms. Poke poke poke and you had it. And when you went out on a weekend bender you passed it on . . . Death had no mercy, not in L.A. Death wanted to fuck you right in the ass—BIGTIME!

Morrison was pissed, someone had fucked up L.A. His L.A. All this grime choked the hope right outta everyone. Proud Black reaching for the Dream had become Nigga out on a suicide drive. Translucent kids were dry, too full of been-down-so-low to look up or think about standing up. There was a ton of this-will-make-you-a-fortune and celebrity-is-somebody. If you survived the slaughter of your Welcome to the Jungle and the noise of the drums didn't fuck you up you might get to watch, but if you touched the wrong thigh or the wrong pile of MINE! you'd be a dead kid. Go ahead take a hit off the Storm . . . Yeah, Morrison was pissed. The ceremony of breathing and living and shaking dreams from the sun had turned into this? He saw it—racing and mad and buzzing in and over and around everything, but hoped he was wrong . . . Fuck this! He was gonna turn it around. Come Hell or whatever else they parked in his way. Morrison had had too much Darkness, he was sick of it, the doubt, the wild rot, all the destinies and kites soaked in wanton blood, he was gonna turn on the Light . . .

Morrison wished he had a cigarette. "All you ultraviolent vampires thickening Babylon in crude-chickenshit hardcore take note—WAKE UP, ASSHOLES, the Lion Hunter has come home."

The sun went down on L.A. and Morrison walked the streets . . .

❦

She was funny and fresh-faced, and this was The Day. "It all starts here," she said. "I've got all this stuff and so many others have nothing, not even hope." *I'm going to save the world. I'll start after breakfast.*

Clare had just seen Al Gore's global warming commercial and thought Save The Planet, Save The People. Do good work, be straight with people . . .

If I were the President I'd show them how . . . So much seems stale and wrong. Mom's a leader and an organizer and a caretaker. Just what the people need to free them from all the rust and crime, maybe even fix the planet. It would be good to have a woman president . . .

❦

It was all a fucked-up mess. The whole place drippin' with rusty cars and curbs that were living rooms where people tossed their ratty old sofas, beer cans, and cockfights, stucco till you were dumb with it, pools filled with personal problems, every dark or blue thought dyin' a little every day, every beautiful, unhappy hand reaching for the keys, everything in sight grinding and overlapping, everyone clawing to get to the top of the heap . . . He made a wrong turn. Where was the Blue? And the clean girls and the crystal waves?

In the City of Angels and not a clean heart in sight.

Dig-Her (& her & her & her—) thought L.A. would be Hollywood, all the gold just sitting there if you put your hand out. And the Beach would be Surf Heaven, all the girls just waiting there if you put your hand out. All he got, saw, was bullshit and junk. And weeds. Fucking things found every little crack and settled in for the long haul.

Outside a bank with a mural that hit you like a crowbar forged with Fuck You Motherfucker there were weeds and a girl. Not fresh, but not beaten with too many requiems and too much of living the HARD life. Blonde, smooth curves—not too fat, not too Hollywood celebrity skinny, right height, he liked them half a head shorter than him, and she was standing there waiting.

She must be one of The Ones.

They were waiting for him. He knew it. That's why he came here.

But she wasn't. He left her in an alley. Opened her up and looked at the meat and the shame. Nothing fresh. Nothing clean. He wanted clean. Fresh. Wanted them to fall in love with him and then fuck like crazy. And he wasn't going to pay. Maybe for dinner when his ship came in, but not for a blowjob in some alley.

Dig-Her (& her & her & her—) made his way to the beach . . .

❋

Tommy looked at the body. Fuckin' Jack-the-Ripper bullshit. Why can't these psycho-ratbags stay in Kansas or Georgia?

"Somebody signed her guestbook in red ink."

"Yeah. Probably a dispute over the quality of the blowjob," Tommy said.

"You ever wonder how many dipshits we've got in this town?"

Tommy half laughed. "The big brains over at Northridge can't even count that high . . . This ain't yer common fucked-up street shit. This fuck likes his work. She's just the one that popped his cherry."

"I liked to cram a couple of rounds up this fuck's ass."

"Get in line. I'm first. This one's goin' outside and there ain't no door to get back in." Carter said.

He was sick of being the nightmare detective . . .

Tommy wished he was seventeen again. Seventeen and not not buried neck deep in two-minute dramas that ended in requiems. Seventeen and listening to The Doors swim to the moon, right there climbing up to top with them. Seventeen and far away from these strange days of freak shows and next mornings emptied and the meat-eaters home eatin' donuts.

Tommy looked in the dead eyes of the dead girl. The music's over and someone turned out her light . . . All these lost, unhappy little girls forced to play hard games, to scratch through if they can. L.A.'s a fuckin' prison. We lock the lambs up with the monsters on streets and take away their prayers. Who the fuck are they supposed to petition? God took his music home . . . And we're fucked . . . Time for six beers and a few pairs of shots.

"Bag her and sent me the report, will ya, Doc?"

There was a bar called The End around the corner. Tommy headed in that direction . . . Fuck, he might even have a burrito for lunch.

❋

Seven nights and seven days Morrison had walked around L.A. Saw everything . . . Made him sick. The shitstorm had come—in full force. Raped the Earth, raped every soul, raped the dawn, buried in under years of NOW and ME! NO ME! FUCK YOU, ME!

Jim decided if anyone was going to save this mess he was the man. He come back from Death, so how hard could it be to set things right?

First he'd need to get the music started again.

That would turn the lights on . . .

Time to put a little inspiring color back in the tapestry.

Morrison looked down at all the beer cans in the curb, he wondered if there were beer cans on the moon these days. He should have looked when he passed by last week.

A dead rat, beer cans, and condoms, and a heavily scared crackwhore with cum-AIDS breath sleeping against the curb. Stolen shopping carts with bent wheels headed for the other alley, where maybe the imitation-Jack or Mad Dog was smoother going down. Yeah, the world was fucked. But Morrison had seen the bottom before . . .

And he'd gotten up.

He was going to go back to the beach and sit in the sand and figure this out . . .

✦

Venice Beach. The poster hit Dig-Her (& her & her & her—) like a winning Lotto ticket. There it was. All of it, just like he imagined. All the California Girls in bikinis, the open big blue sky, the waves ... There'd be the hot dog stand with cold lemonade and maybe ice cream. Two-dimensional today, but tomorrow his carnival of fun would be there full size and summer bright, waiting ... Ready to run to him.

Dig-Her (& her & her & her—) was adding water, palm trees, and a lot more girls (sexy smiles just for him)—mostly blondes, but some with dark hair for flavor. He smiled and started taking out the men. "Very-very-*very* cool," he whispered like a hot slow breeze.

"You're perfect," he said to the young girl in the poster. "Baby, my eyes have adored you. I'm coming." *And I know you're ready.* "See you tomorrow."

✦

Jen called and canceled. Clare would be a solo beach babe today. Maybe the towel with the soft, wide blue stripes over by the pier in Venice, maybe a hot dog. Maybe she'd meet someone nice ...

✦

Tommy Carter wanted a day off, so he took one, called in sick. Sick of it all. He was going to watch a few beautiful girls in Morrison's old haunts. Maybe hot dogs for lunch ... Maybe have a cold one in the shade near the Pier. Maybe just stroll around like Morrison used to do ... Fuck all the strange bedfellows on slabs. Fuck all the dramas in this shitty erotic prison. Just bring on a few hours of blue skies and quiet and maybe a pretty smile with pretty eyes ... Someone nice.

✦

Midnight and yesterday made passages in the shadows. The moments wound from now to once. Morrison spent the night sitting on the beach, the tango of the Milky Way an umbrella above, the waves at his feet. Bare feet, he couldn't remember the last time he felt this calm, this good. Everyone should be free of the ghost dance and the curses of Babylon. Everyone should have it this good. An hour of freedom, no blues, nothing loud, no stupidity, no knuckles, no guns barking pain, just

one filled with the soothing poetry of the world. No TV, not even radio, just the sound of the waves and the poetry of one's own heart.

It had been a long time since he'd sang his songs of innocence and
experience, but not so long his hands couldn't still grip the poetry . . .
There was still a little color in the tapestry, still some gentle laughter,
enough to weave with. All the people out there were still waiting for
summer rain. He would be the rainmaker . . .

Morrison was home. And when dawn came he was going to
smile and say hi . . . Maybe he'd meet someone nice.

❋

Tommy walked west on Horizon and hit the Boardwalk almost
perfect center. There was a crowd, a forest brightly feathered. He felt
sixteen again, all the color of a new language waiting to be learned,
experienced. His smile was his first word.

How many times did Morrison stand here and smile? he wondered.
*How many times did he open up to the sun and the color? . . . Look at
'em, Morrison. They're awake. And they have stars in their hair. Man,
I wish you were here to see this.*

Beyond the Bike Path there was a red kite with a yellow tail soaring. Girls and women and children and men on rollerskates and dogs
splashing in and out of the waves. This was Summer, luck and gold
grinning on the breeze.

❋

Dig-Her (& her & her & her—), unmoving, just standing there
soaking up the rays. He didn't need to add water and the smell of salt
to the blue warmth. He could smell hot dogs steamin' in beer. He
saw the guy in the bright white coat under the striped three-colored
umbrella . . . And he heard girls laughing.

"Very-very-*very* cool."

Then he saw her . . . the perfect California beach angel, pretty,
just the right curves, blonde, young, 500-watt smile, long legs with a
light tan.

"Very-very-*very* hot."

❋

The clouds sang and made moving pictures in the blue above. Morrison smiled his approval.

Back, baby. Back . . . And I dig it.

He heard a young man's voice laugh and turned into it. Proud, intelligent, handsome, Morrison flashed on a memory of Ray. Beaming, tapped into the energy, he was a gift. John and Robbie too.

We did light a few fires. Maybe if I hadn't fucked things up . . . Fuckin' booze.

And right there under a cloud changing from wild horses running to a ship with sails unfurled Morrison decided he needed to find Ray and Robbie and John. Needed to apologize, needed their forgiveness.

Tomorrow he'd go looking for them. He was here to fix things. Starting at home seemed natural.

He stretched. Felt the sun. Turned to look at the people. There was a man, the right age—he'd have been just coming of age when they played The Whiskey, on the boardwalk. Just standing there smiling, Summer, luck and gold grinning.

That's what it's all about.

And there was a young girl, just coming of age. Her smile and her eyes told him she wanted to share the gifts of this life with all the people.

She's got it. Gonna take it somewhere too. There's still things here to work with. The music's not over. Not yet.

❖

The sun was slipping into the waves. Tommy's shoulders slumped. The end of a near perfect day. A few beers, a few hot dogs, and a ton of pretty girls. Not one fuckin' murder, no batteries, no rapes, no little old ladies shoved to the concrete for $14.68. It was the first day in a year he didn't have a headache. He lit a smoke and wished there was a rewind button.

Fuckin' Bill Murray. Gets to go back and do it over. That's about all I want. Do it over again . . .

Fuck. That's guy's a ringer for Jim Morrison. Christ, looks more like him than Kilmer did. Strange, a guy like that here . . . Morrison was right, world's a strange place. But it ain't all bad. Not when you can squeeze a day like this out of it.

Clare was stowing her stuff in the trunk when the hand clamped over her mouth. There was a hard arm around her waist. A knife was in its hand. Pressed to her belly.

"Say a fucking word and I gut you right here. Nod if you understand."

"Good. Now you and me we're gonna have a little fun. Goin' right over there, past the dunes and play beach blanket fuckee-fuckee."

"I've been watching you all day— You got a great ass and I'm gonna go surfin'. You and me we're gonna make waves."

A nasty low laugh full of venom. Dig-Her (& her & her & her—) kissed the back of her neck, licked the bottom of Clare's ear lobe.

She wanted to scream, but the promise of the knife kept her quiet. In full panic mode she was desperate to sort out the flood of images and thoughts assaulting her.

Wait, damn it. Just get through—that's what they say. Just get through. Nothing stupid—nothing stupid. If you get an opening, run. But get through it.

"You smell nice. *I wanted to fuck you the moment I saw you.*"

"You play nice you live. You fuck up and the music's over. Now walk."

She'd forgotten the rules. Wasn't watching. Was too caught up in the quiet joy of a peaceful sunny day. She'd parked too close to the trees and the brush. This was normally a safe place. But there were lurkers everywhere. You had to watch.

She had forgotten to watch.

They were in the grass behind the dunes. Dig-Her (& her & her & her—) pressed the blade to her throat. He was in her. Saw the blood.

"Motherfuckin' jackpot pussy. First time. You are one lucky little super-tight pussy, got Old Dig-Her to play can opener."

Racked by pain and shame and self-anger, Clare slipped. Screamed.

The blade tore across her neck.

"Told you, Bitch." But Dig-Her (& her & her & her—) didn't stop. Not this close. He'd fucked the dead before and never a virgin. He was high.

Tommy heard the scream and was lightning. At the top of the dune he took it all in—the gash in the girl's throat, the knife, the triumphant savagery on the monster's face. His gun was out. The first shot put a hole in Dig-Her (& her & her & her—)'s temple. The second ripped him off the dying girl.

Tommy was on his knees. Clare was bleeding out. She was a goner.

And Morrison was there. On his knees. He looked at Tommy.

Clare was gone.

Morrison closed his eyes, folded in on himself. Started walking, following the warm imprint Clare left. She wasn't far ahead.

Then he was beside her. His hand in her hand.

"Not yet, Clare. There's things need to be done. *By you.* It's not time. Not yet."

And she followed Morrison.

Morrison's hands came away from Clare's throat. No wound.

"What the fuck?"

"How in—"

"I learned a few things in the desert on the Other Side, Tommy," Morrison said to Tommy.

"But."

"I'm not sure I understand it myself, but I came back. I think saving her was the main reason . . . She's a lamp. Like Martin Luther King she will shine a light in the darkness and the people will be better for it. Don't ask why. It is what it is. Simple as that."

"Are you?"

"Yeah. Still me. Just got over the storm is all."

"Morrison."

Jim smiled. *Yeah, laid my storm to rest.*

"C'mon, Clare, time for you to go home," Jim said. "You're whole again. Go and tell the people after the storm there is light. Be their light. That's why you're here."

Morrison and Tommy put Clare in her car. Watched her drive away.

"I still don't understand."

"You will. You will.'

"C'mon, there's a few things in the desert I want you to see before we begin."

"Begin? We?"

"We've a few fires to light."

✷

Jim was singing "Waiting for the Sun." Clare sang along with the CD.

"I love you," she said to a poster of Morrison on her wall over her bed.

"Love you too, sweetheart."

Jim's standing in her bedroom by the open window. He smiles and lights up the room. Clare's beams back.

Almost laughs to see a poster of himself on the wall. On her desk sits every Doors CD.

"That's not my favorite shot of me. Never was."

Jim walks to her dresser and picks up a pen, turns to the poster. With the wave of a magic hand he autographs it and draws a mustache on his face. Writes Clare Gets My Vote.

"Kinda dashing, don't you think?'

"I know you don't understand it yet, but we're both here for a reason. Do good work. Be true to the music."

"I will. I'll try."

Jim laughs softly, gently. "I see your future. You'll do more than try. Trust me."

"I've got somewhere to be. There's a shaman-in-training and we have an appointment in the desert with an old friend. Take good care."

"Will I ever see you again?"

"I'll be around. Count on it."

"Got a few friends who'll lend a hand if you're ever in a tight spot. You'll do fine . . . Just fine."

"The light's on now. Never let anyone turn off the music."

"I won't."

"Moonlight Drive" comes on her stereo. Morrison sings a line to her . . . And like Peter Pan, he's out the window . . .

She's Waiting . . .

So long. So long . . .

All this . . .

pain

The air is full of Waiting. Waiting, heavy as tortured birds denied the sky. The day stretched out over a thousand tears, burning with will it ever end.

Night comes . . .

A hushed guitar haunts the radio, its sad gull tone out of lost sun and psalm. Her shoulders slump under the weight of the dirge. It becomes a path to You, but she can't find him. Momentarily has one and only, but she's denied his coming, lost the key to the garden.

The night is long . . .

So long . . .

Sad.

Lost. Stunned by *this* Eternity on the meathooks of lightning, but not blank. Out of words. Even broken ones . . .

Wrestling with undone.

Trying to breathe.

This long night . . .

of waiting . . .

Was she ever a peacock in spring?

Did she ever have a friend that brought her roses and laughed like answers from the Tropics?

Did she?

Was she?

Ever?

Carry Emily Dickinson's melancholy under the boundaries of voiceless stars?

Choose the right color?

Well?

No breath to give, no word for wind or the devil that smells like burden, the hard corner with its broken streetlight stands outside her window, constant, branchless, no air of panic or wild regret bends it. She's full of time that tries to remember That Prayer . . . Any prayer.

The phone is cold; can't put her arms around it.

Once cooked in blossoms, the room has lost its language, the invitation of wholly, the walls have lost their color; can't even see the small nail that held the picture of him with his arm around her.

Good, You & I, turned into lost words, without a what come next.

Waiting with her tears. Trying to take it. Trying not to fall FURTHER.

Waiting

in the dark. The malefice trumpet blast burning inside her, breaking clear and mine and heart of peace and sun.

One block from the church with its locked door, and no bell in above its sagging white rafters.

Waiting.

The night breathes.

Crying. One tear falls and hits her bare foot half curled under her. One tear falls to the floor and the dust claims it.

This emptiness is a stake in her heart.

This loneliness is insanity.

She trembles. Tears fall on her breast.

She looks at the face of the clock. Its hands hardly minutes from her last gaze, which feels like hours ago.

Tears, but her mouth is to dry to shriek.

Sits in her chair and waits.

The hole in her heart fills with fire. Cold fire.

The blood crawling through her veins burns cold.

Lonely. Lonely. Lonely.

Love as tears

and nothing to carry her back . . .

looks at the outline of the frame that held the picture of him holding her in his arms. Moonlight crashes in, slaps the dust/age-stained outline. Another hole, another lonely place, hollow . . . lifeless . . .

Wishes she felt like her old self.

But none of it lives in this waiting.

Herself. Lost.

Polite. Straight. gone

Soft pleasure. gone

The scent of the sun's lyrics on the horizon. gone

The phrase of bride white. gone

. . . Notes and Paris and Yeah (on the rug with wings) and Diony-
sus and Exquisite happened in the bedroom above The City . . . and
Hell and Tenure and Sugar and Monk's hands playing piano and Tur-
tles and Ducks and Flow and Dots and . . .

. . . and giggling when he wore the wrong color socks . . .

gone

Herself, as she was, as she wanted to be (to and for him) (and for
herself too). lost

Knows she will never see the sun shining again. Not in this cell.

Waiting . . . with her tears. Enough tears to drown in, but they
burn.

And the dove-soft guitar in the radio cries . . . never again . . . no
here again . . . no later . . . or just in time . . . or advice . . . or Valentine
moon . . .

Trembling. Near the edge of panic. Its teeth ready to unleash
hunger.

Waiting.

Trembling.

Blood running from the corner of her sad mouth.

The hole that is her heart burning.

Her blood is a burning noise . . . crawling . . . crawling . . . spreading its secret . . .

Her tears burn.

Night. Nothing feels right. Her loneliness unlocked. Nothing feels
right.

"This doesn't feel . . . right."

Never before.

Never before.

Never . . .

Going back . . .

Can't never . . .

Something under the cold kitchen floor groans.

Night breathes.

Something really feels strange.
Something in her belly . . . tight, hard . . . piercing.
And her heart burns.
Her tears burn.
Night drinks its fill.
She's sprawled on the floor . . . crying . . . her blood burns . . . she
hears her bones groan . . .
PAIN
biting burning
brain and fingers and toes
the backs of her knees
and
bones
predatory enemy that weaves and lynches with its tomb-salt
splits
and writes
its mortuary inflammation
and vertigo
gnawing
grinding
Afraid (it's Daddy's CANCER—passed down and growing in her)
Afraid (he's gone and Daddy died)
        (she should have seen a doctor when it started)
        (he should have seen a doctor when it started)
alone
(missing him . . . missing knowing Yes, and those eyes sweet with
                 YAY!)
in trouble
and
in pain . . .

and every tear burns.

and he's gone.

Waiting

hoping for the sun

and

maybe

the new day can cure the creeping clock and being alone and she'll pick up that phone and cure the mistake of not calling Daddy's doctor.

She's forgetting his open-window eyes, all his pariah poems of pain . . . the tilting, his darklight breath splashing hand-picked stars and flags of thunder upon the borders of her being, all his birds angled-in-cheer and their summer caressed by the tide-sky . . . his hand that would not leave yes . . .

Waiting . . .

Lose.

End.

Blind and waiting . . .

And this ash tongue streaks her in punished.

Her fingers—worn to crushed slaves, curl . . . the PAIN—whitehot poison whizzing (primal and stratified), demands rough in her . . . Its strangling hunger of kisses swarms, slices, deteriorates, but will not leave . . . It digs a grave and clots as it forges . . .

She's sprawled on the floor . . . Feels like she's being boiled alive . . . crying . . .

Tears she can't swallow . . .

✦

There's eyes outside.

Waiting.

A stray. No pack. Not yet.

Waiting.

Knows the burn crawling through her veins. Put it there.

Waiting

with her.

With her he'll start a pack . . .

He'll have a home . . .

With her.

Just like he did before . . . Before he was bitten. Changed . . .

Won't be shot by another's pride. Welded to bluffs, blame, and tension.

Won't be scared-blind by another's teeth.

Moonlight crashes on claws. Claws that remind him of thorns on a road that can't be rescued from war.

He hears her murmur questions in the dark. Looks at her window, says, "Come with me."

He breathes in night. Notes lies and indecision, and barren shadows . . . And all that was soft, yet tried. His chest swells. He could howl.

Lips and teeth and strong heart and sharp mind—Alpha! Leader—no more hours in line waiting behind the others at someone's else's water bowl—no more scavenging what few scraps were left after the Big Dog's banquet and feeling as if he was kicked in the stomach.

Never yelp or whine again.

Alpha—A#1.

He could howl. Could just howl.

He waits . . .

The pack, HIS pack—will sleep in cool shadows when the hotstock sun rages adamant. Trotting, tongues hanging, stretching across The City when the mundane daywalkers lay their weary down to sleep . . .

He remembers Warren Zevon's song. He'd smile if he could smile . . .

He's waiting . . .

For HER

to come out and run with him . . .

Waiting for the tears of fire to change her.

Twitches his nose. Sniffs the air. Knows it's close . . . Shifting . . . Moving . . . Scraping, grinding her questions to Been . . . Hot . . . Spreading . . . Adjusting contours . . .

"Exhale . . . Cast off mute and thin, and we will write history in verses of blood."

❋

PAIN
(and she's waiting . . .)

and
she's afraid she can't hold on.
and
her tears—of END crawling slowly—

burn

(King Crimson "Matte Kudasai" and
Warren Zevon "Werewolves of London")

First There Is A Mountain . . .
Then

Across the river . . .

The golden goose for the taking.

Treachery . . .

Mistakes.

$29.95 rooms. Girls half the room rate to right on up. Girls with world-class tits until the bra comes off. Girls named Candy if you don't mind strychnine or cold blood, or the crude stories that slip out between sips of beer. Lots of Chevys and Fords, white and black and rust, your choice—not many imports, cars that is. Bars and vagrant dogs and Beatles songs that sound like Saturday night on border radio . . . and the same old faces that no one sees. Shakes and Charlie are crazy this week. Baby's splashed this time around. It's like a city down by the airport. A city with no upper crust. No good side. Like most cities it's a city of plenty if you've got hard currency.

And The Need.

Middle of the night ain't any different than any other direction here. This side of the stolen truck or that, neither leads to morning . . . or better. But a hell of a lot try it on anyway.

The line of motels on the south side is death row. Behind a locked door, blue or burning, up to you how you go. What you're worth when you go don't mean shit to the streetlights or the shadows.

Honor among thieves. Yeah, sure. And yer ship docks Tuesday. No need to move off your stool it will walk right through the door. Yeah, with bells on and loaded to the top sail with silver and gold. And the blonde over there with the million-dollar soul kitchen and the features of a *Playboy* centerfold will spread her legs for free—for love, but only for you.

Trouble and that girl named Maggie and Judgment walk right in, rub up against you with dark eyes and only a week to go and your twenty-dollar hand of blackjack has taken to the highway without you.

Breathless have-nots learning wolf lessons and no one wants to get involved. The demons have had too much to drink and can't stay quiet just now. School's in session, sucker. Got a lot of ain'ts 'round here, not much on religion. But the Devil's wind slips in between the cracks . . .

Stirs up the dreamers . . .

Harper was higher than high—six martinis and a bottle of top-shelf whiskey and a very good bottle of champagne, paid good money for his love—eyes deep as the night in some romantic poem, million-dollar Jayne Mansfield tits, and those swaying thighs. Paid for the room too. That's the way the broken, blurred pieces he recollected seemed to him. But now . . . Sitting here in his underwear and bloody . . .

Sitting with his back to the body . . .

Sitting with his shaking hands holding his pounding head . . .

He didn't know what to think.

He didn't know what to do.

Direct action.

A bad taste in his mouth. Smoke. And ashes. And blood.

Lying there . . . the body just lying there.

Start somewhere.

Start now.

There was some whiskey left. He poured it in a glass. Couldn't remember if it was his glass or her glass. And he sure couldn't ask her.

Baby steps.

Two slugs start motion. Wash the bad taste down.

Part of it.

"Fuck.Fuck!Fuck."

Baby steps.

Maybe a shower?

If I can stand.

Did I pay in cash?

Show my license to the clerk?

Which way to go . . .

He coughs. Head feels like a walking bass line thrAkking it out with a kick drum.

So much for moving right this minute.

Baby steps.

"Shit."

Can't even remember the cock dance. He did? Didn't he? Must have. Had to.

Had to.

Paid for it. Paid good money. Up front. Just this minute can't remember her tits. Can't remember her lips. Her name?

Can't turn around and look.

Can't.

. . . There was a Sinatra song. She said, "I love it when he sings. Makes me crazy right down to my clit." That smile, right on cue, the tongue sliding along the underside of her top lip.

Remembered her eyes in the bar. Remembers her hand on his thigh. In the bar. Remembers her smile, those winning lottery ticket lips. The sultry voice. *Alto.* Low. Made him high. The promise of a "*good* time."

Can't move his feet.

Remembers the snare, "Want a *hot* night?" The tingling. The swell. And she hadn't even touched it yet . . .

Can barely open his eyes.

The night got fast . . . her narcotic perfume intercepted his romantic "IS?" with "Yes," hell-warm, deep as a secret. He grabs the passport, sees her in garters, bra, and panties . . . Perfectly beautiful— so perfect, all that lovely skin, miles of velvet—sweet velvet, it seems untouched—he wants to get his teeth in it . . .

Can't stand and look in the mirror. He'd see her face, blood on those million-dollar Jayne Mansfield tits, or painted on that blue-ribbon ass. See that sweet, buttercream cake frosting mouth slit open, see the crazy-fuck Joker smile. See violence. See . . . his dream come to an end.

See blame . . . in the mirror.

She had her cherry-coated lips wrapped around the neck of that bottle of whiskey. Moaned. Dribbled. Two drops slid between her cleavage. "Want a taste, baby?" licked her lips. Her index finger traces a little heart with the two drops.

Want to?

Did he?

He wanted to. Must have. Must have.

He paid for the pussy. Paid for the skull-fuck *Special*-special. Paid to get lost . . .

"You want *hot,* baby?"
He must

have.
pale sheets (he's ready to take his shot)
  . . . red panties off / blind fingers free in open doors / on the beach / groin / legs / tits / melting / waves / a thousand curves / "So fucking good." / winning lottery ticket cherry-coated lips / open / circling / the swell / the lightning / melting "Daddy. Daddy . . . *Daddy—yesss.*" / hot / hot / hot . . .
Eyes closed. The lights on.
He must

have.
  . . . teeth / teeth / teeth / white teeth / pearl white / teeth / shining . . .
She had.
Had to.
Wanted to.
Told him.
Pushed for it.
Pushed.
He.
Loved it.
Loved it.
Sinatra on the radio. "From Here to Eternity." Piano.Strings.Siren song.
Her breath sounded like the summer wind.
She swayed.
The star, top shelf stuff. "Who loves you, baby?"
Hand on his thigh.
  . . . teeth / teeth / white teeth / shining . . .
The stars come up. Glitter. Dance.
In her eyes.
Flame.
Hollywood underbelly rhythms.
Pushing.
His heart bit off a constellation. Hot and sweet. Wants the touch.

A thousand curves. Six martinis in the bar. Three for her? or two? One way ticket. 25 to 11. The clock stopped, locked in his wallet. Something in her eyes . . . something . . .

The sea comes in.

He must have.

She . . .

The stars go.

Fail.

All this blood. On his arms. His hands. His legs. All this blood. Her

blood?

He can't look.

Can't!

Six martinis and all that whiskey and the champagne . . . Can't remember.

Couldn't hurt her.

Couldn't?

Not her.

But she's not moving.

And there's all this blood. Here . . . and there.

On him.

On her.

And she's not moving.

There's her toe. He almost brushed it with his hand. What pretty toes. Cherry-coated red. Like a red Coupe de Ville. Cruising so fast . . . outta here . . . out . . . fast . . . Let's go . . .

"Let's go, baby. Somewhere quiet . . . Somewhere—" Her hand on his thigh.

Slow circle . . .

The tingling. The swell . . .

Mouth open . . .

"Somewhere where we can go *fast*." Thousand-miles-an-hour smile lit up like a rocket ride.

His head was full of goop. Iron cobwebs. Fire and Hell and a thumping electric bassline and an ape thrumping a kick drum with a sixteen-pound hammer.

Bottle back. Gulp. One for the road . . .

A velvet kiss.

Around his soul . . .

Melting . . .

Fire and Hell weather riding a Hell's Angels chopper 60 /80 /200! /1,000! miles an hour around the inside of this skull.

Devils and comets playing fuck you in his head. Pissing acid in his eyes. Drunk hoedown hot line stomping—lava on the bottom of their iron-shod shoes.

"I can't."

"I don't remember."

"Yesterday?"

Can't.

Before . . .

Wrong. After.

We climbed in bed . . .

. . . *fuck that sweet hungry pussy daddy* teeth . . . *god your cock is hot as a star* teeth . . . *your fat cock is* teeth . . . *stick it all the way* teeth . . . *IN* teeth . . . *huge* teeth . . . *elephant* teeth . . . *magnificent cock* pearl white . . . *my lucky pussy* shining . . . *a fucking hurricane* shining . . . *crazy hurricane fucking my sweet pussy* teeth . . . teeth

Can't . . .

Look over his shoulder . . . but

Have to.

Must . . .

Got to.

Eyes open.

And she looks a hundred years old.

No. Dead.

A hundred years dead. And . . .

Blood. Someone wasn't kidding. Peeled back the skin . . . all the sides shattered.

All that money—out of hand . . . those million-dollar tits—something got out of hand . . . reality, pleasure, the cocksucker sighs—got out of hand . . .

Fuckin' drunkin' night . . .

Something got out of hand.

They were dancing . . . She played it simple, straight up. Her heart was a piece of candy. Hard candy with serious thighs. Beautiful thighs, ready for work. He's ready to go down to the river, to die. He's got serious money to say thank you for the holiday . . . And they were drinking. And he was holding her tight. And they were high.

And she's smiling . . .

Teeth white as an angel cloud.

She laughs.

And he laughs.

She pulled him close.

Tight.

And Sinatra, sang ". . . Eternity."

Dead stop.

Fuckin' bitch tried to bite me. "Bitch was a fuckin' vampire . . . Tried to bite me." She . . . She was gonna rip out my throat. Drink my blood. Steal my dreams. Shitass-bitch. Fuckin' wanted my blood. Fuckin'-shitass-bitch . . .

Didn't have a reflection in the mirror.

Didn't.

Didn't let her.

Fuck that.

Fuck her. Shitass bitch.

Turned.

Right then.

Right on him.

Right into a . . .

Saw the blackness in her eyes. Saw Hellfire. Tasted the brimstone on her lips. Heard sultry turn into a growl—Black dog hellfire mean.

Saw her lips part.

Saw fangs.

Her fangs.

White.

Shining.

Hungry.

Cocksucker turned bloodsucker.

Teeth, wolf sharp. Up close.

Loud.

White.

. . . as an angel cloud.

Everything tight.

Up close.

The hot out of focus blur slashed away.

The press of the wild kiss. She's high—the vampyr kiss—one more second and the hot flow delirium will blast through her.

Black . . .

in her eyes . . .

Sly. Ancient. Aggressive.

Something black . . .

deep in her eyes . . .

The stars gone . . . from her eyes . . .

The heat—

the frolic—

gone . . .

His high.

All that money.

Gone

—Fuck!

The promise—LIE!

Fucking

gone . . .

His alarm goes off.

Harper's .38 throws damage . . . And the faux-brass lamp remodels her wrinkle-proof skin . . .

Red.

Red. inches

RED. inches and inches

here

and there

spots

curved inches

of

red

RED . . . filthy

Red and black. An inch of white bone after the last hammer blow . . .

The exorcism finished in seconds . . .

Got to get up / get dressed / and get out. Before the sun comes. Before cops come. Before some . . . She . . .

ACT . . . now! and be gone . . .

Gone . . . back / right / left / any direction—

now

Blood and mascara and happiness smeared—broken . . .

Speechless . . .

Now. (out!out!OUT! someplace. someplace not here . . . somewhere . . . fireproof. no place like this blast, strewn with THIS outlaw
waltz . . .)

Finally, *slow as fuck*, up.

Washed off some of the blood. Washed the splattered red mask
off his face . . .

Dressed. Half dressed that is. Looks in the mirror, the gorge of
mystery . . . black and deep, forgotten by sunlight . . . the gorge of
murder . . .

Blood.

Logic and memory rumbling.

Blood.

Some message jutting out?

Those million-dollar paradise tits—still perfect. Almost distract-
ing . . .

The tanned dancer's legs—still perfect. Parted just enough.

Hole in her head. Just above her right eye.

One in the throat.

. . . Where is the sense in this forest? Who can make sense of
these impulses of black and RED thrown and splashed this way and
there . . .

Two in her belly.

That smile. LIE!

She's still smiling that cherry-coated smile.

"Lyin'ass cunt."

Gonna wipe that sweet cherry-coated fucking lie off her face.

Moves in.

red

Close.

RED

Looks for her fangs. There are none.

None?

Oh-no. No! There were teeth. Shining. White . . . incisors. I saw them. Fuckin' saw 'em. Up close. Close. Shining. Right there. Angel cloud white teeth and those fuckin' fangs. Shining.

Fangs!

FANGS! Sharp as a scabby rat. Sharp. Functional.

She had fangs! A terrible fury, white as the inscription of razor moonlight. Ready to feed, flourish, glide through his scarlet. Glide through the ring of his scream ... As if he were a table, or a fillet.

I saw them. Fuckin' saw them.

Sharp ...

White. Pointed ...

Fuck. I saw them. They were ... There ...

I—

Sharp voice. "Fuck me."

This side of the river ...

3:57 A.M. ... all the lullabies forgotten ... Heaven is Hell ... everything confused by bullshit and drink ...

Saturday night dead as the sound of a silhouette in a puddle of blood. The streets possess the occasional wandering, hurrying dog, the occasional cop cruising, and a quick, fearful shout in the floating darkness ...

In a death row motel room on the Southside ...

Desire. Burned out.

Cold.

Standing there. Just standing there. At the foot of the bed. His feet won't move. Her pretty toes—cherry-coated red, like a fast Coupe de Ville itchin' for the highway—almost touching his shaking hand ...

Shaking slightly.

Staring ...

At his mistake.

Fuck ...

In This Desert Even the Air Burns

(for Karl Edward Wagner)

Early one vicious morning. The air a thirsting panther.

"Me and . . ."

All the old man had was a black-and-white picture of her, the broken yellow lines in the road headed to who knows where, and the need to put the heavy stars to sleep.

"*her.*"

A ghostly incarnation of Dylan was on the radio singing about love driving him insane. Not his first time. Might not be his last. It wasn't the old man's last. Not by a cold million miles. The desert motels, desolate nests burning in the solarfire, and the dry brush blew by, looked as if they were headed somewhere. Everything out here looked as if it was once headed to someplace else. It just never got there. Most often it paused in the long empty, ducked in a silver of shade to escape the absolute sun, got snagged on memories and never got up.

The old man stopped and got gas. $15.23. Bought a Coke and a pack of smoke. $3.74. Almost out of silver. Completely out of gold. Opened the glove box and checked his gun before pulling out. He was old, yeah OK, but he wasn't stupid. Not this go-'round.

There'd be a doorway before it got too dark. A bed. A TV with old news he wouldn't really listen to. He'd get eggs with cheese and onions or a burrito for dinner. Coffee. Black. Hopefully fresh, but if not . . . And he'd lay there in the motel room (or pace around in circles) and wonder.

Third of a bottle of whiskey and he still wouldn't be able to forget her. Not on this road with the phone poles stung out like prison wire and haunted complaints of tomorrow on the wind. Not while his eyes could see the shadows and the things that were locked in them.

It was a room for not going fast. A room of narrow failures.

The wind was outside walking the road. By a broken gate that had never seen an island it turned, howled for an old lost love. He pulled the covers tight. A song from yesterday's jukebox moved slow in his thoughts. He burned in the cold. The ghost of midnight cried questions of right and wrong. Church bells were ringing.

The old man turned on the light. Looked at his boots. He wished they knew different habits. Wished they played dumb and just went along with the dance.

He turned off the light. Wrapped his head around her face. A million miles back and still he had to face the lie. He took. She took. Neither could wait. Neither did. He didn't dream. Tossed and turned. But didn't dream.

When he woke he was still sick. Love. Sometimes it was six foot long and just as deep. It came. You said it would put your mind at ease. Then closer got closer and things got blown into a million pieces. Rock yer baby. And she rocked you. And there was paper. And scissors. No one won. And a million miles had passed.

Before became nowhere. Then was outta doorways. So you left. Didn't take anything but a broken heart and a maybe a picture of the fire.

Then came the trains and the river and Baltimore. You sleep when you can. Tried not to gamble.

Tried . . . to drive straight. Begged night and the painful kisses of the whiskey to bury the bewilderment.

But on some dirt road where they closed the door, you found you were headed back to the last time. And yer boots started leanin' back and that black-and-white picture turned in into a bird flown away.

Yer standin' there just taking up space . . . hands lost in your pockets. Thought there was something there, but no one was talkin'. And there's no one to trade places with. And there's a sunrise starin' at you, offering no future and no sermon, and the appetite of the hole just gets deeper . . .

And the ramblin' starts again . . .

Fargo . . . Ensenada, mariachi, and wanna-be matador too hungover to play . . . Austin . . . Eden—someone thought it looked like it . . . Eudura, a lightpole by the jail . . . San Antone . . . Towns little more than small hives outta words and for old time's sake . . . oceans of sand without limits ... alone and gaunt, a little ranch squeezed hard ... a little one-room shack, might be a coffeepot and a cup and a saucer come from the East years back on the small hand-hewn table—the nails that held it together might have started rusting ...

Ramblin', hardship to next tomorrow morning, and all the mistakes down the line. You see sin ... and ashes. See old ghosts—too hot to run from close-range conversations with old lies, sitting on weathered old porches ... waiting ...

Indigo darkness stretched out thick, swollen with dry. Half a mile stretched into half a state. Impulses sick of hide and seek surging to move on ...

Sun a lion that won't let you run away. Sand and desert sky with no history ...

The road ... flat today for a while. Rocky later on ... all day too hot dragging on ... the sun's a scar and the sky's got nowhere it needs to be ... there's no water out here. No world to get to here ... the cactus laugh when your burden goes by ...

Time comes. Whispers. A hundred years. A hundred years traveling with an old injury. Barrels of whiskey gone jar by jar ... A hundred squirms, aches, crawls forward weakly and the inexhaustible details of the puzzle last longer than a long time ...

The old man looks at the black-and-white photograph of her. Even figuring on the clock her once-saintlike face didn't look a day over a million.

The wind offers no warm embrace ...

It's late. His pistol is sick of waiting. He smokes his last cigarette ...

Looks at her picture one last time. The wind whispers, "Once in their castle beyond night ..."

Dusk. The scent of alone thickening ... twenty miles from Calexico. Far away not far away ...

You won't be wrong this time.

Not this time ...

❋

Once in their castle beyond night . . .

You were out . . . burning affairs filled with darkness. She took off with your brother. Headed west into that rotting, small-fire sunset . . .

Never saw it coming.

You looked at your hand. Didn't have a needle's eye of light between your knotted fingers. Picked up your gun . . .

Put on your boots of Carcosian leather.

A million miles ago the door closed. You remember what went. But you still don't know why . . .

"Cassilda . . . Why?"

Sunday waist-deep and thick on the ground. The tired old sun setting into the ground. Night winds with blood on their lips soon. Outta whiskey and full of

"Why?"

(After some Dylan and Happy Rhodes's *"Winter"* (looped) and breathing "Eno-ambient" low)

Even Night

Even Night,
        as radiant
        as a star and a kiss and a rose
                and the colors of a peacock,
    with her white moon
      and sad fountains
      and frayed rope ladder arias
   to absent, deceiving Oblivion—out sighing with the angels of
Doom,
      has prayers.

They flutter atop
    the sounds of bones and flutes and lost bells,
        as she dreams
              of gentle Morpheus
                and
                    sleep.

Crow in Trick Town

Weren't no blankets or umbrellas or soft shoe shines for sale in Trick Town. But cold blue steel, Crow could hook you up, pick your caliber. Or Crow could obtain certain Umé sorceries bottled in Pengtin, or any of a variety of spike-powders brought across the frontier border near Mule Fork, or thin young funboys if you wanted 'em.

Crow also engaged in another service—

He strutted out of the cold; oily feathers like frayed rags in the wind. Right into the crack rim shots poppin' and slidin' that in & out syncopation in the Honaloochie Grill on the hard corner of 9th & Dull. A new girl—well, new sometime back, before the unanswered letters home and the 29 heartbreaks and the wrinkles set in—was peelin'. Another sad bouncer with thin lips and gorge-deep cleavage reduced to a G-string, and just in off the streets, but for how long he wondered, as she wagged her pliable bottom.

He nodded to a few of Downtown's mad just off from work seven hours ago, and the jacked up Hennessey Bros. Breezed passed Gin & Rainy After Hours (still married at the hip and to the bottle) who sat with Poe Eddie; none of the three were as cloudy as the weather just yet. Gave a knowing wink to the barman, Fitter Stoke, who was busy pouring pardons for those going under for the 500th time. Crow walked the length of the well-attended bar that smelled liked decaying fragments and spilled ruin. Walked right in the back room and picked out a cue.

He had an hour to kill.

Crow ordered his usual and broke the tight rack. Two light-colored stripes down the hole. He pressed the flicker of a flame to the tip of a smoke. Out front the band—a drummer named Styx and a tenor player dubbed Cheops—thought about tellin' the new dancer a certain bedtime story about a vampire and her chastity belt, while she rubbed her ripples. In the back Crow played himself twice in short order.

Four smokes—ground under heel into stained linoleum—and three single malts later Crow sank his last shot. Weren't no tick-tock pop up to announce the hour, but Crow knew it was time to open it up. He put the cue away and slugged back the half-a-finger swallow. Dropped a neatly folded bill on the bar on his way to the door.

Eleven sharp. His step was explicitly assured.

Half a block east Crow ducked around the corner of the No Deposit No Return First Reform Church of Babylon—out of the wind—to light a smoke. He couldn't hear the tears of the steeple over the rain's busy business, but it didn't matter, he'd heard every ripped up Christmas card wheeze till a cough busted their chops or swept them off their feet and over to Rest Lawns.

Quick to be out of the blow Crow winged beyond Ma Zye's Newts & Roots and Frownland and Sue Egypt's love factory and Café Morphine and Uncle Meat's Muffin Kitchen and the Philosophy Agency and Fat Theresa's Bootery.

Three blocks.

Four.

Seven—bitchin' softly about his laid up transport. Further down desolation row, passed the infested galleries oblivion's helpmate mutability muscled out, and the padlocked park with its rusted jungle gyms and the junkyard where the bored dogs slept. Walked right around the distant aria of a screamer beggin' for the fever to break.

Crow crossed Suicide Bridge and turned down the path by the river. There were bodies out tonight: the thin rats in thin shoes rained off Fairfax were milling in mounds for something to show or trade around the barrel furnace, and the Mysterons and Mad Dog ghosts floatin' without the moon to illuminate their maps of purgatory; on a bench below the Statue of the Bulls, Cherry Red tradin' her version of private poetry for the promise of a shot glass of heat and a beer; and an old man with a stray dog, both having forgotten their way home.

Crow saw the match light and the half-shadow of a jowl-supported face in profile. Walked right up to it. Neither nodded. They stood like two great weights sleeping as their eyes clawed for space in the shadows. The taller—and wider, Cikada, wrapped in a greatcoat of heavy black, looked as though he could vanish in the dreamfog being exhaled from the slow surface of the river as easily as the 18th Duke of Pedpott had dreamed himself distant in the Valley of Fragments—Crow thought about all the other pockets-full-of-burning hopeheads that had crashed headlong into the shanty town of impermanent ecstasy.

"Sloat has played without paying," Cikada stated flatly in a voice as sonorous as the aftertone of distant thunder.

The freewheeler counted the currency and the complexities of Cikada's employ. He turned his head to the water.

"Overdue." The long slow word a death promise. "And he suggests I jump through the hoops of his excuses awhile longer. I cannot have things not the way they were." Cikada ground the cigarette to a cold butt between his thick thumb and thicker forefinger.

"Would you like your message delivered with pain . . . or should the red song run swift?" Crow asked without facing the man, though he knew the ruin-allotting kingpin normally dispatched his cumbersome wrecking balls for simple whambooms and thrakings.

Cikada exhaled, adding the heat of his anger to the incident in fog. "Both recipient and onlooker alike must understand I may be silent, but I am not *delicate*. Be certain the headless chicken dances long." His whisper softened and grew colder. "And frame by frame." After a smile, he added, "I've heard it said style is everything."

Stimulation changed hands, agreeing on reconvening after Sloat was rubbed raw and snapped. Life on the bottom wasn't Nirvana, but business was good.

"Most importantly, I believe the belly of Sloat's safe holds a morsel of mine. My possession must return home."

Crow nodded and left Cikada standing on the cold stones. He would have whistled but Cikada found all music maddeningly annoying.

His confidently heeled urban step played quick across shadow and crack and his blood felt like Tabasco laughing at the chilled air. Crow moved through the shadows like a rat—fast and close to the walls. His heart beat like an excited talking drum. Crow dearly loved reluctant brides—penetrating the compliant would make for sleepy amusement, and he wasn't in this biz just for the folding green.

Sloat lived below the level wall some not too few blocks from the south end of Sherborne near Hell's Gate. The uninspired gray dwelling, here and there smudged in darker tones of gray, cracked along the base and soiled with decades worth of raining coal soot, was a poorly shaped rectangle. The door—cut out in the right corner nearest the corner—

was a slab of time and weather-softened oak covered in a dented metal skin secured with now rusting nails. The single scratching on the door simply read *Hermiston Sloat—Relics & Arrangements.*

Crow ran his long thin fingers through oily black hair. His finger traced the S, O, and the top of the T. He liked Ts—two sharp lines; a slash across the throat and a vertical opening of the underbelly. "Anubis calling," he whispered before rapping firmly.

Crow knew the fence and spell-trader's residence well. He knew about the guard dogs, and the safe in the cellar. He heard the fanged barkers announcing him before the door swung wide to flood him in electric light.

"Ah, Crow. Come in, my dear friend. Come in—always a pleasure." Sloat, in long-ribboned curls and love's war paint and soft layers of re-vealing pink, closed and locked the door. His quick smile greased by greed. "Have you some *borrowed* bauble seeking a new home?" Sloat's wet bug-eyes shimmered; gems transformed into money, and money bought thin young boys, and thin young boys brought pleasured grunts and squeaks and groans and sighs and the fighting bang and fury of the love tumble. "Perhaps," his fat hands were clasped as in hungry prayer, "you've come to arrange for a *new* young lad's shedding of childhood?"

Crow smiled darkly and replied by shooting both sitting dogs in the skull. "Sadly, Sloat—*for you* that is—not today."

A wave of fear the size of a flood left Sloat momentarily dry and breathless. His eyes darted about for pardon or exit.

Crow's laugh was low, calm, and even.

Sloat caught his rushing breath, hoping for a punch line despite the grim tenor of Crow eyes. "I'm not ready for the Well of Souls."

Crow smiled in reply. "Few are. All the bothers and the blood and the unfulfilled loose ends—"

"If it's money?" the fat man squeaked—frantic for any slight op-portunity that could be cajoled wider—knowing Crow loved the in & out and slash & rip above all other pursuits, except perhaps Crow's bitch-twins, whom he'd boomingly slighted once for their street-slut costumes.

"Moneymoneymoney! There are other jolly pleasures—"

"Of course there are my boy. I've just—"

Crow wagged the pistol as if it were a fatherly finger of admon-ishment. "Cikada—"

At the name the blood rouging Sloat cheeks fled to shore up his failing heart. "—requires the return of something misplaced."

"Crow, my dear-dear friend. I hold nothing of Cikada's. Had I stumbled upon a wayward child of his I would have certainly returned it with the utmost haste. You are free to audit every crack and crevice."

"And so we shall. Beginning with your *fat* safe below."

Sloat's expression remained a fixture of fear, but inside, behind his eyes, he sighed. Crow's love of currency was known in every den in Trick Town. The gold coins and platinum rings and neatly banded bills were all the opportunity he sought.

"As you wish."

Hermiston Sloat sidestepped his dead pets, making a note to have the ruby-studded collars cleaned before acquiring an unspoiled pair of guards—much larger ones. He felt light. "This way."

Through the lavender and canary velvets of the parlor and down the hall. Through a door. Down. The worn stairs gave audible objection under Sloat's great weight. Stone and mortar and the thick press of damp—Sloat's susceptive plums rested upstairs. Beyond old crates and empty casks lay piles of small bones—cracked and chewed litter in disarray. The remains of young boys Sloat had promenaded with until yawns replaced grunts and then had allowed the dogs to sup upon till bloated.

Forward to a wooden door with a padlock and a iron bar. Sloat, eyes holding the reserved hope of inducement, turned and presented Crow with the keys.

"Open it," Crow said.

The lock and the bar and the safe door unlatched and set aside, Crow eyed money, gems, and—

"It's all yours," Sloat begged. "If—"

Crow saw Cikada's purloined article. "Betwixt yesternight and the promise, I might have been tempted. But."

Sloat's dilemma choked on the flash of an alluring smile and tenderly-honed knives. Nip and dart (around back) for two quick pokes and one firm shove-it-right-in puncture. Sloat prided himself on being provocative, let the vivid whispers of the street make it so. Crow amputated The Finger finger and the right eye and the tongue—he paused, fingers to chin, holding back the bold strokes of the T, to consider the design alterations made by his wet work. He regretted the dogs weren't here for a fatty snack. Hermiston Sloat's wheezy moan brought him back from what if & maybe. Crow concluded with the finishing strokes of the T.

He found a hammer and a nail, and left Sloat's discorporated prick tacked on the door. Two quick finger-strokes left the Mark of Blacklist Condition—in Sloat's blood—above it. Satisfied, his gaze returned to the depths of the safe. Cikada's cookbook of charmwords and sigils was in his hand. Crow picked its lock with three fleet words Ma Zye had once swapped for a certain three-toed, one-eyed frog from the swamps of Ba-Benzala said to impart astonishing vigor to the melodic flow of lovemaking. Cikada's collection of hallowed and blasphemous enchantments unfolded, and Crow's finger traced the ivy of sweeping script as he calculated and absorbed, skipping the grimoire's common conjurations and drolleries. He saw stars of the whirlwind realign and power and money (should need require) and—

He pocketed a pair of spells for the lean days where fickle turnabout pushed hard—he'd had to reinvent himself a time or two in the past when forever changed and one madness was shed for another.

Crow resealed *The Book of the Dominion of Mysteries* with Ma Zye's Fettering Web. He cleared out, leaving the gems and the jewels and the tightly banded stacks untouched. Message sent.

Crow leisurely strolled the wet-skinned pavement—these were the nights he liked best. He whistled brightly as he headed uptown to the gilded turrets of Trick Town's oldest, at present, vampire. After his meet with Cikada he would stop in and play here comes sweet suck-kisses and juicy & thrust with Polly Jean & Shu-Shu.

Tomorrow was The Day the Risen Bones Dance; Trick Town's most celebrated holiday. He had a fitting rendezvous with "He's Shade. I'm Shadow." Crow decided to wear white to the funeral. Life on the bottom was better than Nirvana, business was good.

When the Deal Goes Down

Table with two hardback chairs. A man and a little girl.

Men from the local flops and the gray stoops that leave their consequences in the streets see her, a little girl on the outside. Inside, beyond the cutting stretch of thirsty eyes, it's bad news. Raw. And uncut.

Small hard lips. "Payback." That never use lipstick.

Blue eyes nod.

She's a ghost—hands full of losing, out of short cuts, but hard as a feral street bitch. Harder. Colder. Her cigarette burns out in the ashtray. "Worse than meth. Much worse." Voice tougher than a Link Wray guitar line.

He nods again. He's seen it. Up close.

Maybe before the burn she was beautiful. But the cigarettes and tequila and the 52-week eternity of pain had worn the edge down some. Way down, some might say, careful to stay out of range of her rage.

"Money or pussy." Exhales blue smoke. "Or both if you want. I've got plenty."

Sips his hot black coffee and watches two outlaws at the counter, brutalizing their French fries with ketchup.

She tests the weight of the half-empty beer bottle . . . One finger taps the edge of the table. Lets it come to a rest. Doesn't shift in her chair. Waiting for the price.

Terms.

Barstools or street corners, it's all terms these days. Always has been. Always will be.

He hasn't moved. "Ten. Up front." Plain as day.

No smile. Says, "What the hell." Instead of too much. "Done."

"Tomorrow. Not here."

She lights a smoke. Doesn't ask where.

"Call the number at eleven. I'll tell you where."

She scans his hands. Results. That all she cares about.

He drops a ten on the table for the coffee and the beer.

Her expression doesn't change, but she wishes she'd met him BEFORE . . .

❖

She comes out of a hole in the ground. Two punk kids flee from the blow-torch glaze she levels.

She's seen him.

He starts walking.

She needs no roadmap. Follows the blood track . . .

Two blocks.

Left . . .

A dark street that's never seen moonlight, and rarely the red lights of a cruiser. An island of seriousness that's seen bleeding, choked the fragile on regret and bartender's lies, and 110% of the time didn't give a shit about right or fair counts. Its capacity for death measured in deals that slowly nodded yeah sure to subtlety, then fucked it with a wrecking ball. A place where no one sees anything move, not even the water under the bridge. A street where the crazy sit and drink coffee with fate while it tells them their ship's not coming in this week. Dirty and naked and filled with episodes out on bail, the new arrivals didn't live long after the first sentence . . . The accommodations here were peppered with roaches and lice, didn't come with Gideon's bibles—Hell, there weren't any drawers, and had never heard the word softly . . .

A small, shabby joint. Today—feeling bleached out, as if he can't last any longer, and yesterday (even naked and willing, not a beauty)—mouth working on breaking the cold iron silence with half a bottle whiskey, were drinking, celebrating after having decided to pardon tomorrow for skipping out on redemption. The bartender, counting the small change that still leaves him a million miles from cozy, stares at the walls of this primitive box of disease that's ruining his dream.

Blue eyes is sitting by the jukebox, hard and beyond compromise.

Dylan's singing about "someday baby," but none of the regulars in the joint are buying. A rough cough ejected over false teeth tells the fat blonde at his elbow she should have played "Freebird." Unsmiling, she looks at him as if he's an old gray building in need of an army of janitors, electricians, plumbers, and morticians.

"What do you care? I'm only passing through."

"Then hurry the fuck up and get gone."

Then they both laugh. And order another round of shots . . . He brushes a lock of hair from her cheek. She leans in, whispers, "Bedroom."

She comes in, looking like she just crawled a million miles. Sees him before the door closes. Eyes and the organ that beating beneath her breast measure him, spend a second imagining he could mend her broken heart . . . In the haze of cigarette smoke she believes in some Force, some Power. He can see in the dark. He can knock on the door. Open it. Walk in that place of weird, in the halls of blood. Rules be damned, he can go in and come out. In him she can win.

Finally.

And maybe . . . After . . . (the deal goes down.) She can look in the mirror again. Maybe. She might be there—whole, or mostly put back together—rediscovered. The true Me. Returned the girl, brought back from the archives of insatiable nightmares. Blonde, and clean. Hinting at pastoral. Free to no longer impersonate a killer.

Maybe, for once, she could sleep. Just a little bit.

She hands him the envelope with the names, the descriptions. And the money.

He smokes while he looks over the roadmap of Hell.

3 to 1. They'll bring fangs and claws, and blood fortified by all the powers of Hell. He'll have his guns. His knife. And a tombstone soul that will never knock on Heaven's door.

He leaves.

She finishes her beer.

✦

Midnight skipped out of here two hours ago. Raven shadows sit on their perches waiting for the stains of chaos to break the momentary calm with minds and souls undone.

Three, nearly identical on the dread scale, demons out of their den—gravedigger heigh-ho glints in their cold eyes—looking to whip up a fuck-you-up-bad, lowdown bone-spree, firing 100mph on all cylinders and grab a bite to eat . . .

Soulless to soul. 3 to 1. The little ugly one smells blood. The leader of this pack of pitchfork late-shifters laughs. Singsong thunder, "You're really fucked here, asshole." The fanged smile.

Two clawed hands high-five.

Grunted. "Meat, we're gonna suck you dry." Eyes, fangs glint.

Blue eyes serpent-silent. Doesn't smile. He steps into the fire. He's in the shit, waist deep in hot stuff. His panther eyes stay dark.

Teeth and surgeon's scalpel claws are bared. Lightning. Shots are fired. Eyes full of confused, the thin one goes down first. The talker next. On his knees, without a howl or a hiss, then face down. Swallowing his surprise, the one in the long black coat wants to run. Four bullets convince him to stay. He's on the ground, babbling, shaking, the poison of the bullets deep inside fucking him. Consequences he never banked on sit heavy on his brow. Time, moments ago steel to him, runs away.

Blue eyes goes to work with the predatory edge of his knife.

Boundaries flee the hail.

Skin changes.

Not stopping in disgust or to catch its breath, the razor kiss of the steel executioner works, slices deliberately . . . Pushes, sculpts deeper. Nothing it injures, dissects, wriggles to get free.

When he's certain they're no longer there, he stands.

They got a few good ones in. The rib's going to hurt like a bitch for a while. He'll need stitches. But he'll make it. He'll pay for it tomorrow, but he'll make it . . .

Her Mustang pulls into Tombstone Alley. Its headlights find him, one hand pressed to a wall to help hold him up. He's bloody. He'll have a few new scars.

Soul to soul.

"Was it bad?"

"Some rollin'. Some tumbling. Ugly . . . With lots of noise. More blood. They went down. Hard."

"Let's get out of here." Her arm around him for support.

"Think you could find a place that serves coffee at this hour?"

"There's a quiet little place across the river."

She pours gas on the bloody slabs. Her dog barks from the back-seat.

He flicks his cigarette. The bodies, held tightly by the flames, burn . . .

*

A year after the deal goes down.

The desert. Painted by untroubled winds. Things not missed, blown clean. And smooth. Not a broken tombstone in sight . . . Not a siren or a scream in earshot.

A porch with two rockers and a mean old dog, napping in the setting sun. Same spot every night now.

She smiles. Pops the top on a cold beer. Her once uncomfortably close, wounded memories are back in The City, gathering dust.

Blue eyes nods . . .

The sky here is blue as far as you care to see . . .

The moon will stop in for a visit soon.

You can get beyond the horizon, get beyond broken, hop the last train, get reborn. But you can't leave your skin . . . it always wears the lessons it picked up before it slipped under the bridge . . . A shotgun lies across his legs.

Devil's Got the Walkin' Blues

Weary tonight. Right down to the bone.

But his ghost heels' got miles to go . . .

Worried mind of night winds blowin' under a white Stetson with a turquoise and silver band. The once sharp white, faded some by travelin' in rain, by walks under bartender skies, and raw, stuttered pleas when tunes of assassin dust laughed treacherously. Thirty miles from a thing too hot to touch and the water under the bridge. Thirty miles of lonesome, can't escape mistakes.

Unshaven these last three days. Eyes eyeing strange and the wrong side of town. Nose broken, heart too. Ears filled with a thing of cold reason that turned around. Mouth choking on yesterday's tears.

Dead lizard, third one today. Half buried to the dents a chrome hub cap. Each forgotten by what went marchin' on . . . Sand. A tumbleweed flat outta tumble. Sand, with no future. Sand with no past. Sand that don't know just how jumbled-up-tight Now gets. Bits and pieces of motorway travel cast off at 75 miles an hour . . . And more sand. Sand that never scraped the sublime. Sand. Sand that don't follow no star. Blind empty sand. Sand that don't hear them bells, don't care about his shadow, or the cost of love always comes out the same . . .

Sand. Same shade from this very spot to there . . . Today still, not straying. Not moving at the wind's behest.

Looks like all the parts here were taken away. He wonders why the takers didn't walk off with the sky.

Been driftin' a million miles. Little towns with nothin' on their minds and sand. Sentinel cactus and lamps turned down low. Gas station carnivals—filled and poppin' with circus color signs, 25¢ cold pop bottle crazy-lemon-lime thirst quenchers, and laughing postcards, and sleeping dogs—closed down. He's stopped off at his share. Slept on the benches or broken old wood chairs by the broken cash registers a night or twenty. Broke a backdoor glass and hid out from the criminal turbulence of the rain more than a few nights. Found three dollars in quarters in one that couldn't wait for time and crossed over (without dignity) . . .

Tomorrow . . . Something will live. Still be haunted by the raw end of the deal, but it'll live. Sort of . . . Something, maybe a dream, will die . . . Tomorrow there'll be more sand to drive him insane. More miles stretching under the moon's unhurried glow. Might find a quiet hour or a meal. Won't find the answer to the deal. Might stumble on a sign. Won't be able to read it.

Walkin' the line. Followin' hot dust . . . Step by step. Trouble at his heels. Trouble left back at that backdoor that won't stay down . . .

Walkin' . . . from wrong to wrong.

Walkin' moon to noon on sand that don't collect. Sand that don't gather up pins and needles or try ta please ya . . . Sand that don't remember a single name . . .

There'll be another horizon show itself tomorrow. But no rainbow. There'll be desire stirrin' somethin' in his guts. But no fire or temple of the Cross will burn it away . . .

Sees a rough bird on a wire. It doesn't believe in rainbows, knows all too well in this dead or alive, its rough out here. It checks the horizon and wings off the shelf. Looks like it's in a hurry. He wonders what, if anything, it'll find down the line. Doesn't envy it or offer it a wish. Why bother, it won't escape this cage.

The sun tires of being here all day. The shadows are almost here. They'll pick at his pain. Breathe new life into his knotted scars. Risin' vines full of snakes, snakes with storm eyes that punish the frail things living in his brain, they'll see him wherever he attempts to hide. He'll pretend not to care . . .

Hears a sleepless train lost in the distance, in a private conversation with itself. In English or in Spanish the same hollow midnight thing rolls off its tongue . . .

It's late, no river or valentine for a hundred miles. He wonders if there were people, cousins or sisters (in mousy brown hats and plain brown shoes, hands folded politely in their laps) responding to letters from home, on the train. Wonders what they'll partake . . . or if they found ways to deal with their loneliness . . . maybe one morning they just walked out the door and in a bluster tore it down. Maybe they held a gun of vengeance to their troubled agony . . .

Maybe two old men, faces lost their steel to struggle . . . Wonders if they smoke cigarettes or have bad habits . . . wonders if they ever stood on a ledge, squeezed by decades, but could not commit . . . thinks maybe the conductor's snoring in the last car.

The train's madrigal dies . . .

He sighs. Scratches an old ache.

Night at the bottom.

Entangled in his hunger . . .

Cold will come, charging or in slow strokes, and wall him in. Get in his head. Grind his bones . . . Strip him of past and reason and rhyme and sail. Strip him sore. Distract him from sleep with poison. Even if he curses at it.

Cold just like severe weather . . . nothin' calm in what it tears down . . . Cold, it don't gleam. Smashes, swallows you whole, but it don't gleam.

He'll go down to the bottom of the bottle. Hear all the voices. Stand in front of his burden and when the levee breaks, listen to it cry . . . The hours spent roaming the drunken dance will alter, waver, crawl slowly . . . there'll be pressure and spots of murk and monsters created then lost when the rhythm of concentrating slips on alcohol and laughing and maybe a scream . . .

When what comes after Before—dry and rattling wall-to-wall—leaves and he shakes off the crumbs of crust and spent embers, burns the canvas, he'll lock down his memories.

The sun will reappear.

Then he'll hide his knife . . . and the gun.

And stick out his thumb.

(Bohren & Der Club of Gore "Texas Keller")

Dead 'Round Here Tonight

The day (a poison fast as $20 sex with eyes stained by desperate and cruel, and full of shitty street-junk) ends sucked up by darkness. No one notices, no one utters a huhmm or laughs or clicks a tongue . . . Pain and wounds stand handcuffed by yesterday's rat-infested smile to tomorrow torn down by tragic . . .

Someone is killing someone now. (A gun—the bullets howl, twist, rip, germinate.) A crowd of blind, aggressive hearts don't even pause their chitchatting about the broadloom temptations . . .

On a dog-eared handbill for Jesus an abandoned loser, never beautiful, or daring, or poetically suited for the spiritual, has scrawled Disenfranchised by CHAOS—will work for food.

"If I could."

Coming and going, sure and NO and why(gasped) and Boom!Boom! Boom! over small teeth in Don't's tear-blackened opera, the blight—the visit of void, looped with grieve. Nomads without means to gain or weapons, shrunk and lacking hands to comb the hemlock tides . . .

The day ends sucked up by darkness.

"If I could . . ."

. . . Lower-Class Were (bent by tests and hammer-hard Rule) and moths tossed in the windstorm of flashing city lights, wounded lives that are called back to days lost in the slow-suicide lonesomeness of dreams gone by . . .

The shell of a man, worn by decades of suffering and monstrous Hard prevailing, "If I could."

Arguing with things hard and Pit-wailed . . .

Shadows hunting the shadows for shadows . . . Things fluttering . . . leaning, waiting to see full-blown, or to score . . . Bad, dry things waiting for money, or flesh . . .

A little man, thinning gray hair. "I would." Nods sure, like in maybe-I guess. Sure. Doesn't remember angels or good hearts.

A dim corner of shrugs faces a darker one of frantic with unbearable leashed to near-panic ... Cheap dark streets ... Golden days, sick and insomnia-white, moaning behind locked doors ...

Black hat. Black coat, dead man in it. White. Sick. Out of illusions and full of old lies and trapdoors of got stuck that festered into fear, he's tired as last week. "I ... would."

No good.

Nothing here to grasp ... not even the wind ... Some settle for words full of themselves, or

fake kisses ...

A hundred shadows, not a smile ... and souls strained by "No."-"No."-"No." ... (Every sleeve has tracks of grief.)

Some await the sun ...

... Swollen clocks ... damnation and rot and no ceasefire ... toxic disappointment and volcanoes of pus ... and beer and beer and beer and beer and beer until you forget about careless if it will make SOME-THING happen, or let some gesture leak half a Edenic chance ...

Nights of cluttered never-never.

"If I could ..."

Sign says, NOW! NOW! NOW!—hand behind it say, if you have the cash. But all the pockets are filled with gone-gone-gone. Or DEAD and GONE ...

The blonde with heavy, dead eyes is hunting. Cash to buy meat in hand. Teeth that began their journey to The End, ready to chew it.

Face to face. Ghoul and half-dead ex-dreamer meet on a street corner. Both back again ... Only one will walk away.

Hard done up pretty (over the flesh covering ugly inside) flashes that wicked smile. Lets her brimming cleavage stimulate judgment intercepted by unexpected.

Glazed eyes take both in. A mouth that barely remembers the sky opens. No word comes.

"Care to have a drink?" she asks.

Head nods sure.

A hand on an arm. Images of the heart exchanged.

"This way."

A straight line through lights that curse ... She leads the live corpse. The wind hisses ...

Without a "Thing is ..." he follows. Mouth open, lonely trickling from it.

Stairs, banister, dirty cracked linoleum. Broken bottles of too late on the floor ... A canceled place, poor beyond blandness ... Third floor. A doorway that doesn't need a key. A bed in an empty room in a shabby shell of a building behind 20-dollar hotel rooms ...

She hands him a pint bottle. Half full of fast.

He takes it.

Fingers slow to unscrew the cap.

Bottle back. Swallows the burn.

Coughs.

"Take off your shoes and get comfortable, baby."

Something from his past trying to claw its way up his throat.

She takes off her dress.

Drops it on the dusty floor.

His eyes burn.

Hers are cold. Even as they lock on the veins in his neck.

Takes off her bra. "Like?"

His starved eyes are locked on her hard nipples.

Mouth open. No word comes.

Nods sure.

Tart, she laughs. It sounds lived in.

Eyes still aimed, he doesn't hear the tenor of her cold hiss.

Stares. His breath is loud, short. Feels something like heat trying to get up from the floor of yesterday.

Slides off her dark purple panties. Shifts her hip. "You're trapped now." Causal as the gruff "Come on up, get it!" of a carnival barker.

Takes another swig. Tries to burn through dull, remember saturation and fire and vibrating deep. Wants the future to let him expand and spark.

Wants one more taste of something new. Thinks even ten minutes will do.

"Want me to cummon over, baby?"

He nods sure.

Something like spirit appears.

Forgets errors. Thinks motion. Take.

Nods sure.

He looks at her plush outline—wants to contract warmth (not a banquet, just something to eat), sprouts.

The room starts to drip with desire.

Fifteen slow steps . . .

She sees him trying to live on one more time. Lips barely parted. Smiles. "Good boy."

Her fingers on his two-day sandpaper face.

"Gonna feel so good, baby."

He nods sure.

Snaps his neck. No victoriously or mercy in it.

No kisses . . .

No soaring on fire . . .

Little left of the cadaver. Bones. Shreds and stray bits of meat. Face and scalp. Genitals she never touched. Tossed aside guts.

Naked. She looks in the dirty mirror.

Sees the blood.

"This dead body."

Sees her breasts, her belly.

Hands cup her breasts. Something that passes for disgust on her bloody lips "My dead body."

. . . Remembers a sweet young boy (hands of fire, eyes of tender desires) . . . the freshly repainted red convertible with the top down, brushing up to the night . . . Making out, tongues and lips and finger-tips, locked in a first kiss where youth dreams as one . . . A barked storm-growl, and the red eyes set over rotting fangs, some of them black . . . Young love meets cold, venomous hunger. One ache meets its opposite. Lover's Lane becomes a Dead End . . . The Thing with red eyes and fangs, and tearing claws, eats most of the boy and leaves her awash in blood . . .

trembling, in streaked tears . . .

And with her life wiped out . . . *infected* . . .

She looks in the cracked mirror. Sees the smeared grime, the blood . . . But no vestige of What if . . .

She doesn't tremble.

Or even nod.

Doesn't shed a tear . . .

Or a cold, heavy "Fuck."

[*Bohren and der Club of Gore "Dead End Angels"*]

The Delirium of a Worm-Wizard

Small, shrouded in pure white cotton, I have come . . .

Far
from the lush shades of the palm-girt wells, and
the designs of the watchmen, women, and
merchants of the great market by the sea;
beyond
pigeons on ruffled ironwork and curses sung,
and my simple neighbors splashing in their fountains of drunkenness,
and the cock-a-doodle-do greeting of glimmering dawn poised upon the
windowpane, and the rushing electric clock that skips softly and wishes
no one well . . .
beyond the twisted gorges, winds crying in their ruining bellies,
beyond the courtyards of hunting birds and
the paths left by scorpions with murderous appetites, and
villages of insects leaking like pain onto the sands, and
the stony hills that hold no blue pools . . .

The endless bright sun on my back,
my naked shadow, head down, pulls me along.

On the way,
forgetting the waters of the Jordan.
All the shelves flooded with obsessed and woolly mumbo-jumbo
the champions of truth have not yet burned and
the hungry, bickering Jews behind me . . .

To each vacant mirage,
cold, stillborn Nevers bloated with sizzling laughter, I walk.
Oh how I damn each arsonist, each poisoned chalice!

My clipped litany of venom sweet as a moist fig upon my tongue . . .
Roba El Khaliyeh is a cruel empty pot,
           dashing hope with sultry lies of ease.

How I long for the calm pronouncements of rose-scented moon-
flowers
                              and silk divans—
                              For sweet air and colors,
and the ribbons of an angel's laughter raining upon me,
or the sculptured hum strolling the ornamented sidewalks of Vienna
and Berlin,
or one more closing time with the anthem of friends cloaked about
me
                              like a miracle cure for disorder,
                       but I am only thirst's bloated anguish,
                                     staggering drunkenly.

           On the way,
centuries traveled;
shadowed by the temptations of Christ stretching;
the polished avalanche of ambition-anointed chiefs and kings and
wizards
discovered to be useless exercises . . .
All born of heaven or earth, dust in the wind, indeed.

Like camel-footed caravans whose destinations lie in the East—
           each laden with yard goods for the unmarried daughters of
shepherds
           and Tomorrows destined for homes in old photographs—
twelve and twelve sunsets leave me . . .
The wind and I continue our steps south.

Each footprint I leave vanishes like a solitary drop of rain.
Each moist breath exhaled, expects a reply, a signal on the horizon,
                       but the long road will not compromise.
I wonder if my map of these dry seas was rendered by an imbecile
                              or a poisonous snake.

And my pleasureless companion and I—
and my shadow, glowing in the full-light of day—arrive in Irem.
     Yet only I am worn by the cruelties of ever-attendant, animal
       heat . . .
I would collapse like a sick-thing failing,
but this strange city of enchantments
falls upon me like the silver drafts of the wild moon—

         The burned avenues of many-columned Irem,
              its linear corners hiding assassins;
        Sublime trees—limbs blended like flocks in flight;
  Shapes and sand-eroded spires as seen in fogs where demons traffic with
                          wraiths
    or Chinese paintings filled with festivals of love and death and war;
      Ziggurats forgotten kings borrowed from Paradise . . .

Here, I, the nimble-fingered hunter, will fill my pockets.
I will never grow old, or suffer the black condition of Doom's web—
I am thunder singing.

Then: touched by the swell of night, the world,
       suddenly chilled as if by a pure frost feeding
       or the crippling pecks of a lie of love,
       is unsettled and confusing—
As one in a dream I walk in the Garden of Sin with jangled senses,
the jubilant flies of Doomsday, binding
as a malignant weight or unexpected enlightenment
       —light from lamp and star, playing
       like drunken shadows in a flawed mirror, showering believing
in a different now
       —outnumbering scents as strong as death screeching from a
crossbow
       —sounds on this island of scorched dust, an unrepeatable
river of reverberation;
     The Noise of Heaven?
This flailing ode of death,
roaring like the thunder-heart of a gluttonous city of famine
rotting with snapping mouths, or the Devil's disobedient laugh,

just imagined to lighten the darkness?

Having looked into my heart, I hesitate—*I know the dark, the Perfect Emptiness,*
and conflicted, harnessed in tremors, fear.
I pray for fog and thunders.
I kneel on dry earth cracked like old skin,
feel winds playing after the heat.
But all is dying leaves, blazes in miniature.

I—refusing the pungent sleep of the deadman—
cling fast to the mage's discipline,
find myself,
and ride from distress . . .

Darkness into light—

Beyond the south wall I ascend three-hundred and thirty-three steps of red stone.
I rise at a right angle to the east;
pass through a confusion of chambers old when Zoser rested in his mother's womb,
seeing unsealed space in the disposition of the copper pins and dials.
Ceilings which must have wings soar a thousand miles above me.
I listen to the carnivorous quiet reflect off sand and stone.
I proceed by vestibules whose stories were demolished by sand,
march through corbelled arches and vaults inlaid with ancient scents;
past unfamiliar engines,
surely for measuring the attitudes of prominent stars, and
broken furniture and orderly mosaics shaped from memory.
Within a stunted tower I read inscriptions ripe with malice on a wall,
each, loud as the glare of a severed head set upon a spike
when Death's bright tournament concludes,
speaks of Terrible Visitors in the house
and the beginning of the Sleep of Ruin.
Decay surrounding me, long do I toil in the cursed halls of long-night.
I stand within the annular central pillars,
examining the perfection of invading starlight on masonry . . .

My fingers slide over the stark blaze of the sigils.
I place my hand in The Hand That Reaches for the Key to the Gate
and speak the Forbidden Names
and talk to cursed spirits risen in the temple.

Into another fierce darkness—

Night is a hissing swarm.
Surrounded by the shining of things without shadows.
Bells, and
a return to a theme towering like winter open on the north shores of
the Norsemen.
Ghostly moonrays and wind—
Nightsick with storm-dreams, the poison bride of flesh,
her fire-flowers writing on me

deep—

The arrows of secrets, vibrations;
unmistakable, a shower of lions loose in the lost land.

Where is that vesperal testament of my youth which sings of divinity,
that postcard painting the coils of home,
the day little hands clapping was enough?
Where?

I smell the horde of corruption resuscitated
—tangle of smoldering notions flickering,
gushing,
a galaxy of nails speeding from towerblocks—
Tomorrow's funeral today.
Yesterday and peaceful memories
are now,
things without muscle, ambushed
in the rushing, the first wave.

Filled with voices, each in their own tongue echoing, "*The blood is water.*"
I greet what I can't hold back
—Dazzling details.
Under the Dome of Dreams, conquered—ravished by shapes of terror,

                              my tongue dries and curls up.
Irem's enormous inhabitants have come, furrowing talons firm in prey.

Like every vanished rainmaker before me
I have learned . . .
                    From the desires of my soul, holding it
                                        (gestation)
                                        love, fear, need . . .
Time is not weeks dragging flung open days into months,
            or the rumbling mountain of history
            or medicine.
I, betrothed to the Dragons In the Stars by a vow of death,
feel its blast.
It, the Hidden-Abundance Swelling, has arrived
—Here, now and forever, Oblivion's riddle solved by the worm's
eternal elegy.

Compliant, I formally bow;
beg to be enraptured by Their Secrets.
            "O Lords, Most High, all praise to Thee . . ."
All the pious elder phrases shouted in the stormy air . . .
The sentence passed.
With a wave of my hand the blade, lightning to a surface, arcs—
                                        I have ended the story.

As the Sun Still Burns Away

for David Prior

The Great War had ended, but summer, this year vigorous as a swatted hornet, was here again and the tail-end of September was far away. One crime ended and now a new one swaggered over the border.

An empty whiskey glass on the porch railing in the sun . . .

A sign face down in the sand . . .

Hours drifting . . . Problems nested in barbwire and sagebrush. "Somewhere," a *sotto voce* dream, pushed out warm as the hot weather.

Bitter.

Hurt. Broken. Hit too hard by what slipped away.

Spilled.

No rodeo come to town.

Nothin' to be late to . . .

Nothing changes here. Not the immobile animal sun, not the hot dust. Not the tarry braids of long cold nights. Not the flat and torn carcasses littered like dead-end signs along Route 93.

The dark. A lonely place of waiting. As It Was fades. The hunger does not . . .

The day's immense light pinches the terrain here. Beats it down, chews it with wild teeth. No one here can recall mild. Most believe it to be a lie. No one here gets to fallback, the frontline has always been the frontline.

You don't see a wild eye or anything sprout here . . .

It's a small town, barely a town by modern standards. Two streets wide—east to west, five long—runnin' north to south, no downtown. Not a garden to be found. No newspaper. No stoplight. No need for a sheriff these days. Everything burning, but no fun. No excitement, closest jook joint 30-odd miles away. Lots of half-crazy sittin' 'round here, trying to sidestep the seeking sun. On porches, on fences with the broken bottle wind chimes and steer and coyote skulls. Out behind the shed, hiding in the weak, limited shade . . .

Light . . .

And dark . . .

The course, head devouring its tail, flows . . . repeats unchanged . . .

✷

They laid the flowered heart of innocence in the ground last week. Anointed her eyes with silver coins, whispered a dry prayer. Threw in a good handful of salt.

And hoped . . .

Hoped the magic cloth they wrapped her in would keep away Blue Dress Annie. Hoped the salt would keep Annie's tongue in her mouth, if it came to that. Didn't really think it would work, but Hayes said, "Fuck. Can't hurt. Can it?"

Maria Luisa cried at the thought of more violence. Cried through the remaining hours of light and when the stage roared with darkness kept right on crying.

A shot glass and a bottle on the table. Six lonely feet away, sequestered, a cup of black coffee; hot an hour back.

Hayes looked out the window and mumbled something about the plastic bag keeping the smell contained.

"Maybe," he whispered. "Might?"

Maria Luisa wanted to laugh. After the tears she wanted anything that was not a crown of pain. Her hands were on her knees. Kept them from shaking.

"Shoulda burned her. Ain't no music in that black bed . . . $40 dollars for a dress she'll never dance in . . . A waste." *Out here everything's wasted. At least we didn't waste money on shoes . . .*

It was almost dark. The crimson scar of sun was losing its battle with night. It didn't want to ship out, yet what could it do? The black came tumbling down and no one could fix the broken sky when the black thawed and stretched out.

Maria Luisa took a sip of cold coffee. Feared to look up, to catch a glimpse of dark staining the window. Coyotes would be prowling soon. The full moon was coming. Blue Dress Annie would be wandering.

He saw the black. Feared it. "They should have burned that shack and *her* in it when they had the chance."

"Should have filled her belly with rusty nails. She'd be full then."

"She'll never be full," Hayes said. "That old bitch is as empty as 40 miles of barren sand."

Maria Luisa remembered the bells of a church in Boston she heard when she was a girl. Haunted, lonely bells. No one had offered a hand to calm their dim mourning. She could hear them now. She wanted to get up and turn on the radio. Or the TV. Maybe bake a pie. She didn't get up. Couldn't.

Hayes was pacing 'round the room. Walked the worn hardwood like he was a rodent on a wheel, mindlessly racing toward an escape it couldn't see. No salvation in the circle. Wanted to go to back to the window and see if anything had changed. Didn't. Wanted to. Really did. But he didn't. Couldn't. Stunned with violence, or the language of poison and splinters he knew hope and a prayer and all the wishin' in the world or in a jar of homebrew wouldn't change shit.

He looked at Maria Luisa. Frozen in all that's hard to bear. Still as a cold evening without a breeze. Shackled, tortured, bound by a noose of leftover shame. Looked at the plain gold band on her finger. What good had it done? Didn't fix it. Didn't bring grace. Didn't even make him stop drinking. Not for long anyway . . .

Lot of fucking good it did. This place sucks the energy out of every-thing . . .

He turns his gaze from his wife's quivering hands.

Sucked Amy dry. Dry as a bone.

He'd tried to love her. Really had. In his fashion; quiet—closed at first, trying not to step on her toes as they danced.

And she tried back. Hard sometimes. Even when the parts were uncomfortable and worn thin. Some days, playing the role of an enemy at the gate, she pushed hard. Ragged sometimes.

Weary and sometimes scared of the next page, he pulled back.

He walked the walk.

She turned and walked away.

The sun had watched it. The moon spent hundreds of nights watching too.

Jibes, smoke, and lies. Mercy no part of it. Ashes to ashes and no map in the king-size bed. Flat out of treasure, full of time and the ruins of bridges burned.

Lonely afternoons when the leaking sun tired of drifting and drifting and was shutting down, her eyes searched the highway, or his locked on her throat. Never a fist, but that didn't mean it didn't bruise deep . . .

September and April, sometimes gently in the orchard of distances they stand. No sentimental day trips, no translations . . . Moments—ill blossoms, blind and pensive, whisper forever in the mirror. Silhouettes of the nightmare loiter . . . After what's happened, they folded, turn away from the open book, there is no strength in the echoes . . . Alone and alone—ghosts landing, tiny hands on a bleak avenue where the sun was turned off . . .

The hours, emptied, pass, leave poison.

Shadows hang on the wall. More than a lot of days they didn't have the ammunition to meet the lingering shadows head-on . . .

. . . Some nights the whiskey rubbed hard.

He shot her when she rattled. She shoved her dreams in old boxes of then and wondered why he couldn't get anything right.

That night. Both were whiskey-fueled, drilling, waving off consequences and other arrangements. They were fighting again. Revved up, screaming like horns of accusation and doom. Their daughter at the top of the stairs, crying for them to stop . . . begging—for the hundredth time . . . she slipped . . . tumbling . . . a short scream came all the way to the bottom and touched their feet . . .

A week gone by and Maria Luisa hadn't got out of that chair. Didn't take to her bed, dozed right there at the table. Didn't think a single word that didn't scratch, tighten behind her eyes, her shoulders, the grieving in her chest. Day and night wrapped in lost love and gestures, now smoke awakened in a mind of bloodfire.

She glanced at every side, every nook, saw little but too late . . .

No noises.

Voiceless, the shaking of broken dreams.

She turned away from the *failed* declaration on his face.

A week gone by and Hayes still paced. Walked to the window and stared. Walked to the cabinet over the sink and got out another bottle of whiskey. Day and night soaked by the view out the window and the naked whiskey.

Not a bird or pickup or car passed.

What passed for a tree out in the yard of sand didn't sway. Couldn't. No probing wind weighted in heat from farther down the line came.

Yesterday and anguish, wounded matadors drunk on their own inability, couldn't work up a "Yes, move on," remained rooted to the floor.

The sky could not even summon a cloud or a silver bird . . .

Dust came and settled wherever it liked . . .

Barely a sound.

He turned away from the hard time on her unmoving lips.

Both broken.

Disintegrating.

Rigid. Unsteady. Trembling.

Blind. Pride wrapped in something they couldn't swallow.

Without a crutch.

Morning the seventh day. The coyotes had gone to bed. She made him eggs and toast. He pretended to eat. Washed down the few bites with a few shots. Went to the window. There was no music in the air. No wind. Each memory in the shooting gallery cried.

Noon came and burned out. The sun lost its grip. Evening was slain. Wind and blackness came.

Over a scab of rock the moon came up. Sat there—still as any dead man or junked wreck—without a word.

For the first time in a week he went outside. Walked through the back gate to the grave. His face turned to the small swell of sand.

Lost. He didn't kneel. Didn't think to pray.

Smoked with one hand. Drank with the other.

Wanted to say something to her. Couldn't tighten his fingers around a single word.

Maria Luisa came out. Stood there. Could have been a cigar store Indian after a fire. She had words but they were caught up . . . Her hands held nothing of use.

The weather was almost black . . .

And they heard the voice singing. Parched, like a scratch or a blade, or dangerous wings stained in cold and dust.

"Sleep all day. Sleep all day. In that box of dust. They took me away from my babies. From my life. My life . . . Sonsabitches and whores, cheap fuckin' whores. Took away my life."

Come up from the blackest deeps of the dry earth, she walked. Comin' toward the wire. Toward the fence. Comin'. Comin', in the full light of the glaring moon, arms rattlin' and shakin'.

Wasn't a ghost. Wasn't dead dead. They killed her sure. Sent her down into dangerous ground. But she didn't lie down and take it. Not for long.

With curses of hellfire and abhorrence, curses woven in the grimy inferno of greedy hearts, they dumped in her grave, one nail of spat venom with each shovelful of dry sand. And all that pain and hate, mixed in that awful fevered darkness, they'd got up in her bones. Oozed through her arteries and veins and cavities. Molded and remodeled her. She shook with each black pit thorn as it rippled through her. All her hate and longing and all their wide-lipped curses bit deep, bit and bit over and over, and over as the moon shone down.

Eighty long years and no rattlesnake or coyote or bird or lizard would come near the cursed ground of Annie's grave. Eighty long years she laid there, festering in the sunless deeps. Each night waiting for the next to fall.

Then she came. When the moon came up and shouted. Stepped right out of that desert-oven grave as if it had a door on it. Came and took what was due her before a single week had passed.

And this night of wide-mouth moon kissing every weakness, exposing every silent stain of shadow with its great silver eye, she was coming again. Comin' with her grunting procession of babies followin'. Her babies, not a one with shoes, some naked, every one dead eyes locked on the hem of her threadbare, faded blue dress.

"Took away my life . . . Took my babies from my bosom."

Comin'.

"Took and took." Hellfire eyes ripping the night.

Hayes emptied his shotgun. Maria Luisa tried to scream.

Comin'.

Hard as he could he threw his shotgun at her. Missed.

"Took."

Comin'.

. . . from a hell—a sewer blistered in sin—beneath a hell . . . stained white bone showin' through sunken, split cheek and gashed forehead. Cankerous skin on her hands and chin nibbled on, dripping with the filth of death's wasteland. Dry, split skin spotted with the unholy muck of ebony pastures . . . Smoldering with repellent things broken free of their moorings and crawled up to her as she lie in her box shut below the cold night air, crawled up and rubbed off . . .

Comin'.

A corpse of disquiet. A twisted corpse of blood-red gestures, murmuring and embroidered with the unearthly . . .

Comin'.

A black lump of hate and desire comin'. One slow hard step. And another . . . Comin'. And no man or damnation would turn her . . .

Comin'. A slowfire hell train . . . Nothing but moon and sand in her way.

He looked for a rock or a board to throw.

Nothing . . .

Maria Luisa knotted her fingers to pray. But she'd lost her use for it and couldn't remember the way.

Comin'. Close. Too close.

They could smell her ruin. It bit like spurs.

He made a fist.

Blue Dress Annie laughed. A leather hiss, low and hungry.

Over the shaking stump of her fingerless left hand: "*On another night you will ride with me . . . Both of you—hearts and foul flesh.*"

Every heart-stopping, babbled lunatic tale of Blue Dress Annie's black dagger claws-to-dig-deep and glaring, vicious teeth full-blown animal terror in their minds, they ran from the grave of their daughter.

Ran like they were runnin' from their own sin . . .

Annie stood over that small grave and her babies fell down to their knees and with small leathered hands and black-razor claws dug. With nary a bark or a screech, ripped that hard-baked sand from the ground until they touched the hardwood box of empty space.

Then Annie wailed. And the top of that hardwood box flew open and she spread her arms.

"*Come to Mama, Child.*"

Maria Luisa and Hayes's six-year-old daughter, Amy, white Spanish lace, Sunday school dress and box-store cheap, faux white pearl barrettes, broke neck and all came into her arms.

Her iron, deadwood arms pulled that girl in, flesh to coarse flesh, hugged her tight, gripped the small of that child's back with the one good hand, the one the town folk had not sheared the fingers from, and she bent and kissed the child on the top of her head. Kissed her like she was one of heaven's perfect angels.

Desperate for real love, the girl clung to her.

"Mama loves you. You be a good girl now and do what Mama says."

Annie's pointed nose twitched in disgust. Her long tongue slid from rank autumnal lips, licked the salt from the dead girl's face. Another agonized twitch and winch, she spat twice.

. . . Carrying that girl in her twisted arms Annie walked into the desert night. Back to her bible black funeral nest. And her babies, seventeen scabbed, dirty cherubs she had come to claim over the years, followed . . .

Nose in the nape of the child's neck, a gentle nudging: *"You are a gift, child . . . A sweet gift."*

Nothing here changes . . .

Eighty years ago the town folk took her life. Said she was a whore and *brujería*. Said she poisoned the Reverend's wife with terrible and esoteric *hechizos* so she could get in his bed. Cut her. Beat her. Opened her flesh in a hundred places. Put her down in a hole. To rot. Down in a hot, dry hole—with no coffin—for the insects and time to feed on.

They took her from her babies. And when one of theirs died . . . Annie came. Came straight away for her baby . . .

Came to get a piece of her life back.

When one of the town's folk died Blue Dress Annie came. Came from that dark sand where dark dreams roll to the repast with her starving, jackal-faced babies—need hissing over withered, tiny dry tongues—and did something different with the flesh. Lips parted in death over the prize, her dark, lean children leave few shreds of meat for the empty sand's other scavengers to unwrap . . . Leave bones for the sun to burn away . . .

[Harold Budd, The Serpent (In Quicksilver) / Abandoned Cities]

Caligari, Again

It was after the Peter Lorre film . . . I think. A piano was playing. Some-thing—a quiet thing, soft and alluring, breathing slow. Almost a death march. I felt I'd heard it once before . . .

❦

The moon is a window of ice wrecked in soft embrace of the river of midnight . . . its banks couldn't hold the invisible . . . it had rained earlier . . .

A show was in town, between the weeds, love and wonders for sale. Color and motion for a few coins. Everything—women, remarks, glowed like hot coals. Tight white sweaters, fingernails painted red, holding tickets. Men were drinking, their libidos diving right in . . . Children laughing back and forth. Candy wrappers and popcorn on the ground. There was a fire-eater and a dancer with silver bracelets on her smooth ankles. Brothers and sisters, whispering. Monkeys. Riddles and games spiraling. You could buy fruit, thought you could buy the stars if you asked.

By the spinning wheel a woman called a man's name. Only a burst of charming music answered back. Under a wooden bench small birds with dolls eyes fought over donut crumbs.

The colors laughed as they escaped their boundaries. The lights flashed. Out past sunset and the line where cement gave way to barns, little plots of pasture that could be, Shanghai (in that tent), or Paris (under the Ferris wheel), or Hollywood (behind that frayed curtain) . . . Things from out of the past, something eternal twinkles here. Food, the smell tumbling over you. Moths seeking The Grail, no end to the maze. It was all here.

No speed limit here.

Eyes. Their first time. Eyes. Traveling back in the textures of re-membering. Eyes, sweeping the future. Eyes everywhere, being drawn together. Some were frightful, vivid paintings, the eyes of fugitives. They ate the light as if it was text—I could see the words in the whites of their eyes . . . One long walk of activities, stories, jostling . . . I had a glass of wine. A woman offered me a seat. Her hands were old, grotesque. They were demons who wanted my equilibrium . . .

Darkness spread from the lacquered door. Nice falls under the turn of the spider, the kaleidoscope blooms. The funhouse in the mirror . . . *a blur* . . . *movement* . . . Hands. Tiny flames in the soul . . . A splash of shifting red. A young woman. The pain sees me. It takes hold like winter's bitter breath. It bites, takes . . . I hear The Voice . . . The lights go down. There on the stage again . . . The show must go on . . . I hear The Voice . . .

You must [a dove's wing whisper]—

You must [a dove's wing whisper]—

The storm churns. I follow the steps of the young woman from the funhouse . . .

Labyrinth streets, crooked ways. No fog. No trees. The sweet chase. Cast-iron shadows jabbing . . . the shape of simple clothes backlit by far away lights . . . splinters . . . Lights and sounds, a one-two punch, leak out of bruised neighborhood . . . A man, one of Eternity's stray dogs, drops a brown-bag bottle, curses . . . The transmutation of voices crossing . . . Cabs, carrying the refugees of weeping meadows, roll by . . . In and out of valleys. Around corners stained with the whispered names of children . . . A prison to some, I know the curves of these shadows . . . Small waves, I can't see them, but they want to tell me something . . . Something uprooted waiting . . .

An old building, missing pieces of its nineteenth-century face of uncomfortable gray. Magic windows, lights fanning out. There are cigars and bourbon and good cheer behind the lights. She is upstairs, gone the red working dress. In pale-pale blue now . . . I am a blue-black shadow in the sea of shadows . . . I am the breath of the night, moving over scars. Slowly. The air tingles with her scent . . . *She is so young* . . . Alone, a hummingbird in the gladbush. Her neck is a delicate vase. Her lips are cherries, roses. Roses. I can smell the secrets of the garden . . .

Her eyes, doe soft, doe brown, are the eyes of innocence . . . her hands are doves, soft soaring doves . . . Soft . . . *soft* embrace . . . soft . . . as dust . . .

I am hardness.

She can't see me . . . yet . . .

The soft cushions. White. White. The hills of her breasts smoldering. Sin provokes the dance . . . The bride, moments ago a calm swan, shivers . . . *as if she was allergic* . . . The overture. Her eyes are closed . . . noiseless tears . . .

Her shoulders of moon flesh make me drunk. The moment, a flaming lullaby, shining up. The moment. The moment. The moment an instant later—beauty conjured, there on the platform its meaning possesses me. The mask off. The real face, I break from the hypnotism. Her trick. We are side by side—joined by the pulse. The gestures of the blade on white sheets . . . Afloat, I sing the dearsong . . .

Red. A dark spring underneath. The flower bending, cracked open, hot, and sweet . . .

All that glitters . . .

Red. I glide. Sketch in thunder.

All that glitters . . .

Red. Breath ruptures.

Red—little birds flying, smiling at the spider. Little birds dancing. A festival of naked fire, she and I danced. In silence.

Autumn touches me and I depart.

❊

I lie in my room. Two voices from the television enter the room . . .

"She was nineteen . . ."
"Warm to the touch . . . But . . ."

"Caligari."

"From the shadows . . . Knife . . ."
"Carnival . . . Behind the curtain—an oblong box . . . Twisted . . ."

"Summer silenced."

"Guilty."

"Sickness. That and the grave are countries creased in his face."

"Society must protect itself from this darkness. Your future hours end here."

I'm floating ... burnt murmurings carry memories on their tongues ... In the black chamber I see lights ... the dusts moves ... I hear The Voice. I hear The Voice—The Voice right behind me ...

You must [a dove's wing whisper]—
You must [a dove's wing whisper]—

❁

Out in the open I hide behind sunglasses. I have a beard now ... Faceless monsters, flapping newspapers, babble all around me. A red dress, red handbag, red shoes—a slender vase to win. She steps off the streetcar. Sunset Boulevard. Her ankles convince me to follow ...

(after Supersilent "c1.1" and "C-5.1")

Long-Stemmed Ghost Words

(for Alanna Quinn, the Mistress of the Yellow Chamber)

Weeds . . . a world of doors . . . cracked open shirts . . . tarnished faces of buildings . . . strange drumbeats of love . . . ghosts . . . ghosts of . . . passengers in an empty square (with no trains) without codes . . . mirrors and doors . . . alone . . . strange ghosts . . . dead door buzzers in dead doorways . . .

The phone called disturbed her. With just her coat and bag, walked out of her office to chase darkness again. A few quiet drinks in Ionesco's first, of course. She hoped she'd find a little stardust in the skeletons and minutes there . . .

Most nights boredom brushed her sleeve. Yet every once and again, on a street invaded by the uncommon or iron silence, or at the top of the stairs, she brushed up against darkness . . .

The second-floor reading nook of her favorite bookstore. A group, huddled, hunting fans, each gaunt and darkly beautiful in funeral black on black . . .

He was holding the thin book open. Reading his poetry aloud.

Alanna moved in closer to hear.

> *From each death The King's misery narrows.*
> *He breathes*
> *And phrases of Oblivion*
> *Fall from his spreading wings.*
>
> *Before his eye days collapse*
> *And the blue stories of evening,*
> *Once loved as spring flowers by the light,*
> *Weep no more.*

His gin-and-embers voice falls off. He looks right, down, as if he's lost some history. Looks like his head is in a noose.
What is that? she wonders.
Sotto voce: "It's so sad."
He read another passage.

Lost, yet . . .
not afraid of the soft blackness of the stars . . .

She saw a tide of clouds come. Saw him, kissed by the void, lose a few more tears. He is the son of a rigid lightless sky. Motherly instinct kicked in. Alanna wanted to comfort him. Take him in her arms, his chin on the soft whiteness of her shoulder, and tell him he would be o.k.

Last night she sat in her apartment and listened to the strange beauty of black moth guitars and circling cellos and candle-river pianos sow rapture from thoughtful yearning. Sipped tea . . . and drifted.

Now . . .

Once upon a time at dusk and the interludes of Truth find her . . .

In a hard chair in a dim corner, she sat in the last row. Listened.

> *Star of my exile,*
> *echo the heartbeat that breaks,*
> *with each rushing wave,*
> *upon the shore*
>   *Of Carcosa*

A flutter of applause . . . the assent into air, chairs are freed of the weight . . . eyes shifting, watching, accelerating . . .

An exuberant few rush to him with copies of his book of lost days to sign. She sits in her corner. She is good with coffins and gravestones and quiet storms. Many times she has waited before. Waiting again does not change or harm her.

The labyrinth of limbs gone.

—Hello

—Hi

—I saw you
—I was listening
They talk. Chance between them.
They go.
Drinks in a soft blue corner in Mur.
Slow. Both are.
Then
a threshold, a spark—solid,
corks uncorked
. . . pouring out.
—Camus
—spaghetti
—M
—Kwaidan
—The Pillow Book
—*beautiful things*
—*you are*

Masks set aside. The madness of yesterday's carnival, that masquerade of uneasy undercurrents—deluded whispers of dust spilling, removed from lids and bosom.

A new sea. Sparrows of Now, running wild, wings clear of mourning . . .

Closer.
Each chooses Now.
Fingers woven in fingers.
They bind the interest between them with tomorrow.
Eyes without excuses.
—Voluptuous Panic
—The expanded edition.
—Yes. Kakadu
Laughter . . . each gives a little . . .
—Steppenwolf. When I was lost in hungry childhood days of thunder, and graves . . . Young
—You still are
. . . The bottle empty they go, strolling, taking in gentle rewards.
Alanna's apartment.
White tea.
He watches the teacup touch her lips.

She watches the teacup touch his lips.

And more talk . . . magic unlatched and humming in the room . . . They do not hear the language of the clock . . .

A raw sun comes into the room. Opens its yellow throat . . . stretches into fire . . .

The poet, smitten, leaves Lady Luck.

She takes to her bed of quilts. Hugs the fluffy whiteness of her extra pillow. Wonders if he can write beautiful things on flesh.

❀

Waiting.

For the second date.

Ready. And nervous . . .

Her hair.

Her eyes.

Her clothes.

Just so.

Waiting. Anxious.

An interlude of amore becoming visible . . .

She blushes . . .

And he—music, a kiss, is there . . . Leaning in her doorway.

In his good pants and good shoes.

—Hi

—Hi

—Ready

—Yes

. . . driving through the city . . .

Weeds . . . a world of doors . . . tarnished faces of buildings . . . strange drumbeats of love . . . ghosts . . . ghosts of . . . passengers in an empty square, waiting . . . mirrors and doors . . . strange ghosts . . . dead doorways . . .

Laughing.

The top is down. The moon up.

Alanna holds the single, long-stemmed yellow rose he brought for her. Smiles. Laughs with just her eyes.

Miles. Other cars fall away . . . their ship sails to a different port.

. . . secrets begin . . . dead doorways . . .

Journeying. No compass. The streets and roads swallow them as they invade autumn in his automobile.

Shadows race . . . they are the wind breezing in a pleasant country . . . each passed tree, the moon's softly lit rose . . . a gate in the knot of wild green . . . a garden spot where the moon's restive soul is reflected in the still water . . .

She spreads a soft green quilt of unbalanced borders in the tan and yellowing grass.

He lights a candle.

An unopened bottle of wine sits on its side in the thick grass . . .

Without faltering he removes his boots. Her blouse comes off.

. . . Open to his voice. Open to her touch. She collects his soft whispers . . . The energetic web, long-limbed, beautiful with their clothes almost off . . .

Flying . . .

Gestures drawn . . .

He touches the griffin tattoo on her left shoulder. "Yes, treasure you are." Her finger traces the scorpionlike, red etching engraved over his heart . . .

They are star to star—sparks and bells hunting soft fruit . . . adorned by a trailing razor of beginnings . . .

She fills her blue eyes with his form. Lets him mesmerize her with his meadowlark gaze. Takes him inside. Inmost, passed little and the barbwire clutter of things of ash and death filtered by a glass darkly . . .

The jewel box opens . . .

His lips are roses. Hers, shimmering lanterns of evening stars . . .

Arms a liquid shadow. Thin fingers stretched, singing—weaving . . .

Breath. Quicker . . .

The journey of searing, a hymn from heel to eye . . . The form of joy.

Fingers brush an upturned face . . .

Faster. Deep

. . . and deeper.

Revelation.

Beauty, wings and laughter, captured . . . absorbed.

. . . at peace . . . driving passed open fields . . . the top down . . .

the delicate stars above unnoticed . . . Fast and faster . . . Free . . . And wild . . .

. . . Laughing . . . as one . . .

A deer in the road.

The left.

Hard. SUDDEN. Too sudden. Too hard . . .

Savage chaos.contortions. a constellation of glass spattering/a blindfold of diamond shards. cheekbones.shoulders. bent.limb and metal splitopen.UNGH—skin splitopen—torn/raped by a metal rod.blood.PAINroiling. blood-death . . . furious bites,skinshifts . . . PAINa vicious gangpushing, finding an assault of lava flowing in her veins. seconds hiss.sink in a puddle of shadows.

BLOOD.life unfastened-quickly.blood. Gone, extracted.a moment of howling . . .

"need"

. . . bleeding . . . succumbing.to the burn of harm . . . a glimpse left—lost. BLOOD.

Love (inside out) and out of light.

"help"

Alanna wakes in a sterile white room. Nurses in sterile white dresses flit in and out. The world is thick, cloudy. A distant masked pain, a quiet storm waits to thunder in her shattered ankle, in her shattered knee . . . she collapses in the undertow . . .

She awakens on the second day. Remembers fragments . . . Through a veil of fear and tears discovers she has left her left hand somewhere other than in this room with the rest of her.

Pain takes her . . .

A nurse in a sterile white dress doses her . . . the undertow pulls her into the shadow depths . . .

The world is yellow and darkening . . . Black moths lie dead everywhere . . . the great black tree is dead, scarred. In blood . . .

He is gray . . . Dimming . . . His words distant . . . graying . . .

Alanna walks in a somber hollow of autumnal grass. Black birds—Death's eagles, wings made from old manuscripts, circle in the murmuring air . . . she comes to a garden wall, stops before a masked figure.

In a dull monotone: "The world waits beyond."

"What world do you speak of?"

"The true world, Camilla."

"And he, so beloved?"

Cold: *"Walks in Carcosa."*

The phantom stranger points. His long skeletal finger, white as the thickest winter, stretched along the path.

She takes her first weary step . . .

✦

The treatments. The tests, shots and pills and salves and questions. Nurses and doctors, their beaks open, rambling, directing, waiting for reaction.

Recovering . . . They call it.

Dealing with what has run away. Saying, the last thing I can remember,

the last thing I can remember

the last thing I can remember

the last thing I can remember

and again . . . digging for the moments before the storm, forgetting to pause.

Softly: "Starting again?"

Pain scraping against movement. Gathering, immediate complaints.

How?

The constant examination (slowly scanning—measuring agony) (in a hand-held mirror) of a quadrant of her face that arrogant red scars own . . . Seeing half a world. So small now . . . putting a bra over the bruised breast his warm lips touched. Trying to find answers, or windows, or a lust for life . . .

Wearing excuses to numb details confronted. Searching space and mistakes as history quakes for a place to assign blame.

Trying to get steady again. The body feeling better . . . but no less tense.

Lost.

A last silent night in a hard sterile room . . . long groans born in pained bodies she can't fathom and rushed soft steps down the precisely lit white hall . . .

Discharged. Through the exit. Alone. Alanna emerges from the hospital. The sun is a small lion in the blue above. Birds burst from shaded tree branch to sun-touched branch. A loose dog barks at cars pushing their vivid colors through the crosswalk. She swings a small hook, resting where her left hand had been in the other life.

She wears a veil of soft yellow silk. A simple disguise, it covers the large scorpionlike scars on her right cheek. Over the hollow where days ago a clear blue eye nested she wears a black silk eye patch.

The taxi, yellow and black, deposits her at her apartment . . .

. . . alone . . .

After ten days dust speaks its truth . . .

His pale bone china teacup still rests across the table from hers. His yellow rose gift lies withered and dead on the table. She picks it up . . . and the petals fall to the floor. Tears rain on them as she gathers the lifeless mementoes.

Wine. Her days alone pass . . . the sky grays . . . more wine. Less light. More wine . . . Blackness holds court.

Swept away by despair and fatigue, she stumbles from room to room searching for his face or something of him to hug and hold dear, some element to flood the room with . . . From candlelight and incense smoke and remembrance she creates a ghost . . .

Bursting from her mouth: "I am so tired without you."

. . . clinging to his ghost . . .

She tries to take it to her bed but it is too softly formed to lie in the dead leaves with her . . . a frothing wind, shuttering, she leaps from the bed of dead leaves . . .

Unnerved as it—inept in this light—dissipates . . . Stained by the fullness of her agony in the air, into the night she rushes.

Quick over the ground to his apartment.

A fist-size rock in the green bushes under his apartment window. Raised. Its heft is right. Smashes the window. Rustling through his door. She's in.

Loud as a drum the size of an elephant, she stumbles in the dark.

Rushing through his book shelves, casts Trakl and Rikle and Baudelaire and a hundred golden journeys and death-slow nevermores to the worn carpet. Razing objects. Leafing through his clothes, touching some to her nose, to her lips. She is a cyclone without a path. All need, no thought to it, she absorbs and casts off . . . Gathering to feed her ache . . .

Looking in envelopes and storming through drawers . . . finds $850 dollars in bills and casts them to the floor with the other unwanted remains.

A photograph of him at a wedding. Slips it from its frame. Leans in, kisses his forehead . . .

She leaves with a threadbare yellow robe and his thin book of poetry. Holds his antique gold timepiece clutched between her breasts . . .

✶

Night becomes her day.

She reads and rereads every line of suffering he's poured into his collected translation of the cold autumn silence and the black tears that burn, sealed in soft constellations of madness, in Lost Carcosa . . .

> *cloud voices in the water*
> *they sing of glamour & finished . . .*

Her third night. No end to her desire. No healing in sleep. She brings out needle and ink, tattoos a line of his poetry on her flesh. Recalls the dew of his breath on her skin where his words now breathe.

> *Night walkers*
> *frolic in the dreams of the changeless spectral flame*
> *of midnight . . .*

. . . wine to soothe the ache, the empty dance of whiteness . . . and sleep after the forced fire-foam of wine. Dreams, the swaying of a light madness, of him lost and walking the leafless, twilit lanes of cold Carcosa . . . she follows, but cannot catch him in the stone autumn air . . .

Arisen from the embrace of her dreams the next day rings with thorns. She eats bread and honey as evening sings . . .

Reads (and rereads) of sonatas echoing weakly in dim yellow chambers and dynasties breaking . . . reads (again) of thick fingers muttering in the lonesome valley, and eternal stillness, and the leprous hole the worm keeps its secrets in. Reads on worn, narcotic yellow pages of the dreams adrift in the deeps of night's river . . . and the utterly lost.

The next morning comes.

Licking a drop of honey from her palm she notices his words have expanded . . . One line etched into her white flesh has become two.

From the One-joined, spirit in spirit, flesh on flesh, light . . .

More light!
Bring your quivering brush to the silence where deeper ends . . .

He's writing on her.

She reads the ivy path of his plea. And with needle and ink, writes back . . .

Each new day additional words appear on the white emptiness of her skin. Each soft curve of skin has become his garden and row after row he plants benedictions and communiqués until she is covered with his desire, his determined, yellowish trails of beauty that can not be erased . . .

"Come to this silent dim glade, My Sweet. Come glow. Soothe the stain that follows my every tortured step. Come soon and heal this leper lost in dim yellow fields. Follow the arrow of the winterboatman's long, threadlike finger . . . Mercy, My Sweet, before I fade out entirely."

Naked she stands before the mirror in her bedroom. Her body, laboratory, monastery, garden, bed of heaven, sings with the voice of another. Auguries of pure poetry radiate in circles from her nipples. Bracelets of embroidered language are buds on a vine clinging about her wrists. Valleys and peaks of his winter night words of solitude are a scroll unfurled across the velvet plain of her belly . . . webs of transforming text along the inside curve of her thighs . . . his confessions at the corners of her mouth. Her calves adorned in wispy lace, each character a translation, a bridge, a seed, a wave of love's lore. The candid and the poetic expressed, she, his lighthouse, is soaked in his words, words that fit her like a glove. Her armpits, back, reveal the route of his desire. Each of the places his lips and fingers had touched—gloried in, bare the written ointment of his longing. Alanna is a traveler, and a map, reading every sweeping word (taking in the bittersweet fragrance of every letter) before putting on his threadbare yellow robe.

Succumbing to her need wrapped in his, she closes her beguiling blue eyes. The back of her eyelids glow with his fiery rain of *you must.*

She can no longer sleep.

From a closet shelf she takes a picnic basket woven from twisted roots. Fills it with staples for her voyage.

At the bottom of the stairs unlocks her bicycle, rolls it to the pavement. Lashes her basket to the rim behind her seat.

And she's off . . . riding from catastrophe . . .

Leaning over the handle bars, mouth open—a glare of intent, she pedals her bike furiously through the heavily shaded streets . . .

. . . a world of doors . . . tarnished faces of buildings . . . strange drumbeats of love . . . ghosts . . . ghosts of . . . decayed doors burning in shadow ink . . . strange ghosts . . . faded hopeless windows . . . cold hands empty and silent . . . dead doorways . . .

Street by street . . . Buildings. Houses, some single family, some cheap. Brown and black. And white. Or brick. Feet spinning. A half a block of empty . . . the exposed hollow of a home gutted in a blaze . . .

Each black street echoes with the last exhausted shadow of times and beauty lost. Dim dreams turned by the spade of soil and disuse are flooded by the velvet weeds of night . . .

Doors (and sin and troubling views, haggling, sleep, vain murmurs, the bare shoulder in the gallery of frost, going left, going right, sullen sighs, mornings after the vino and the hollow laughter, which sweater with this skirt) behind her, trees—sentinels, line her road . . .

The last hard mile.

Her eyes are older . . . and full . . .

The cemetery is quiet. And dark. Not as cold as she'd imagined.

She finds his grave, her garden, in the dark with no light at all.

Laughs sweetly as she stands before him.

On her knees with a pair of scissors from the drawer of her sowing table. Fingers waltz. Snip by sharp snip she evenly trims the grass of his grave. Her fingers as rake, she removes every loose blade.

When she is certain she has stripped away every sheared blade Alanna lights a waxlight then spreads her green patchwork quilt of lost and found on the spot beside the coffin-ground.

Red string. Blood red string. Slowly uncoiled from the ball. Laid out in the exact outline of his form. From her basket she takes two small glow-in-the-dark stars and sets them where his eyes would be.

Alanna smiles.

Whispers, "I have come, Dearest." as she places wilted petals of the yellow rose he gave her in the shape of the Yellow Sign over his heart in the shape of blood red string.

Her robe comes off. Naked she lies atop him.

"Read me, beloved. Take my nightwalker song into your heart. I give you my complexities. Summon them to your shape . . . Each fits you."

No moon to help light her way, so she invents one. Gently casts it into the sky . . . Places it just so.

Candle light.

Close. But incomplete.

"Read me," an alto whisper from mending lips. "I stroke you with my flood of night-tongues. Let my rose words fill the emptiness in your dim heart . . . Banish the sleep that clutters your eyes."

Cloaked in cold. Her skins tingles as his breath moves over every ivy arc of etched black marks.

Pauses to smile. Knowing he is reading.

Whispers: "Find peace in me."

Blood, bone, and desire, she is an open page. A sequence unfolding. A bridal chamber, hips and banquet flower awaiting the cut of light's liquid arrow.

"Let my skin be your road. Come across the savage ground of Down and Last that I may carry your burden."

Tears. And far cries.

Candlesoft: "Rest your hand in my hand. I give you my warmth."

The prosthetic moon, pallid and weak, looks down.

She looks up.

They share tears.

With a small stone she smashes the face of his timepiece, freezing the moment . . .

The gun—loaded with the unmistakable power of the afterlife, is in her hand . . .

"I believe."

Light sheared, Alanna and her moon depart for a far cold country . . .

In far cold Carcosa
The King sheds no tear . . .
Knowing
There will be another needful thing,
Another jewel needing repair . . .

And another after that . . .

From the wake of dark clouds massed, the solitary moon arrives. He looks down . . . Sees what has drowned. And again, awash in alone, cries.

(Bob Dylan, "Dreamin' of You")

When the Moon Comes to Call

for SCS, the storyteller

Days backwards to yesterdays on the page, a gray page of madness. Maps and images and dances—preludes and bittersweet thoughts, for one. Poem-tangos gone. Lost. Missing. The moon, full of the pain of a final page, came with its ghost stories. Cried. The gray clouds below caught its tears.

Sorrow. Roses and January passed on. Ends of summer in the currents of autumn. Night as a lullaby of doom, again and again . . . and again. Interiors without doors or stars.

October, blue and unwilling to fly.

The promenade of shadows. And his last lonely dance . . .

The case of his trumpet open. An invitation. Unanswered these last nights. The distance crossed, the moonlight finds the bell of the horn. But no music of soft and lonely goodbye is made.

Hasn't played it.

Not since the girl in the sunglasses came in. Sat there. Right there.

In the front.

He played it.

Played it for her.

Lonely. Twilight slow. Sexy in it.

He saw her head tilt toward it. She breathed in its gravity. Liked the view. Let the sultry caress her.

She had it all the way in now. Liked it there.

Really liked it.

Filled a hole. Something forgotten put back where it belonged.

Liked it a lot.

Like she hadn't lost wonder.

She had.

But it was back.

He put it back.

A cat in warm moonlight. No need to prowl. She could just curl up. The perfect fit.

Secret hours brushed with a glow. She stretched into it. Rubbed it. With her neck.

Reached across the table and the club.

Hand and hand. Walked with it.

Invited it home.

He went.

In a room without a roof. In a bed without borders. She took off her limits. One at a time. Slow.

Let him see her beautiful skin. The gleaming bronzed poetry. Silk inch by silk inch. Heated up and reflected in his eyes.

Both barrels.

Raw. Animal. Basic.

Primal.

The dance.

Swept this way.

Swayed that.

Each curve.

Sleek fingers steering.

Nothing slow. No failure on this map.

Lips and eyes. Traveling miles of warm velvet.

The hunger in her belly gleaming. Holding the whispers tight. In the center of a birthday. And a box of chocolate. And a rose. One perfect tender summer rose.

Beautiful discovered.

No war in the long gestures.

No spiders close by.

No knives around the next corner.

No other world.

No other edges.

Simple as the heat in her veins.

Blood simple.

Beautiful discovered.

He felt . . .

Good.

Strong.

Wild.

She

smelled so good. So . . .

Wild.

Lips a swollen blur of here and NOW. Lips as horizons. Eyes taking in every color she is. Fingers full of her sunlight softness.

His hands on her.

Whispering.

Warm.

She smells so good.

So wild.

Full of moon-time he changed. Shifted.

Teeth bigger. LOUD.

Boiling over.

Hunger bigger.

She smelled

weaker.

Her lips in his teeth.

The softness of her, now red and wet. Open. On his tongue.

She smelled so good to his wild.

NOW. Exhaled, free of its soft-shell cage.

Nothing casual.

Beyond consequences.

No excuses.

No confusion. Not scattered or tricked. Not pausing to consider, "Do I dare?"

No faint to it.

Nothing to prove.

Just the bite that won't hide.

NOW expressed. The pure YES. Impulse/desire manifested.

No grappling with last or old or maybe.

No IF in the language.

No lies to seal the mouth.

No Future/Next.

NOW the place with no season. Pure. Unfettered.

NOW faster.

Red.

Full of her smell. The smell of red and wild. Raw. Wet. Primal red. Wild. Beautiful discovered.

A blur of teeth. Teeth conquering horizons. Quick honest teeth taking in every warm color she is.

WAS.

Soft.

Smelled so soft.

So good.

So good not to be hungry . . .

The curse back.

From the dead place.

The hollow filled with blood.

Every cell nourished.

Red and wild.

Every cell.

Wild.

Again.

Then comes the scream. Wants to cry. Wants to rip out the face of the moon.

Doesn't want to feel this.

This full.

This satisfied.

Wild.

But he does.

He does.

Likes it.

It fits.

Fills every cell.

Been awhile since he was alive.

An eternity without NOW.

Starving.

Without The Joy.

An eternity of moonless dreams he couldn't feed.

An eternity with only the weak pinprick of scattered constellations and no glowing master.

❀

Morning. Alone.

Again . . .

NOW
gone.
No weeping.
No ode of tears.
No bye-bye sweet summer night . . . No kiss from a rose.
Just the end of the world . . .
Just alone.

✦

A small hot club called The Zoo.
Animals out. Strut
and sally. Spin
and wish—crazy with capacity and The Game—and
FLASH.
Parading.
Showing their colors.
Preening.
Pecking.
The hunter turned loose, full of Laugh Now, cherishing the easy fun of the hot rhythm—*Shake* . . . Take/Take/TAKE!
Fire
rising . . .
Forging languages of hope from their addiction.
There are stars above their erotic sentences. And too busy with their wounds and portrayals, a moon they're insensitive to.
His Miami-moonlight-sliding-along-the-bed-sheets trumpet is filled with stories.
Above, the moon speaks the language of hunger.
Hard and wild . . . and cold.
The bell of his horn filled with immediacy. Rising to speak of silvery stars and warm seas of clear blue day romance you dip your toes in . . . and *Once* . . .
She sits at a table.
Alone.
Lovely. A quiet warmth from mouth to toes.
Auroral eyes shining.

Her face, blushed with excitement, whispers with the echoes of golden spring mornings. Her breasts are meadows.

The voice of his horn runs . . .

Something within her smells wild.

(Sha's Banryu *Chessboxing Volume One*)

After Reading Michaux's
"In the Land of Magic"

The night is ice
& full of eyes. Winds that will not cure speak of November.

There are no white halls in the hostelry. The tin ceilings are low, the
carpets an exaggerated foliage of blunt faces. The wallpaper is sick
with the smell of twilight spreading endlessly.
Even the shadows rot.

Up forty-one stairs that whisper like migraines to a door closed on
the rumors and fragile madness of the stiff warblers outside. Behind
the stained and chipped panel with the tarnished knob and the loose
bolt that passes for a lock, the smallest rented room. Below, the Tav-
ern of Ruin, where time & dreams happened a long time ago. Sitting
on the edge of the bed where a restless thousand have disintegrated, a
curled figure in threadbare clothes

—*his consciousness no more fluent than a haze of aimless dust*—

gazes at a flat spot on the wall where a soft avalanche of hollowness
reaches out. The man named Uphill isn't paralyzed, simply too empty
to move. Lost to his ordeals in the abyss he's even forgotten the little
secrets children consider run-of-the-mill, forgotten all phenomena
not terrible . . .

. . .

. . .

A croak of bitterdesire punctures his interval of nought. The man
named Uphill turns from his nightlong narrowing. Stares at the keyhole, as if he could find luck or the interest he lost last yesterday or

114

sometime ago beyond it. He feels the pangs of thirst. How many hours—days?—since he has eaten? Perhaps among the covey below, he could order something . . . But to sit among them—despair and everyday-wretchedness served to the chuckling shadows, jostling with their tortures—to watch them paw their garbage, could he endure it?

. . .

. . .

. . . The man named Uphill closes his eyes, hoping to silence the poison downflight of thoughts. He hears darkness move and knows the murderer will soon get his bearings.

"Let sleep come," he whispers

, wondering what the dead do with their   time.

(for my friend, the DaRKaNGEL, Michael Cisco)

The Walking Man Walks

When the twilight is painted in soft shades . . . and some, those not driven by the unobstructed humming of their hunger, are soon to take to their beds . . .

A one-man carnival walks the road. Tries to stay in or near the desert. From here to that motel, or beside a boulder or cactus, if that tonight's chosen bed, he wanders, hoping to excavate mysteries. He has his diary and moments in whorehouses or bars, things to pass the time between performances. And he has America and its ghosts and graves and its old iron chains. And he has skies. Often when exhaustion comes over him he sends up greetings to the gently circling hawks. Their lack of reply never angers him. Had he wings he would not lower himself either.

Some think it's a lonely road. He invents murder or beaches or subtle tragedies to pass time. Before every performance he finds a bar, full of mundane twists, or injured judgment not bound by scholarship, and orders whiskey. Somewhere in his second glass his dairy comes out.

Pen in hand, he begins the show.

Blonde. Nice legs, long. Good shoes. Laughs if need be. The long scar on her cheek does not detract from the magic in her eyes. Calls herself, Libby, but that's a lie. When he saw her four weeks ago, in _____, she called herself Naomi. Fit.

It was all the usual. "Hi"—"Hi." Drinks. They danced to something slow and voracious in the corner. She stepped on his toes. One or the other laughed, forgetting seedy and grim for a moment.

At 2 A.M. the bar closed and the zombies and their hard-luck operas limped home. They stood at the door of her rusty, white Chevy and shared a smoke.

She kissed his cheek and told him she had something at home that required her care. He smiled and said, "Good night." She smiled back and drove away.

He slept under a bench on the porch of the bar. The dead leaves in the corner did not disturb him. Listened to the coyotes exchange opinions on the unsolved murders at the bus station. He could have set them straight, but his mouth was full of stars.

Over coffee (he thought about having the pie, but skipped it) the next afternoon, he opens a book. Reads, "The playground was just across the street ahead of me." from AFTER DARK, MY SWEET. He liked that line. Liked it quite a bit. Gets up. Leaves a small tip and exits the dinner.

That night he met Susan in a playground behind the schoolhouse. She had on a lightweight red blouse and a black skirt. Mentioned, in passing, she had lost her shoes. For a time they pushed their toes toward the stars and laughed. Susan confessed she enjoyed mazes and history. Asked him if he found it easier to breath after he solved a puzzle. "Yes. I think so." At 3 A.M. he left her. Gave her a gentle kiss on the cheek before departing.

Wrote a poem about the rare luminosity in her eyes the next morning.

On a sandy, haunted plain he found a letter. He camped there and waited for three days before opening it.

Dear _____,

Your father reached the last page and with no view left to examine, complained. Nurse Abbott sent him off to bed with no supper.

You may contact us during regular business hours to register any complaints you may have on the subject.

It was not signed. He shrugged and tore it into small pieces. Every fifth step he dropped one alongside the road. Laughed, when he imagined a Hansel, or fair, lovely Gretel, might come across his crumbs.

The congregation of cactus presented no schemes to deal with the inmates, so he suggested a phrase or two to get them started. When he returned to bed down for the night six hours later they thanked him and showed him the dead roadrunner. He was pleased.

After a fairly quiet dinner of beans and bread, served by a demon in a hellish fat suit, he found a bar. Inside a dozen authorities on glimmering and disease lectured and conversed. He told them he was a pilgrim who was still surveying and had no real opinion on matters as they had been presented.

Over half of the twelve thanked him for his politeness before they retired.

The next few days he spent behind a dirty window writing about the pitfalls of paradise in his dairy. When he was finished he flipped back a few pages and saw her name. *Naomi.*

"Such a lovely name. And truly a delight."

He's under a voluptuous display of stars. Walking. Passing open gates that have granted entrance to rust and crumbling homes. He has no illusions in his pocket.

There's a light in the window. He steps inside the bar . . .

"Hi, I'm Libby." Blonde. Nice legs, long. Good shoes. The long scar on her cheek does not detract from the magic in her eyes.

"Yes you are."

They have a drink. Laugh quietly. Go outside for a smoke. His performance begins.

1:15 A.M. He gives her a gentle kiss on the cheek before departing.

He has his knife—pen, so often outstretched in conversation. And when the road turns from soft silence to vivid dream—there'll be a small red mouth (and maybe red nails and a cheap ring) and the curling smoke will suggest a dance . . . After a deep breath someone will whisper fierce . . . And he'll perform another show.

(*After a dream that placed Thomas Ligotti and me—in full bEast regalia—in a park at midnight talking about things that frolic.*)

Silent No Longer

Morning's warming sunlight played outside the loft, yet little of it passed through the heavily soiled windows. Inside the tormented song of long night choked the air.

"'His grievous seed drowns my burning need . . . I'm trapped between his hard ardor and my torn dream . . . as the bones of compassion settle into the awaiting ground . . . and the sun becomes a shadow of itself . . . About me the tears of saints run errands for sin . . . while the cancer of pettiness rules with a twisted stick . . . You've hired perversion as governess for my dreams . . . and God has cried himself out of my tears . . . Has all hope been called home . . . Overlord, of thee I'll sing . . . Noo . . . No . . . Noo . . . No . . . No more. No, No, moooo'—"

The fuzz-distorted riff was abruptly silenced.

She knew why he stopped playing. It was always the same, whether it was his music or his sex, the nuclear burn of his anger, erupting like a behemoth from shallow depths raging, hungry. She was afraid to turn, to look. Afraid of the coming storm—the sharp, heavy-hand and the fanged threats.

And the storm came, swift as buffeting winds.

A bolt of fire blazed up the arm slammed between chest and floor as she strained to become controlled motionlessness. Clutching survival fantasies—*"To be a silent shadow in the unlit forest of night"*—she mentally chanted as if the mantra would form a protective umbrella over her, she feared hope would turn to dust or abandon her. It had before. Full lips, crudely painted in warm blood, lay shrouded beneath black-rooted, blonde Medusa-locks dusting the wooden floor, hiding burning tears. Imprisoned in the looming shadow of an always-wired taskmaster who demanded nothing less than his limited conception of perfection, she gazed at his far-to-near black boots. Silent prayers streamed from petrified lips.

"Get up!"

More searing pain. Burning eyes watched the silver-accented boot tips for signs of motion as death strode the heavy pause.

"Shall we try again!" The boots moved away.

Later, when she was wet and almost fucked raw, he'd hold her. "I'm sorrys" mixed with "Never agains" until he fell into drunken snores. "It's just my music . . . It has to be right. There's no room for . . . You understand."

She didn't, but she found ways to justify it.

❀

"This is the place." The calloused fingers tightly guiding her arm pulled her inside the caged shop. "You're gonna look great in this shit . . . Too bad you couldn't sing in that! Fuckin' thing is hot . . ."

Face to face with the empty-eyed, full-head mask of leather, neither she nor the sown shut mouth had words. He's not content to control me, he wants to silence me as well, she thought, fearfully encountering the fact for the thousandth time.

"Fuck me! This is it! They'll go bat shit with your tits trussed up in this rig."

I won't be able to breathe in that—

Thirty minutes later they left the fetish emporium with his choices in black plastic bags; a leather Zorro mask, a red, wet-look leather thong and a black leather corset that pushed-in and pulled-up her pale fleshy breasts, transforming the cup size to a false, but visually convincing D. He'd also picked out a cat-o'-nine-tails and cuffed thigh boots to further stimulate the vampiric twenty-year-olds they played for.

With this S&M shit and her sex/pain lyrics, which I always have to rewrite, the hard little drooling-fucks are gonna eat her alive, he thought as dark fantasies of playing (headlining naturally) The Bank or The Shuttered Room in New York whipped in his head. I'm the reaper. Soon to be rollin' in money and willing wet pussy.

Quick as a lie, he left her outside the shop. "Gotta see somebody about mixing the demo." Another cold falsehood and she knew it. At least this one didn't raise visible welts. Lighting a Kool, she watched him turn the corner. Concentrating on not crying, she thought of stuffing the bags of S&M crap into the trash, but that would only invite another bestial dance. It was time to run, submit, or strike back. *How could I strike back?* she wondered, exhaling the cigarette smoke from her nostrils as if she were an angered, awakened dragon.

EVOLUTION THROUGH VIBRATION promised the yellowed sign taped to the window of the adjoining shop. *What the hell does that mean?* Curious, she let stiletto heels cross the threshold of the occult shop. *Maybe I'll find some little witch-trinket or mystical toy to embellish this outfit with,* she thought, enjoying the freedom of making a decision of her own. She didn't, but among the assorted hermetic clutter assembled to help usher in a new, or bygone age, she found an odd music book. Transcriptions of light-speed, avant-garde compositions for flute—one, entitled "Calling Him," caught her eye. She could hear it. *That prick wants raw, then we'll play it raw.*

"Ahh," the aged proprietor sighed as his long-fingered hand caressed the worn tome she'd placed on the counter, leaving a strange marking in the dust. "*Songs of Desire* . . . An interesting choice for one so young."

"How much is this?" she asked the dark-skinned bald man, his eyes hidden behind dark glasses.

"It's worth nothing to me sitting here clothed in dust. For you my dear . . . It's free," his distant sounding monotone replied, before turning back to his book and whistling an unsettling melody, part of which seemed familiar.

"Thank you."

"Sing them well, daughter," he whispered to her back as the door closed.

In the dining room of her spartan-to-the-point-of-seeming-empty, squalid fifth-floor walk-up, she sat blowing and trilling harsh notes from her flute. Working the raucous phrases of "Calling Him" into the current arrangement of "Of Thee I'll Sing—No More!" she felt elated—almost vast and powerful.

✸

This Teardrop Wasteland's first set had rumbled through subterranean darkambient drones and blurred, coarse calls to despair. Post-industrial odes, saturated in self-doubt, self-loathing, and razor blades, grated against goth/speed-alternative war chants, occasionally slowing to passages of sparse ethereal whispers as the crowd drank bitter brew and milled closer to the stage. Vulgar litanies promising banishment and death against the incapable-of-understanding-anything and aged living-dead collided with the pained cries of the directionless and alienated as her fluted pipings screamed in response to his feedback accented chords of metallic groans. Their sweat-driven nightmares held the audience bound in the mummy cloth of sound they sprayed, like aural napalm, into the diminutive club.

The second set ballooned. Stark cacophonous tableaus of pain rode atop storm trooper beats of unrelenting cadence which raked ears and set dark desires in motion. She knelt, legs spread—forcing their wishful vision to the delta of her sex—before the horror-film-clad youth, stroking the insides of her glistening, taut thighs, offering blunt taboos. Receptive as an engorged cock, the predominantly male audience was hot, hard, and ready, as she let her hand rise to her abundant breasts, encircling and kneading them, then, like a moist breathy moan, she pushed the dry-mouthed youths closer to promised pleasure, sliding the microphone's shaft between her damp cleavage and laving it with her tongue. Near ecstasy, their screams of "more" burnt to moans. They all fucked her—from above, from below, as drums and heartbeats set rhythm to their illusory pleasure taking. Mouths open, savoring the sex and doom show, hungry males watched her heavily painted face pushed into the rough wooden floor as they took her gyrating ass from behind. They all used her, to squeeze the last drops from their sweating fantasies.

And she used them. Tonight she gave as never before, needing their energy to feed her conjuration.

"*Bound in a corset of obedience . . . Command me! I'm your whore . . . Shape me, take me . . . With strap, with whip . . . Make me whole . . .*" The whip sang it. She hissed it. *No more*, she thought. "*Nooooo . . . mooore . . .*" Her voice diving into unbridled rasps and raw whispers, then sharply rising, nailing their ears with heated needles of merciless emotion.

Snake-legged, in shiny leather skin, she writhed and dry-humped the floor, as the Munch-eyed voyeurs stiffened. She teased, pranced, and strutted—lashing at them with the tongue of black leather fire. They were hers, stiff cocks and conquered souls. It was time to use the energy of her slaves' labor.

Across the stage she crawled to him—slowly twisting and grinding—pulling herself up until her head was beneath his guitar. Softly her gloved hand reached out as if she were touching something holy and cupped his balls. Through the black material of his jeans she kissed his swelling member, marking him. In the full-blown equatorial heat the crowd worshipped their sweating demon whore, their fuck-me-all, rock-goddess slut.

As she slid away from him he slapped her pale tear-shaped ass. The painter's red signature colored the pressing crowd's vision. She was certain they wanted more.

No more! "*No more,*" she sang. "*No mooore,*" she wailed, her voice fueled by the memories of a thousand slaps. "*No mooore,*" she sang, her stomach lurching in fear of the black boots which had trod miles of her intestines. "*No moooooore!*" she screamed as she gathered all her pain and focused it into the notes. Years of denied and compressed pain were unleashed—howling dogs slaking their thirst on pheromones of lust, oiled in fear.

Across inhuman distances Cerberus pinned his ears back in fear and something heard her call. In the patternless electro-chemical mire of a cosmic pool vast in its strength and texture, its ageless depths continually erupting and feeding on itself as if it were a hive of cannibalistic maggots, the nameless thing tensed and lashed out, feeling the sharp weight of the tugging.

Her back arched—she rubbed her sex into his ass, the summoning notes streaming from the flute like the scalding liquid song of mating banshees. High-pitched wails ejaculated from his Les Paul in response to her impassioned playing. Heat, tension, and tempo increased, as the lovers mock rutted in reverse before the prurient crowd.

Eating their energy, she attacked the piercing notes, repeating the sequence, calling—*No more. No more!*, sacrificing something within herself, adding her pain to the arcing wail.

He looped out the fuzzed riff while she repeated the quick, harsh notes again and again, as if she were trying to learn a foreign phase or she was calling to someone who wasn't quite listening. Then ending the refrain as suddenly as she began, she spun to face him. A bolt of lightning flooded the crowd's vision as the flute, caught in the spotlight, became a compass needle aimed at his heart—a pointer marking a destination on a map. In the hushed pause, the drummer struck a gong, its sonorous toll hung in the air like a solid form, weighted and defined, as the spotlight remained fixed on the flute, glistening like the silver arrow of justice.

In the wavering heat of the overly hot club, a glimmering vertical pool, a wet passage to damnation, appeared between her and her tyrannical paramour. Within the liquefied aperture something revolved. An amorphous phantasm of cyclonic bubbling thrust out an elongated appendage, petalled at its end. With the blossoming fingers fully extended it closed about the guitar-playing rock lord. Completely engulfed in the spheroid-shaped nimbus, her suddenly all-too-aware, master-cum-victim felt like a fish trapped in a glass bowl. Within the globular chamber, suspended by invisible tethers, he slowly rotated, his asking eyes ballooned, pleading with her contented stare. Sweat appeared on his brow, grease escaping roasting meat.

"Don't you like it hot, baby?" she hissed into the microphone, uncertain as to whether he could hear her.

Transfixed by the deliverance of her justice, she watched his eyes. The tiny veins popping like pinpoint paint splatters, dotting the inner walls of his intensely bubbling cell. The walls of which absorbed the fluid as if it were sustenance. Was he screaming? Above the howls of the crowd, she heard broken, fragmented crackles and the choked blats of a frightened infant. Was he calling for his mommy, or some god perhaps? Sexually stimulated by the tortures her summoned executioner imparted, she saw his mouth forced open—the soft flesh of his cheeks ripping to accommodate the ever growing mass forcing itself within. How many times had he forced her jaws open with a sharp hand or the threat of or else? How many times had he laughed; told her to not miss a drop, as she choked on his musty semen, or fell into a teary-eyed jag as she vomited his warm seed into cold porcelain?

"How do you like your wet womb now?" she silently asked, not expecting or caring about his reply. "Tight enough for you?" she asked as the guitar's strings popped and swirled before him, lashing out, stinging and cutting, as they probed and tested orifices. Two strings, low E and A, pierced his wrists, burrowing up his hard-veined arms to the elbows, where they cut their way out opening eleven-inch-long gashes. The remaining four strings, needle sharp projectiles, plunged deep into his throat and knotted together before they were pulled out, rending the muscular flesh as surely as a honed blade.

Splattered blood sprayed the bubbling walls of his prison. Seconds later his shell was spent, his thick claret consumed. With a violent thrash his amorphous captor withdrew. In its wake the aperture shriveled and winked out, leaving him momentarily suspended above the stage.

A heartbeat later he fell like so much discarded refuse, thrown before her—a gift or perhaps a trinket for her inspection.

No more, she thought, releasing her pain, casting it into the withered shuck inches from her stiletto-heeled feet.

The Maiden of the Pines

I had come north—from the sweltering thickness of the gray cities—
to the secluded house of the Rainmaker to escape despair for a time,
to wander among the oddly appointed rooms of his otherworldly
abode. In that great gray mansion, under the expansive sweep of its
gothic canopy, moments, like brief rehearsals for eternity, would pass
as I lost myself in a room filled with levers and tanks of a bubbling
crimson liquid, too thick to be water tainted by dye, too scarlet to be
blood, or in an L-shaped corner room filled with hundreds of cobalt-
blue globes, every one the size of a newborn infant's skull.

I drifted, as if taking in the galleries of an exhibition; through a
room where lenses and eyewear of every size and thickness, and from
many ages and lands, were suspended from the ceiling by colored,
silken strands like some celestial mobile; too, I found hours pass like
minutes in a second-floor room where the walls were completely papered in half-finished anatomical portraits sketched in ashes. And in a
fashion, married to extinction as I am, I returned many times to gaze
upon the slate-hued walls of a basement room where grandiosely il-
lustrated seventeenth-century death certificates hung, each with perfectly round holes exactingly punched out, illustrating a different
astronomical constellation. There were other rooms in which I loi-
tered as the days and nights slowly traveled by; behind a door painted
burnt orange, a room of broken wooden toys; in the basement, behind a door perhaps imported from a 500-year-old German castle,
was a damp room with a dirt floor littered with empty gin bottles.
Within it, there stood, in a circle facing one another, eight particu-
larly small gravestones. Instead of being inscribed with a name, each
upright, granite square was inscribed with the words Pennies For
Heaven in Cyrillic. But my favorite chamber was discovered behind a
large tapestry of a snowy owl, a white mouse, and a murder in the
snow, hung on the wall like a curtain. It was a vast white room where

on the walls an oversized map of a land-locked city was being created, all the north-south streets were named after pirates, while all
the east-west routes bore the names of steamboats. Landlocked myself, for I never learned to swim and fear water, I was often drawn to
dreams of black-cloaked sailing vessels and the brave, Eldorado-
bound men of the sea who made their mark and set forth for glory.

From high noon to the wee small hours I roamed from room to
room. Obsessed with doubts cluttered with the drama of small epics
and raging yesterdays, I was a ghost in a dream dance of chilled fogs.

Behind the violet shutters of the Rainmaker's teeming residence,
with the gentle spiders spinning and quiet dust dervishes, in the ab-
sence of a clock or a single mirror, I hoped to come upon, perhaps
stuffed on a shadowy high shelf or slouching on a mantle like the forgotten handiwork of an old adventure, a path from the cellars of silence. And it was there, on the rear terrace, which overlooked the
edge of the invading drift of the pine forest that I first gazed upon
her.

She seemed to me—to my weary heart, battered as it was by the
cheap, gaudy riots of a dozen urban netherworlds, seething with the
tragic and the obscenely stupid—to move as if in graceful flight, as
she skirted the border between summer-tan grasses and the wall of
towering deep green. Her dress was blue, pale, sky blue; rendered
lovingly by the brimming heart of a watercolor genius. And her hair
was as richly dark as starless midnight. I put a flame to the bowl of
my briar and watched her move west.

Then, as if she set as softly as the sun, the twilight of pine absorbed her.

I sat and watched the ink-black breach where she had entered
the undergrowth and imagined her to be a white witch on her way to
an appointment with the moon, or an elf-maiden returning to the
riches of her robust kingdom of secret hours and laughing woodlands.
Moments later, I found myself briskly laughing at an image of her—
sans crooked-peaked witch's hat or elfin crown—executing a pagan
jig with a portly hedgehog and a stately heron; the Minotaur, some
floppy-eared puppies, a whip-long yellow snake, and a band of
amazed but critical ducks, watched and laughed at this dance of the
new moon as well.

After a time, the heat of the day wandered off in pursuit of Father Sun and the Rainmaker came and sat beside me. I nodded and offered a half-smile. His huge eyes, themselves so like quiet storms, laughed at me.

"It is quiet here," he said.

"Yes. Thoughtfully so." I replied. "Perhaps an hour ago a young woman with skin as pale as Christmas snow passed by . . . She had long, curled tresses of jet and moved as if on gentle wings. I would have thought her a gypsy, if not for the pale splendor of her coloring. Do you know her?"

"Yes, after a fashion. It is said she is the daughter of an wicked enchanter . . . Whispers—local legend—have it that the apprentice of a great mage—cast out by his master for waywardness—while passing the home of her parents, who were newly wed, became enamored with her mother and attempted to seduce the new bride one night while the young woman's husband was in town carousing. She is said to have flatly turned away his lusty propositions, and a few nights later, when the husband was again out wenching, he returned and took her against her will, cursing her when he was finished. The next spring the maiden was born, and as the infant let out her first cry, her mother died. They say the young wizard had cursed the young bride to transform into a crow on nights when the moon rides high o'er the deeps of the heavens."

The serious eyes of the Rainmaker looked straight at the New Moon. As if receiving confirmation of bad news, he cast his gaze toward town. "The townsfolk say many things about the forest people around here—after all, they need to fill the slowness of their sad hours . . . Did you notice the bridge by Hugh's Pond? The children of the town believe the bridge has a great warted troll living beneath its span." He smiled. "The maiden you saw lives in the stone cabin on the hill east of the pond."

The Rainmaker looked off to the east as if a storm had turned him. "Her father is a cruel man." And with that he fell silent.

Soon after he stood and left me.

At eight I rose from the rough-hewn chair and walked the short mile into town. The night air was crisp and the fogs so normal for this region had chosen another province to haunt for the evening. At The Owl and the Faerie I ordered a jar of single malt and began to observe the patrons. In these past few weeks they had begun to accept me as just another quiet object not to be moved by. Whispers and the occasional word or two came to my ears, along with a modern variation of a poignant madrigal sung by a woman whose voice, it seemed to me as I sat enchanted in the soft frost of melancholy, had heeded the "come hither" of Misery. I hoped the bitter cold where dark hunger dwells had never touched the fair heart of the maiden of the pines I had seen earlier.

Her delicate image, to me at that moment as much a miracle as any rainbow, was in my mind's eye; hands like floating larks at play, elegant shoulders worthy enough to be portrayed in fine marble like the rarities of Europe's foremost museums, breasts as round as the softly glowing summer moon, ripe rose-colored lips. But Cruelty and his associate Misfortune tapped me on the shoulder, dislodging me from my tender revelry.

I heard the name Cassandra, and knew it to be her, and it was followed by a chortle of depraved lust. I went to the bar for another single malt in hopes of overhearing another utterance concerning her.

"Her father's daughter she is indeed." Followed by a hushed round of crooked chuckling.

"Witches and thieves—"

"Worse!"

"Yes—decent folk don't live like that."

"Certainly, not I."

"Are you saying I do? That I would?"

"No, of course not."

And the indelicate voices, noticing me listening, fell silent. I went back to the nightshades of my corner and once again, head down with my thoughts, became an object. The men returned to their cups and their repellent whispers, and held their dark laughter to little more than lewd smiles.

On the days following, I queried the Rainmaker, but he was uncommonly quiet regarding the maiden. So I began spending my mornings in town in hopes of learning more of her. Though known to some as a master of subtlety—something I require for my vocation— my questions only received sharp frowns and terse replies of, "They keep to themselves. And we're thankful for it."

Every evening I sat on the terrace and watched, for her gracefulness had awakened a shimmering candle of affection in my heart.

Once, as she passed by, she turned as if I had hailed her and looked at me. I thought she was about to smile and I rose and waved, but as quickly as a startled fawn she dashed into the bramble of thick pine. I stepped off the porch and walked to the border between field and wood, but feared to enter the labyrinth and frighten her further.

"I would cause no harm to come to you," I whispered. "I . . . merely wished to say hello, dear lady."

All I heard in reply was the calls of a few small birds and the fluid rustle of the breeze in the leaves.

That night I had dinner with my host and again inquired after her.

"Some affairs here are best left to only those embroiled in them." And with that, he would say no more, quickly asking after my journeys in his myriad rooms. "What illuminations have come to you?" And as soon as it was out he regretted asking, knowing the maiden to have cast aside all other discoveries.

Believing he had no experience with love at first sight, I let it go. Before dessert or after-dinner drinks could be brought out, I retired to my small room to read. Though affecting and cheery, the collection of verse I was reading, *Silver Kisses & Other Sonnets*, could not keep her from my thoughts. I put the book aside. Settled in the warm glow of the down bedding I dreamt of her in earnest.

So began my vigil, that long train of waiting in which moments that can find no way forward descend into a vague sadness. I brought my chair closer to the low stone railing and turned it so I might view the whole of the field without difficulty. But the days passed and she did not appear.

One night as the moon watched me as an undernourished cat watches a mouse, I knew I would have to fashion a change of fortune. The following afternoon I could wait no longer and decided to walk to the bridge and wander up the hillside. I would start with hello, and, I wonder if I might have a drink of cool water to wash away this dry heat?

Perhaps she would smile and a conversation might blossom, I thought.

After lunch the next day, I put my heels to the path. I was not swift as the wind, but my step did brighten as I neared her home on the grassy hillock.

Feeling uneasy about just walking up and speaking to her, for I am no quicksilver-tongued poet, nor am I a handsome cavalier who finds it easy to be in the company of ladies, I lingered on the bridge and looked over at the rapid flow rushing toward the unknown bends and wide waterfalls waiting downstream. Both sides of the river were overhung with thick green foliage, which shifted in the wind like sly snakes moving toward tasks that ended in doom. Good cover for the murderous fancies of a troll, I mused before moving on.

A few minutes' walk brought me to a pastoral view of Hugh's Pond and the diminutive stone cabin. I packed my pipe, put flame to the bowl, and pressed my back against a firm oak, awaiting a glimpse of her.

A big sky of open blue entertained me for a while before she came out and began working in a small vegetable patch. I was little more than a rolling dialogue of opening lines and should I?, could I?, for more minutes than I can remember.

I moved closer, yet somewhat nervously remained hidden, so I might gain better sight of her.

There was no sound, no breeze, and no leaves bobbing like playful fingers, no clouds in the vast blue that brought to mind other objects. Just her image—working, scratching out an existence in the dark soil. Scratching out a living did not belong here, it was the way of the gray cities to the South, but in these lush green hills it did not belong. She was meant to walk on clouds, to enchant deer and soft-feathered birds, not to slave in the dark loam of the earth. She should have rings and happy, devoted servants. She should be effortless, soft and bright as the song of joy.

As I watched her, and thought of the freedom that should be a rich cloak about her, I realized, one such as I, a shadowy creature of the bitter and indifferent darkcity, could not offer—or share, the sylvan ease she deserved ... My thoughts blackened as she continued her toils.

The embers in my bowl went cold and I continued to observe her tend the garden plot etched before the squat face of the cottage. But before I could marshal the nerve to approach her, her father came out, stamping and huffing like a minor lord of Hell. He stood before her, a flood of angry sky. There was a mad shout, a rancorous pronouncement—"Again, you get it wrong. You are no better than your whore-mother!" and he bent and struck her. A red blossom appeared at the corner of her mouth. Without hesitation he jerked her nearly fully erect before casting her to the ground as if she were merely a soiled rag. Down upon her rained an outburst of everything vile.

She cowered. Tears of distress staining her cheeks, she shook like a timid youngster in difficult weather. As if stirred by his thunder, the wind rose up. It raised the hem of her dress above her knees and he shouted, "So it's *that* on your mind again, is it?" And swift as a debaucher taking what the soiled fruit of the city streets offered for pennies, he—vicious as any harpoon—was on top of her. His foul, bruising heat was on her mouth, in her loins . . .

Her own father? And indeed he was none other, for I'd heard him described in town on two occasions. I thought my eyes and ears lost to some extravagant lie of madness. I began to vibrate as if in a dream of hate. I saw him—no longer thrusting, but gutted, neck snapped, dangling from a tree, carrion crow, the "sleep later" behavior of their black beaks exposing ivory bone.

My hands were fists, my eyes fire . . . I—rigid as flawed glass about to shatter—snarled like a wounded wolf, and she screamed—

I ran, yelling for the rapist to desist, and he rose from his assault and came at me with a great woodsman's axe.

From a sheath tucked beneath my coat I drew a weighted dagger—so often in my hand for villainy—and with the skill of an assassin, which I am, cast it true. It found his heart.

A dozen steps brought me to his prone body. I looked down into his hateful eyes—met them with an even hardness. That darkness I'd encountered previously and often. I took my pistol from its holster by my heart and after a single word, "Sadist." put one round between his eyes. Then I went to her.

I knelt and cradled her, and she wept for a time. The heat of shame in her tears burned me. Above, the sun moved in the sky. And with the coming of dusk she found strength and stood. She smoothed her dress and looked at cooling shell of her father, then at me. Shadows began to take her face and I could see all the questions in her eyes.

I did not speak, but walked to the corpse, and she followed. Standing above the body of her tormentor, we exchanged not a word, but her eyes thanked me for her new freedom a thousand times. I dragged his dead body down the hillside and cast it off the bridge. Perhaps the troll will find it of some use? I thought, as I tried to recall if trolls dined on only children and lost Billy goats.

I was quick back up the overgrown slope. Lost in the echoes of my actions, she seemed unable to fully comprehend that which I had written in blood. Unused to the sensations within me, I was a rush of words, fumbling with what was in my heart—

"You must go. I'll tell the constabulary someone—a stranger—raped me and murdered my father."

My feet refused to move.

Trembling, she said, "You have saved me."

I fought to tell her the summer dreams that were in my heart, but my voice could only find, "Come with me. I have another life. And money—enough for many lifetimes. All I've ever lacked was a heart to share my hours with."

"I cannot. Go. On the Night of the Full Moon at the eleventh hour I will come to you."

"But—"

"Wherever you may be, I will find you. Now go."

✦

In the cold of night I left the Rainmaker's house. Leaving one funeral for another, I returned to the ink-dark winter of the gray city, to my habitation devoid of lullabies or perfume. For days and weeks, draped in the indistinct murmurs of this gutted forgery of orderly manners, I walked the tilted pavements. Amid the shadow dances of those trapped in their immovable iron masks, I wandered from ill-lit alley to deserted cabinet to the complex bottom where the unhinged, the Underneath, pitch their sleep chambers. I lived as if in a desperate hallucination; about me, the etched gray—hard and unfailing, peeling from the weight of its insanity. The bone music of dark forces filling this zero of ever-gray, I waited—counting the monstrous hours—for her pledge to be made flesh. Every night I stood at the window holding the jeweled words of the maiden like an incandescent star.

✦

Thirteen months have passed since the afternoon I sent the monster who called himself her father to his just and proper niche in Hell, and at the appointed hour on the night of the full moon each month she comes to me; for one breathless hour. I hear a fluttering of wings on my balcony and know that in a moment she will enter my barren rooms.

I, in my fashion, far more evil than her sadist-father, for I take men's lives to earn my keep, know only this one single hour of grace and peace . . .

On this night, as on each of the others before, the soft, icy light of the full moon is overhead, and I rush down from the heights of despair as I hear a soft beating of wings outside my door.

Is she truly a child born of some dark sorcery as the town's folk tell furtively, or has her freedom given her wings? I know not. Nor do I care whence my angel comes.

Last Year in Carcosa

(Cold days biting . . .)

(Having inherited the hunger of the cold stars the moons dip low. One moon whispers, "When this is all over," the other—a twin phantom of truth, whispers, "This will play on . . . and on—on and on . . .")

(A man and a woman seated at a table on a high balcony, overlooking an empty beach. The air is dead calm, the sky a corridor of walking clouds. There is a gun and a pale rose on the table. The rose has shed one petal . . . She glances at the strange clouds as they ride off . . .)

THE MAN:	Spring, and all?
THE WOMAN:	*Then . . .* Perhaps. *(She turns her face to the beach and its blankness.)*
THE MAN:	Some may remember it differently.
THE WOMAN:	The slamming door and the ebbing foot-steps?
THE MAN:	That too.
THE WOMAN:	And the Brother?
THE MAN (*frowning*):	Turned around . . . Lost to some meadow of winter.
THE WOMAN (*regret disturbing the shipwrecked ghosts her tears so often see*):	Today walking in the footsteps of to-morrow.
THE MAN (*frigid, stern*):	And Forever.

(The woman looks at the gun. The man covers it with a pale linen napkin. It resembles a mound of windblown snow. She shivers, as if someone has placed a knife to her will. The clouds, touched by her October breath, push confused birds toward the spreading shadows of the lowlands.)

135

THE WOMAN: So the mess, and this Game of Truth, end?
THE MAN (*who the inhabitants, on the day they remove their masks, will call The Golden Lion—the Last King, worn and almost a reflection, smiles dimly—glacially*):   Except for the shadows love leaves in its wake.

(*The woman turns away and looks out over the empty beach. There is a long silence.*
    She sighs, turns to face a mask cold as the empty black stars. The man picks up the gun . . .)

(*The gun cares not for time . . . or reasons . . . or worlds, or dreams that could.*)

THE MAN (*standing at the railing, alone*):   Desire is the future.

✿

A gun in the mirror.
A gun in the mirror of a mirror . . .
A gun in the mirror of a mirror of a mirror . . .
Each mirror is an island. A parade of scars.
Each mirror is a face—a secret or a remembrance, bad blood, a tomb. Each face a mask.
A soulless mask.
The gun has no soul.
But the eyes looking in the mirror, looking for the gun . . . There's a soul in them . . .
And it's a dark one.
And it dreams of blood.
And the rhythms and canvasses of The Past . . .
U: "Desire is the future."
The mirror . . .
sees.
U: "Desire is the future."
The mirror . . .
Sees—
the thin lies that loved her.

"Desire is the future." (He whispered it Then. He whispers it Now.)

The mirror sees—

something has changed since last year.

U sees it too. Sees far away . . . And a face in the cold dark (hatching from days he left in time covered over by shifting sand). A soft face trying to hold on to dreams that would not heed swollen cries of the scavenger-wing blackbirds. But it's the same face. The same soul. Same eyes—angelic eyes. And he remembers holding on to the time. It was so simple . . .

Walking the corridors. Again. Like last time . . . and . . .

And the galleries . . . Long . . . Silent . . . disguised in a gray stillness they tug . . .

Chilled. Black mirrors. Doorways. To other eras, eras filled with detached voices, whispers in ink . . . Endless gloomy doorways to silent rooms.

Empty space reflected in empty mirrors, silent entropic coves . . .

Silent corridors. Shadowed halls . . . where no one walks . . . deserted corridors . . . portraits of dead men from eras gone by . . .

(old bonds broken by falsehoods)

(doubts) (faces turned, taken down)

There . . . in things the shadows imply . . .

—Now

a hand . . . Eyes . . . That face . . . (Did it forget?)

The voice (whispering of different times) (of frozen gestures) (hollow sounds)

. . . of kings and queens, princes—frozen, and princesses, and the impossible . . .

Columns. And shadows. In the gloom.

(and whispers) (of roles)

(and days of silence) (and the Garden of Day After Day when dark men walked in cinders of yesterday)

(and the eyes that turn away from the mirrors) (and the pillars that are only visible at twilight)

And the tall, dim figure in the painting . . .

Watching her from a distance . . . Watching her watch something unmoving in the whiteness . . .

She watched him, wondered what became of him.

Did he marry?
Did he find a way to be free of Today?
. . . or is he the same as ever?
The same as when he came down the stairs . . .
The stairs she sees in the mirrors.
Did he remember?
Were his hands still waiting?
For pleasure?
For the secrets of shame and destruction to dissipate?
Did he remember the dance? The thunder?
Did he turn?
See it coming . . .
Did he know?
About her mistake . . .
Did he guess?
(Then . . . the sound of her laugh . . . it sounded far away)
(everything in the mirror sounded so far away) (and deserted . . .)
　　　　　　　　　(the long corridors)
　　　　　　　　　(the chairs)
　　　　　　　　　(the game of silence) (cold, love and fault)
　　　　　　　　　(the gloom)
(cold) (tears—shame—fear—the act bent with fury)
(always seemed so cold)
(it did not leave one alone)
(like a persistent question)
(—please)
(—please)
(—please) (the mirrors flooded with desire)(like the corners of a
dry page stained with disappointment)

Mirrors . . . filled with shadow moths with phoenix wings bend-
ing to embrace the blind midnight stillness held in the jet trenches
. . .

Mirrors that slowly erase . . .
Mirrors that take your breath away.
Mirrors of afternoon.
And twilight.
And the dreamer in high heels that whispered, "Time . . . Time
. . . time poisoned . . ."

Mirrors of flesh and blood.
Mirrors leaning . . .
Mirrors hatching shadows . . .
. . . watching it all . . .
in mirrors flooded with desire . . .
Desire . . .

It was so simple Then . . . simple as the lines twilight paints over the place Day will never come back to . . .

Back Then. On the Other Side.

U sees

Then

and Now.

Feels (almost) the same.

Something's wrong.

Something.

Wrong.

Wrong as his hand, as the broken glass, as the blood.

U sees the gun.

Feels something's wrong. The lines. The shadows. The mess that was made. Torn up—("It all went so badly.") The way the lines sit on the page.

But you play the hand you're dealt.

Win.

Lose.

Or wrong.

Wrong—

. . . The corridors . . . (something cruel—something cool, that word, "Nonetheless"—something beautiful . . . so far to fall) . . . The shadows—the flock of abyss-dark shades spreading. The kaleidoscope of merciless centuries in the mirrors . . . The doors opening—in the same room again . . . The plague. The choices—a hundred silent autumns on her lips . . . The sigh, the crash . . . the line and the wheel (and what it all came down to) . . . what the voices carried . . . guilt spilled, dispersed . . . The shadows. The weariness—the angry face in the mirror, its vanities bullets . . . The corridors . . . Rowing in the dragon's fire. . . the stillness of the long

corridors . . . All the dead days and dead months, lying in the ever-
lasting shadows of another here . . . the narrow light on the beach.
The balcony . . . The final sunset (without a tear).
"Wrong?"
Maybe you get kissed.
Maybe you get dead.
That's the dance. Then.
Now.

All these mirrors. But not a single clock. It's as if time has
stopped, took the easy way out, filled the mirrors with ghosts.

Was it Monday?

Was it New York? (Couldn't have been Paris. All he could recall
of Paris was the cold and the rain.) (Wasn't Mykonos.) (Not barren,
dusty Cairo with its rose.) Or Marienbad—the mind, picking at the
scabs, pushed around by illusion and deadly acts?

(Strange, dark clouds—Autumn's vagabond clouds pushed along by
fear.)

(The labyrinths and what the weak lanterns etched.)

(The jealousy.)

Maybe someone said he was a hero.

Him?

At *that* moment?

Some savior? The Last King? *Him?*

It all felt so alien.

Then.

     . . . History flashing in the mirror . . . Her open mouth, her open
arms in the mirror . . . shining black shadows—smooth and deep—
a state of asphyxia, waiting in the mirror . . . the mirror watching
night and secrets at the door, watching small variations meet, fade,
in the twilight of far away . . .

Now.

Not the song. They didn't turn away from it. Couldn't.

Not the feel of her skin. How it turned him around.

Not what they'd done in her room—he sees it distinctly.

Not wrong.

The endless dark hall . . .

The stairs (facing southeast)—37. Long and slow, going up, leaving today for tomorrow. The hollow sounds.

The door. Opening, on visions, on shadows hand in hand. Just them alone, far from the world.

The sighs.

(That golden age.)

(Summer.) (The moons, a prince and a princess, each wearing a yellow veil, filling the blank window panes.)

(Summer, held fast in his clenched fist.) (Every ounce and secret and feat, even the air—right from the first page.)

. . . Her sighs—stirring when she trembled, his sighs—stirring as he trembled, then fierce, clear. Delivered from the air of different cultures.

Not wrong.

The reflections . . .

Not wrong.

The echoes . . . of Infinity. Stretched out, a sea of night. The urges of imagination—Lips open. No limitations.

The garden of flesh . . . the path . . . beauty you could smell . . . (Even in the Garden of Dead Moths—that lawn of dead verses spilled from a mouth slammed shut) . . . Night on his tongue . . .

Not wrong.

Then . . .

. . . *(walking the Hall of Mirrors—endless—endless. Standing at the door to her bedroom . . . Desire, the unspoken agitation, in his hands, pouring from his heart . . . the moment formed of purpose . . . drop by drop the toil of divided thoughts . . .)*

Now.

Wrong?

Vivian?/Delphine?/Clarissa? U remembers her eyes. The gentle feel of her skin, every gesture—every second of the event *(her skin of stars leaning)*. How she was of a mind to . . . The shadows cut by another reality.

The mess . . . (her secret heart—touched by lies—crossed the room) . . . What was erased in the dimness . . .

(Then—) Vivian? *(once crossed the room . . .)*

(Then—) Delphine? *(once crossed the room . . .)*

(Then—) Clarissa? *(once crossed the room . . .)*

Different names in different times . . . A million twilights ago . . . *there were sticks in the grass . . . roses with blackthorns—blooming, their little mouths of color sweet fruit, a waving jungle—showing their contours to the morning . . . Four hundred nights ago . . . the dry thirst of the raven dying in the fragments and silent smoke . . .*

But surely the same place. Surely That Place . . .

Paris?

Last year? . . . *(the canvas . . . the pearl-handled . . .)*

The moment she turned away at the ancient gate . . . The terrible murmur, soft as the desolate contours of the coffin's dark lining . . . The emptiness of his fingers, hollow inquisitors . . .

How the moons came down and dropped their tattered light on the dark street of ash.

Last night? *(by the window . . .)*

Or a night a year ago? *(on the stairs . . .)*

Or a hundred years ago? *(in the mirror . . .)*

Some lost Then. *(blood inscribed on the pages . . .)*

So close . . . *(close enough to see the trouble in her face)*

So far away . . . *(all the walls . . . and dark doors . . . locked doors . . . and unfinished visions . . . the velvet work . . . the shame.)*

The curled shadows of ghosts spilled by the blade of destiny's sword . . . And cold, blue hands . . .

"It was so simple. All . . . so simple." Whispered, grainy, tilted. (His lie . . . dripping with ill shadows—The crowd of lies, the crystal-lized regrets.) (His eyes stung and drifting along the dry streets of Eternity.)

But this is Now—This time. *(Then, distant and steady, frozen . . . the flowers motionless)*

Ripe.

Open. With light. And space.

Time

that's not torn up.

Not filled with shadows—witchlike things of fangs and tortures slipped from eyes rattling with infinity . . .

NOW.

TODAY.

A day not to forget. *(not to)*

Like the last day. *(forget)*

The day *(the last day)* she was here. *(no one notices the last day)* Laughing. Her eyes flashing in the bedroom.

Her lips were red. Her eyes dark and worldly, filled with rigid phrases. There was no ring on her finger . . .

Her mouth open.

(the grave . . . motionless . . .)

Speaking.

Something. A trick, or a door.

(a fog of ashes . . .)

"Not"

(gray . . .)

"that we could."

(almost mean. sticking . . .)

"Did."

(blunt . . .)

"Then."

(cruel . . . struck.)

U leans in, over the edge—all the way, looking.

She sits straight. Not accepting his hand, the bridge, he thrusts in the silence.

(struck.)

U sits back. No might on his brow. *(all the years to fill in . . . communicate . . . to break the silence . . .)*

The slow sky of almost . . . a sky with shapes that remind him of belonging . . . a sky of echoes and things half open, things took from her, things he lost . . .

Rain, no longer under cover of distinct heavy grey, ended. No bridges between. Across the room . . . scarred flowers . . . sprained candles, losing their wax . . . a heap of intentions that almost fooled time as it sailed to moments collected in the mirror . . . the fuse of boredom and the flash of a dark afternoon here again . . .

A muted trumpet makes a fuss. Things close.

An angel's teeth and no talk of heaven.

A clock too tired to navigate.

Over the railing, a garden of empty seats . . .

He closes the faded, brittle Midnight Parchment. Leaves his room.

He is no stranger to the to and fro of winding shadows, or the voyage of sorrow and fire, or the unheard footfalls of darkness, or the doors between the self and The Other . . .

or the pallor of madness unreconciled . . .

There is no sound in the long corridor . . .

The mirrors here do not forget the past . . .

He stands before a mirror. Adjusts his tie, whispers, "Wait for the harvest?" Smiles . . . He inhales the time scratched in the mirror. Imagines his powers, an infinity of starry black his prey will scream under . . .

He steps away . . . And his hand, an iron vessel filled with everything—and nothing, shakes . . .

. . . U thinks he's seen a ghost, a silhouette of something that was never evergreen. Decides it was a gesture of her hand, or a smile painted on a mask, hiding a lie.

He hears music and wings . . . there is something simmering in the air . . . her eyes are large, jewels scarred with wishes, they trigger a current in the air . . .

He has seen it before (*A cloud of wings and black cloaks. And no mouth and no eyes. Braids of grief and death. It bends and shivers and roils . . . Gathers ashes to its dance . . .*). Fears he will see it again . . .

The world with its holes and worn hills, clawed by every empty hand that lost, is awash in stained silver windows mourning plundered promises.

His mouth opens. Silently rattles. Closes . . .

His mind races, picking at strands . . .

"Clarissa." His tongue knowing the name he forced on it was wrong. "Camilla."

Then remembered fully.

(*A room of tables and windows and puddles of light. A room of weakness . . .*)

Turned around.

"Now I remember," Camilla says.

"Last year in . . . *Carcosa?*"

"Yes, the coast . . . Hollow. So hollow and thin those vast rooms. So dim. Silent."

"But not empty."

"No. There were things—lies and treason—in the dust. Cold, angry things." Her eyes searching, returning to something that haunts this unfinished time, something that was there in the space captured in the mirrors . . .

(The man and woman standing in the garden by the fountain. He is firm, dark. She is dressed in white and set against the stony spine of a huge column . . . The sky above the House of Suffering is gray (again.) . . .)

THE MAN: (*Pressing. His hand upon her breast, his hyena breath in her ear.*)   Please—Please.
THE WOMAN: (*Her head turned away, her eyes damp. Her mouth open.*)   Please—Please . . . Stop.

(He is cold—firm, a knife spreading her troubled days. She is surrounded, shouldered—thrust, in to a labyrinth of difficulties and cold, angry fire.)

(Neither finds pleasure in the eruption . . .)

(. . . He is walking the long, shadow-laden corridors. From his lips, in fever-painted whispers, slip gray words from Midnight's Parchment . . . He is waiting for his time to come . . . the long staircase . . . a route of blackness and alien distance . . . and the skeletons of storms . . . The black-soil shadows are filled with dead moths . . .)

(He passes a mirror that time and the walls cannot control)

(And another . . .)

(A mirror—raven-night deep, where time does not count . . . where somewhere is impossible . . .)

(And another . . .)

(filled with the blood of the dead)

(and the gnawing chapters of gray married to claustrophobic waiting . . .)

(A mirror where you find yourself alone.)

(The Hall of Doors, lined with mirrors filled with space, their blackness expanding . . . Walking . . . The endless repetition of corridors and stairs and mirrors that hold and stretch time . . . ancient mirrors that un-shape dimensions—that illuminate darkness with an immense silence, that disorient and disturb sensation . . . The long corridor (leading somewhere, to some brink) that ends at her door (again.) . . .)

(Forward noiselessly—a tall dark shape in lace of intersecting shadows . . . The key talks in the lock, its language a recitation of unspeakable things . . . The shadow of his hand, a wavering stain, on the knob . . . Her room (again.) . . . She turns from her winter travels in the mirror. She is dressed in white, a white nightgown . . . His darkness, built of Then and This Present, and the closing line from the Midnight Parchment—'It's the one who starts who wins,' pressing, spilling, overcoming . . .)

THE MAN (*Dry as the impossible distance of centuries, the shadow of his hand stains her breast.*): Please—Please . . .
THE WOMAN (*Exhausted, wounded, burning in his fingers . . . Her head is turned away. Her eyes flutter.*): Please—Please—Please, stop.

THE MAN (*From his lips a rush of words from the Midnight Parchment.*): Black moths cry your name . . . the years and The White Figure damned and torn stand at the coast . . . waiting for midnight He cries your name . . . THE marriage . . . the stars become black moths . . . there is light . . . and darkness . . . Never, swollen with His Mysteries, leaks . . . the flesh expects . . . wishes to . . . walk through the door—

THE WOMAN: You're raving!

(But she cannot turn away . . .)

(Her eyes and hair and gown in a state of disorder.)

(Ten dead minutes

—the masquerade of hope flickers out . . .
    She trembles, groans, grows dark, spends her
blood-stained tears of failure . . .
        they nail her dreams to the rusted mouth of
silence in the mirror . . .
    Consequences reached . . .
    Goals no closer . . .
    Gluttony has conquered all—the tips of her
fingers, her mouth of empty names . . . left her heart stale . . . and
frayed . . . left her heart a grave-shaded verse of blood and sand . . .
        . . . Wantonly gorged deep—confused,
alone, she can find no star in the full cry of evil)

(. . . Ten dead minutes, continents dying in the sun . . .)

His hands, in other times rough seas a thousand secrets deep, rest on the table, palms flat on the smooth, cold surface. Over the dying edges of the rose petals he searches the riverbed of her eyes. "They didn't have to be. There were seeds." A strange sentiment—A plan for escape?—flashes in his eyes.

"Colored by things that crawl in smothered hearts and paint the horizon with bitterness."

"If you had only found a way around. It could have been so simple."

"Around, Day?"

"Another would have followed . . . If you had just waited. A few seconds more—"

"You are wrong." The bent shadows of her hands tell of power struggles.

Uoht whispers: *"Wrong."* He pauses. Lifts his palm in an empty gesture. Looks both surprised and threatened. "Again?"

Eyes slaves of fleeting lore: "Wrong? . . . Then?" His thoughts slip by silhouettes of minutes . . . weeks . . . months . . . years . . . He finds shapes in the loam of memory's shadowy creases . . .

Negations
Sides . . . lines . . labyrinths . . . splintered, seized
Ascendency
the orphaned words of the old regime weeping

Wrong—for each other—joined together, that surge
On the wrong day—the caged breast overwhelmed erupts,
screams for To-morrow
With the wrong need
holding the wrong flag
Wrong question
from the unmoving mouth
Blind eyes colliding with a heart of poisoned fire
     —Too wrong to be this anxious after all this time? After be-
ing excused from Paradise, sagging and torn from grotesque shad-
ows in this gloom . . . confused and molded in misgivings—Where
is the sunlight?
Wrong
     . . . time (to think there was still time—still a path—to wish
Now was not cold and false)
     . . . year
     . . . and no where to run . . .
The claws of truth, the syllables of dust
     . . . and—no where to run . . .
Wrong
gestures
gamut
intentions manifest in gales, hissing, melting in chaos—
combinations sunk in impotent, painted flesh of never—never—
never
     flung
     solid
     too far to climb
     too many mandibles spitting . . . the arcane fever
Wrong
when he said, I am yours . . .
     . . . To stand there mocked and condemned as the sun falls . . .
unable to change, to fully live . . . helpless and alone at the end of
the road haunted by repetitions . . . to look back and look back and
see . . . surrender . . . and empty mirrors . . .
     . . . Did he miss something? some remark or detail . . . some
vague corruption of compass . . .
Some interwoven shadow in the mirror?

Wrong to reach for that face in dark space—Wrong to want to know—Wrong to notice, to name cadaverous night enemy . . . Wrong to try to wake her . . . to carve inspiration from the cold currents of irrevocably gone . . .

Wrong

Productive as ashes,

or old thoughts deceived by their own fear . . .

Wrong

to seek her door—that famished thunder where the light vanishes . . .

The disguises of the King's puppets peeled away . . . The myth in shards, the Mother (in silken robes and the devil's mask)— laughing—crumbles, the sister knotted, her balance collapsed . . . the dead-bird bastard brother swirled in war . . . the high tide of grave music dissecting the ancient walls, pushing . . .

Wrong

Hands screaming like lepers split with illness and colors silvered by the cunning of madness

Wrong mother

Wrong kinship

Being the WRONG brother . . .

Wrong bed—side by side mayhem and fancy . . . wrong bedroom

Scalded, dancing, begging—every deafening limb rotating—

its thirst advancing with the wrong desires

—Jealousy pleated and striped with ecstasy

—Taboos—teeth and tongue snapping for the love of the threading spider

At the wrong door

Hunting, the clamoring teeth—wrong

Lost, tongue crumbling with hate and fear

Sick . . .

and

Wrong. Wrong . . . the blur of the devil's eye . . . WRONG.

Lies . . .

Every . . . sweet . . .

lie . . . dry, methodical . . . (in hallways, up staircases) . . . (the unspeakable silence of the waning moons) . . .

Lie?

Wrong? Almost spoken, but his mouth, each corner dry and leaning toward the consequences of motionless blackness, can find no door in the clutter maze of shadows . . .

In the mirrors filled with the unforgiveable, the dead—drowned in laments of desire, dance with the dead . . .

Dead wrong—

Wrong—

the venus sex lips language of sin and memory sacrificed— Liar! Liar! The last dying breath of delirium—empty black collision . . . To remake the nightmouth terrible-news boiling in the arteries of her cold body—Vanished, every trace of angels closer— Dust militates the wrist—Hollow dust stains the curtain-leech sky of impossible memory—False!

Liar! There are no revelations quartered in limbo.

Liar!

There . . . a mask—a tattered costume—pretending (twisted spheres scratched by the crowd of cannibal chance and indiscretions)—every finger bone white, whispering about execution and time silently clamped to raw flesh . . . and then she never even existed . . .

Scraped hours . . . The hole with no mercy.

The slow grind of dark. Flesh in the custody of the grave. Decay succeeds.

Disappear . . .

The mirrors . . . the face of the Black Man in the mask she serves . . . entangled—monstrosity—retaliation—talking backward in slow motion . . .

Liar!

Killer!

. . . the shadows corrupt . . . lengthen . . . dark . . .

and more dark and no where to speak . . .

And endless night . . .

—Told me you died

—Told me you died

—Told me . . . You died

—Told me

. . . Empty black tongue churning

Black . . . the crawling cyclone . . .
Black . . . every crack in the heart . . . the tide of shadows . . .
dead . . .

Wrong.

The endless faces of yesterday splashed in that black hole . . . waiting . . .

(A man and a woman seated at a table on a high balcony, over-looking an empty beach. The air is still, the sky is a mire of steel clouds. There is a gun and a pale rose on the table. The rose has shed one petal. He glances at the dark, strange clouds gathering . . .)

THE MAN *(wanting to say, so beautiful you are . . .)*: These wounds we share . . . They could heal . . . In our morning silk we could find a place where we can hear the flowers bloom—Our garden would never be finished.

(She removes her pale hand from over her heart. Where it was placed, as if to shelter it from another lie. It slowly moves to the cold black gun lying on her side of the table.)

THE MAN *(eyes desperate)*: A year isn't long—

(The gun is in the inquisitor's hands. Hands of scarred alabaster, billowing with ancient minutes, filled with Today—hungry and ready to burst. Filled with the ruin of Then. The inquisitor's yellow eyes, filled with Tomorrow and the exhaled cellar air of the Next World, are suddenly permeated with thunder.)

U turns from the din of thunder in her eyes, sees a demon(always new again)—with sunken eyes shudder in the mirror . . . It smiles . . . and whispers, It all slips away so fast . . . The mirror cracks.)

THE WOMAN: There are no second acts in Carcosa.

(She pauses for a few seconds.)

THE WOMAN: Only . . . dust . . . (Whispered, grainy. Filled with ice and ruin, and a quivering, gray hunger.)   And things that never return. (Is all Camilla says.)

(The gun and its dividing volume offer no farewell.)

(Then—There was a glass and a rose on the table. There was lust . . . and blood . . . A red desert in his pale eyes . . . Now—the rose is dead. The glass is empty.)

(Poured out bit by bit (too deaf to seek, to conflicted by madness to cope), he in the vapors of agony, a scarecrow lost in the haze of a silent mirror of mistakes, its little mouth filled with plague, its stony limbs punished by Eternity's cannibal worm clinging to the spoils of regret, vanishes . . .)

CAMILLA (standing at the railing, alone.): Desire . . . *is the future.*

(She turns, looks in the cracked mirror where a dry darkness moves. Pauses . . . as if looking to see if something will appear.)

(Camilla's thirst, driftwood dry, finds The End. The hollow sounds of her shoes, the color of crow's wings, dissipates as the Last Queen takes her exit.)

(The black mirrors are empty. Silent. The dust they hold grows deep. The strange shadows they devoured have grown long . . . The silent black mirrors are empty . . . As they were Then . . .)

(The Queen's mask—a scene stained yellow by lies and regrets, her calling card, mirroring the lifeless color of the pale, desolate moons—lies on the table . . .)

(All the far stars cry)

(. . . the wind carries secret tides of lies . . . no one notices the black moths, jewels for her crown of blood, lured to the lizardbreath shackles of Forever . . .)

CAMILLA *(silken yellow lips dreaming.):* But to desire to-morrow. . . *(Eyes embroidered with some time ago transform, reflect a lost object . . .)*—in this time of blackened branches . . . *(She looks down. He lies there unmoving, his eyes and hair in a state of disorder.)* is an error.

(after a rainy afternoon viewing of Last Year At Marienbad)

(Fleet Foxes "Mykonos," Joe Henry "Scar," and Beth Orton "She Cries Your Name," looped)

Scarlet Obeisance

For Frank Belknap Long, Poet at the Gates of Wonder

When he comes from his sleep in the dusky havens
To the squat foothills of Tsang
At the base of the dolorous mountain
Ringed-heavy with moisture and green and silence,
To laugh, to feast—that insatiable visitation upon opulent flesh,
The poems, the music,
Will be as a hurricane
Penetrating from life to life to life.
    Only bones and dim stains—the truth of dark chaos,
    Shall he leave upon the rocks.

In the empty space of his temple,
Cluttered with dust the winds have not swept away
And deranging secrets from moments long ago
His immortality measures, and remeasures in dreams like illnesses,
Images, tainted by time's grave,
Of lustrous dark red currents of reluctant fragile things
Rampant with ruin's lesson.

In the primal forest, dense of teakwood and bamboo,
Where stalking shadows like serpentine coils weave undulant tex-
    tures,
And even the great cat painted in orange and night-line stripes
Fears to pad,
All lesser creatures are loath
To summon up their voices or breathe,
As the vapors of his inexorable hunger arise
From the ebon caverns beneath.

O Elephantine-headed Father
Of the Miri Nigral and Tcho-Tcho man-demon,
What doom-destined om sounds in thy vast webbed ears?
What cosmic wheel spins,
And in its ageless dervish rotations
Brings the days closer
To the call to swift running harvests unending?

O Chaugnar Faugn,
Bloated Feaster of jet-tusks and conduit trunk,
Fattened on oceans of claret red,
What darkling meditations dost thou beguile in,
Sitting, lotus-poised, before the scarlet mandalas
So long ago employed as stepping stones
To ford the cold heavens?

O Grim Legend of the East,
Slumbering on thy pedestal of foulsome dreams aflame,
Awaiting the White Acolyte's coming
And thy journey from cold, far corners,
Wake from thy unbending contemplations,
For the ripe fruit of your garden gleams.
Rise from that perfect darkness
To the dense woods of confused blood dreaming of escape.
Rise up, Idle One—
Multitudes, phantoms of nothingness though they know it not,
Await thy taking of softness and fear with particular pleasure.

Come to me now, Irresistible Mountain,
    bring Thy new day of barren, terrible night!
Come to me, Sleeping Emperor,
    refresh Thyself.
Hear Thy acolyte, Chaugnar Faugn,
    meditate no longer in Thy exile of inanimate solitude,
    come laugh the conqueror's laugh that rends all asunder—
Lose Thy roar, full sore, that all may become omnipresent silence.
Open Thy great hand—man's grave,

that all may see the vicissitude illuminated.
Here is the map drawn of my passions,
      come from the labyrinths of Hell
      and collect Thy accounts due.
Take their wits and ingenuity and emblems,
Take their memoirs and melancholies,
Come Immutable Triumph—
      bind all to thy maw of annihilation
      for clemency has been irrevocably damned.
Come with the ferocious tools of Thy holy frenzy blazing,
      and overturn their vulgar wisdom.
Come, Lord of Desolation,
      Thy brides despairing, bloom!

O Swollen One,
Vast in thy abandonment so like a dance,
When the Night of All Nights,
That perfect nothingness after thy feasting,
That void as barren as the very beginning, is the All—
Will you then, reclining in repose, be contented,
Or will you, Elemental-Predator, once again beset by
wounding thirsts, dream
Of bones and dim stains upon the rocks?

Rendezvous Under Shadow Bridge

The Night Watchman checks his flashlight, clips the turnkey to his key ring. Puts his notebook in his satchel, examines the level of ink in his pen . . . Finishes his cigarette, puts on his coat. Adjusts his cap in the cracked, dirty mirror in the washroom. Checks his heart at the door. Turns up his collar . . .

And he's out the door . . . into the Deepest Season.

First Night:

Under the bridge of a cold northern town. Crime as a form of witchcraft coming from opposite directions. Grill to grill twenty feet apart. Lights off. Two parked cars. Two men with guns, the big one smoking. Translating the obstacles. Agreeing, this time without blood. They leave—back to check their traps.

When the tail lights fade to black the homeless drunk hunkered down in the bushes stops quivering and tries to sleep. In his dream he's talking to Last Summer. He's got curly hair and an all-the-live-long-day smile, says, "I could have been somebody, if I wanted to." Without reply Last Summer just continues to polish the anvil they broke human kindness on.

An hour later the excuse they use for a taxi in this neck of the woods passes by. The driver, maybe off to breakfast, flicks his cigarette from the half open widow. They never hang around here.

Another night:

A piano—Bill Evans she thinks—crying, "Who Can I Turn To?" from the car radio. Fog working over the hymns of the weary sentinel street lamps. A woman smoking her last cigarette. A pint of whiskey and a bottle of Seconal—the finishing touches, on the red leather seat beside her. The lips of the executioner at her throat. She left her alibi at home, or in the bar, she can't recall.

"I know," she confesses to the eyes in the rearview mirror.

The open mouth of water soft as the laughter of leaves. She leaves her string of pearls and her shoes and her dress in the car . . .

She's dancing on the white moon lyrics her hand spilled from the window—bare feet, without hope, tracing the velvet sky turned ice in the letters from Knoxville, crying—not now, not ever, down by the river . . .

Down- *where* . . .

down- *grief* . . .

down- *slumbers* . . .

Wild night:

A knock at the solitary door of midnight. The boombox blowing, blarin' big ugly beats. A girl—a misguided angel deceived by a fleeting smile, paying Hell for the error in the bottle she swallowed unknowingly. The hurricane of blind carnal force flashing and sweating between her legs doesn't care . . . There's a chain of lightning waiting behind him, whoopin' and ready to dock.

She's carrying the load. Thinks she wants to say No, but can't find anything but ends that don't end at home and dark corners of nothing in the witch-smoke of the chemical labyrinth.

A crowd of stranger's maws all round. Cadillac cowboys, laughing, drinking themselves to death, one big pool at a time. The last hour of their vacation was almost over . . .

Fuse blown, the last storm finishes. Weak, head full of cotton and kaleidoscopic fog, webs and flat tires, she can't move. He drags her to the edge of the water and spills her in . . .

"Jailbait—*Fish bait!*"

High fives all around . . . Then they're out riding with the wind. Headed to the crossroads . . . where there'll be Hell to pay . . .

A night so sad:

A boy and a girl—lovers, fallen off the hilltop—sit on the iron bench. Hand in hand, tear to tear. Five hours ago she had her feet in stirrups . . . And he waited outside. Both were scared.

A doctor made adjustments and the road stopped going on forever.

A soft kiss. They part . . .

One west, to home.

One south, to the bus station.

Fifth night:

Rain tired of trying to grow things in the vacant lot, but it still scratches out a downpour now and again . . . pulls a little wind out of the cupboard to turn things around . . . and there's the thief coming out of the tunnel with his pot of gold . . . and the New-York-minute gun . . . and the hand of a fisherman who dreams of sunny days going well . . . but Yeter'el, the expenditure consultant for the Slaughterer of Souls, has other plans . . . his talons click and out comes a signed copy of the grim reminder that laid claim to delusions—the terms and conditions agreed upon way back in a honky-tonk in the dark . . . Garden party cancelled . . . One burned. Excited to let it bleed, he turns to the second. Another stipulation to level. "Fair my ass. NOOno-noo you indignant little bastard. This ain't Waiting For *fuck-ing*Godot, ya don't get to fuck around here forever. The more you stupid ratfuck assbags get, the more you want." Another rubber-stamped Jack Flash flesh in his lamprey hands of gallows spice. Yeter'el turns on his automatic-midnight smile and without further fuss or gulp of air dissolves another trophy. The hangman slides his tongue over his top lip, sucks the sweet moisture of a fat drop of blood, wonders where the closest bar is . . .

Friday night:

Awake. The stone paws of the gargoyle have come out to play. The 103 lbs. blonde in the cheap fun-zone dress finds him hard to handle. His spark starts a fire. She seems to like it rough until he starts breaking her bones . . . When he's done with his take out he burps.

Final night:

Under Shadow Bridge. A hint of yesterday's gloom in the weather . . .

Baggage and bottles with a lot to learn . . . The lies never stop promising . . . If reverse could fly the blindman's unfinished business might understand the joke and the fire . . . A stain, vacancies and ve-locities, will landing in quicksand, the dim echo of a conversation between grace and guilt . . . A doomed overture cracks . . . Buried in a laudanum of maps of unbridgeable amnesia the sweet forest that can't extricate its eggshell heart from autumn stumbles from a white square of responsibilities . . . All the pretty little working class Fausts outta money and cigarettes, running for their lives . . .

The Night Watchman, having reinstalled his heart when he came in from the cold, makes the week's final entry in his journal . . .

Just another midnight. Nightwolves and street demons out to tattoo themselves with angel's tears . . .

The ghost dance. The usual suspects churning, cold hands grasping or frightening the overloaded innocents. Red screamed, another slow pulse slammed into gravity with a dull thud. The sirens didn't seem to notice the debris—Guess they were too busy rowing through all the temptations . . .

I wonder why no one understands beauty is fragile, even if it's covered in war paint? At about 2:30 I thought I heard an angel cry, but it passed by . . .

An editorial in our local toxic grudge last week said evil is so civilized these days. Don't know what portion of spice that fool was sucking on. 'Round here, the FIRE EXIT sign's been out since God ran out of silver bullets. And some damned-fool thief chiseled Buddha out of the green stamps and rent money he was saving for a rainy day . . .

With contempt, the cyclones lean in . . . the windmills never change.

He turns his key, hangs it on the peg. Makes a mental note to check on his transfer to the desert . . . Whispers, "Adios," flicks the worn light switch by the door and the stars go out. The Night Watchman puts on his sunglasses to add some hint of color to the blackness, turns up his collar . . . His shift over for the week, he lights a cigarette and goes in search of a stiff drink . . .

His back to the bridge, letting the wind add his thoughts to the leap-frog rustle of leaves, he dreams of some time ago when there was silver and gold in a May day.

"Whores and winos and pushers and stoned underage girls and every cold-handed demon, just popped out of the shithole, or some burning sewer, pissing blood and trucking in witchfire and spooks . . . Some nights it's all too much."

In a bar crowded with flat-broke last exits elbow to elbow with hearts of stone who never bought into the tales of light he hears a sax/piano duo play "Someone to Watch over Me". He'd laugh, but knows even the shadows of the sleeping moon need a hand to hold every once in a while—Even if it's all but a dream within a night-mare.

And so far, this one's been Hell.

(Bohren & Der Club of Gore *Midnight Radio*)

in front of an empty house in dead city

The poison hour ended three minutes ago.

No river. No lighthouse. No one fine day. Post-whirling. Post-gunfire. Post-lightning, post-spat/protests. Post-beginning, post back-lash. The haze and blur of the red path darkstorm quiet when the crazy crests of black-round&round-&strange stop . . .

In the middle of the street.

"Close one." The owner of the voice examines a scratch on his partner's neck.

Knee deep in loud blood and transfigured-flesh by the pound. Bullets holes where eyes were. Earlobes and lies in the gutter. No for-giveness in this bloodbath. One spent brass cartridge on the tongue of a death thing, looking constipated now that it has stopped throbbing. Two empties lying in a knife wound to honest to be an accident. Pieces of things and exposed bone (more than a few broken), here and here

and here,

and there

and there . . . A riot cooling . . .

The houses on the curb quiet, sinking. Windows dark. Shut tight. The gunpowder cloud gone. A tri-colored cat pokes his head out from the bush he hunkered down under. Weakness—dead. Nothing created. Blood (and a little more) on the killing floor. A field without ghosts. No radio. Very little light in this dark hole. No more things speaking with foul tongues. No more vampires this weekend, not on this street anyway.

The big man covered in tattoos and battle scars slides a fresh—full, magazine in his weapon. The smaller man, still wired, still sharp as his knife, plunges his stag-handled, 18" Arkansas toothpick into the back of a slab of dead meat, lights a cigarette. Exhales. Grins.

Ear to ear smile—cold smile. The big man covered in tattoos and battle scars shakes his bag of new fangs. "Mojo workin', brother."

No innovation. They hit their work hard. No buzzing. No chit-chat. Strong arms made no noise. A left-hander. A right-hander. Former Marines—Recon (hard as sapphires, as outlaws). They'd shed blood before. Gallons and gallons, if not rivers, of it.

A big black boot toes a skull aside. "Let's go get a drink."

"A cold one."

Sweating. Hungry. "Done."

Sapphire hard smile. "Good. Then let's get over to Lex & 9th. Might snag a few more Fangs before the sun pops up," said the smaller hunter, kneeling, sheathing his Bowie knife, before stringing the last (a greasy, black ponytail) of fifteen scalps.

There used to be a candy store on the corner and the musical promise of happiness ran up and down the block. The bus driver that was born in Vermont used to drive by here. He'd tell people about the silver moon and apples (he could carry on for an hour about his Mom's pies) and salamanders and the concerto of vivid autumnal colors . . . Leprous, peeling paint, weathered shades lighter. Knee high weeds and cigarette butts. And empty, broken bottles. Bits and scraps of paper—of no importance now, with nowhere to go without the aid of a stiff breeze. Dozens of spent brass cartridges. A rusting mailbox with six bullet holes in it. A severed hand flat out of the sin that animated it. Blood (and a little more—dead now) on the killing floor . . .

The hot sun will come. And in their turn, so will the insects and the rats and the black-eyed crows . . .

(after listening to some fondly remembered oldies on WTRY)

Ain't No Love on the Street

[for a certain gent, WHP, esq.]

... it's a slaughterhouse.

Chicago (after a week of tight skies suggesting rain): The jury's never seen an innocent man. Empty pockets and empty guns are loaded with bitter gestures ... Suicide, blues and rattles of trouble. Yes. Sin. YES. Resurrection, redemption—NO.

Across the street from the abortion clinic. The lobby and the precisely ornamented rooms behind it closed for appointments last week by protests and a bomb ...

Under the first floor window—closed, blind. Flowers. Plucked. One. By. One. Dead ... *she loves me ... she loves me ... not ...* and the head. Her head. Discorporated from the body she carried below. Bloody. Out of breath for over an hour. The flowers seemingly spilled from her open lips. The flowers a final scream. A river of silent pain. An invitation ...

Dry. Drops of blood, smeared—by a painter's hand, on the grey wall. Not a word. Not quite a picture. A constellation

... she loves me ...

... she loves me

not ...

A narrow street (of knives and whiskey as courage for the marauders poised to rise from their insignificant rituals of broken light and blind eyes). Loud yesterdays blow. At night, filled with Lucy (fingers locked on a horizon with no stars) and Wendy (stopped. Searching for herbs or words in her pockets) and Lily (no longer a Mrs. She freed herself of the battle of secrets and violence) and raw unsweetened sugar and one hour weddings where mother's daughters meet lions in shadows. In twitching, knitted scenes, two-legged dancers. Skin . . .

House. Place. Cars and birds passing. White birds. Black cars. A leave or two stops. Then continues on, trying to keep pace with the wind. A summer afternoon off the tracks. Unsure of its footing. It too passes.

Her head has not moved. No insect has come to it. No ray of sunlight found it in the shadows. No one has stopped to take note of it . . .

Fragments and sobs.

Maneuvers that do not take long . . . Currents and wits and wine spilled. Thieves out of myths . . . Unsteady panhandlers and drunks and eleven-year-old kids that know you don't need a pretty face or to be a genius when it comes to fucking . . . The old and young and the broken in between, knowing you don't have to be a genius to keep your skin. You need to be lucky . . .

Needles

and AIDS

and skeletal paychecks

and unfinished weeks cut short by nightmares and curses and quack friends . . .

Scraps and hard words forming harder sentences . . . The tongue of zero playing for keeps . . . Tangos and recreations with starving little girls (and desperate boys) for money, or because they couldn't run fast enough . . .

Closer. Very close. A landslide of deafening dry weather.

Jealousy on stop sign faces / crimes of insensitive touch / and heated hate phantoms / greed under a thousand masks, in a thousand colors / mouths stirring years with their doors kicked wide open . . . from park bench pew to lonely, convenient doorway flop to the TV glare on unmade beds of overgrown anxieties and rust to alleys caught on afterwards of drunk and bruised and sick to cracked and chipped kitchen counter an unbreakable tug of war.

Up is down. In is out and has fallen down. Right doesn't give a shit. Left pretends to. This way or any way, kicked out is kicked out.

No getting over it . . .

Night again comes to the narrow street. Wolves with their cigarettes and their lies prowl. Night signs coming to life. Not a place to run. Gone altered . . . Luck slapped . . . Shiny-new-red-car-fast dreams too s l o w to avoid the outlaw arms of the void . . .

Tangles . . .

And death.

Four floors up. A corridor of bolts. The door is a closed mouth. Dust and plain truth darken the hall. Night comes in his window to caress the candles.

Stretching corner to corner to corner the bathroom lights burn. His hand moves over her ribs. He washes her. Gently pats her dry . . .

The tub shines. Light glitters again on the chrome drain cover. Thoroughly rinsed of the soiling red he puts the mop and sponges away. Smiles at the pleased, expectant face in the mirror.

Motion. Desire. Silence.

He carefully paints her toenails. Red. Fresh red inferno. Puts her open-toed shoes back on her feet. Folds her skirt, bra, and panties. Places them on the chair beside the bed. Just so.

Arranges her (on the bed, carefully sprinkled with rose petals). Just so.

She is almost . . .

. . . she loves me . . .

He brings out the head. A mannequin's head. A cheap porn-shop vinyl girl-face cut and glued to it. Places the Betty Page wig of jet tresses on it. Pins it in place. Just so.

He places the head on her neck. Adjusts it by pushing the steel rod in the bottom of the head down her windpipe. (Wipes up the blood with a clean towel.) Turns her face slightly to the left. Facing him. Looking up. At him.

They are alone again.

Not a drop of blood on her shoulders. Not a speck on her breasts. Her pubic hair combed. Just so.

Her eyes are clear and wide. Open. She waits for him.

. . . she loves me . . .

He has shaved. Combed his hair. Bleached and trimmed his fingernails.

His shoes are off. His belt too.

. . . she loves me . . .

He removes his shirt. Folds it. Places it beside her clothes. Just so.

. . . she loves me . . .

Removes his pants. Folds them. Places them beside the neat pile of her clothes. Just so.

. . . she loves me . . .

He takes off sox. Wiggles his toes.

. . . she loves me . . .

He strokes her tiny rigor-firm nipple.

. . . she loves me . . .

HIS EYES LOCKED ON HER
                    TUMMY.
His breath is small.
BEHIND HIS LIPS TEETH. HAPPINESS. LARGE AS A PYRAMID OR A LANGUAGE IT SPLASHES OVER HER. HE'S COCKED. READY FOR COMMUNICATION.
Her hand—conducted by his hand—stokes his firm length.

"You *do* love me."

His dead moments end . . .

(listening to *Buddy Guy, Sweet Tea. Silvertone Records 2001*)

Perfect Grace

for Grace Jones—flesh, and Patti Smith—spirit

Love—*everything*—gone in the rain. The gray distances drifting . . .

My joy snapped . . .

The bonfire mask of evening sky gone. Night unlit on the wind—the fruitless sigh . . .

So well composed. The angels on the other side of the bridge which few may pass. The girls, cloaked brides pledged to eternity's solitary king, come to the park. To sit. To walk the flowered, manicured avenues, row after row of soft white lilies on exhibition. In their soft skyblue dresses. In their soft yellow hats. In their silent midnight shoes . . . they discard the frost. Their hands, having chosen Forever, are so clean . . .

The flowers on the other side of the bridge which few may pass are so soft . . .

so soft

There are no birds in the park. No glimpse of sin here. No footprints are left to despair in the shadows.

The dome of the chamber—passageway, holds No Longer There in its soft, stone shadow . . .

One block East of the hollow months of yesterday I come upon it . . .
Black as coal.

So elegant. So soft her jeweled eyes . . . Soft as the midnight hour under soft black stars.

She lays her golden crown at my feet.

All my windows are open . . .
Fragrant yellow gloves off . . .
Soft yellow blouse unbuttoned . . .

Perfect.

Perfect. Animal grace . . .

Hot to touch . . .

I touched her—Hollow. Every elegant shadow . . . echoes. Hurricane of mouth shapes . . . singing. Chewing. Voice as ritual. Perfect. Grace. Running. How far? Near. Near.glued to her touch. How far? Not.far.enough . . . lips consuming sun. Giving birth. A face under the face. Giving birth. Hurricane. Echoes. Giving birth. Perfect. Grace. Every elegant shadow . . . Hollow. How far? How far? Under the shadows. Under the face under the face. Lips touching. Ears, lost in the ritual of echoes. Ringing from the distant dust.welcoming dust.

Sleek coal black limbs. Touching. The kiss. The kiss. A revolt. A celebration. Mouth on shoulder. On earlobe. Mouth open. The kiss, the kiss. Touching. Hollow. Shadows. Hurricane of mouth shapes . . .

Ripe and full and soft. Ripe and full and soft . . . soft.

Hollow.

Brushing. Touching . . .

Ripe and full and soft. Hollow. Chewing. Never stop. Never stop. Chewing. Full and . . . soft.touching. day sliding. Coal black soft. Hollow black.fulland soft. Ripe.

And soft.

Black. Hollow.hurricane mouth of shapes . . .

Touching.

thee.star-salt on the curve of a cheek.

Touching. The season of her face, breathing . . . The illuminated face.

Running. How far? How far? From the arms. Why? Why? Rippling . . . echoes—the swell. Touching. Taking. Consuming. The face. The killer. the kiss. Echoes . . . electrify . . . me. me . . . the face. The lips. The long-stemmed kiss, pressed. The touching. Echoes, sighing . . . in and on and over. Me. me—a sea of echoes. Touching— unbroken. slave. Slave. To the echoes. To the rhythm. Drums. As fingers. Touching. Me. slave. To the sweet evening fingers of the echoes. The mask open. The face under the mask throw off. Open. Rolling. Mouth open. Lips calling. Rolling. Over. Me.me. slave to . . . the echoes of the face. The thunder . . . rolling. And rolling. The swell of perfect shadows. Rolling. Perfect. Grace. Consuming. The lips. The star-weave kiss. Chewing. The hurricane.

Of shadows. howling. Hollow breast. Hollow eyes. Perfect shadows. The face under the face. Under the mask. the kiss of echoes. Black blooming . . . Yellow. The hills, the sky, the sunset . . . Yellow skin, casket. The yellow flow wrapped in stars. Deep blooming. Shadows deep and echoes wide . . . the kiss. The kiss . . . hollow . . . hollow. Deep. The kiss as roses, as threshold, gathering.whispering eyes. Echoes bite. Bite and bite. The face.desert. The kiss. the lips. Blood flows.a prayer.red & deep.Echoes deep . . . hurricane of mouth shapes. The kiss, the edges of the moon dying in it. the face seen. And seen again. And before. The echoes of night preying in the nest of day. Yellow closing. Consuming sun. Grace. Perfect. Perfect for . . .

Fire. The face of black fire. Echoes. Tastes. Love. Hot love. The fire. Burns. The kiss of love blooming. The echoes of love. Love bites. The face under the face uncoiled. Unwinding. The kiss of love. Love tastes of fire. Fire. The lips—The gift. The kiss. The feast. The bite. Unwinding. Yellow shadows. Cold and deep. Fate on her hollow lips. Perfect lips. Consuming. The echoes consuming sun. consuming me. me. cold. And deep. In the rolling shadows. Coal black fire lips. Chewing

The defects.in me. the light in me.weak . . . Sliding. First time. Echoed. On her lips—The gift, black and black. The black gift in her kiss. Born again. Echoes. Rolling. The kiss.inches.bending in the parting lips. The kiss.hymnal sail of lullabies transfused. The face under the face. Layer of shadows under the shadows. Echoes. Preying on day harvested, kneeling. The face. Seen. The lips coming in, tasted. Chewing. Deep. Black and deep. Blooming. The fire mouth raised.open. Cannibal yellow. Lips, inkwell bridge. The tongue of nightshade mysteries. The mask of shadows under the face. In the perfect circle of lips the kiss of no colors, told and retold—oh, yes.oh,yes. Lips blooming, blackness burning. Curved with a thousand oval, flitting poems whispered these trophies—Ribbons and pens jeweled, trembling, drowning out the musical miracle of sleep. The wave murmuring. The wave of sleep, the kiss. Chewing. In the kiss. A kiss inside a kiss. The flow. The wheel, the vow of falcon lips. The chain of future orphaned. The voice of bare branches never stops. Never still.the echoes. Blood flows.a prayer. The lips. The kiss. The spider eating moments. The spider black, opened, pressed in the inmost, the secret place of desire whispered and adored. The kiss. The feast—foam. The

kiss. Silk. Silk on my cheek. Delicate perfect kiss.waves.spilling love.
Slave.burning…the tears of eternity.billowing foam burning

Stretched.spread.

Exposed.hope and suffering . . .

The kiss. The stroke.of black black light.lyrical consuming light.

The swift kiss. The hand still.closed . . . carried away on a burning
kiss.

Spilled into the black stream,

the weightless dreaming. The tender curve . . .

overcome. . .

by the flame

. . . naked

night's lawn

touched by fire

rippling . . . the drifting distances . . . twlight.touching

The face under the mask thrown off in the soft midnight hour . . .

Mouth open. hollow. Man.chased to Paradise. Chewing. Still . . .
the chain. Slave. The kiss. The sigh of action. Chewing. Breath in
breath. Birth breath—the hurricane. The birth of the mouth open . . .
Live. The hurricane. Chewing. Chewing. Echoes, coming in.on a tide
of you and you and lips inscribed. Papered in moss . . .

Warm surrendering to the technique of cold . . .

. . . a silhouette of ice, a cloud, a fog.a bed of leaves,dead and
beautiful. Cut down, spilled by the sword of nothingness.

The moment. Pushing.

Pushing.

. . . Pushing. The scent . . .

Heavy and sweet, rose edges open . . .

Lips. Troubadour sweet. The oracle kiss. The sport.shouldering
the death of flowers. Chewing. Chewing. The face under the face.
Laughing at beauty. At day. At light. At shallow images . . . Echoed in
shadows. Hollow. Shadows. Cannibal.shadows.chewing. sweet this
kiss of lips of abandoned voices.chewing. The touch.of ash, of opals.
The fear, the death of flowers. Chemical. Touch writhing. Echoes of
long-stemmed constellations writhing. Chewing. Sweet lips, sweet
kiss of tears chewing. Everywhere. Tears rubbed with grace, with
ashes. Across the nameless emptiness. Tears. Less. Less. Less mount-
ing, blooming the dark thunder now. Chewing shadows. Echoes. Roll-

ing.rolling. noise. Chewing. The kiss. The cannibal kiss. Chewing . . .

Time.dreams.vanishing . . . the heart. The eyes to see.the tongue.

The kiss of drifting distances. Soft coal black. The teeth. Chewing
. . . softly.

Falling.slowly . . . softly . . .

Twlight stained.loved.

Removed.   detached.pressed   in   the   regards   of   coal
black.nothingness.hollowblack. Her coal black legs.her coal black
skirt.nature redesigned.black and black . . . spread.beautiful. caught in
the black ribbon. twig.wrapped in the cold soft curves of an indifferent hollow sea. Deep.

falling.

Still life. Less.Out of breath. less.Out of next days. less.less.slave
bidding.me. To the echoes, cannibal echoes of fever. To the kiss. The
perfect coal black sweet kiss—chewing. On my knees.flat.the chewing. The face under the face. Perfect. grace. Chewing. Man as sun.sun
as day shining in the deep kiss of hollow shadows. Consuming the
light. the day. last day of all days.the man.the body.the leatherette left
behind at the world's end of its dry tongue. Every elegant perfect coal
black shadow.Hollow. Chewing. Consuming woven day.slip away
softly. Blood-prayer.Close in the yellow blaze of the magic iron
mouth. Laughing—the shape of the tempest this kiss—the quicksand
wounds of chaos—alone in the embrace of death.soft is the kiss. The
hollow kiss of grace, princess—priestess of flowers.and ghosts. Grace.
Perfect. And sleek. Soft black . . . And hollow.

Hollow.

. . . these pearl wings of rain.

hollow . . .

slowly . . . falling.vanishing.

Less.

the sweet last kiss.a tide of eyes sighs.looks out.look.out. faithful
and deaf, wanting. Wanting, to lunge . . . across. So slow.this nothing
. . .

The grey distances drifting.

Stretching . . .

The kiss. Long-stemmed and black as coal. Cold.to touch . . .
Black is the color . . .

Immortal black . . .

falling.truly . . . THE KISS.

Echoes in a different tongue *Goodbye day.* Echoes on the tongue *Goodbye sweet man.* Echoes.cold dry echoes *Sweet meat . . . So sweet. So soft the taste of goodbye . . .*

Across the drifting distances . . .
The kiss
of the perfect face
black as coal
under

the face . . . to the gate of last goodbye. unraveled.

coalblack horizon. still.ravenwing-silent. shut. close.closed.

the final page on the other side.the black incarceration

                                  slave in tatters of darkness

                                  emptiness . . . irretrievably

(after the video for Grace Jones's "Corporate Cannibal" and Patti Smith and Kevin Shield's beguiling & brilliant THE CORAL SEA 22.06.05)

Kynothrabian Dirge

For Antas, Eibon's seventeenth male issue,
shorn from the world by the Dogs of Tindalos.

Sa-læh il. Sa-læh il. Sa-læh il.
Li-pacn-sul kaviin väul.

On this long day when death resounds his unchallenged claim,
Let all the lofty titans in the heavens hear our hearts decanted,
And let all unbecoming men stand in fear
When rings the baying clamor like raging confessions,
Along the paths that surge
From the jutting spirals of Tindalos' bitter towers black.

In the curved beams warming this world,
Given from the sun, bright and brighter in its span,
Stand acolyte and abbess, lord and vassal,
Herdsman and headsman,
Feeble and becalmed
With their dwarf wits blind.

Little do they fathom of Grand Impurity and
The ambush of line, and crack, and angle sharp,
And cavernous shades deep,
When the beacon of light bleeds to death on the horizon.

Nightfall is not a quarry,
Nor a seedbed,
For the sons of men
And divined yearnings sought.

The coming Marvels of Judgment,
The burden and the yoke unfailing—
Awash in that vessel of earth and spirit joined,
Spilled and wrecked upon doom's door—
Hunger for the salve
Breathed by all the sons of men in sum.

When iniquity's transgressing devils cast nets unfurled
And wrathful rods of thunder and affliction,
And reap the spoils foretold,
Taking back to the realm of nothing
The sons of men, carrying no blood to the ending,
Man shall lay as bones set in the places dark
as he was Before.

All powerful Thou art unto all ages, O darksome Lord Zhothaqquah.
All powerful Thou art unto all ages, O darksome Lord Zhothaqquah.
All powerful Thou art unto all ages, O darksome Lord Zhothaqquah.

O Ebon Conqueror Eternal,
We pour out our praise on breath untainted and unfailing.
To delight thee, O Great-Slumberer, Zhothaqquah,
We sculpt mountains,
From Diarciholn's Peak in Eabdamar to Intviilui where white webs
    spiral,
In thy toad-shaped countenance tremendous.

O Ageless Zhothaqquah, Daemon-Sovereign of N'Kai and Yoth,
Forsake us not, and vouchsafe your solicitous servants,
Barring us from eternity's darkened torments.
And when the office of the dead hails us,
Grant us a good end

Li-pacn-sul kaviin väul.
Sa-læh il. Sa-læh il. Sa-læh il.

The Exorcism of Iagsat

Wrathful Assailant IAGSAT, see what power I lay before Thee in force!

ATEI   ATEI

KU

KU

KU

KU

ATEI   ATEI

Hear me, Risen Avatar of Brute Afflictions! My voice animates the lore—

NDE OO CA NDE

AR-BHAB

ASL OO PYS-A PR'ILLI

NDE

Vile-Troubler called up, I send Thee back—

OGTHROD AI'F

GEB'L—EE'H

IAGSAT-yog-sothoth-IAGSAT

'NGAH'NG AI'Y

ZHRO

Haunter Unseen, take thy life back to the core! *Tlexant sint sn sut amn*! Depart, O Iagsat! *En Y! En Y! eIkI eIkI Di-tua eIkI! En Y*! I have followed the formulae writ true, and set the symbols, vital and empowered against Thee, Bold Iagsat—Smell the blood that grants them power! Evoked—*p'he hwe'ev*, You have risen from the malodorous gulfs Outside the Spheres. I cast Thee back, Unwanted One! *Hoxevei lm zO zwlelcth hR eistemiis*! Take Thy mysterious goals and traverse that Space Unclean and full with the odors of the crypt piled thick with that which Worms, and Ghouls, and Daemons, and the Earth have not taken unto themselves, and return across the threshold that stands between the worlds! Hear me, Unwanted Lurker, I am the salted-blood that speaks fire! Hear me, Unwanted Iagsat, I am the salted-blood that speaks fire! I bid Thee stir and depart with Thy strange processions and contortions! *Tetentaz eniitharl!* Depart, *En Y! En Y! eIkI eIkI Di-tua eIkI!* *En Y!* Iagsat, transgressing-iniquity of malice invited not, I make no Scarlet Sacrifice to keep you! Withdraw from this light to Thine own nation! Ride swift before the words I set free to drive Thee! Feel the lash upon and within Thee as great fires of venom! Flee before the word of power I place in the air!

```
        H
      T   I
    M   S   N
  O   T   H   S
    A   K   R
      A   L
        C
```

    a-GLE cAALN pHA! a-GLE cAALN pHA! a-GLE cAALN pHA! Hear it and flee!

    a-GLE cAALN pHA! a-GLE cAALN pHA! a-GLE cAALN pHA! Hear it and flee! zO!

Shuddersome One, touch me not, for I am Power, and full of seawater and salted meats, which leave in Thee a taste sore! Depart, O Iagsat! *En Y! En Y! EIkI eIkI Di-tua eIkI!* *En Y!* Take Thy blasts and rancors and tortures and fiery deliriums, and whirl through Space and Abyss and swirling storms uncharted, or face the harms of doom thrust by the eleven I serve and adore!

By the powers of ZHOTHAQQUAH,
By the powers of YIG,
By the powers of ATLACH-NACHA,
By the powers of HZIULQUOIGMNZHAH,
By the powers of NUG and YEB,
By the powers of BUG-SHAGGOG,

By the powers of THUSA,
By the powers of OKKOKOKU,
By the powers of AULANIIS,
By the powers of UBBO-SATHLA,
a-GLE cAALN pHA! a-GLE cAALN pHA! a-GLE cAALN pHA!
Hear it and flee!
a-GLE cAALN pHA! a-GLE cAALN pHA! a-GLE cAALN pHA!
Hear it and flee!
Ban oo G'uiin-mim!
zO!
Ban oo G'uiin-mim!
zO—IAGSAT—zO!

Lonesome Separate Ways

Downtown ghost town—skeleton town/vague doors/abandoned windows—empty galleries/smokeless chimneys . . . every other block or so, a winter barren, melancholy tree . . . alleys to darker streets wounded and rumpled . . . a blur of car's headlights . . . Pretty sure history ain't feelin' too good tonight . . .

Drizzle.

Endless cold drizzle . . .

Lawless pistol in outta the rain. Sat the damp, raw weight of my bones in The Nazareth—I forget the regulars' unfunny joke about the barstool pews. A cold beer and two smokes before the shots start. Poor Boy Troubadours start inta the slow toe-tappin' "Southside Albany Blues." Two shots, "She's Gone" hurtin' me. Hardcore valentine heart down in the bottle. Bonnie's gone. She slipped away a day before my eyes saw what was in my hand. Without a prayer, no big surprise.

Upside down and the company of the bottle's come back again.

The itch—stiff as fuck and screamin' over your explanation for being late—goes off. Two more shots. That's how it goes.

Grieving, you say fuck it and just go along . . .

The hours play for a bit and drop off . . . someone will sweep them up with the cigarette butts and the spent vowels later . . .

Thugs and drunks and cold decks bump into ends, burn for a soft bed. Like some eerie dream of cigarette smoke fog and sorrow-carved light, the lost-most-everything autumnals, afraid of morning's edge of thickening sunlight, thin out. Midnight rambles out of the joint before a handicap can handcuff its one remaining wish . . .

Depleted, last wanders out with a willin' hometown girl.

Mercenary beerlight got no regards for anyone.

Old Ironweed wipes down the last glass, turns out the lights as if to say closing time . . . And I'm still sittin' there thinkin' about a

179

young girl's heart. Toe-tappers—weren't really very good—packed up the guitars two hours ago. Seems they forgot to take your memory . . .

Ghost of a girl who never said goodbye still standing there.

Reunion.

The hand that threw away the key is holdin' that devil gun. Her ghost starts laughing. Three shots and it's still standin' there. Still cryin'. Still unrepentant. Still hasn't made a god-damn sound.

Shot her Then. Just shot her now. And no one's heart will rest in peace.

The light in the place goes from grime-dim to bad. Ghost ain't feelin' all right, got the mercenary blues. Paid in rain and cold ground. Something insane got me and that young girl she was is sleeping in pain. Locked down. In some black dark.

All that cold black nothing might have drove her insane.

Ghost left the flesh. Ghost forgot love. Ghost just remembers TAKE.

That's what I did . . .

Done—freezer cold and spilt down to the black:

> *open revolution of ringmaster words*
> *. . . thorns to soul*
> *. . . joy and care not remembered*
> *. . . beratements (just another hurricane I was too drunk to keep*
> *my eye on) spilled*
> *between Jesus H's and FUCK's*
> *. . . whiskey fire*
> *. . . dreams evicted, in shreds*
> *. . . gunfire mistakes*
> *. . . blackened butcher rage*
> *. . . frail came apart*
> *. . . deep jagged currents*
> *. . . red everywhere*
> *Transfigured . . .*

TAKE.

That's what her stark ghost's here for . . .

Didn't come back across the river bearing a cross. Came a thousand miles—More? Came, mad death winds at the stained hem of her burial ground cloth, as truth with eyes of doom . . . Came back from that nameless tombstone place heart and mind aflame.

Smile torturing me. Silent laugh torturing me.

My mind's weak. Full of a scarred wind. Ready to explode.

Hard to breathe in this place.

I stutter something 'bout nothing I can do now.

Still she won't speak. Eyes tell me it's time to hang.

Lawless devil pistol in my losing hand.

Something's on the wind . . .

Something's cold today . . .

That damn ghost, can't decide if she looks thinner now, might be 'cause she's run out of future and been isolated from her past . . . Thinner, yeah. Might be just this light . . . I'm looking through her.

She's looking right into me . . .

One who can't hide and one who came seeking.

Somewhere there's moonlight caressing fresh smelling trees. Somewhere there's a porch swing holding on to love and rainbow ecstasy. Somewhere, that's a place I'll never be . . .

Not here.

Not here.

Not with disaster loitering . . .

Place gone cold.

And grave still with haunted air.

Was flat out of any salvation. Now 'bout to go down the drain . . .

Should have known she'd come back. Come to settle up for all the lonely nights my spilled demons burned her days. Come ta deal straight with what she went through wedding night to pills and bottle to fuckin' all out of none.

Come to even out the constellations and rolls of quarters I stole to cool my hungry in some shithole-gin-joint hurricane pussy . . . fouled every one of her soft spring kisses with fleshy, beer-slopped snatch . . .

Think her altered tongue might have a word to say—maybe from a cold mouth spit, "Why'd ya do it?". Maybe give some back.

Guess this other time needs no words. Guess the closing in is enough.

Not for me.

No.

Gun's got three truths left in it. Two for her. One, I'm thinking, for me.

Maybe over yonder the lonely anger dies ... and there's a boy who didn't grow up hollow as the hangman's noose ... no bitter tears in his heart or on his tongue ... who, in a fit of fuck-it-all blues, didn't sign away his soul and come out the other side in a bloody mess ...

Ghost, gloves off, brittle dead lily hand, points at me ... Smiles.

Too tired to take another shot at her ... Too tired ...

Too drunk?

Not drunk as that last time ... Not drunk enough to ever forget that

... *It was 'round midnight* ...

It was cold that last time

... *the television was on* ... *smoke* ... *liquor—I was full of bourbon* ... *couldn't find the remote* ... *empty-handed quakes* ...

Heart boiling over ...

Ready to punch something ...

Bit ... *forgot to count to ten* ... *revved-up wild* ... *storms in my weary hands* ...

Fueled by all that trouble—teeth and hide, strangling me ...

And she just stood there—like a faceless, mindless onlooker, trembling, without a word ... *Didn't have a word to say* ...

Trembling ...

Poison hand raises the gun that's out of lies ...

Smiling, 'cause I can't hurt her no more, the ghost, finally not disappointed, turns away and dissolves.

(an hour down in the blues and grit and tears w/ Steve Earle)

Just Another Desert Night
with Blood

From nowhere

　　to nowhere . . .

Devouring yesterday. Dissolving innermost longings with blood
. . . Walking. Not pointed. Not pressing. Slowly . . . carrying something that burns, a language not of the physical . . .

Walking . . . from the middle of a hole . . . remembering the devil
. . . and dread . . . and the wings of the locust . . .

Slowly . . . walking . . .

With its long hours, night, large (sideways and up) and thick,
again falls on the galleries of life . . .

He comes to it. Finds . . . Sometimes a storm. Sometimes a
town—poor places . . . of shapes and floors and directions. Numbers
and alleys. Glass—reflections and portraits, and bric-a-brac. Some
things, different by day, open. Some entangled. (heartbreak against
the horizon.) Never, in recent memory, a song of rain . . .

Stands in it. Face, body, breath, every demon-stern impulse,
reaches for life . . . Good heart (strong and sound). That's black—been
dragged along the blade of night's knife. A one trick pony out of work.
Hands—sometimes an epidemic of fists—free, with nowhere to go . . .

Bend, man made slow, in the road. Traces and codes . . . Passing
under windows, translating. Boarded-up wind out free on a walking
holiday. Thinking of touching dreams.

Front-porch light bridge no witness. Sleeves, over hard ground.
Slow. Hands of a blacklisted tiger (without love), red.

Permanently tilted-open gate, rust, slowly gnawing at its hinges.
House. Needs painting and a few new screens. Waits at the knob.
Tests its weight. (Locked the unlocked door behind him.) Stuffed

with the smells of living. Valleys between the sofa of crowded, stuffed playmates and the chairs. Cataract fingers sweeping the spines of a fence of books. Takes one out—blackbird ruin haunts the cascading ivy woods crawling with lines . . . shadow foam corner to corner, what is real buried beneath . . . The itch. (language wrought of loneliness and sunder in his fists.) Steep stair trail . . . winter comes to the shoreline. Breathing. Hunting. Listening for yes or foliage or rivers or absolutes. Visualizing. Breathes in the false words hiding in dream.

The prickling. (language of fire and wind in his hands.) Curves. A nightgown (It's been awhile since he's seen a nightgown). Sudden momentary anguish. Said and done hiding under the bed. No warnings. Thief of emptiness in the sheets. Mother (breezy thighs)— smoldering—fangs and wounds—scorched—lion's rough teeth on her breast, no gift—can't run, can't run—(done with her) . . . and child, sized and overcome—a splash of fun (something in the eyes as she dies) (done with her) . . . and under wings and clouds a smaller child, snuggling satisfying Honey Bear, pushing at sleep, down and down with her tiny spring song of balloons. Happy little lips. The nape, sweet—candy dreams in the red hands . . . small shoulder, small elbow, tiny fingers, lost in the battle. (Done with her.) Despair, desire, in the wolf's eyes.

Blood on his shirt. On his belt buckle.

Wounds . . . no confessions. no notes. no ghosts.

Wounds . . . no poetry.

High . . . gets there for a few seconds . . .

The empty chain . . . a well-worn path . . .

Down among the rooms of day . . . Stood on the faded remnants of grape juice. Stood where the littlest one did the Snoopy dance—there was sunshine that morning. Moved, not curious. Stood where Mom and big sister laughed to tears, hugged. Stood where things started. Stepped over laughs that hadn't been vacuumed up with the cracker crumbs. Walked through hollow air that would never again be filled with chain-linked hollers of Mom—Mom—Mom. But he didn't care . . .

A long red finger on the white keys of a piano. A mysterious song of knives and misery . . . Walking . . . humming something that's not warm.

Hungry.

A window with nothing to say but sand and sky. Clock noise. He eats a sandwich. Never turned on a light.

Sits and looks at horizons gone silent on the ceiling.

Chews. Sips from a bottle of cold water. Carves an X in the table top. No dawn escapes his mouth . . .

Calm.

Drops a vase shaped like a fire hydrant on the hardwood floor on his way out. No answers in the jagged pieces. Never are . . .

Leaves the back door open . . . Deeds. Handprints. A mouth of secrets leaving.

Home, once common maybe. In the aftermath it's quieter, a lonely place.

Out in the folds and contours of simple chilled black hung over everything.

Afterwards . . . tears and fire.

Slowly. Passing a black stone, echoes of a distant storm. Night, needle tapestry stars, no back and forth (the moon turns, bends gently away—off with some other song). Tears form.

(Raven apron night doesn't taste like summer.) Evening disappeared before the blood. 10 passes. 11 comes swinging—48 . 49, trying hard . 50, knees buckling. 12 (watching—waiting) will be here for hours . . . transcendental and slow.

Lies. Landed. Lies. Here. In the open, under beds. Littering the scrub bramble . . . Glasses of blood and lies . . . lonely, but not the same . . .

Skirts a poor side of town trying to hold on . . . Austere parking lots and things that used to be girls. Ghosts bought and sold. Not a nickel and out of dimes. Below a cross that couldn't hold on. What was pressed there—fast and spurs and comfort and forever and heat, gone.

The bells lie silent.

He slips away . . .

Moon-gray sand. Blown here to over there . . . common sand knows no doors . . . a patch of something with roots, holding out for September or water . . .

Crazy blood. Dust (between seasons) without explanations, repeating itself . . .

Demonic coyotes, weary of the truth dripping from the stars, have been around. Howling, lonely and mean. Took little. Left nothing in this long wheel of forever headed nowhere.

Out in the middle. Leaping bottles empty of gestures and earthquakes. Never thinking about it.

ACTION. Burn it all away . . .

By a large hole and a troubled-by-rust (and the crash) auto car-
riage, stripped of tires and chrome and silver bells, comes upon a
frightened young woman with pale blue corpse eyes—a runaway
from The PAIN and sadness and the ridicule. Not hidden well, but
she's trying. Her scent is a temple . . . And he just did.

Does it cold. Want, the lion's fire, comes forth—all the thrashing
(skin off the branches of the bride—not difficult after the face is kicked
in) . . . as it tries hard . . . her cries are fire, but end is END. Heat to cool.
Blood to sand. No one raises a glass. Tomb games of HATE/Love(fear)
fast . . . and gone . . . Final here . . . and gone. (Done with her.)

Something outlived. Forever comes with no comfort.

Gravity takes the last of the blood.

His blood runs . . .

He drags a nursery rhyme from somewhere deep . . . it lives,
spreads—an injured dream, until he snuffs it out. No stain or echo of
the dance.

Looks to town . . . a difficult thing.

Walks (east tonight) the other way. The birds and the coyote and
the insects and the desert sun will come hunting the dead. Lips will
part. Bellies will be filled. Another night will come. It won't cry.
Waste or silver or precious gems, limb or bone, it won't be impressed
by the sight or the name.

Two vagrant cats and a solo moon. Dead brush. Hands in his
pockets. Swaying. He sees constellations thrown wide. Hears the song
of a different night—a night without saints. Can't explain why it
laughed. If he knew, then . . .

Pure sand. Cut with ghosts and pieces of time . . . nothing in it to
spoil.

Sand with no offspring, too barren to be wild.

No lamps, lighthouses. Ears filled with empty fire and boredom.
Hands paralyzed by whispers and names . . . red memories in his veins.

No bedtime. No reptiles (*Do the snakes sleep?* He wonders.) . . .
no ladders or angels or crowns or tenderly . . . so tired . . . no water or
sunshine . . . locked, smothered in this endless nowhere . . .

In the breath of starlight unleashed, a glimpse, a dead roadrunner
that hasn't disappeared yet . . . no more circles for the sleeping dead,
blackened and finished . . .

A free man. No friends, no laughter left behind. Time his stage.

Chance his key, his flood. Blood and cotton skirts on his mind . . .

Outwardly restless and . . . inbetween . . . No anchor in this grave ageless Nothing.

Takes in a view without solutions . . .

Laughs in the face of the leviathan . . .

Highway. Ditches full of seasons (and the cast-out containers of thirst quenchers). Winds traveling. Red taillights—moon sold souls—bound for somewhere (*easy?*). Night's not going anywhere. Never does. The lies cooling. Not going anywhere . . . moth and spider goin' nowhere . . . phone booth with a broken interior light . . . owl . . . clouds, not built or elaborate, flat on the dark rug of sky . . . asphalt—solid ground has no point . . . boots notch the dust on a road goin' nowhere . . .

This nowhere land, a flat leviathan wearing blades and puddles and smudges of black, seamed with memories, holds no scavengers, no mirages, no vultures. No windows surging with lines or glows of wishing. No talisman or seed, or coat of arms. This solitude does not murmur . . .

Laughs at the 3 A.M. moon. No mirror, it don't laugh back (but he thinks it would like to).

Walking . . . from nowhere to nowhere . . . devouring . . . A slow voyage of no real reason. A haunted man, swept up. Throwing loose questions, thick in sin, at the moon . . .

"So tired."

No one hears.

No one answers.

All this empty space. No thin plants. No struggling flowers. Nothing upright. No color here to take in. Nothing cool but the bite of air, some nights . . .

Night (maybe soft, maybe not) after (always indifferent) night . . . walking the rim of the land of the living lost to their dreams . . . Blood . . .

Blood that roars wild . . .

And open sky.

(lost in the rare beauty and haunted magic of
Neko Case's *Fox Confessor Brings the Flood* and *Blacklisted*)

After Death

(for ~K)

*They were talking one day . . . Talking of wolves and deliverance, of
the many faces stained in limbo and by pain, and the crisscrossing of
circumstances . . .*

And of Grace.

*Far beyond the neon strip promising QUICK . . . and scrapbooks of
dreams that disappeared in hollow apartments of disgust and pain waiting for the FUCKING-SCREAMING-YELLING arguments next store to
stop . . . Passed the chimneys and the streets thickened in slow ruin and
dusk where the trees ended they walked the row of crypts, two lambs cut
by shadows . . .*

*At the tomb of the poet, Tara took Nikki's pale hand in her own
pale hand, said, "Here is where we enter."*

*Leaves and small white bones in the tunnels . . . no bread crumbs
the tiny, emptiness-changed things . . . hidden from the expression of the
moon the spider captures its pleasure with silk kisses . . . something dry
snaps . . . two witches seeking souls without bodies by candlelight . . . a
thick chuckling, swollen with crimson joy . . . a gray night-thing in rags
scurries in the sour air . . . yellow eyes that crave . . . "Seekers," a hungry bark of hell-tones . . .*

*Still dazed, bloody—the gash in her head would heal and scar,
Nikki climbed the stairs. Found herself in the cold light of the dying
moon . . .*

Tara did not return . . .

✦

Alone . . .

A twilight of thorns and worms . . .

Alone with her open casket of winter, starving wounds and nests and dreams of purity, she sits in Tara's library with her dead lover's books on Egyptology and Houdini and the moon and reincarnation and ghosts and black magic. Tara's paintings of nightshades, unleashed and vibrating with pain, hang on the walls unseen . . .

Whiskey, no justice or courage in it, to quiet the ticking of clock. A white cigarette in bone-white fingers. Watching the blue-gray smoke coil and rise aimlessly . . .

Echoing pain, the speakers washed the near blackness with sorrow spilled. David Sylvian sang about darkness hiding in its own shadow.

When Tara's cassette of *Secrets of the Beehive* was eaten in the car's cassette player Nikki bought another copy. Played it until it was a ghost. Both dead copies of the tape she buried in the yard. In Tara's flower bed. Tara's favorite singer with Tara's favorite flowers.

She was listening to a remastered copy of the CD.

"You would have loved hearing this . . . This way," she whispered into the empty room. "His poetic textures are so . . . *alive*."

When "Let the Happiness In" started the memories came and she cried.

A few more hours until 11. The agony would stop then . . .

For one hour . . .

"Tara."

❂

Thirteen black candles burn.

Raven shadows haunt edges and undersides, fill corners.

The flat surfaces in the room are altars of roses. Red roses. Roses and thorns. The thorns draw blood. Blood is life. Blood is fire. Fire is life. Life is subjugation. The rose is a wand.

Medusa has the room ready. She always has everything ready. No detail escapes her eye. Or her hand.

The stage is set.

The players present.

A fat man. From London. A banker, or so he says.

Doesn't give a name.

They don't want one.

Sits in his chair. By the little end table.

He's a got a cmaera. A flask of scotch.

Lights a cigarette.

Loosens his expensive silk tie.

Unbuckles his belt.

Medusa doesn't let the Watchers get undressed.

They read the rules or they don't get in.

The fat man with siege eyes appraised the flesh he bought.

One girl, taller and slightly thinner than her partner, is an albino. The other woman's complexion almost as pale.

Abundant white flesh in black bras and black garters and black hosiery. Stilettos black. The albino has ass-length white hair. The other scarlet dreadlocks.

The redhead called herself Medusa when he paid her. Her back was tattooed with an inverted cross. Her left leg, ankle to hip, was inked with delicate and ornate spider webs.

Two ravens were inked on the upper arms of the albino Medusa called Nikki.

No jewelry.

The animal that was still and waiting inside is awake. He, more than a bit pissed there's no touching permitted, offered to double his price if the albino would blow him, or if Medusa would dance for him and sit on his lap and grind that shaved, tight cunt on his meat.

Medusa turned winter-hard, cold. Hissed, "To touch . . . is to *Die*."

OK. So he'll watch . . .

Next time . . . He'll get to touch . . .

The fat man likes the red-haired witch, nice piece of ass. Toned and tight. Wonders if she's ever fucked on cocaine. Thinks, she thought it was nice. Thinks, she's a wild fuck. Likes it in the ass.

He can see her dancing, sweating, primed—thinking about fucking, thinking about a hard cock parting her pussy lips. He doesn't give a shit she's a witch who channels ghosts. Fuck all that weirdo sex magic shit. She's a hot piece of ass with big tits, nipples like jewels. Thinks, she gets hot, she begs for it. Thinks, crawls across the floor and begs to be fucked. Opens her delicious cherry-red lips and begs him to slide his throbbing cock into her mouth and she'd suck and suck—every sighing, loud inch, and suck and she'd stroke his balls and swirl her tongue around the head—as if it were a flicking snake's tongue seeking heat—and he'd give her heat, and suck and suck until she gobbled down every howling spurt of his red-hot load.

He'd conquer her dancing lips, feed her gluttonous tongue, and she'd smile. One pearl drop of his lava on the corner of her lips. One drop she wanted him to watch her tongue take inside.

He knew she liked it.

They all did.

Every last . . .

The albino is tied up. Blindfolded with a black silk stocking. Sitting on the edge of the bed.

Medusa slaps her.

Peels of the blindfold. Casts it to the floor.

She pushes Nikki down.

Slides her lacy panties to her knees . . .

stops . . .

then slides them

to her ankles

and off.

Roughly turns her over . . .

Punished, the albino raises—offers, her ass.

A whisper of D/s to stir Nikki and the fat man . . .

Medusa slaps her pale ass . . .

Bends

and kisses the red blush . . .

Then slaps it again.

A whirl of blood-red dreadlocks. A bra comes off. It's thrown to the floor. Medusa bends to cup Nikki's pale white breast in her gloved hand . . . Nikki's eyes close. Her red mouth opens . . .

The edge of a hand whispers under an alabaster ear. Shoulders . . . a kiss smeared . . . Nikki's scarred cheek covered by the streak of lipstick . . .

Medusa's hand spreads Nikki's thighs . . . quick breath . . . two long, fluid fingers circling Nikki's clit . . . pressing . . .

Heavy. Dirty. Slow. He thinks. "Like that. Yeah."

Tongue, rare fire, dancing, speaking in a tone of hummingbird lips and sunshine . . .

Time vanishes in this garden of longing . . . fire plays hide and seek, reverberates with petaled myths in the tunnel of desire . . . sparks of motion . . . magic heats the blood . . . wings of breath blossom . . .

The hissed howl of passion's earthquake . . .

His dick is hard.

"Hard for you."

Hand damp.

His ears open. Straining.

Nikki's drumbeat heart . . .

Eyes over flared nostrils, hungry. Sipping the motions of love on the bed before him.

His breath a rush between mumblings . . .

bare shoulders pinned to the bed

breasts

wild eyes

"Come on—Come on," he crackles to the canvas.

a wiggly ass

He's impatience. Enthralled.

"Stick your fingers in her cunt."

The fat man's drumbeat heart . . .

He's snapping shots.

"Good God, that's . . . Fucking—beauti. . ."

Fat bald head. Sweating.

Almost panting . . .

"Swee. . ." Telescope eyes. Radar lock. "Wet cun. . ."

The fat man. Sitting there under the canvas shoreline of a painting of a tree. Its shade spread, a tangle of black hair, a demon's mane. And a broken wheel and birds—two, resting on a broken spoke—the color of rust . . . His small prick in his meaty hand.

He thinks these two are better than the pair of nineteen-year-old German starlets he arranged roles for in *Im Garten der Nacht* last autumn. Better with each other. But the tight-little German gash both licked him dry after they finished putting on their little leather straps and miracle pussy show for him. They winked and bounced, tickled him, pushed their tits in his face. Called him Big Daddy Wolf. The tall one, Renate, a slobbering dog in cocaine and champagne heat, took his barrel full-bore in the mouth and giggled when they passed his load from tongue to tongue. Licked their lips when they were done milking him.

Thinks, these two are better.

Be better if he could fuck them.

. . . Legs. Exquisite objects.

Medusa's hands, red-hot angels of fire, are hinges. They open death's door.

Breathing ghost poems.

thighs

"To be taken."

open

He thinks it's the most beautiful thigh he'd ever seen. He'd pay anything to kiss it, to touch it . . .

Nikki burns for the return.

Nipple, flower of desire, traced by the tickle of dipping lips . . . the kiss of a new language on the slope of Nikki's pale breast . . .

Energy.

Energy and desire.

Massaged.

Honed.

Building.

The rush.

Hot blood. Burning.

Climbing.

One nipple stretched by Medusa's tugging, ripe cherry mouth. One heat-tipped nipple stretched by Nikki's own fingers . . .

Inches of smooth white flesh bending to the touch . . . hands sculpting, spilling down thighs . . .

Hard muscles . . .

curves

nipping white teeth

Secrets hurrying to be naked.

movement

Stretching. Surges. Reaching.

Jolts.

Flesh listens to the heart.

Leaning into Now and More . . . unrestrained. Brimming with clarity.

entangled skin . . .

He focuses on a nipple jutting from a coil of scarlet dreads.

Mouth etched. "Sweet hot bitc. . ."

The rush.

The rush.

Supple white flesh sliding . . . teeth and shoulders and erect nipples . . . long arms gleam . . . the canvas of an eager, pale breast brushed with open lips . . .

Briskly. "Flawless double-D."

Nikki's drumbeat heart . . .

More and every side of motion . . .

In his frozen stare the women glow . . .

His ass shifts in the chair.

Ripples . . .

Medusa mounted Nikki, shifted. Snow-white tenderness swaying, tenderly grinding and thrusting, Medusa rubbed her shaved mound to Nikki's. Inflamed, unleashed, thrill spasms seethed where the lips of womanhood brushed the sweet scented wings of her partner's night garden. Swiftly the fires merged. In Medusa's hand the petals of a rose whispered on Nikki's nipples, now swollen with fire.

The irresistible, delicious perfume of desire, sweet as an hour of wicked kisses . . .

Every glimpse of the skin ceremony imprinted with shiny, wet kisses hotter than the last . . .

calves

to touch

to devour

A long sweet sigh, a blizzard of white hair covers the plain of a shoulder . . .

Medusa's tongue slowly arcs across Nikki's alabaster neck

ear

to

ear . . .

The muted sound of a serpent discharged from the predatory throat of the fat man.

The candles flutter in the swollen air . . . Energy swirls in the room . . .

His hand strokes his balls . . .

Fingers circling a navel . . . a moving sculpture . . . shoulders . . . hands . . . tongues pressed to desire . . .

The flickering light . . . the fragrance of the roses . . .

His camera lying on the carpet forgotten . . .

The back of a bare calf, so white, so smooth . . . divine.

Trembling, damp flesh murmurs to him . . . he's tingling. `Tits. I love those tits.` He'd kill to rub the head of his cock on that tiny nipple.

Medusa

kisses

Nikki's

belly . . .

thighs open . . .

Her

tongue

finds

Nikki's

swollen

clit . . .

ass lifted a little off the bed . . .

Hot hunger lips carve flesh . . .

"You are so beautiful," Medusa whispers.

Nikki's eyelids flutter . . .

Close . . .

Spirit.

His hand stops. Shakes . . .

Lightning.

Touched, pressed . . .

Smooth skin . . . Knees . . . nipples . . .

thighs . . .

Tension.

He grunts.

Throbbing . . .

Delight . . .

Breathing coming faster.

The blood pulse drumming in ears . . .

Delight . . . sparks . . .
Close.
rhythm
whipping
whipping
"Alm . . ."
grinding
shifts his ass in the chair
rhythm

hot skin

in her

mouth

smooth sweaty skin

A sleek finger stutters, swarms, infests the flushed sails of the soft garden with incandescent satisfaction.

Do it, from a silent, oven-mouth. "fuck."

Submission.

CLOSE

Adoration.

The storm, part sigh, part sonnet—thick and intimate as silence, flares.

Flash/liberty . . .

The fat man groans . . .

Nikki sighs . . .

Post-orgasm. His fever-glazed eyes squeezed shut. His thoughts clawing to hold the heat and the beauty before it's lost.

Medusa is across the room.

A lightning glint. Her knife flashes before his breathing settles.

Arm. Quiet fire splash, slashing his throat.

Hostile. Goal driven.

ear

to

ear.

Blood.

It's voice free of flesh. Red without boundaries, the crimson roars . . .

A quick death. From the surface falling, the filth-song from his wolf mouth disappeared. His flesh opened, a crack in the horizon.

Hot blood.

A lot of blood.

Just the way Medusa likes it.

The air, a cauldron rippling and full, takes a chill. Vibrates with the keys and elements of frenzy and focused passion.

A door tightly shut glows . . .

The essence of heart and soul and life lost rise . . .

Through the entrance, running, yearning, the appetite comes. Purity touches flesh and blood. Tara's loneliness ensnares the energy of the cadaver before it's lost. The pressure cyclone of her desire surrounds it, absorbs it. From the lost midnight darkness of woe Tara crosses over, comes in.

Being. Touched, risen from shadow by love and care, bright and full of plenty.

"Alive."

"Yes, Dearest. Alive once more."

Eyes, measuring, beautiful—star-bright, feasting.

Radiant hands tethered together, clutch Alive, and Oneness reawakened.

Medusa turned and left the room, leaving the body where it fell.

The embrace. The warmth of curves.

Nikki, dazzled again, is filled with questions . . . the cold laugh of, Forever the Predator, there between them . . .

Whispered, stormy: "Why?"

The air is tomb-still. Forever's barren tapestry never enlightens with words.

"Why?"

"It is and that's all it is."

"It's not enough."

"It's all we have, Love. This. Here in the dark . . . for a moment between the Frost of Ends."

"We can have more. I will use the knife and join you."

"No."

Pleading. "Why?" Asked again. And 50 times before.

"You are too frail, My Love. The foul hours of doubt and longing on the Other Side would break you."

"I can be strong *for You*."

"And you are."

"But not strong enough."

"Hush. Just hold me."

Tara kisses her mouth. Not drunk with Mine or hunger it is a simple, tender kiss of love.

"Beloved."

Floating . . .

Endless . . .

Tara, both sparrow and firebird, kisses the tears from Nikki's cheeks.

There are few others words . . .

Isolated in the solitude of nothingness the lovers bloom, its echo races into the vampire blackness of Eternity's desert . . .

The void does not lie quiet—

Tara ripped from her arms . . . *again* . . .

until the next time . . .

Alone. Dead. Mouth filled with the loneliness of the grave.

"It is not enough." Weeping . . . on her knees . . . fierce memories leeching the love she had been decorated in . . .

Naked and streaked with blood, Medusa sat in a hardback chair in the hall and very slowly wiped the blood from her hands on a white rag. Wiped it from her breasts, her arms, her face. Sat no sound to occupy her. Smoked. Sat for an hour in a tar-black scar of shadow with no one to talk to. Waited for the agony to stop . . .

Her heart breaks, it does every time, as the muted howl of Nikki's brushed against the door when Tara is torn from her arms.

A hall of muted gloom that leads to a stairway and rain . . .

Tonight Medusa will not sleep.

Tonight Nikki will cry until dawn sends her to bed shivering with voracious grief.

I Often Dream of Words

Blood on my nights.

Black

      and red . . .

Strange shapes erase deep blue day.

In all the excitement I forget I'm me.

Ever happen to you? Does it?

The train goes by. Winds along the river. People in pursuit of pleasure are on it . . . Perhaps they're on their way home from Tiger Mountain? I often watch and dream of their soft lives.

I live in the red house. I'm a lodger.

Sometimes I sit on the stairs, on the landing by the planter, and focus on one word. Most often the word is DYING.

Yellow summer or grey winter I sit by the small oval window and dream . . . of dying.

I have heard the words of a hundred dying. Took their last words deep within and brought them back here to look over. To care for . . I wonder what, if any, my last words will be?

Their words put me in a different place as they are now in a different place—there. Not here. But their words are. Here. Within. Saved. Collected. Orphans taken in. By me. They kiss me. I'm their hero. It's very satisfying.

Very.

Go back.

Through the echoes and the repetitions, behind the eyes—in, where you hear, rainbows and webs and the ghosts of memory, bat-winged, possessed, that army with half a face, and greed and grief melting, barking at the cage of heaven, hunched, splitting, legs, and fire, in burned out eyes, and laughing headless thighs—thighs, Jezebel, *Jezebel*, temptress—slut, my life, trouble, again, again, again, again, needles, bells, and trumpets, tolling, come with us, come with us, the

waiting road, carrying secrets, I'm sorry, very-very sorry, the mindless
blur of drums turning, the goat attacks, sir, sir, sir, sir, I am too, I am,
too, I see, I see it, clearly—bible black fire, I can serve, can, serve,
help me serve . . . through the layered loops . . .

To the basic elements. The core.

One.

Then another.

And a third.

More if needed to come upon the sum.

And it's done.

As it should be.

As was intended. By me. By the words.

Leading me.

As if they're carpets . . . or drums. Talking drums. The texture
comes to me. Forms. Releases. Like a fine perfume.

I breathe it in . . .

Must follow.

Follow what guides me.

Sometimes shirts and blouses come off. It's all like Picasso. Bits
and pieces.

This goes here.

That goes there.

Just so.

I merely follow where the drums lead. Follow in their footsteps.

Guiding me.

Fire drums.

From one to

                another one.

Bit by

        bit.

Piece by

          piece.

Making things fit.

The Plan.

Yes there is a Plan.

I formed it sitting on the stairs. The words became a strategy I
discovered while unfolding the words.

It became a fan. Letting in a fresh breeze. The wind of change.

Words formed in the change of this life for that.

There was no rain. No choir of angels. Just the words slowly unfolding to reveal the whole.

It came so softly.

Like the spreading wings of night. Floating. Drifting. From here to

there.

Surely you've been there?

The clock stops. The blue sky turns bluer. Clearer. The radiance comes to you. Enters you. Fills you.

With dreams.

The words are now music.

Rhythm.

Multiplying. Living—free of its tethers.

Comes for you. Enters you. You dally in it.

There is no shock.

Just the movement. The groove. Flowing . . . Smooth.

Colors and action. Defining the patterns.

I love how they slide into place. Red. And black. Filling the pattern. Creating the whole.

Smooth and soft and perfect, all the red and the black. Moving past the idea and doing it. Smooth and soft and perfect, all the red and the black.

The ideas. Hands. Ready to work. To knit. To discover the whole by shaping its creation.

Thunder. Swirling. Winking. Thunder. Tones and lights—a river of lights . . . Shining. Singing. Hands remaking/remodeling. Shaping fire.

You don't need to know what you're doing. IT knows.

And guides.

Comes from the distance . . . to . . . Hand and heart and head . . .

The words come for me.

And I embrace them . . .

And in the deep quiet, dream of beautiful deaths . . .

(after snippets of many homemade Eno videos on You Tube)

Forever Changes

Room: appearance of pain untempered.

Below: street corner with a lamp post—a blonde, eyes to belly a poem, magnified—more than life. Both glowing, drawing the world to them.

Day the resident of light, played his part, met the end, went out.

Night, the desolate river faithful only to shadows (and passions, and crime, and blasphemies, and those bruised souls caught in the juju of inflamed black dreams), came.

The blonde, red rouged lips, blue eyes, blue eye shadow, sleek black dress that promised journeys in meadows of burning sun, came to stand. Didn't have to wait long. Never does.

Above: the room of winter. And the heavy man (his crime, sorrow), rigid and narrow—condemned in a grave-room without bridges—whose last-puff-voice spent the stars on wayward empties.

But he remembers orbits, and threads, and the horizons of summer days, dripping with light that could not be withered by black rain collisions. Once he dreamed of flowers—soft peach petals, and easy chair futures . . . *Once*. He remembers . . . Yearns for more again, for flame.

At his window of steel he sees it.

Flame. So warm . . . *so warm* . . . to reach out . . . fingers free of millstone pockets, stretching, surging . . . to touch . . . something of the sun . . . again . . .

Presses his palms—exclamations, flat to the glass . . .

And she looks in his direction. Up. Smiles. Her gaze lingers. Invitation.

The instant dream, a tide of music fills him.

His feet a fever rolling, he leaves his room of warped confusion, of rags and cluttered ashtrays, and blank pages . . . The bird free. Its diamond eyes soar . . .

Through halls of dust and squabbling whispers of hunger.

He believes today is not yesterday returned to bestow attacks of splintered and broken.

His breath and dreams in the street of stakes, straight to her side.

He leans into her bubbling cheer. Hears answers flutter. Follows the wake of her chariot of light.

Her phantom-white hands open a door. He enters the bright shore of her pretty, glossed rooms. Shore to corner her castle is set with lace and rainbow flowers.

By the French doors to the balcony he sits. Has tea. Delicate, spiced and warm. And is drawn to her smile of spring in high places.

The night is young and sings of her. The smile of the moon, a spirit bird resting in its white nest joyously beguiled by her warmth.

That warm smile, the sweet thing of Earth that begins in her laugh and sings promises of redemption and more opens petrified places within him . . .

Drawn to it, as he would be drawn to anything or any presence that could turn him from ill star-winds and bleak phantasms of foul decay.

From her mouth and breast charms flow.

She laughs.

A pretty little web she spins.

Her sculptured sweater of All For You comes off.

A shoulder. Salt-white . . .

And soft. . .

His émigré eyes tremble.

The big electric moon colors the meadow of her breast.

She turns and laughs.

Opens the doors to her balcony.

Whirls in the naked moonlight.

The spaghetti strap of her clinging black dress falls from her shoulder.

She laughs, strokes the pale skin of her shoulder.

Her fingers dance in the pallid light.

He wants to say, "I have dreamed of you. Of your cotton candy kiss . . . Your gaze." He remains silent.

Staring at her. At—

Her fingers, secret songs from far corners, touch ghosts captured.

Spills them like wine.

They're in his hair.

Sighing in his ear. Charming him with delights spilled from the moon.

They trick his eyes.

She blows him a kiss.

Rushes to his side . . .

The scent of his blood, kissing the animal in her soul. It rubs her in her dry places.

Her ache for blood-comfort throbs.

She sat on his lap. Put her arms around him.

Whispered, weaving her spell. Soul-stealer, cooing lyric yeah-yeah-yeahs in her game of I will love you . . .

Promised . . .

His barriers broken, swept away by the bottomless Paris hours of pleasure on her death-silent lips of rose.

Her face is a lake of open summer sun . . . He tilts into her eyes. In his midnight core cries her name . . ,

Her fangs penetrate the smooth flesh of his neck. Get hold of his vein . . . the pleasure burst, the flow—enchantment—of sultry fire . . .

He opens his mouth of sad dreams to speak.

NO words

NO smile

His voice of NOTHINGNESS drowns her voice.

Paralyzed.

No trance, no wine, this pain, This HOLLOW vulgar language of NOTHING.

TERROR, the journey of pain. Burning in her.

It, the black drift of the hardest truth, scrapes through her. This sharp pecking, tearing crow leaves her tongue a black dry rag.

She tastes her own FEAR. Tries to pull back . . . Too late. It has touched her in her deepest places . . .

She begs, black fever in her inmost deeps . . .

Her arm and her hand go numb, fall away lifeless.

The toes of her left foot wither in her shoe. Fingernails dry and split . . . Her skin goes grey.

It, the HOLLOW NOTHING, moves. Consuming. Not harpooned. No BOOM—no BANG—no boots splashing, no hulk shambling through the labyrinths of her mind . . .

It takes NOW, and ME . . . Scatters all the grains of I. Broken shapes the lost in ashes countries of her memory. Takes sorrow and fight. Leaves holes in images/concepts.

Losing the places and things between the lines. Words are broken, guttural fragments . . .

What parts of HER the indifferent destroyer leaves burn to run, but there's no where to hide.

THERE disappears as it erases every "Mercy" she barricades herself behind.

Bones snap.

The dead blood in her veins sours and burns.

Facts become unstable. Incomplete.

Fear becomes pure.

Being's gallery is full of holes, tiny infinities of emptiness. Identity, pieces of it, now a difficult narrative littered with craters of blind motionlessness . . .

Some bitterblack, silent tiger crisscrosses her thoughts, mind— Soul. Takes sad and dreamy and past of wishes and stories. Its mouth of nothing takes, invades, leaves barren EMPTINESS. The nightmare beast feeds . . . No pretty smile, no tone, no knife or fork, no jaws, just takes . . . and takes . . . There and gone . . . Takes any something into its hollow and leaves HOLLOW.

Quietly it numbs. No method. No precision. No fitting or connected . . . no cracks or mysteries to hunt for information . . . I, or some part of it, transformed, into NOTHING.

It cuts.

Mutilates.

Turns off edges, pieces, leaving NEVER BEEN.

It, the soul eater, is moving the borders of her mind. It ripples, rends, burying what parts it takes in absolute of DARK . . . Self divided by SILENCE, but it's not an impact, not a surface pulling, it is just something that exists, something without heat or consciousness that leaves gaps . . . holes . . . HOLLOW . . .

Fear builds.

One I crumbles as terror presses.

Another piece/section/pattern GONE.

Panels woven of iron-and-steel-I and undying, monolithic-Me

that could not be dislodged and had outlived one vampiric death, feed the cold expanding BLACKNESS.

A slender piece of Me (perhaps it was a foreground, perhaps a translation, perhaps the memory of a woman in a painting, or a flood of baggage fighting for escape in a song), out of bridges and keys, reaches for a wavering candle of hope that dies alone in the saturation of blank space.

She, summoning a dimming I, shivers as things close, as interiors lose their center and are sucked into Never Again. She can almost see them unwind . . .

laughing when the old man's false teeth fell out as he tried to scream / the way home / the dark tunnel in the fog and the snob / the message rushing in Babi's chest / the early autumn chill on the marble floor, her bare feet leaving bloody footprints / the New Year's mimes lying silent—truly silent / the hottest blood of all / the pretty black-haired girl in the devil suit on all fours, begging / amazing / intricate / the game of nursery rhymes that ended with a half-gurgled grunt of a scream / how warm it felt / bees and marmalade / being informed it was not the end of the world, merely the end of summer—all the clairvoyant nights after / Miles' hushed bye-bye crying / needing math / . . . *impulse* . . . / absorbing expressions / existence struggling in the white steel hands of the incomprehensible

how simply amusements arrived

flanking prey (wide-eyed Casanova, or courtyard-smooth, god-like thigh of pungent poetry sick of her husband or boyfriend's urge storms—blood's BLOOD) before sampling

the quick fix of BLOOD

sureness/pleased/when I was/reached/solved/every minute of faith closed by this coursing never again of atrocious emptiness . . .

A tear scars her cheek as she tries to recall things now not simply forgotten, but wholly eradicated.

Where first and before were, now is no after, no moments of

concern, or doors. Where the authority of solid and known stood, now is things no more.

Losing: all the howls that climbed the walls . . .

        presence

influence

        control
        of her
        universe

what she made

    wore

her achievements

    notions/conceits

what she has seen

        documented

the Frankenstein mind of 200 years [feeding/hunting/shaking that fine, tight ass for the prey] 200 years The Thirst drinking hot, gushing BLOOD—200 years of hard, ugly mass murder, dripping (and smeared) with scarlet red BLOOD . . . 200 years of corners and lies: she has been a bitch, a breathtaking syllable in a poem, a coyote, a vagina, an altar, a killer of men, anger, and not quite sure (learning to redecorate after the new clock stomped out the sun) . . .

it's her world

as SHE understands it

    HER examples
    HER points
    HER illusions
    HER conclusions

HER

mouth putting an end to

their thirst

she thrived on their fire

. . . preface/possible

nothing is

SAFE

    She is losing herself—

                —for a second
                —dirty rags of silk
                —impassive

—for the living there is only death

—sticky

—natural

—conviction

—had to have/not asking/wanting to ex-
plode/every juicy little tidbit

—so help me

—what do you mean

—his gray and green rotten fangs

—salt

—bullshit

Losing all the pieces and threads of 200 years of power . . .

Her mouth hangs open noiselessly. It can not find or form words. Not the ones she requires.

The gestures and posture of appearances, the muscles and foliage of time she could return to, not cast off, but zeroed!

Her passages erased.

She is naked.

Crumpled.

"Fuck." Sputters out . . .

Rain . . . The promise broken with pen and ink . . . The lush paradise the silver lady visitor used to spill over her childhood dreams . . .

Hindsight.

Reckonings . . . the murmurs of listen here . . . the listings, note-worthy and those that no longer play the mainstage . . . each and all no longer contributing.

Once and coupling and directions and spent slowly, or ruffled, or carefully, have parted from consciousness . . . even "It was just of the tip of my tongue" is now lost . . .

Where she was sharp and unflappable, brambles of fear ring the hollows.

Predator is PREY. Not embraced, yet drained.

Less and less of herself to deal with . . .

Less and less of the I who is Me to protest/sustain, to know I and all its senses exist in the future—Any future . . .

Less and less of her very essence to rely on . . .

No stars within to find . . .

Her hunger taken from her.

Oh, for an angel . . . for a line . . . for a sky . . . but—

NO

crumbs to follow home

None and

NONE

No rope or white horses to ride to freedom and faces and life . . . No bone-faced winter clock of slow to snarl at. She has forgotten joy and how to scream . . .

No womb

No survival guide

No child's books

and ever-soft Mama's voice, so alive with beauty . . .

NO

shades of life unfurled

NO

complexities

or blood—life saving BLOOD!—soul feeding BLOOD!

or flames

in This END

NO

ME

or how to say it

The last fragment of her/I/Me/the vampire thing does not snap, or sink, it is not of birds, or Socrates, is not worn out by running through 100 strained lives . . .

The agonies of this spilled void—that does not call or sleep or move straight across

TOO CLOSE

TOO DEEP

Auroras and places . . . NO.

Memory banks, various montages, streets, personalities, years living and morphing, interconnected to ideas and descriptions and inspirations unwoven . . . Empty.

No lore and its offshoots . . .

No carpet of cowards awaiting her sunrise grave-mouth . . .

Cognition.

Identity—first shy, timid life, and this fearless passage.

The Whole.
No longer unified.
Quietly there . . . and gone
This incarnation of her collective moments slips . . . away
bare
broken
changed
an uncommon death, no thunder, no muttering, no black-wing
worm thing from the stars—its red lust a fist of sickness—hunting
mortals
broken
broken, out of bravely and finally . . . she no longer knows want
. . .

Her heart, a clock without real numbers, stops.
Not even a last breath to gain . . .
dark

NOTHINGNESS

Done
(No LOADED right side of the brain. Nothing crosses the corpus
callosum.)
Empty takes EVERYTHING.
leaves a grey husk of flesh (No other Me on the other side of the
wall of Self; No I to have faith in Me; Not alone (inside) with herself,
keeping her secrets; No other coasts of thought; Me not waiting
there; Me out of trouble and miscalculations; No Me to find Me; No
Me expecting, rising to deal with important matters and truth—
imagined or saw; Who I am, as lost as the words of the Purple Sage;
Forgetting the addiction and the whip. Forgetting what the black
magic d(ID). No I'll committing . . . or thinking . . . or interfering . . .)
No clues; no headlines . . .
a gray husk of flesh

He inhales, takes his nothingness inside—back. Closes his puppet
mouth. Wishes he could find a smile or a friendly hand to sever his ties.
He puts his hands in his pockets. Dust and forgotten tides of silence from his world of pain gets under his fingernails . . .

Back in his silent room of bitter autumn pain he tries to recall her smile . . . her eyes—tender birdsong echoed in their soft-fire starlight . . . thinks he remembers her clothes were almost off . . . maybe his gloom blushed as her golden grace gathered . . .

She laughed? Yes. Yes, she did, (it was real) he was sure of it . . . It spilled yellow/white/soft/shining light, warm gardens of light . . .

And was there . . . a kiss?

"Who cares for me?"

So full of teeth blazing, the sun (just this moment risen) is silent.

(*LOVE* ~ *Forever Changes*)

In the White Walls of Silence

The puppet-faces with teeth said: *"Guilty."*
Morals and dogma, pointing: *"Sickness."*

all white here

I'm weighted with its lack of shadows. so BITTER its bite of silence. so PURE its circling syllables. WHITE lights to make me forget. WHITE powders to make me forget. WHITE hours to make me forget. WHITE these walls that chain me with teeth. WHITE these walls that chew with animal heat . . .

so white this brittle page without words. so white, straight & even—stiff without apart. so white, divorced from the hues of yesterday. Where flickers even the smallest thread of home? Where flows sky of dark and wind, where flutter whispers from throats warm?

Slender this truth laughs at me with its SILENT white smile.

When comes the *dove's wing whisper* and the *soft* embrace of departure? Where is the road? And the rooftops and the sash?

Where is the dream?

I am Caligari. I rule the trembling hummingbirds curled in the smooth glow of their lamps. I rule the angles that lead to their thresholds. Bring down the dark. Open the curtain of shadows. Night longs
. . .
white

        `"Please. Make it blink."`

white
this leprous skin.
white
this shepherd who will not sleep.

Give me the eyes of the moon. Give me the cool stars. Let my soles travel the narrow language of the roof. Let me drift like the frayed mists of autumn. Give me the inmost dark. Give me   space black as the milk between the

t

s

a   r

s

Where is the next day? Where is wide open, the shade, the shape—evening full of slender laughs and quivering, and my art demanding no error?

Take me to some other lodging place. One room for the dust, one for the stars & one room for the voices . . .

"Please."

"Please."

Trees. Ground made gentle by the weeping moon and doors. Walls—penetrate—entwine. Solemn mouths of streets, storybook calm in the garden of midnight. Vanishing, seeing clouds, windows, smoke, the faces of ghosts . . . everything softly asleep as I cover my nakedness in the alchemical braids of blood
& dreams

I am a stranger here.

"Turn off the lights."

"Please. Turn off the lights."

(for Robert Bloch, Master of the Knife & the Scream)

Mother Stands for Comfort

She gave up on God after he failed her. Failed to kill her father with a heart attack, or in a car accident. Suicide would have been alright too. In fact, preferable—he deserved it. And it suited the incestuous swine who stole so many hours of light and replaced them with sand and cold grey roots of shame. She gave up on Eckankar and Buddhism and twelve other disciplines she investigated. Cast off every tourniquet of maybe, and Not. Found the drugs and booze didn't do shit either.

Walked and walked, in shades of afterlife, through fantasy, until she found there was no Promised Land.

Slept alone and with sharks of revenge and bareback confusion. Lived, for a time, a small-skinned life with no wings . . . Poured crows and blue into every dirty girl hieroglyph of dust.

Quivered.

Leapt.

Went from fat-slut-jockstrap to skinny to apple-cheeked to sick and tired . . .

Prowled.

Found she was not immune to the rubble.

Built a house of cards then found she couldn't live in it without a gun.

Murmured when she knelt at the threshold where self bleeds because it can't find a good thing.

Conjured. Cracked.

Made furniture out of the neon blur . . .

Spat at houses of Someday and Sure.

Fell off ladders . . .

Then, after being given over to the gale-force wheels of a certain drama, she found Him and was delivered.

The night, colored with the throat and roads of goodbye, had come. It brought rain and other things . . . Things that were born against backdrops of darkness.

. . . She was lying in an alley. Raped. Bleeding out—three bullets in her chest. Left for dead. Her small hands were weak fists. She was full of the coldest shadow-kiss—freezing, when she heard his wings beat softly.

"Stay calm, Child, and we will find a way around this trouble."

She heard his voice clearly, but couldn't make out his features, couldn't focus. Cobwebs and shadows fogged her vision.

"Do not be afraid when you confront youth. They are the bridge, My Sweet Lost Angel. Do not forget summer when you sleep in the quietness."

The wind is filled with his scent. She remembers how much she loves red summer roses. The memory of their tenderness anoints the shattered contours of her lips . . .

She can hear dim drums. See a light. A pulsing yellow light. The light of a heartbeat. The heartbeat of the drums.

The drums sound like the fluttering of his wings.

There is life in the light. Wings. Faces. Sigils and skulls and darkness . . . A gathering darkness filled with teeth and thunder . . .

Things—life, is being born in that moment when the light dances with the crawling darkness . . . Things with faces of fire and volcanic laughter . . . Things of night and desire and clarity . . .

And she is their mother. The blood that flows from her breasts their milk. And they grow, reach, stretch, shoulder—lunge, dance . . . ever up—ever onward . . . they call her name as they flutter and flicker and ascend . . . She is the sea, the womb . . . She breathes and they sing . . .

And she reaches out with liquid finger to stroke the coming . . . The beginning.

She is the sea, black deeps and lava currents—a bounty of salt and temperament, her seeded dreams and memories, her arteries, groundwork and poetry . . . From her fists grainy flocks form . . . Pale yellow-white shapes—sculptures, collect, rushing and thrusting for her attentions, for her love . . .

She hardens, firms. Her hair is tattered. Her lips tattered . . . and torn . . . She sighs . . . and writhes . . . Her fingers enjoined with those long-stemmed horizon-limbs of the King . . .

"Sweet Summer Knight," she whispers.

Voices full of different words and forgotten colors journey from the interior of some lightless, lost between and explode in the garden of her tears . . .

She whitens as they, burning with her velvet love song, feed . . . They, the tide lured from sleep, are bewitched by the peace of her golden mask . . .

The King lays his solemn white fingers on her empty heart. Takes in her last breath, smiles as she sleeps

(after the Q6 film Din of Celestial Birds *and*
Kate Bush—"Hounds of Love" and "Mother Stands for Comfort")

Blow Wind Blow

Under an empty sky. Not a cloud or a mountain in view. The birds that broke the early sun with the—higher—higher—outward tracks of their wings had passed by.

All in all, most locals would call it a fine late morning. No wind blew in the near-silence outside the roadhouse dinner . . .

Nice hands. Smooth and soft. Refilled his cup. The coffee, black. And fresh.

He didn't look up from his French fries and cole slaw. Ionesco knew what he'd see.

"Would you care for a slice of pie?"

Still didn't look up. Just shook his head no.

Took a sip of the hot coffee. A slight smile that said, "That's good."

A leisurely full smile after the 2nd sip.

A third sip and laid a ten-dollar bill on the counter.

"Thank you, Dear," she said.

Looked her right in the eyes. Saw the evil framed by her eyelashes.

Then he shot her. Two in the center of her face.

The cook in the back was hugging the floor. Praying. Hoping he wasn't next. Muttered, "Please just the cash and leave."

Ionesco opened the screen door, stepped outside. Turned West. All the grass around here was brown. But the weeds were tall. Green.

❋

Chicago looked like Philly looked like the Big Apple. Miami and L.A. didn't look like this. This was a fertile hunting field.

Ionesco lit a smoke. Watched a young blonde girl with a ponytail cross the street. Fifteen, sixteen, by her dress and her gait still a good girl. Saw what passed for a man with a knife in the shadowed doorway.

There's no science to evil. Bad company is bad company. He ground the cigarette under his heel and crossed the street. Stopped in front of the doorway.

Looked in the shadow.

The shapeshifter masquerading as a man knew who Ionesco was—they always did. He closed his eyes. That didn't block or blot out all the stories he'd heard. Didn't utter a prayer. They never do.

Ionesco shot him in the face.

The moon was off tonight. The shadows found their work easier. Ionesco didn't care one way or the other. Day or night, God or no God, it was all the same to him.

❦

Cold blue steel. Drifters. Dogs. Wind blow. Bums. Wind blow again, same old, same old. Bums, sleeping until the sun goes down. Wind that never changed, never stopped. Ups. And downs. Bullets. All packed tight. New arrivals with $73 left after bus fare. Detours. A coast of its own. Poolhalls and bullshit. Chalk marks, gatherings, and sighs. Bluesmen. One old master said the blues could heal you. All the hungry wolves plowing these streets leaving the leasts and the mice and the lambs on their knees in excrement, blood and poison, that didn't heal anything ... Hustlers uptown. Surprises. Policemen with Mississippi delta blues on the take. Streets, ugly as the souls of the politicians that helped ruin them, packed tight and ready to blow. Backstabbers so thick you couldn't go out your front door. Churches that sleep at night. Bars and alleys and makeshift doctor's office that didn't. Wind blows. Wind blows. Sad and mad—just a touch or full blown wired, and plenty of bad, Chicago had it all and then some.

Ionesco walked twelve blocks. Found a room. Went out. Bought a razor and a few basics in a Mom and Pop.

No radio or TV on in his room. Sat in the hardback chair and sipped a glass of whiskey. Watched the smoke from his cigarette curl in the curtain-filtered sunlight.

He looked at the postcard. Read the address. The time of the meet. Exhaled and shook his head. He'd never received an invitation from one of them before.

A request to meet. More like a suicide note.

Good penmanship. A steady hand wrote this. A woman's hand.

Ionesco looked out the window. There was drunk in the parking lot across the street. He didn't have a shirt but he had a bottle. He was yelling at God. Yelling it was unfair he was stuck on this side when He had all that easy living up there. Two drunks who weren't drunk were eyeing his bottle. Their eyes said he wasn't going to have to suffer this life much longer.

Ionesco sat back down. Took another sip.

His watch said he had four hours before the meet.

He smoked and drank whiskey.

The sun dropped from the sky.

An ancient gray street in an old grey city. Black pouring thick hard shadows out of every nook. The weak smear of red neon in the small window said The Waterfront. It looked like the sun never vacationed here. Ionesco flicked his cigarette to the curb and went in.

Another shithole cheap bar. If there was a little used backroom in Hell that smelled like a cancer ward in a psych hospital this was it. No TV. The grime of tens of thousands of cigarettes hard and thick as old paint. A thirty year old jukebox, playing an old blues number. The old black voice, in a near whisper, said, it serves me right to suffer. Anyone in here was suffering alright. A tombstone-on-the-side should have come with the beer. Should have called the skeevy joint No Future.

One customer in the bar. Looked like he carried the plague. Looked like he spent the better part of his days in dumpsters sifting through regret. He was scrying yesterday in his beer. Those days weren't answering, though his silent, moving lips called and called. Ionesco knew what he saw in the flat golden glow was no good.

The bartender was a mean old rat existing on a diet of hardcore and mean. It stretched over his round face. In some past he might have had teeth. He was smoking a cigar thick as his scabby, dirty fingers. Behind ½-Coke bottle granny glasses his disease-yellow eyes were hot stars of hate. When he went down for the dirt nap and the worm came it would stay clear of the poisonous orbs.

Ionesco saw his host. Not much more than a boy. And a young woman with him. He stopped at the bar and got a beer.

Walked to the table and sat down. Sat the long-neck bottle to his left. Didn't touch it.

At close range. Waiting for a word.

No hello. No thanks for coming. Right into it. "I didn't choose this." Showed his fangs. Waited for a reply.

Ionesco didn't indicate one was coming.

The young man in a hurry. Looked directly in his eyes. "It was raining that night. Hard. It was cold out. I was delivering a pizza. Working part time to help pay for tuition. They took me—like a rape. Two of 'em. Grabbed me. Cut and bit and chewed. Felt like when I burned my hand when I was kid. Only a hundred times worse." Waited for a sign of understanding.

"I can't even remember what kind of fucking pizza it was.'

"I never wanted to hurt anyone. I wasn't a bad guy . . . I'm not now. I only do what I have to stay alive." Eyes pleading.

"I'm tired of hiding. Tired of running. Looking back and wondering when you'll show up. They told me you would. Said you always come—laughed about it. Death and taxes. And *you*. Guess they think you're the death part."

The young woman set her hands on the table. Palms firmly pressed down. "This is not my fault."

Ionesco looked at the woman, signs he was finished listening in his expression.

Frightened, she inched back—squirmed—in her chair. Opened her mouth. Couldn't find words.

"She's the same as me." Filtered. Fingers to lips. "We didn't choose this life." Fingers balled into a fist. No threat in it.

"Yes. I didn't get a say. *They* jumped me. Came out of the dark and raped me—both of them. Made me do *things* . . . And then, *They* changed me. They laughed because I was a virgin. Twenty-four and a virgin—doesn't that matter? It should. I was school teacher. Third grade. I taught Sunday school too."

"We came to you because we don't want to die. You know more about *this* than anyone. Can't you fix this for us?"

"They ripped my crucifix from my neck and threw it in the sewer . . . I never even got a speeding ticket. I delivered Meals On Wheels when I was in college. That should matter. It should. It really should."

Ionesco eyes said no. He shook his head slowly from side to side.

"Please?" Wasting breath in the effort. "I don't want to be Satan's child." Three teardrops on the sleeve of her blue blouse.

"We didn't choose this. I was in the wrong place at the wrong time. That's all. It's not my fault. Help us."

Stone cold. And still as a photograph, still no.

His honesty no help to either of the children who had been stripped naked, contaminated, punched, slapped, taken and taken again, and reformed as things whose situation was beyond their control.

"It can't be undone?" Came out breathless.

One last no. No hate in it. Just fact.

"Why did God abandon me?" She searched Ionesco's eyes for an answer.

Cold as a brick. Ionesco's eyes, expression said nothing.

She opens her mouth. Shows her fangs. "This can't be God's work."

Dead air. The man and the woman didn't move.

She put her trembling hands in her lap. Started to cry again. Wanted to pray. But she'd forgotten how.

Low tones, crawling from the fearful crack in her lips. "Will . . . I . . . go . . . to Hell?"

Dead air.

Two kids, staring into a space filled, choked with their disappointment. Hope for a remedy or sympathy turned to gloom.

"Can't you do something?"

He nodded. Slowly. The motion frightening in the weak light.

Ionesco stood.

Put two shots in the man's head. Two in the woman's.

The bartender stared. Gruesome and cold didn't phase him, he'd been part of it a hundred times. He leveled a shotgun and smiled. His greasy smile of scorn and obscenity tried to bite Ionesco.

Ionesco normally didn't kill humans, but the bartender shed what little—if any—humanity he'd possessed decades ago. Ionesco sent him away with a hollow point in his brain. No big deal. Bad is bad. And until you move it from this place to that it just keeps pouring its black laughter and crap over everything.

The lone customer shook in cold terror. Didn't move from his piss-soaked stool.

Ionesco did not close the door on the way out.

The cold Chicago wind blew.

The moon was off tonight. The shadows found their work a little easier. Ionesco didn't care one way or the other. Night or day, God or no God, it was all the same to him.

Wind in his face the walking man walked.

8's & Aces

No whiskey. No days at the track these days . . . Pool in the back-room of O'Connell's Grill, no.

No pussy.

Cruisin' all those nights, up and down the strip in the souped-up Chevelle—hopin' for easy and cash and speed and surprise parties with dancing and honey and big comfortable summer with bells and the top down and everything in the whole god-damn world placed at their feet . . .

Misadventure ringing, lost that map.

Outta laughs . . .

They wander ended story to story run its race. Simon Bartholomew Wormwood . . . Annabelle Buck . . . Starling, Snow, Cotton Fulton II and Case and Joris and Porfats and Polliards and Barretts and Burgess and Estrada . . . and 137 others. All have reached their destination. Many were not whole when they got there . . .

Plank and the Belldog steal from the Lord. They get born, live for a time and come here in the end.

In the old lives they robbed graves for gems and jewels and rings and bodies to sell. In this incarnation—after a night, many, many years ago, of drunken missteps—they steal from graves. They skip the gems and jewels, pass on the rings or just throw them out, they're after bodies. Dinner.

No bones to gnaw on in the casket of Sarah Joris. Plank spits at the moon for enjoying the defeat.

"I eat one of yer old boots if you hadn't burned them last winter," The Belldog said.

"Reanimated in the odors of death and twenty years on I still have to hear about them shitty boots."

Scratching the itch of a horde of fleas, The Belldog attacks his crotch, behind his ears, and his armpit. "If it wasn't for you and your tight boots we would have gotten away with it."

"She was sitting there naked as the fucking moon. Waiting. Remember that? Sittin' there grinnin'. You brought the goatskin. I only drank to keep you company and this is my payback?"

"Do you remember what it felt like?"

"What? Whiskey?"

"Yeah. The Buzz."

"No."

Two markers from the one that was their downfall, Paul Jos. Whittam (*Time Loves a Hero*), they sit. Quiet—vocally—as the moon.

Bent shadows move. A rustling, something good size.

Red, night-eyes open wide. Meat. The thought strikes both at the same moment.

"Maybe a stray dog?"

"Maybe. Most likely a cat or 'coon."

They're up. Mostly silent. Moving. One right. One left.

Flank it.

Cut it off.

Maybe kill it—smash-smash-smash . . . maybe cut-cut.

Dine.

Plank has his old dirty knife out. Ready. Doesn't need it with his predator fangs and brittle claws, but old ways, fun ways, die hard. And just because he died, they didn't.

The Belldog leaps. Elbows. And a high-pitched wailing. He comes up with hair in his hands. A head attached to the thick red mane.

A girl screams.

"Young, pink, and pretty."

"Them's nice tits. Good size," hisses a smiling Plank.

"Sweet."

"Very."

"Nice meaty ass too."

"Dibs." Out fast and greedy.

"The fuck you say."

"I caught it. Dibs."

"I eyeballed it first."

"First come, first served."

It moved. Plank smashed it in the head with a chunk of head-stone.

Blood.

Limp. Lying on the dry grass.

"A live one."

"Yeah?"

"Fuck."

"Fuck? What do we do with a live one?"

"She never said a word about eating the living. And she sure as fuck didn't pass out no handbook. You killed her too soon. She might have told us things—"

"Might have ate *us* if we let her live. That bitch-thing was never gonna tutor us. All she was gonna do was plate us up."

"Then we kill it and *then* eat it."

"Finally you got something right."

"Bet yer moldy ass, 'cause I caught this here goodie."

"And I dug up the last one. Partners?" Plank's expression says it better be, or else.

Why the fuck not? "I get the heart and the tongue." Comes out like a crime from his furnace of desire mouth.

"Liver and brain."

"Done."

They spit in their hands and shake.

Plank hooks his cadaverous hands under the girl's armpits. The Belldog grabs her legs, licks his lips.

Back down the black hole.

Down a winding path of sour, decaying earth . . . Under the pasture of dead flowers plucked by oblivion.

Stepping over the splinters of broken bones and creeping roots. Kicking a rat or two out of their path.

Passed shovels and picks that had not clattered in years. And more piles of bones. And moldering walls. And tossed rings and jewels and flags and a few stuffed animals . . . Through the tunnels they dug on their hunt for meat and to pass the time . . . One's whistling a children's song about teddy bears having a picnic. One grinning, death-cold desire melting to frenzy. One's hellishly thin and desiccated. One's bloated and puffy as a well-fed graveworm, somehow the gasses of the metamorphic, decompositional process hadn't dissipated from his corpulent body.

Home.

Deep in seedy shadows . . . Nest, warren. Tomb under the tombs. A ghoul's retreat.

They drop their battered load in the middle of the large, self-expanded cave like it was a sack of dirty laundry.

Plank lights a candle.

Maggots glimmer. Shadows play on the scattered gallery of mask-hide portraits peeled from faces and tacked to walls.

The Belldog lights two more . . .

Skulls shriek.

Face, chin, half-bloodied from the granite-whomp, slumped on her chest, they've unfolded her and tied her to an old wagon wheel they can't remember why they hauled down here. When the rope ran out they tied her left arm with wire to a cracked spoke. She's hung like Christ.

The Belldog pulls out a hardback chair taken from Pearl Hoover's grand mausoleum and sits at the table made of two oak casket lids.

Plank follows suit. His seat, a cheap plastic thing some kids had dragged in the boneyard one night when they came to party.

Both stare at their catch.

The Belldog: "How long after do you figure we have to wait to eat her?"

"Fucked if I know. All the other stuff we dug up was dried out, like jerky." Runs his fingers through his beard. Scratches his chin. "A week maybe?"

"Would it help if we hung her feet up and slit her throat, so she'll bleed out? I think that's what they do to deer and pigs and shit."

"Do I look like the town butcher?" Waves his knife at The Belldog. "This look like a clever to you, Foolish?"

Plank shrugs. "Gonna have to take shifts watching it while it cures, or the rats will be at it."

"Fuck the rats. Maybe we should try to cook it."

"Slow roast. Hmmm. Might be good that way."

"Chop it up and roast it a piece at a time? Plenty of wood here."

"And where does all the smoke go? Ain't no figgin' chimney down here."

"Asshole, yer already dead. You ain't gonna choke to death on smoke."

"True. True."

"Well, lookey-lookey, our dinner date is awake."

"Welcome to the world, missy."

"Yeah. The new world."

The bite of sense erases the dead-world hallucination abasing her eyes. Seeing madness in the black room. Hearing cheerful appetites drunk on contemplation, laughing doesn't drown out the scream.

The room of pressure and teeth and spiders searching for banquets and . . . fear, stark hysterical terror, prodded with needles of momentum.

"You's keep that up and I'll carve ya up right this second."

A second scream, compressed, ragged and soaked in hysteria.

"You heard him. Shut yer pie-hole."

"Pie-hole." More laughing, breaking into self-pleased cackles. "That's a good one."

"Yeah, I could always come up with a goody."

"You're the funny man all right. Funny as a half-staved hyena at a corpse party."

Tears from blasted eyes. She's staring at the pair. Some leprous disease wastes their skin. They have totally red eyes. And fangs and claws. Like the ghouls in those gory movies Tommy likes to watch over and over and over.

It's all Stan's fault. Stan told her about finding the Wormwood's graves; Elias and Silas, Millie and Jeremiah and Dorothea and Aunt Isa and Uncle Matthias. Old as shit—seventeen-something, he said. In the bramble overrun, back of Stroudwater Cemetery, by where the big Maple fell and took out a chunk of the stone wall. A dozen or so, planted there all by themselves in a little family plot. And she knew Tommy would love grave rubbings of people named of all things, Wormwood, and the Renfield was a fantastic find. It would blow his mind, having a Renfield buried here. A Renfield grave rubbing as a present to a hardcore Dracula fan, perfect. That and the bottle of absinthe would have been the best birthday presents he ever got.

Happy Twenty-one. Stan and his dumb-ass ideas.

Last time she was in trouble with the cops was his idea too . . .

She should have dragged his ass here. Not come alone.

And it's in her head, she'll bargain with them. She'll tell them she can lure all kinds of people here for them to eat.

She knows lots of others into horror and the gothic. She'll tell them she found this cool place under the graves. And they'll come running. It will keep them in meat forever.

It's all a lie, but she's good and then some with lies. Been lying since she was a child. Lay on the big eyes, the sad mouth, cry some, even her mother went for it. Every time.

She's lied to the cops a dozen times. And they always bought it.

Plank sets a worn deck of poker cards on the table. "I'll play ya for it."

The Belldog looks at the cards. "I deal." Shows his teeth.

"Fair enough."

"We play till it's midnight. Whoever is ahead at midnight wins. Winning hand deals. If it's a tie, we pick a card. High card wins." A flash of punctuating teeth.

"You've got a game."

"Cut?"

"You bet I will." A dry wind filled with shadows and dead leaves.

Third hand. Plank's winning.

Teeth looking like they're dying to tear into something, The Belldog scowls. Spits something more solid than phlegmy on the floor.

She's stopped crying. She watching, trying to make it look like she's not. Wondering what they're up to.

Trembling. Almost ready.

Trembling.

Thinks she's ready to run her game on the madmen—*Not men.*

First breath: "*Ah . . .* hey."

Stunned, they turn.

Door open. "Look. Um, I have this idea." Hands clenching her wish.

Suddenly. Jaws hang open. Ornery eyes, in the flickering candlelight, come up against sheer disbelief.

"Um, if you were to let me go, I can lure all kinds of um, people down here for you. And—"

"If we let you go you never come back."

"No. NO! I *promise.*"

"Right. You'll be a good girl and bring yer friends to, *dinner.*"

Both laugh.

Plank slaps his side of the coffin lid tabletop with the flat of his hand several times.

The Belldog, eyes hard: "How fucking stupid do ya think I look?"

Plank, almost a bark: "Right. Fuckin' right. You'd run like hell and brings back coppers and dogs and priests with God in their fists and torches and shit."

"Yeah. Burn us out and kill us. Rip us up like we's vermin."

"And where would we be then? Dead crispies."

Spit out. "No fuckin' way. I'm not havin' any."

The dove dares, sings. "But-but, you, um won't believe how many, um kids I know would kill to see this place. It's just like a horror movie set in here. It's so cool they'd have to see it. Have to. I'd like tell them it's a tour. Um, horror is um, really big these days. Cannibal and zombie movies and books are um, a big part of the culture. They're like so popular they keep remaking new versions of all the old horror movies. There's like nine or ten Night of the Living Dead movies now. Everyone digs *raw*. Kids eat it up . . . They'll go for it."

"They might." Expression says, he's almost willing to go for it. Then. "Nah. Stupid-ass kids come around here to drink sometimes—don't even leave a little taste. Just piss all over the place and push over markers, smoke their weed—shit smells like shit. I'm not buyin' it."

"Yeah. Yer lyin' to save yer ass."

"So's shut the fuck up or I'll shut you up." No mercy in his eyes.

"Got it, Missy?" Waving his knife.

Five more hands. The Belldog's currently winning. Two games up.

She's listening to them talk about seasonings and which parts to cook. Or if they should even try to figure out how to cook her.

Half out of her mind with fear, with wrong and worse, she's got to make them believe her. Got to.

Now.

Before—

She's trying to stay calm. Working on her speech. Got to bend her pitch so they'll fall for it.

A larder that's always full. Boys, or girls. You pick. Other things if you want. I'm a good thief. I can get things.

It's got to work.

Got to.

"You're playing to see who gets to eat me first? My plan's a lot better. Think of all the kids you'd get to eat. I could never to turn you in. I'd—I'd be an accomplice. And I could get you others things. Booze. Whiskey or rum. Wine. Whatever you like. My Dad owns a chain of liquor stores. Eating me is a bad choice." Quivering, heart to lips.

Both laugh.

"Not like that at all. This ain't about eating you."

"We're playing to see who gets to *fuck you*, before we eat you."

"We eat the dead, but they're no fun to fuck."

"Yes, we likes 'em ta squirm. A lot."

"Ain't had no pussy since the old bitch turned us back in '73."

11:59. Not enough time for another hand.

"And we have a winner." The Belldog lays a trio of aces and a pair of 8's on the table. Smiles. Pushes his chair back. Rubs his crotch, the old, threadbare fabric of his pants splits, exposing his grotesque genitals. Smiles wider, thinking he won't even have to unzip. Blows a kiss at the girl.

Plank, truly sour: "Fuckshit."

"I'll be skippin' the shit. Just want to get to my fuckin'. Might chew on a nipple while I'm havin' my fun." Winks at the girl. "Or maybe plump-little Missy u'll slip me the tongue."

Both roar.

As does she, many decibels higher.

A One-Way Fare

for Derrick Hussey, a great tour guide

Wasn't the public library.

Wasn't summer.

The safe parts of downtown where you didn't see the roaches were fifteen blocks east.

In here you wouldn't be sitting beside a lawyer or a cop or an English teacher. 600 to 1 no one in here had ever heard of Jean-Paul Sartre, or Ayn Rand.

Betty, the bartender here at the end of the world, smoked Chesterfields. No filter. She had a knife and a loaded .45 and no one had called her Baby in twenty-five years.

There wasn't an unshaven soul sitting at the bar drinking Coke, or one that remembered what crickets sounded like . . .

The small black and white TV over the bar hadn't worked in a year. A vintage-'51 Victrola ran a needle through B24. Vern Gosdin and ET. A hard case working on his fourth boilermaker (this hour), who claimed he was chiseled in stone, but in truth had spent too many seasons in the crazy rodeo found a tear in his beer. The needle zeroed in on its next victim. Sammy Kershaw walked down a road, took a left at Yesterday . . . and found his haunted heart in a living hell.

Someone laughed about "that fucked-up" fist fight over the 50-cent bankroll that tumbled out the door of the laundromat into the street last night.

"Yeah. Last night was a hoot. That fight next door. And the gunshots."

There were nine midnight riders in the bar. Every one of them was white . . .

❋

Cigarette smoke hovered over the glass of whiskey. The corner was tight. Black. The wounded did not enter. They were throwing back beer in the light. Those pockets that passed for light.

Excess enters. Her legs went on forever. The almost-dead gorge. Lifeless slimy eyes rush to seats and windows, searching the secret recipes of experiences they never played. Their bedroom dialogues did not reduce her. She didn't need followers.

Ionesco had experience with demons. And a lot of the other things that didn't walk in the light. He'd followed them. New York, San Francisco, swampy, scabrous flats in Florida, he walked in smoke and shadows. Killed what he found. He'd stood in the rain and put poison in the veins of murderous. Didn't laugh. Didn't feel bad about it the next day. Just stopped the feeding.

She was in the bar looking for another life. Another meal. Loneliness made easy prey. Open, her angel eyes. Warm, her mouth. Right here and now you can have it she said. Her silent night voice whispered. Then it laughed.

Easy pickins. Just like they told her. Look in the isolated joints by the river of tears. Played out . . . Frayed. Sitting alone. Praying over their beer . . . Put on your lipstick. Put your hand out . . . A big smile. They never see it coming . . . With that body they'll never see your fangs . . .

Ionesco knew what laid under the fresh paint. It wasn't a strange place for a rape, but the expensive paint job seemed out of place. *A new actor in the play,* he thought. *Hasn't read the whole script.*

Easy. He thought. She thought, easy. (. . . *as stealing candy from a baby,* she laughed at the thought) Neither gave a thought to who'd mop up after the wedding.

An old lion who suddenly remembered his loins were capable of sensation elbowed his way to the seat beside her. Put his cigar in the ashtray. Fluffed himself. Said, "Hey."

A big smile. It said, "I Do." The mark had taken the con heart deep.

Ionesco's fingers tapped on the table top. Greg Allman sang about a midnight road that went on forever. He tossed back the whiskey. Took a last drag off his smoke. Ground it out.

Stood.

It heard him. Felt him moving from the shadows. Turned. Re-

membered what they'd said about the man with hurricanes in his
green eyes. Then they'd freeze, stumble over the words, and say no
more. Ionesco, the solitary man . . . Couldn't be turned. Can't be
stopped. He comes . . .

You go.

"Stone cold." . . . *"You can't reason with him."* . . . *"He never says
a word."* . . .

"He's the worst thing in the world."

"Really?"

"Truth."

It wasn't easy to put together this deal. She fought for it. Made
hard choices. Walked dark hard floors, crossed bridges. Gave it all up
and made the deal. And He was going to erase all that. Now?

She looked at the door.

Looked at the gun in his hand.

"He can kill you a hundred ways." Everyone had said the same
thing to her.

She begged with her eyes.

Accused. Tried. No border to escape over.

It was only a month ago she'd watched herself die . . . Downed
one last glass of gin and let The Pain burn the haunted brutality of
the old life away . . .

She was still getting used to the rules

. . . too young to

. . . just

. . . vanish.

There must be something . . .

If He killed you there was no coming back.

There must be something . . .

He was too close.

"Gone. For eternity."

She needed time. Wanted time . . .

It couldn't be too late . . .

Once, she was one of God's children . . .

Weary . . . sure . . .

But . . . There was a field where strawberries grew wild . . .

She was twelve. Once. She had a picture of Jesus holding a little
white lamb. Once . . .

Before sneaking out at night with Tommy. Smoking pot . . .

Before the night in the woods with George, drinking beer in the backseat of his father's shiny gold Buick . . .

Before skinny dipping under the Georgia sun . . . Before the taste of gin . . .

Before Ken's frost and the tears and the holes in the plaster . . . Before he started slapping her around and the punch in her gut . . . And the black eyes . . .

Before the stained, bare mattresses. Fucking a hundred drunks. She didn't even know their names. Never bothered to ask . . .

Before she turned the cash to the meth . . .

Before the abortions . . .

"Whore." Snorted. Felt like an elbow . . . "Whore." Hissed. Felt like a slap . . . "Whore." Ashamed, but not surprised. Bit her lip. Wished she was holding cold blue steel in her shaking hand . . .

"Cheap fucking slut." . . .

"Two-dollar crackwhore." . . .

Robbed.

Raped.

She'd wanted to go home a hundred times . . .

Wanted to go home . . .

or get high.

Wanted to get out of this dirty room . . .

The Life . . .

Wanted a tub of hot water and a hundred bars of soap . . .

She paid.

Cringed.

Prayed. A hundred times . . .

Put up with the cocks and the dealers . . . Let them take their greasy pictures . . . Drowned in their laughter . . .

And paid.

Worn thin and tossed around, she'd paid. Enough.

She'd wanted to go home a hundred times . . .

Her lips part. "I." Passed over her fangs. Came out dry. Alone. Out of other words. Out of grammar and room. And understanding.

Ionesco put a silver bullet in her left eye. Didn't smile. Didn't say a word. Didn't look at the scared-shitless losers huddled on the floor hoping they weren't next.

The door closed behind him. He turned southward.

Three lifeless blocks, stops for a moment. Back to the face of a grey building that hadn't served regular people in thirty years. Ionesco lit a smoke. Stood on a corner where grass didn't grow. Wondered if there was any place around here he could get some French fries and cole slaw.

Don't Look Back

Coming down from his last fix . . .

Dry as a bone . . . Chills, a hard river flood. Trying to think through the confusion . . .

The yoke. The lash. Spread-eagle mind trampling time.

Shaking. Crazy with what's gone. Missing humanity. His humanity. Missing it bad . . .

All starts with a John Lee Hooker song coming from an open second-story window. "Don't Look Back." No good. No good. Looking back. Poking and poking at what's inside. Even if it's buried deep. Almost lost

. . . almost.

But the dreams of living come. Break through rust and no relief. And that voice tells you, No!-No!-No! You can't go back. Not for minute. Not through THAT gate. Not ever. But those days of way back call. Call. And call . . . For a self disappeared. Call for you to come back . . . Way back . . .

At the glimpse of a man departed, just a simple man trying . . .

It felt so good. Breathing. Walking her home. Her smile glazing his eyes with sweet. The kiss . . .

She laughed. When the world slept. Sonny Rollins sax, sweet slow steps, verses above earth, climbing the stars, strolling . . . She was close. Blushing. Comfort . . . Paradise. Maggie in twilight. (Maggie, he whispers. In a hush. The breeze. Tints the air with her name. Maggie . . . Tints the air . . . turned inside out.) Never won . . . In a garden, outside the storm, with a dream . . .

That was before the madman. And the illness his wicked touch passed on. Before you broke down on that back road. And He came along . . .

The strange things . . . a fierce foam in the language of light . . .

It had been raining so hard . . .

Dragged back in a city window . . . a reflection. Bait.

John Lee and Van "The Man" testifying and the organ slow and filled with old plans never won. And you're looking in the window that can't say yes. Above spread shoulders in the mirror, a man with dreams . . . without that catalog of woe behind him . . . before the cauldron . . . not much in his pockets but what he hopes to gain . . .

First time in The City. Alive. The skies were tinted with blue. Way back. Streets carpeted with museums and shops of lively good and parades of honey and spirits still beating . . . Ivory towers. Paradise. The tongues of storytellers, flowers in their wallets, that didn't believe in the world's end. Sounds fresh as outlaws performing wild and free. All the people in the street, tickets to somewhere shining like sunshine. Streets leading to different countries that heal the suffering of every writer denied peace of mind with lilacs and rose-colored wine. Every surface muscular—marvelous muscles, poured out, nearby, loud. You could feel it living. Cozy and yours. All the eyes that won't be denied . . . First time alive. Way back . . .

He was happy. Protected, proud. Enthusiastic . . . no defects . . . Feeling how it could be . . .

Drifter. Once a young Irish rover. Traveling where the urge leads. Living ugly and tight. Always in need. Always so cold until the eruption of the dope. A prisoner. Motherless, no one to care for him. Watching got to go back . . . Watching ships and their angel light leave for feelings you can't find anymore.

The long nights longing, ready to explode. Running fingers through your hair. The burning howls. Screams. Fire. Living on your knees. The inferno with no lyrics.

He picks up his sorrow, tears himself from the foreign window of gazing in and way back. Tears himself from the ancient corner so full of his name when he walked in a golden age.

A narrow street. A narrow night. Across a parking lot. Not seen. Long lost the heart. Another lifetime . . . Leaning where free men meet. Eyes pointing at a hole of chaos. Hollow tricks waving, clucking tongues . . . rust in the idiot hours. Wild needs loose . . . The sinner . . . needs . . . pounding . . .

Take me—

Back . . .

On death row. Where rust dances in small rooms. Where gestures flutter and die.

Waiting, expanding to meet soon. Waiting (seething in an unmoving, bitter, to and fro) . . . Waiting for the hour.

Here it comes . . .

Here it comes. . .

The light—

To thine own self be . . .

Slumped in a shadow, carrying a torch.

True.

No exit. Way. Way. Way—Back. Somewhere else . . . No Hell of personal shadows. Back before hard, when you had wings. Back before the mourning sucked you dry . . . Back to gentle candlelight. Back before the miles of dreams got left out in the street, sad and pitiful, thrown out at closing time . . . out of hope on the last page . . .

OUTSIDE looking . . . . . . Distances, small motions humming. Being there. Hearing words said when the siren still had time. Seeing the longest day stride. The waltz, the silk transmission. At rest, warm and connected, in the web of truth. Midnight—the dark temper of the skyline unfiltered, after the slow leaving of tide and the moon raged and the words, dark and biting, unlocked farewell in one long howl . . . . . . IN—headlong—the black chamber, words (oceans—lions—volcanoes—terrible hard little weeds undying, ringing in the dead spots) at dreamspeed.

Don't look back—the thirst. The habit, the twist of the dark flame. Coming out of the woodwork . . .

Don't look back—the thirst, always searching, always waiting. Can never go back. Can't make it back . . . To much unreal made real . . .

A woman—a girl, night-blooming, in a black skirt. In a soft black skirt of musical wings held up like sweet, fresh sunbeams . . .

A step forward. And she comes round the corner. Breasts and miles of legs. Every inch all in colors and jewels. So young. So sweet. Her eyes—her eyes, just Her eyes were that first night. Her lips, soft as Her lips that first night. One tender, sweet kiss. Just one . . .

Tender kiss.

He stays pinned in the shadows. Her skirt flows. Her soul, good and playful and fluid, in the eyes of Leviathan. Inviting him. Perfume, playing with his nature. The dance. Her siren shoes headed toward sunrise. At the gate of the park. The garden free from the ancient snow . . . Ripe. So young. So ripe . . . Shining . . .

Your heart wide open. Your lips curl back, on the verge of a scream, an eternal groan. And your dehydrated, bark tongue slides over your fangs . . . Her neck snaps in your chattering—nibbling, THUNDERING fingers . . . The identity of your monster mouth around her gentle thrush weather. Kissing—I will, I will, sing, compose. Come to bed, I love you so. Veins a road wet, the sweet red dope flows, hot, a saxophone filling you with healing. Blood. The score. Survival. Blood familiar, curing the throbbing—the endless blind THUNDERING. That warm feeling takes you to a sweeter place . . . Healing—the glove of sun singing. Rapture—supreme, bigger magic drawn near. Today—love exists. Now!—love exists. Your long lost soul living for a moment—wide open, finally at home—in the golden age.

(In a blue slipstream with The Hook and Van Morrison looking back)

Long is the way and hard . . .

for Hubert Selby, Jr.

Abandon all hope . . . The Chain—raw/rusty/unrelenting . . . *Abandon all hope* . . . The Life . . . ***Abandon all hope ye who enter here.***
Cain eats Cain.

These hunger days when the bell tolls and tolls again. The emergency followed by the kiss. The blood offers light—Paradise. Heals broken dreams.

Frank. No fancy name in the after-life. For some, but not for him. Frank. Sometimes unwashed. Mostly unshaved. Smells like any street junkie. Looks like any street junkie. Unless you look in his eyes (giant blood-red irises, no sclera). Unless you look in his eyes . . . And they steal your soul.

Frank. Hunter, mouth full of dead soon. Outcast, spinning in broken, odd hours, and cheap whiskey—not that it does a thing . . . Wanderer . . .

. . . Endless night meandering—Fuck-it, that-a-way. Around a corner. Hard or just there. (All the things just there. Like any of it made any sense.) Two Tuesdays back, soaked by a 45-minute tiger rain he didn't even notice . . . Following the heat echoes of blood. Living hot blood. Bumping into wounded pride and songbird hands that will lie for a beer. Screening the human creatures for failure . . . Windows as mirrors, the moon full of hours and teeth, and smudged clouds, within them . . . Walking slow or fast, not exploring, not really. Just following the moving street, or fingers making knives from rotting pieces of prayer . . . This-a-way (dead end maggot tango under a ragged black skyline) or that (demons prowling the trash at midnight stricken by degenerate), happening upon ends to embrace . . .

One shot deals—no rehearsals . . .

Under the mule-gray city sky

—Moments with scared-shut eyes clamped tight so you don't see all the god-damn poison and the bastards pissing in the sea of love. Maybe you miss the stars, but it keeps out the dingy-infested-with-grungy, at least the part that doesn't involve smell.

—Scarecrow deathsongs of shoot—SHOOT! (All kinds of things flappin'.)

—On the bottom of the sea-saw, words as objects to fill endless hours of rrrrrrrrrrrrrrrrrrrrr.

—Questions empty can't resolve ... *Do you DARE* ... maps with long faces that no longer talk of the town ... and every orphan and brawler and cloud would rather be *anywhere* else.

—Hatred in acid gazes and ink.

Wandering (doin' time in evenings he can't postpone). Wandering in things he can not explain ... can ... not ... NOT.explain ...

Frank.

Outcast in a city of scars and infernos. A city with beasts and no sense. Shops and markets of HOPELESS, downhill (open black maw of razor machine teeth waiting) the only thing in any head. Asses and boredom, apprehension and flies and copycat sickness and boo-hoos that ripped up the stars for a spike of junk, and the smell of dead-end goodbyes(wounded, wounded, and wounded) ... and NAKED BLOOD. Shame in every front window. Every eye an enemy and a client.

Dirt.

Shit.

death

Plague. Mindfuck rot eye to ear to written hand—

Headline: **HATE ON THE BRINK**

Headline: **PORNO RICHES**

Headline: **GRACE WRECKED - IRREVERSIBLE**

—to fill the negative space ...

The Game, having blown sanity to shit with staccato interruptions of excess and shattering glass, assaults sad doors filled with blistered birds, putrid and naked.

... constant ceremonies of misery on the dark end of the street ...

Good gone-gone-gone-gone-gone, those days and their fools, gone out. Never to come back. The nail, rusted, fallen from the Palm of

Paradise is a key. Oblivion the Grimscribe, seals the black well coffin with it.

Frank. Outcast of The City's most powerful clan, energy and overpowering edge and tough as anything that walks, the Lions of Night. Cast him out—rapidly aside—when he lowered himself and fed on a street whore with tainted blood. Put a bounty on his head for hunting; only the female members of the pride were allowed to hunt. The males could pick a target, but it was the role of the females to cut it out and bring it to the table.

A life of broken rules followed by an after-life of breaking rules . . .

One night in The—worn to crappy—Sentinel (even the clientele looked torpedoed by too many sunsets) he saw her. (Waiting for word or vistas or any flourish she liked or stumbled into.) Her, eyes and uncovered skin, sitting there, smoking, laughing softly. In that dress; her shoulders nearly bare, her neck, a soft calm sea of whiteness inviting him. Frank wanted her to laugh quietly in his ear. Wanted to go on a ride, letting her sweet breath drive him to someplace without a crying jukebox and sad Happy Hours watered down with ice and tears.

She had great legs and nice tits, but he didn't care about the package these days. Not much anyway. But it didn't hurt. A little something to look at that hit the eyes nicely didn't hurt at all.

The place smelled bad. Insecticide and piss. Old dreams and spilled beer. Hands and dicks and asses gone stale. Eyes on the Grand Tour of Living Hell . . . Half of the creatures in here dead but for the hanging or the no cheer tales and edges of the straight razor . . .

Glassy eyes promising it was the TRUTH to the empty stool at his weary elbow . . .

"God-damn shitfire," over nothing . . .

Needy-Needy telling 10-hour-day-at-slave-wages how she couldn't buy her way out of eternity with a losing Lotto ticket, but she tried, Jesus she really put her ass into it, but the sit-around-lazyass-fuck wasn't buying . . . Celebrating sinking the eight ball, Pickpocketed Wits with holes in his directions—bottle back, thinks it's a lot tougher to get to the top of the anthill these days . . .

One insatiable, backdoor eye glued to the ladies room door, a Hardass Deadbeat who couldn't sit anywhere without one eye on the exit . . .

Needle leaves the grooves of "Should've Been a Cowboy" and finds "Mamas, Don't Let Your Babies Grow Up to Be Cowboys."

"Fuck. Cockersucker's a baboon." Denied (even one small miracle), muttering to the monkey on her back . . .

Greenback passport revoked, Running-in-place at the EXIT. At least his dream, spare-bordering-on-skeletal-and-ragged as it is, is still tied to the end of his leash . . .

Frank remembers a movie, back in the old life, a movie filled with BLACK EYES AND SPLIT LIPS AND ASSHOLES SHARP AS KNIVES THAT SHOT ON SIGHT AND BAD THINGS AND BAD THINGS AND GLARING STREETS OF PANIC AND GARBAGE SCRAPING FOR TIME AND SPACE AND NOTHING IS NEW AND FISTS AND BLANK WALLS shakes his head.

Sat tight. A shadow in the shadows in the corner, fenced in by the bastards and drunks and elaborate plans shot to hell and little drops of gossip. Watching. Waiting to procure. Frank, ready to sail, sat there fingering his ice in circles around the rim of his glass of whiskey, thinking she didn't look like one of the bar strays that would suck you off after two or three drinks, but one never knows. She was soft—her erotic openly winking GO, not one of the moth-eaten pleasures sealed in something tight that looked like they were salvaged from things that didn't last long as someone thought they would.

The sun would come soon. He could smell it.

And he could smell her. Under the corrupting swirl of the cheap booze, the blood in her veins would fit his need like a custom fit glove.

She. No angel. He. No demon. Two things of the squalor, dreams between them.

Me and . . . Me and . . . Me and . . . ME. Her blood.

The sun would come soon.

Fuck *their* rules.

It was there—*right fucking there*, sitting there smiling—and he was willing to bet it was willing. That's all that mattered. That and The Need.

How the hell would they even know? There wasn't another blood drinker in the joint. He hadn't seen one since . . .

Didn't want to wait. Fuck walking the line. It's late and time won't leave him alone.

The sun would come soon . . .

Day's glow soon to be in the air, burning . . .

Take her and run.

Fuck control.

And he did. Did the math, promiscuous and two belts passed a little drunk. Walked over, "Frank." (She turns, gets caught in his eyes.) "Arlene." "Want?" "A lot of things, honey," and reined her in. Took her to his cheap one room. Poured her room temperature whiskey (didn't have an ice cube or a clean glass). Put his hand on her thigh. Kissed her on the mouth. She kissed him back—hard, she had a need too. Had half of her blouse unbuttoned and her hand of moments to come on the inside of his thigh.

Dripping, stunning, in any other circumstance, dangerous: "What do you want, baby?" Brushed him like opium and luck.

He showed her the deep end. The low vibration of an animal noise, not even a "This won't hurt a bit." Showed her where gestures and obsession end.

Trembling tender flesh—hot to touch—sweet to taste. Not even a scream in reply.

Touched, the moment. LUST. The connection—the score-the score-the score-drop by drop. Resuscitation. Drank her dry. Not even a "Farewell, My Sweet."

Frank can hear the emphatic shadowbirds rattle as warm changes the grave thing in his arms.

Gone her X-rated meow.

A full doze of her blood, the overflow, the old language—*anything!anything!FUCKING anything!*—now new, metastasized, takes him over the horizon. Momentarily breathless/warm going hot/going right straight to hot. Sensation—fast. Liqueur. Essence—FASTER—FASTER. Dope. UNCUT. Colors, lizard-eye diadems—living forest fires delivered, blooming, unglued and leaking with tidal cosmic poetry . . . *peaking* . . . LOVE! Love-UNLOCKED. SPLASHED—Expanding, no slow and gentle. All filters shut off. Limits fucked out of existence. HOT-hot-hot/sliding/spinning, taken over—no why/NO fucking WHY. Hot, high as a cliff. OWN crooning, shrieking, vibrating! POWER—pure psychopath cutting the form and fireworks of EVERYTHING INTO MINE. Hero. GOD. LIFE. WILD AS FUCKING. PURE AS THOUGHTLESS JOYOUS

REVOLUTIONARY FUCKING. Nova-wild soul summer—rattling blind orgasm(newly-born)—*YEAH!* . . . sweet fog, vast and lush and open, wide open . . .

Then cool. Post-burn, a mellow madness. Oasis. No corners. No sea of time. Drifting in Mercy—the lonely hunger shed like dried skin/the change—past as future, future as childhood blessed. No wounded surfaces in this space . . .

. . . ceaseless—*the dream within the dream* . . . Floating on the brink . . .

Down in the flood, a season in peak Right Time. A new lifetime. Tart and spangled and *sweet* and incandescent. Every cell massaged, oozing the crackling blood-junk. Enough deepfire seed to take him to the next sundown.

His eyes closed to games to play, Arlene, dead in his arms . . . In his arms. Bled out. Nothing. Cooling and he's holding her, Madonna and child. Not a word between them.

Two errant drops of cold blood on her breast. Two holes, thanks-giving and pain, in her neck.

Blood-junkie. Perception gorged on hope . . . The Call . . .

AND THE AFTER . . . Deflated . . .

The sky goes down.

The river dries . . . the hunger, parasite, flickers, builds in slow-motion.

The animal rises up—screams.

Frank wakes from his blood-daze. Casually rolls her off his lap. A stranger, a river crossed. Drops—deposits—her on the floor. Cast off like he did in his old life when he was done with the evening paper—something for the maid to clean up.

Stands. After a dumb moment, cold blood rushing from his head, remembers to pull up his pants so he won't trip . . . Steps over the un-living doll, blood-partner, broken. Walks to the dresser. In silence he wipes his mouth with his sleeve. Lights a smoke . . .

Pours what's left of her half-downed whiskey back into the bottle . . .

Wait . . .

Trapped in the rat cage with the filthy broken thing that's no use to him anymore. Gone clearlight—lexicon—Now—HERE—*aflame The REAL LIFE!*

WAIT . . .

Pacing. Doin' coarse slow-time the hard way. Staying away from the window and its nasty stain of disturbing light . . . Frank's got two hours until the sun bleeds out. He sits with his feet up, heels resting in her cleavage, listening for the hiss of its last breath . . .

wait

Almost laughs when he can't remember her name . . .
Doin' time.
The air is full of slowly.

Wait . . .

Struck. And wrong.
No transition . . .
The lungs of the campaign, over and cold, find no air to knit into birds of dream.
Picks at a layer . . . hard. withered exits . . .
Reason sucks on the scar for shabby scraps that hang like amputated meaning . . .
The clock, cold, uncaring—pockets full of oblivion, ticking past what happened . . .
The last drop of sun spilled.
Frank's hand finds the door. Arrival on the other side. He'd approach it whatever the rules. Turns the knob. Uncontrollable hungry children filled with loud need, his thoughts race ahead—*Hours shaking shadows from their troubles—injured chapels—eyes with dusty tongues—catching the terrible black poetry that dribbled from windows . . . blood.soon. Blood.*

His first step into night a sentence ... Perhaps the next chapter will end in a scream?

Perhaps not.

(Mott the Hoople "All the Young Dudes")

huddled in rags
in a Kingsport alley . . .

(for Julia)

The ebb and flow of lips twisted by gin . . .

Wounded tongues . . . Drifting, whispering . . . Needing more . . .

Fingers snarling with lust . . .

No hiding places . . .

Crying things that cannot sleep . . .

Mouths haunted by vice . . .

Ships that glide on currents of blood . . .

A drunken musician swallows a gutter of degenerate urges. Its sunless silence severs the prayers from his open mouth . . .

There are no hiding places . . .

The scent of pleasures burning . . .

In their bridal chambers, new corpses lie bent by the dirty kisses of blackness . . .

There are no hiding places . . .

The sea is rising . . .

Kingsport's dark sky answers no questions . . . Its frozen breast of rust is the flag of the bleak . . . Swollen beaks from the rim of death, drape change over the scarecrow-husks hiding in the sludge of madness . . . Wind, scraped with ghost static, delivers rodent eternities that leak blackened colors . . .

Kingsport and all its voiceless boundaries of rain and scaffolds of assassin-shadows are mad things. Its winter mouths—nests of black-black-black, cold as the ice of oblivion-eroded dead mother poems—visit the throats of children, leave the smell of war and lies in the engulfing dark . . .

She, Eva, a slight few named her, O (for Object) to the (many) others who used her and cast her out, sleeps outside poison-clad doorways. The black and white and gray and sickgreen world blurs by—Flicker—Journey to The End . . . She, bitten by traitors and knives—and unwholesome inventings, remains . . .

Cold.

alone

Slight. Worn thin, barely frail. A scar surrounded by cracked, empty bottles and unusable things and the venereal residue of desiccated words . . . and crawling maggots . . .

The graininess here responds to nothing . . . The arsenal of faces, carnival monsters with siren-bullhorn throats erupt—Cough—Wail—Belch and bluster—Call out for proof, but their hands are empty.

And their eyes, bound to THAT darkness as surely as the constrained hands of the prisoner are tied to the jabbering teeth of punishment, rake and plea at the Door of No.

Their puppet mouths (all little town possibilities abandoned to the NOT-latticed mire of some black bog-hole of not getting up again) move, repeating the same worn down phrases of babble, and stretch across the cold, wide back of irreversible consequence . . .

Disenchantment squatted here last year before drowning in a thunder of thorny last words . . . Eva lies in its echo. Raven-shadows, chilled by the wind, offer no pillow, no murmuring crumbs . . . She pulls her cluster of soiled rags tighter. Behind closed eyes, her mind, rooted in things vanished, searches for a prayer, finds nothing scrawled in the wounds.

Time is a bitter stain. Zero a rite, a massacre that has no end . . . it echoes, and gropes its victims, scatters morals, suffocates tomorrows . . . It would laugh if it cared, if it had a voice . . .

Nothing here moves far from the sanatorium hourglass that spills its dim hysteria on the street corner. Nothing crawls very far from the sorrow of blackened fingertips the turbulent waves swallows . . .

Eva has not moved. She opens her ash-burdened mouth and her tongue makes all the gestures of a stone. In harmony with her voiceless nightmare, Night's field of silence drones on . . .

She remembers the green lights and the ceiling of balloons and the warm, soft girls—they kissed, protected her, carved hills of snow and fire and bridged the waters of shame with sweet-scented birds of Spring. But that time did not last. They too were taken from her . . .

Taken to the beds and tables of the ugly-hearted Corpse Men—put under (and inside) bulbous bellies . . .

It's all teeth. Hammering their graveyard plans. Twisting, pounding, tearing . . . Chewing. Moving in the zig-zag narrow streets, destroying everything between the windswept steeples, drawing even memories to the Forest of Dismembering.

TEETH wild as flapping galaxies. A great wind of iron teeth to tear and bend and pull down the stars . . .

The battering teeth of the SEA—articulated, stretching its sour disaster over the places men ruffle with maps and disregard . . .

But she has not forgotten . . . naked and abandoned, impaled by merciless violence and disaster, Eva lingers, thin fingers trembling. They cannot contain the wisp of hope she has tried to keep safe . . .

. . . tried . . .

Slowly circling a sleep she knows will be filled masks of unmentionable design, and dust, dire dreams of corrosive festivals under battered skies, and things—scratched by the grasp of the leering Dog Star . . . and roaring fire and erupted from phantom nests hidden beneath the waves. She shutters . . .

Here in Kingsport, under archaic gables, in sight of the churchyard of the Great White Church, in the mass of this condemning, inhuman blackness, she, innocence broken, worn by leather tongues, hides from the wolves of ice and murder . . .

Hides in the shadows and rags, hoping . . .

Hoping for the ways of flame-fire sunrise, as if she could swim away from the pain that burns and shatters.

On her knees. The battered, black gates to tears open . . . Far from the brine-rotted wharf she's forced to work. Far from the reek of fishy-thing and the coarse braids of defeated men who bargain away their poison hallucinations in Kingsport's worst bars, elbow to elbow with hothouse madness, those who pull back their lips and burning in whiskey-fire, try, if they can swallow enough, to forget the baleful upsurge of things harnessed to the bitter deeps they have been tainted by . . .

On her knees . . . Always pinned down. On her knees, a small, red-eyed fact in the crosshairs of malice, sighted by things with dark dreams. Dreams that cause the sea to lurch and roil. Shivering, tremulous things that carry the stench of water-logged bondage . . .

On her knees. The descent . . .

No, Dear God, help me, swells in her. There is no room in her margins, no room for the devices of Christ-light in her fear-laced deeps . . .

Even here, in this alley of dyed, shifting blackness, the cold sea's contorted waves lick her . . .

Wooden, rigid. Transfixed.

Caught.

The landslide of summits . . .

She tilts her head back . . .

Aeons of silent blackness yawn . . .

Landscape ends . . .

There is a sound, a defect externalized. A disfigured croak of mad laughter, an enemy's narrative. Its wanting squall is an act of war. It seizes her heart.

A draft of its carrion technique leaks out. Its grey-rumble/ghost-gait scent, stolen from a BLACKnova, ambushes her blood.

Hand to mouth to push the coming lurker's black wings to other events, she tries to backtrack, but there is no tight corner this vulgar Babel-trellis of teeth cannot inspect . . .

Afraid to look . . . more afraid not to, she opens her eyes . . .

This alley is a tomb.

At its mouth the street is The Pit itself . . .

In the beaststripe-tinted light of midnight the lurid Shadow Thing comes . . . Wet . . . Creaking with spite and intersections, It—some wild part of it shimmering—dips to erase . . .

The mouth of future closes . . .

No one is spared.

. . . Little but the noise of the moon survives.

(after MorganScorpion's reading of H. P. Lovecraft's "The Festival")

Dead Ends and Empties

Sittin' in the Uncle Jack Hotel. Good a place as any, they don't let the weather in here, and they don't make you check yesterday at the door. I've been to this garden party more times than I've pissed, but no one remembers me . . .

No one in this joint cares who wept.

Whiskey. Dark wildfire whiskey. And a .44. Loaded. Stories get stuck. Eat me outta fortunes. Push. And push. And fucking push, like there's no other place for the shit to go. The demon yearnings. Fast fucking things clawin' ME-ME-ME-NOW . . . Never a quiet minute. Shit. Balance my ass. Gone, all gone. Down the fucking drain. In some blackness too monstrous to bear.

Left. Right. No running from it. I'm fucking running in place. More whiskey—I need it. Helps me keep away the eyes . . . Bad eyes messing with all my plans. Evil eyes. Uncomfortable eyes behind the whiskey.

She was twenty-one. She was looking. Lookin' for fun, 1001 nights of free. Followed me to it. Rode it hard. Both of us. All the way down. Lumps and bumps and wild days blowing. Nights, damned nights, in love with the wild night. Running till we fell or stood still. Took everything, words, ghosts, doors, anything that was in front of us. Pushed it. Pulled it. Stole right outta its mouth. Tore the feathers right outta noon. Every spot under the moon was our dance floor. Something walked by us, turned up its collar and quickened its step, we showed it cold blowing.

Gin joints, sitting next to hard old men who mixed their whiskey with whiskey. Gorged on coffee until we were awake enough to gorge ourselves with misbehavior and someone else's misfortune. Whatever, wherever whim touched . . .

If we stayed in like little birds afraid of the shape of the storm's truth, we sliced heartbreak with spit and lips of fire. Didn't try to walk with crutches. Hell we had whiskey that never took a day off. Big bottles, half pints, fifths, half empties, day or night we paid off tomorrow with loud, drunken who gives a shit.

Played make believe when we were sober enough to stand.

We ate when we got hungry. Drank—hell, we were always parched. Fucked when our solo came in contact with arms or lips or eyes or light or sugar, or if an elbow or knee whispered, even if we couldn't slip out of our socks. If the heat hit an edge we were at it. Never found an answer in it, never looked for one, but we didn't care, we never gave a rat-shit about speed limits. Jam the rules. This was *our opera.*

Ashes and alphabets and circles as bread, as sky, we made fate, spilled it quick. Poured salt over it to keep it quiet. Up the hill, down the hill, carrying secrets and clouds. Did it all. We were not mice on strings.

When the load had picked our pockets clean we liberated whatever we wanted. Whatever would get us over the next border. Had no plans. Plenty of nightmares. They hit us like a cold shot.

Never fucked ourselves on cocaine or pissed away a damn thing with beer. Anointed the insatiable with whiskey. Drowned evening and horizons twice a day. Told Death to piss off.

She stood right there, in his face. A tired old man. Tired old clothes. Slept in, pissed in. The old fart couldn't get in Low Rent's Tiki Bar with two million bucks and a note from God. Told him to fuck off and hand over the bottle. And if he had any silver in those raggy pockets, fork it over. "Make it fast, Asshole. Like now."

He laughed. Opened those scarred grey lips, showed her bare, petrified razor-stumps of black teeth and laughed, and gave her the finger. Muttered, "Time to go home."

Pointed that twisted, poison wire-finger at her like it was a weapon. And it was. She withered right there. Just fucking up and collapsed. Like someone stuck a straw in her head and sucked hard. Looked like someone dropped a stocking. A ripped rag. Peeled, discarded garbage.

Sure as fuck I was drunk, but it couldn't have taken more than a few goddamned seconds. Hair and skin and a pile of bones in that withered sack on the dreary ground.

That's it.

My eyes glued in disbelief to the thing. That . . . useta be Her.

All the air and shit and energy sucked right outta me. Just hanging there, a scarecrow nailed to shocked.

And he started a howlin'. Like some mad-ass demon thing right outta Hell. Laughed till he started to cough. Pointed at that skin-bag of bones and from his tunnel-mouth of circles and primitive hours hissing, yelled, "No-no-no, FUCK YOU! Shoulda watched that *cunt-mouth*. Fuck with me."

Then he eyeballed me. Cold. Fucking cold. Hard as murder. "I'm tired of you street-shits. Run home, Little Piss-boy. Run fast . . . Or." And he laughed his black-fire croak of dust and skeletons again.

Each black crow-thing that sat in the dead tree behind him slashed a broad noise in harmony with his thunder-croak.

Hit me like bricks.

Boxed me in. My feet—black boots, not ruby slippers, trapped, no way home. Shadows whirled around me, autumn leaves in iron-jawed wind, my legs rubber that won't blink.

"GO!"

Somehow I did.

Fast and picking up speed. Around hard corners soiled by languages I didn't understand.

Home.

The *How* for other minds to understand.

. . . ALONE.

Stood there and faced it. No God, but there was my confession.

All alone.

I can go an hour or three without a shot. But alone? Alone is more disturbing than any empty. Take my money. Make me take a bath . . . Pull me from the gutter if you have to . . .

No she at my elbow. No one in my face. No hand handing me the bottle, pouring another shot. No body, soft and hot and full of honey and feathers and scars, to acquaint my suffering with.

Alone. The foreignness of it. It's like a black eye you can't overlook.

Wounded and . . . Alone, some fucking banquet for the damned.

The bottle with as much intensity as I can push into it. Mixing my whiskey with whiskey. Tumbling to the blackout . . .

Woke up crying.

The trouble screaming, hot with stories forged in menace.

And not a penny to buy my way out.

Then as NOW echoing. Torturing. Here for me, its meal.

Alone. Contents burned.

On my deathbed, the Devil summarizing the pages of the plague. Whispers, "Destiny."

And I reach for the bottle of blindness. Right hand, whiskey, the last of my last fifth. Left, doesn't want to wait for the drowning, holds the .44. Loaded.

A pair of her old jeans, a faded blue pool, dropped where she pulled them off the last time we . . .

were together

Forever curves around my sharp empty blank . . .

. . . She was an explorer, some days I was her sail, some nights her anchor . . . Our flock of emotions and notions turned on its head if I needed, if she needed . . .

Just to inject one more "Sweetheart." in this black crop of slow pain . . .

We were coyotes, distorted, restless, punching needles in night to make it bleed so we could live to the next whatever happened. We made our own everything. Tried to.

Good luck? Opportunity? Fuck. It's about WANT. Wanting the experience to quiet the dead seas storming in the soul's sub-basement. Wanting to stop the bum-bum/bum-bum/tap-tap/fe-fi-fo storm-bottom noise in This Trap. Use whatever you come upon before it uses me. Slap the no no outta it before it spits more noise and clouds all the windows with broken gargoyles shitting out earth-quakes and disappointment.

Didn't know then . . .

Didn't know . . .

The kiss of the empty bottle.

I can't do dry.

Not without her.

Awake is too busy with hard and sticks and barren meadows of mute dust, a strange world of brutes.

And I'm dry.

Blathering sweating loser words and naked spit and the hard-slap dead-black forecast and the fanatic rushes and rises. Pushes. Pushes.

Strapped to the jolts. I'm losing my mind . . .

Going through Hell. God-damn-motherfuckin' Hell. Brokedown-fucking-can't move-or-think-god damn-lost and all I want is That Way again. Like it's too much to ask. If there was someone to fucking ask. Ain't. God-damn-shit. No one. Ain't right. The black fucking death, you're OK, just being, maybe dreaming, then BAM-BAM-BAM!BANG!POW! Fucked. Totally lights out black and nothing. Less than shit, less than garbage. Not even a pile. A nothing. Zero. Void. Shit. And some motherfucker thinks it's funny you ain't got a drop to pour over the dry. Some half-remembered shit-ass voice of mom-words or pastor-words, *long is the way and dark*—FUCK YOU! You weren't dead. You weren't there.then alone. What do you know? Shit. Don't know shit about shit. Don't know shit about shaking hands and the howling hole in the center of your skull—that barren DRY . . .

And I'm dry . . .

Fucking drowning dry.

Fifth. Half downed by my tenement dreams, half sucked up by memories crammed with immediacy, cheap, deranged demons didn't share. Fucks don't care who brought it to the party. Don't care if anyone else lives or dies. Long as they got theirs.

. . . And there's that dumb-ass bear I won for her. Owns the whole god-damn corner of the room. Blue Teddie, soft and cuddly, "I could eat you all up." This gets you everything in her eyes . . .

Her eyes. Sparkling like stars.

HER. The storm-wind cry in the desert.

Maybe she was some cold, murderous bitch, but she was mine. Life/love/partner, all mine. Night and day, stuck with me. Hard times and no times. Flat or fat, MINE. We rode through every sunset they threw at us. Every god-damn fuckin' one. Even when we didn't have a car or a horse or sneakers—me and her. And that wasted old, laughing son-of-a-bitch took mine.

He's gonna bend down and kiss my ass then I'm gonna put a few in his skull. Right between those black fucked-up eyes . . .

I can find the street. Find his fucking corner of hell.

After I find a drink . . .

Another couple of belts and I'm gonna show that assbag he drew a real bad one. Thinks he's mean. Gonna be Show and Tell. Twelve bad things and bones. Birthday and sun revoked for his ass.

A pint to work on while my feet disturb the pavement. A pint to bring on full-scale BADASS . . .

After this last corner . . .

When I put the arsenal up his ass we'll see who's laughing . . .

One more turn or two . . .

He sits under that dead tree on that corner of madness by that shitty-little bleak park. Sits there like it's his old front porch and he talks to those black crow-things like they was old buddies. Does little tricks with his bony, bent fingers and the shadows jump around like puppies. Never a breeze or wind on that corner. Like he won't allow it. Like he's King Shit. Fuck that.

I know death too. Passed it out like it was candy. And if they didn't eat it when I plated it up, I stuffed it down their throats.

Six nights . . .

Alone.

Crying. A slave to loneliness . . . falling . . .

One more swig.

One more critical swig . . .

Got my gun out. Loaded. Six bullets to swim in his summer. Six bullets tattooed with my grief screaming for something dead and soft to lie down on.

One winter eye open, he's napping on his bench. A baby in its cradle.

Birthday revoked . . .

"Motherfucker."

(Tom Waits *Bone Machine*)

Sharp Fangs + Blood = Murder

for Bob Price

Blasphemies.

A beast that rose out of the sea of Hell, or nightmare and darkness . . .

They only come out at night. That's what they say, while watching for swooping bullets or the anger on the other side of the door to evolve. They only come out at night. Come and leave

BLOOD.

Then pain. Sometimes with

and more again.

Most times.

Sure there's tears. And empty hands—some knotted by anger. And the spectrum of pain is wide—galaxy wide, limited only by the fear-lessons of bibles or imaginations . . . or simple pleas.

No deserts. No abysses. No barren, dead yard of hard still nothing. Pain is not an empty place. It's a walk of war, survival in a greedy place, teeth and hands that must hold and conquer the biography and sky and the ghosts that walk in the cities behind eyes. Soul that can not bond with another living thing that must possess the air and hills and even simple the humiliations, every old house and bone, every page of destiny won or lost, every fulmination of lust, each and every slice of bread and eulogy.

In their pain they say,

"They only come out at night . . .

and leave

blood."

An old woman. Tears fall into it. Hands run over it. Prayers seek what lies beyond.

Blood.

The child. Eyes filled with old. Voice that would stretch out all the way to eternity were it not trapped in the dry blackness of its own throat.

Blood.

Interrupting a moment of fabulous little changes, a moment of remembrance—the rise and fall of "I love you," with an act of malice.

Blood.

A tideless sea blooming on the lifeless body.

Blood.

Joins them all.

Blood.

Answer . . .

or

end.

Bobby. Whiskey in hand. Eyes reaching for something that ain't out the window. But he's looking anyway—

Broken hearts.

Badlands.

Assholes.

Sleaze bags.

Skeletons—out of wonder and foresight, and living among guerrilla rats that have the power to chew on the sun itself, whacked and frightened, divorced from luck, lost in the back and forth of sadness. Their sanity at risk.

Sin, boxes wrought with danger, and FEAR.

Glory days up and turned unhappy, or worse. A chorus, on their knees—whispering to absent God for honey, one sweet drop of wild honey—that borrowed dreams of happier days.

Half the world, the one that could afford one or steal one, has a gun under their pillow.

Poor. Dirt farmer poor caged in a cold cigarette-ash gray tomb of stone and steel and the bones of hope, waiting for more shit to come and assassinate chance with, "You can't."

Just plain fucked.

And no one gives a damn.

On this street of no secrets and around the corner complications that lead to zero there's no place to hide.

Murder.

Everywhere you look.

In every word and rushed sound that scratches its way to your ears.

Old cop turns from the body under Bobby's window, lights a smoke. Shrugs. "Everywhere . . . *Just like shit.*"

SIN

& ashes.

Bobby's got a gun. Not a scar on it. And blood in his eyes.

Got hands flat outta tender. Hands filled with tragic. And a belly full of anger, a sea of blood-rage turning cold.

Got a gun that never ever answered a question with tender.

Gonna finish this drink and step outside. Gonna see The Thing no one wants to see. Gonna deal with it out on the killing floor.

They only come out at night.

Come fangs bared—no thing of grace and beauty like in the movies. The Dark Breed ready to tear out throats; elderly; young; man; woman; infant; street girl or someone's sister; in a suit, or out of choices. Come and drink

blood.

Another murdered woman-child outside his window.

Last month it was his sister.

Face down. Lying there.

Throat savaged.

Never made it to the movie.

Lying there.

Not bright anymore.

Discarded. So much trash.

Downs the last slug.

Hand twitches.

Looks at the gun as if it were a mirror. *The air is thinner. Something in the shadows at the end of day barks. There's no argument to be settled with words in this universe. No lies. There's tears and cold and the rattle of pain and the hunt . . . Face to face, fangs and bullets . . . and flames crawling . . . bleeding . . . The wounds . . . The howling . . .*

This one was someone's sister too. Or daughter. Or someday, perhaps, mother . . .

Discarded.

. . . never . . . *took a stab at sailing*

. . . tried it again
. . . a summer to write things down
. . . magic wedding hearts beating, whispering . . .

One last look out the window at the killing floor.

The street buzzing dims.

The coroner's bus pulls away.

Who do you call?

"Who do you call to fucking fix *this?*"

There's no Rod Serling the devil reaps what it's sown, no Stephen King everyman hero to blot this stain and save the day.

And John Wayne is dead. DEAD.

Bobby's last warm tear is a scream.

He don't know if it can die, if bullets will put it down.

But he's gonna find out.

Not spending one more night sitting here.

Not downing another drop.

Not one more bent elbow bottle back and go.

Gonna walk out the door into the brutal air, walk till he finds it.

He's not bringing pretty words. No poetics. No civilized exchange. Not going to say a word. No, "Hey." Not even, "Why?" Plain speaking, uncomplicated sledgehammer bullets (won't mumble, won't let it slide— no GO TO HELL or FUCK YOU) will talk for him in cold black words.

His gunmetal black verdict loaded with silent won't look in its eyes for truth or fear. Things are way passed anything that simple.

Shoot it till it falls. Until the gun's empty, had its say.

Gonna spit in its blood. If it has any of its own.

Gonna show it the other side of murder. The terrifying part of Forever.

Gonna . . .

If it takes all night.

(U2 "Bullet the Blue Sky")

Saint Nicholas Hall

for Michael Cisco—
who once showed me a platform that led to dark, nameless places

The old life.

His.

Old life.

No 2 cents for an opinion . . . or an answer.

life

Ain't no ballet . . .

Ain't holy . . .

The sun grows weak. In a locked room he takes off his mask, whispers, "prisoner, chances zero." Dangerous throws failure into the waltz.

His life.

Stolen.

Numb. Scrambled. The torture of no someday soon.

No place to hide.

The breath of Aldebaran howls its ashcan autumnal hunger . . . The weeks around him taste wrong. His oracle flunks the test, swallows the sharp poison . . . Knees that can't escape the killing floor. Mouth punches out "I exist!" Bedlam laughs . . . Winter with no soul. He pleads for fire, or any arsenal of magic words. Looks over his shoulder—pleading, taking every short cut to distance I from the feats of HARM.

A dry afternoon. Narrow streets. Depravity thrives, drains another expedition dry as it shits out a new nightmare. Fat violence slides, rattles. Smashes things till they're raw. Decides it's not him, if it even noticed him in the twisted shade of the dying tree. Rides off, its lance ready for meat . . .

Pushed by a blaze of rust and crippled autumn words he leaves the sun behind . . . Before he leaves There and its Then to its tired stars, he lays his tears (with the horn and the lie) in winter's tomb and burns his maps of delusion.

Shadows accrue, cover him.

The Sparrow Gates close . . .

Three weeks with the riders in The Abyss. He watches the frail, torn and drained, fail. Sees the light flushed from sockets. Watches them kneel, nudge, lose their breath in the silence. Watches the numb scavengers pick at them. For watches or shoes or ribbons . . . A small girl with thin arms and thinner, awkward legs dug through the grave pockets looking for coins or shiny objects or jewels. Hoping, he thought, she'd have something of worth when they arrived in the New Place.

Having made it through decay, all nine layers of distance (and having slept through the Red Cosmos—alone this time), he came off the Death Ship. Most in the hole didn't, they, struggling with the weight of the temptations, fell victim to the Black Shapes.

Shadows spread. From the depths of bitterness evil imaginations create the lurid in gloomy rooms . . . Night is a formless ebony border, part genius, part demon, part dead weight, it takes the weak into its sable chamber . . . The docks where filth prowls. No moon. The damp, hard meadow of the refugee, where the exiled, weeping for limbs and brides (or lovers) lost, come in under cover of mist and oft repeated prayers . . . Running, no suggestions or service, just short words—GO, spat hard as any darkness.

And they do—to hide, or to deal with their mysteries and troubles . . . Running in to the streets of The Maze, all fires and shapes and storms and cold nights dotted in moaning, offering no promises or hope . . . Running (a few—utterly terrorized, wheezing), reeling—dizzy, afraid, the street is a wolf . . . The cruel men with rifles smoking, laughing . . .

Wide open this aftermath between formerly and new sky. Different walks under these streetlamps where the light vanishes. Newborn to this brambled dark. Alone in his black glasses and shaved head. A great black coat covered him. He'd had a hat. But traded it for bread on the 10th day of the voyage. He'd had a cape and a walking stick. But he traded them for a bottle. He emptied the bottle—drank it dry—then, bound in dimensions of fatigue, he cried.

He carried mysteries in his pockets (two in each pocket). And a gun.

And the page torn from a book. One lone page, a yoke with its vague quivering words of shadows and doorways.

And he had two scars. The outward scar, an old one, the one that had taken an eye, had healed. The one in his heart, the one no one could see, had nearly killed him. More than once these last months.

He came here to The New City following The Laugh, pursuing the fire it spread. For three years he'd tracked it. There were those who spoke to him, some firmly, saying he did little other than chase his own tail, or called him a madman and all he would find at the end of the maze was himself, alone in the dark.

Three years of his life chasing it. Pushing other things, the things of friendship and life, aside, he moved further toward the edge.

Before—THEN . . . There was a morning of bells. In plain brown shoes she stood on the path of their small house in her travel coat with her travel bag . . . She wore a brown hat, held a brown package tied with brown twine. No flower adorned her buttonhole.

Tears blemished her dark make up.

He ran to her. Her breath was cool, filled not with its former joys.

Through tears she said, "Nathaniel, the shadows and stains of your interrogations have found my heart. As I tumbled through the chests and chairs of our abode I found myself barefoot in the adders of your madness, I found myself lost to the purpose of ghostly stars . . . They call . . . And I must go."

Victoria cried as she held him, and then she left him—it was winter; it was a divorce, even if they were not married on parchment.

No time for lies . . .

No time for For God's Sake . . .

"For God's sake," his last muttered words she did not hear when the trolley lost present time in the dented, rotting distance . . .

From Border to Meridian and he still was no closer. No reasoning with the fugitive dagger songs in his palms and the unfaithful utterances of shattered harmonies. And Victoria had left him.

Gone.

Carried off.

Left him no place to escape to . . .

Left him alone . . .

The blind busker on the subway platform was playing "Black Is the Color of My True Love's Hair." Could he see? Was he a servant of The Laugh?

His old life. His love. Some whispered, Rest In Peace.

But there was no peace.

Just alone. ALONE . . . (excluded) . . . (limited by anxiety) . . . With his mysteries. And the gun. And a picture of Victoria in an old locket, tucked in a threadbare velvet bag. And the scars his memories picked at, unfolded, seized, leaned into, and then folded, never the same way twice.

He came up the worn and soiled stairs from the transit under-world

      and quickly passed spasm signs pasted over survival codes

      and sentences of diseased rumor

      and the indulges of fragmented stories

      and the solitary solos of motherfucker-crazy shitty little lives

      filling the high, massive tombstone walls of grey,

      Rapidly turning corner and

      corner

      without surveying the discolored and the dust

      until the desolate galleries

      and lanes ornamented with broken oars spilled in dreams of nothingness-wide-open

      gave way . . .

He stood in the grass and looked for color. Grey this harbor of ruined, sunken buildings. The city before him was iron. The cloud-ripe sky was iron.

No birds spread their wings in the torn sky. He wondered if they too, were iron and could not raise their narrow wings to brush the sky.

This was the place. Fabled in every age-worn nook and drying refuge of the Old Country and in the farmhouses and scandalous taverns and inns of The Middle Places through which he had come. The Laugh came from here. Its servants were born here. Trained—rigidly, by a clamor of devout hands, and finished with notation, study, and consent, swore The Oath to it.

This immense edifice, fortification, undisturbed by the rubble

that stained the blocks around it . . .
This was the place.

The inflation of the delirious ..

Mud and winter ..

If ..

Loss ..

Decree ..

Frayed bits and tidings ..

Low, crying from the canvas of memory ..

Shame, every moonlight stroke of its voice, fading
from TRUTH ..

He gazed at the handwriting on the pale worn page he'd torn
from the old book of sad addictions. Having swallowed all the words
wounded in restless ghost echo, he let the yellow page and its trou-
blesome address fall from his fingers.

Yester Park borders Saint Nicholas Hall on three sides. It is not as
green as in earlier years, nor as lush as in earlier years. But in this city
of rough stone and steel and grey concrete and granite that threatened
to ambush the sky, any remedy for the eye was most welcome . . .
The morning doves and songbirds are absent, quickly evicted by oc-
currences that day did not know. Three ravens, sisters who grew
bored with frolic and the spectacles of glamour, now own the park.
Under the dome of Mother Night they whisper and rattle of blood,
of bleak and things stretched and bent and staked, and Ends. A few
fading peacocks still find moments to sail o'er the lawns. Wildfowl
gesture and look about. Thin gray rabbits rush to graze when the fox
bends his shoulder to nap.

Yester Park. Its hours, spread like the voice of light at the bottom
of the sea, are seeds . . .

A twitch of breath . . .

     poems of wind . . .

          portraits in soil witness the journey . . .

Day follows wounds in the park. Night comes breaking all the inches of light with dark indifference. Warm raised, or the flood of chill disturbing the hours, few come to study, to paint nature's hide, or to sit without shouting, letting their breast be filled in a long hour of quiet council. Fewer still move from the green grounds to the yellow and black doors of Saint Nicholas Hall. None—ever—before the toll of six bells. Not even the young who climb the wild fastness of their youth, their faces entirely masked in the plain bone covering of the King.

But he was not young—its punch far from his memories in these days of unreasonable details, and he had never, even in the tugging of loosed dreams, been among the few.

He steps from shadows of the garden vale to immalleable stone.

In the black he came. The doors nearer and nearer, as if they and not he, moved forward.

Straddling the sides of the considerable doors, solid walls of rough-hewn grey stones carried here from places of fallen kings and not a single window to note passing or to gain an interior view.

No lamps were stationed to illuminate the appearance of visitors or impulse, only the solitary doors broke the rule of the gray stones.

His boots at the threshold. He raised a closed hand to knock, but his hand stopped short as his eyes took in a small, black onyx plaque inlaid with a strange character. Foreign, he was certain, but not Oriental, nor a rough etching from the cold northern climbs.

"Come within."

A strong voice, the tone fully satisfied with itself, invited him inside. But no one stood there as the doors swung opened. Nor could he discern any mechanical device to project the voice, or device to open the black doors.

"This is the Hall of the Four Winds," said the lifeless iron voice.

"Having climbed all the flatness of irritation and the implications of misery, the slender roses are invited here. Shorn of their deficiencies they leave the past and exaggerate no more."

He was desperate for words. But his tongue had crumbled.

"You seek."

Head bobs, agreeing.

"In this ancient house those born into The Wild Glades and exiled in misadventure come. They shed their scraps and sky . . . And sigh."

"Who—"

"There is little time left to the day, humanchild. Behind the door you select lies what you desire."

In the still, quiet air he stood. Waiting for another word from the voice.

One did not come.

He looked at the hallway.

It was lined with arched doors, thirteen on each side. Bleached, bone-colored and lined with minute fractures along the wall to his left. The right lined, each and all, with doors heavily lacquered with the blackest black.

And there were

faces

and more faces

outward identities and expressions of nature transformed

tinted

blurred

bruised, matted

alone

webbed and scarred and shipwrecked

shorn of disguise and alibis

jealousy and love and loathing worn from them

portraits lined the walls between each door, groups of four, set two upper and two lower above another quartet of faces. Each wraithlike image framed in rough, dry wormwood and the taint of a spreading green mold. Though masked, he recognized a few poets, Utti, Coscia the Exile, Bärtsch, and Abbuehl, and the autumn minstrels who hunt the soft places of the heart, Sha, Wiss, and Keusen. He had heard Sha play by candlelight at The Wooden Horse on three occasions. Had read Utti and Coscia to Victoria one afternoon as they picnicked by the round lake in the Then before the troubles were first reported.

Most of the faces dyed in shadow he knew not. Each was a spirit drained and vague. No eye twinkled. In the cast of faces peering from the paintings, the leviathan, Silence, chewed upon the haunted.

Hearing a door open and slam shut, he wheeled. But the hall was empty.

A damp chill caressed him.

The statement of another door slammed.

Melville spun.

No eyes or face waiting. No fact to climb.

Another door slams . . .

Another . . .

Each time he spins to find empty grinning, nothing happened.

A midnight choir rose up—"*La-la . . . La-la . . . La-ah-la-a-da-da.*" Light laughter followed and fired the hallway. Laughter drained of the things of the sun. Laughter that filled the air with echoes of twilight and the Ferryman.

It subsided. And now rose up a voice, a woman's voice, possessed with the venom of scarlet and fire.

"*Melville. So you have come. You have taken your time in arriving.*"

"My path was as direct as the terrain allowed."

"*Ah.*" Very nearly a laugh.

"Something of mine has been taken from me."

"*Every soul loses small pieces of itself on the way to The Rendez-vous.*"

A small rage was in his shoulders. In his eyes.

"A rendezvous with some cruel spider . . . I—I have not come to repent, or to hear reviews of rivers run."

A hand upon his shoulder. Thin long fingers in soiled yellow gloves split and frayed at the tips, gray flesh and ragged nails exposed.

Melville turned.

The hand falls. Slowly floats to its side.

There stood a thing of cold calm, of twilight, of confusion smothered.

The curved slope of hip and breast lie under stained yellow robes and the face, a sleek, silken yellow mask with no lips, no mouth, and no grin fitting its autumn stillness. Sharp hawk-brow above lidless yellow eyes. Eyes, fire bright and glaring, fires that absorb but do not reflect.

"Name yourself masked maiden."

In a voice of harsh powers she said, "*By those who have found The Yellow Sign I am called, Content. I am the Dean of Saint Nicholas*

Hall."

Open mouth, hardened sorrow wild and bent, stuck behind his teeth. (He feels like he's overrun with coarse weeds and is breathing stones.)

Closes.

Content raises a stick-like arm, her outstretched, gnarly finger points to the door.

No knob or lever or latch. No keyhole.

Half a thought momentarily played with abracadabra . . .

He went to the bone-colored door.

Leaned. And it opened.

A room stained in dimming twilight. A room lined with long, narrow glass boxes, several feet wide and several high. Row upon row. Each box filled with thick, swirling yellow vapors Melville thought looked like torn curtains flapping in fits of biting wind. He leaned his face closer. The fine yellow currents, rushing—small dense rivers without masters, beckoned compellingly. Their wild yellow art shading out what the boxes contained.

"What—"

"This is The Chapel of the Banquet."

"A feast for whom?"

She brushed off his question. Her finger directed his gaze to an empty box, its lid open.

"This is the world without you."

"And those?"

"Other worlds. Without those who came seeking what had passed."

"Are they . . ."

"Done looking at the undersides of leaves for secrets and answers. Done moving from chair to chair. No longer do they rush low and high for they have finished listening to the hollow words of the self-impressed and the fabled."

"Gone."

"Only from here."

"To where?"

"To The Vale Where the Fog of Mystery Rolls. To The Place Where Evening Falls On Still."

"And the struggle?"

"Over for those who shed careless and curious, and followed, giving

their last words to my brother, the King."

He placed his hands on a box next to the one with the open lid. Its yellow vapors part. Victoria lay in the box. Her face, a stony mask, was dimmed. Gone, murdered by his dark questions, he was certain. Gone—vanished words and manners, happier moods of mind, all the traces and whirling of schemes, and the heat that smelled of sweet flowers and the pretty vistas of dreams unfolded, he had once surveyed.

The lightning flash of recognition that belongs to requiem and the deep bitter ache of lamentation.

Her hands—hands that once strayed on his face—now so pale, were crossed on her breast.

Silent now the contours that never spoiled a morning.

Alone . . .

Turned to cold stone.

The windows of her eyes forever closed. Her countenance sealed by a condition black.

His heart screamed, his hands covered his face. A swift, damning knife had been plunged into his memories. A mob of tornadoes shredded—ripped, all hope of forgiveness and reconciliation.

Gone.

gone . . . never to . . .

Truly gone.

Forever sealed, bolted. Shut fast.

The lifeless image—of her—a fire that conquers, corrupts, crushes, pure acid and ice burning his eyes.

He stands in a habitat blind, alone—ALONE in a mire of agony, distant the golden stream of life. Promise sunk in a fate of skeletons and misery that goes on and on . . .

He had lived with his eyes open. He would not go.

"I cannot . . . Cannot." He shivers. Looks down at the pond that was her cheek, sees his heartbreak. "When Then is shaken from my memory . . . Can—can . . . will not . . . accept—"

"Signs and stars and dreams, all sink into the darkness."

As her yellow profile moved away she whispered, "He *will be there."*

Tired of Everyday he whispered, "Where is my heart?"

Melville turns from the tomb-cold flames of her eyes. He is

flooded with discolored memories: Coherent blue skies . . . a table with wine and cheese . . . her gentle laughter when he stubbed his toe . . . the cats asleep in the sun-filled pasture of the bay window . . . the strains of ecstatic music dancing from tender hands . . . the kitchen table with honey-sweetened tea and the burnt desert and her smile as he laughed at the hard black underside of the yellow sponge cake . . .

"Damaged." The war prayer, ravens' dance melody of the grave is within him. "Light . . . swaying."

His hand is conquered by tremors . . .

"Fall . . ."

There is a twitch below his eye, which has forgotten how to shout . . . His tongue is dry. It tastes of flint and briars and tired flowers . . .

"ing."

His lungs are husks that can not function in this vertigo of deepening ash.

A wave of crowlike hissing in the air, burning, swelling . . . The shape of a woman with no mouth shifts, offers refuge from the threatening shadows . . .

"My life . . . is . . ." The world of heart within—with its blindness, and jars of small lives, and countless bridges—crumbles. Nests and wheels fade. "gray."

"Better off—"

The horizon, a yellow orchard of cancer torn and obscured, hangs upside down. He trembles, veneers and questions out of breath, flake off and fall away . . . And he cannot remember how . . .

"Better off . . ."

Exhaustion and devouring pain unfold, mute hand and eye . . . the bite of steady tears . . . poisoned, summer bled of anger, descends . . .

Images tarred in black spin, speak . . . Silhouettes crossed by whipping shadows . . . Lakes swallowed . . . Goodbyes sleeping in the sand . . . Thorns, socket thresholds full of wasps and malice smiles, come down the ladder from the gloom to find things to keep their feet warm . . .

Driftwood fingers slowly gliding through thunder toward answers.

Melville brought out his gun. Raised it to his temple . . . The echo of the outburst was surrounded and overcome as The King's cold, brutal laugh moved through the halls . . .

"*Ssssh, child,*" she whispers, placing Melville's hands just so on his chest. Her touch soft as a mother's, she covers his face with a thread-bare-thin cloth soiled with dried tears and dust.

"*The gates of Carcosa are open.*"

There was the rustling of another pair of boots or slippers about to cross the threshold and enter Saint Nicholas Hall. Sister Content turned from Melville's glass box toward the door.

"*Yesterday arrives so soon.*"

She sighs, its tone like the retreating breath of a distant banshee, thinking of tides and how all things, the stout, the fragile, those who judge and the blindfolded, those crouched in ill-fitting fear, lean toward the dark . . .

(Judy Henske & Jerry Yester "Farewell Aldebaran," "St. Nicholas Hall," and "Three Ravens")

Funeral in a Hate Field

for Lin Carter, Grandmage of the SASA

Smoke and bodies, bloody and burning . . . Wagons and carts reduced to splinters and horses without legs, some without heads . . . Arms twenty feet from the owners . . . Faces, split apart, dented, bloody, slashed, nearly skinned, eyeless (and the vultures in their funeral finery have not even arrived yet) . . . Fingers and feet that can't run or hold a sword . . .

The sky is perfect, beautiful blue. Cloudless.

A boy cries.

A man who will never return to his home by the river, screams.

A man tries to hold his guts in as he talks to his God. Spittle covers his prattling lips.

Among broken spears and shattered shields two men pass a wineskin.

A soldier who lost his best friend pisses on the body of his commander.

A last word said.

No smiles.

And no wizards left standing. Though each army brought a sorcerer . . .

Dawn was nine hours ago.

Even the pretty ones did not die pretty.

At this hour there are less liars, cheaters, brutes, fools, gamblers, and poor men in the world.

And less warriors too.

Heaven and Hell are swollen with those who did not say goodbye. Some were the very best. Some were crazy. Some, had they lived to see another morning's light, would have amounted to zero.

Misery and despair will not leave when dark comes. And it's coming.

Molds were broken. Continuation stopped. Concertos and tangos, edited by blood work, will leave scars.

Luc stands before Matts Kam.

Neither has been scratched this day. Both have shed much blood on this field. Both are demons fueled by hate-fire.

For two thousand men this day is over. For them it has yet to begin.

What they encountered from their saddles they put down. Their bows and spears and swords and knives ventilated, pierced, ripped, dragged—fortunes both fair and dangerous—from this world of sun.

With their hate-driven orders they stripped morning of elegance.

Eyes mad with loathing and sweating brows and burning lungs they stand ready to bring this day to an end, each warlord certain of his opponent's blood-spattered damnation.

Bare blades.

Boots soiled in blood and mire pivot . . .

There is spit, but no still . . .

Brutal steel weaves . . .

Shoulders and furious arms strain . . .

A blur of blades that hurls sparks . . .

Tangled memories burn in bloodshot eyes . . .

There is no knowing better. No enough . . .

No word passes between them . . .

Impact . . .

One vertical cut, opened deep, becomes two . . .

Spasm . . .

Doctrines are lost . . .

Slash . . .

Flesh tears . . .

Stupid and wrong and careless, each chase a dead man . . . Blind to all but the kill, swords flash, cross thresholds . . .

One stumbles . . .

One staggers . . .

Doom does not delay. Or sigh. It cares not about ambushed flanks and the quilt of atrocity that wounds the knoll. Through torture and pain and idiocy doom comes. It leaves no echo.

A kettle of vultures circle above the dark field where the hate of two men broke thousands. The kettle grows, darkening the sky. Soon to be a venue, ripping flesh from bone, the monks survey the carcasses below. When their crops are full from gorging they will sit half asleep.

The vultures hate nothing.

They come not to bury the dead but to consume them. Let time and the sun and the wind and the soil and the worm put in the ground what their bellies can not stow.

Luc and Matts Kam, conjoined with steel, lay hushed on the table.

Gray legs land on the green swell where the banquet is strewn. . . And the black beaks of death's dark angels begin the funeral proceedings . . .

An Orange Tick-Tick-Tick-Tick-Tick

In the backyears, sure—Yeah. Once ... Yeah I met Old Alex—Fuckin' Ultra-Ultra-BIG CAL! Had a big stinky orange tosby jammed up his bezoomny arse. What a punk! Mr. Futuristic-chepooka. Guess ya drink cal-loads of that grahzny water—all that fookin' plasticgoo and cement taintin' it and you go bonky-bonky.

His clockwork eye was shut. Didn't paint it up nice like the old days. Clamped right up tight'n'tighter! Mine were wide open. I'd thrown me books and hat in the dumper—with a bit of gasoline and a match. Thrilled to the burn-baby-burn.

Old Blue Eyes was a-sleepin' like a wee cal-boy. I mean he was walkin' 'round, but he wasn't fookin' there if ya's taken my drift. Not the droog I met! Maybe earlier? I wouldn't know. Didn't give three rat's arses one way or that.

Sure the Apostles tore the lid off and the flame was everywhere, they'd thrown the bird at the tight-arse Rightside and then dumped a load of cal on top—smokin'cal—just like a bleedin' cherry.

Still not sure why they fooked him up like that. They said he was dangerous—Fook! Dangerous? Just pop out for a stroll. Tell me that's not dangerous? Fookin' devils and darkness strollin' 'round like it's Sunday in the bloody-fookin'-park. Mayhem-mayhem-mayhem tickin' like a young cock's heart, ain't gonna slow that down. It's out to fook and it's gonna fook. YOU or anyone else. Bang-bang yer gonna wind-up cal-full of stinky. Doesn't matter if yer a tank or a norm, best leave them to their vision. A splash of moloko and a tight young Lolita spreadin' wide for yer in-out poke of art and the superfly motherfookers won't give two squats about quiet Johnny Q ... Yer cal—not worth an eyeblink!

Fook-cal! He wasn't confessin'. Fooker couldn't get his brain around an IF.

Hateful little puss—all zoobies, chatterin' 'n clueless on&on&on

. . . That dumb arse was all wet—Singin' in the bloody rain . . .

Abstract cal? What the fook. In yer goob, the pack hunting. It needs to feed—You need to eat don't you? Yer out gathering and there's the pack. Well, the mob rules. And they're happy about it. They'll take yer cal and fook you up all horrorshow this raz. Next raz, it's all munchy-munchy. The Nazis ate everything, the mouth eats ALL! Your mouth, my mouth. We're all hungry—We eat and eat. And fook everyone else.

You think you've got freewill? Fook you and that rat yer feedin' from the cal runnin' out yer arse. You get cal, it hits you, you hit back. RAGE HARD or you go down. Simple as that.

The fookin' mob—it's society. The pack is strong, it lives 'cause it's strong. Rolls right over you and yer cal-little plain life. Fooks you over without lookin' back. If yer quick you're on and yer rollin' with it. Rollin' and tumblin' . . . A cog in the grindin' wheel—chugga-chugga big bad ultraviolent machine. Is it sane? I'll be fooked if I know.

Is any of this ultra-cal sane?

Is it supposed to be?

C'mon yer'a Moraler, lay it out for me. I'm tryin' to stay alive.

Same for you. It's all a big hey-ho! The fookin' dump's crumblin'. Suck it up and take a good eyeball!

Be brave and maybe sneak by—everybody tryin'!

Everybody.

We're all actors and this is one big cal-arse stage. Filly yer part, dance your limp-arse dance 'cause yer young fer an eyeblink and if yer lucky you catch a bit of fun, then they pour the sand on you and you settle in for the long dirt sleep, or cal-ass old crumbly comes. Slow chews and chews and chomps. All them zoobies jawin' at yer weak-arse numbered days. Yer rockin' and droolin' and Mr. Tick-Tock don't even know yer still around. And it sure don't fookin' give half a rat's maggoty-arse.

Old Alex, he got chewed up.

Fook 'im!

He played. Splattered Ultra far as he fookin' could. Got it jammed up in there 'til he went blind. He ain't swimmin' back across that fookin' river. No one does. Never-ever. Poison fook's yer future and cals out yer past. Just moves by quick-quick-zoom and thrackBAM yer left like an old cal-pie something gonna push aside sometime.

Now if you'd like to make it outta this wee-bother and home to-night, hand over yer pennies, before my kindness tumbles.

Why?

Fook.

'Cause yer a gloopy starry sod and I'm the new MASTER—That's fookin' ME! And the whole sparkling fooking thing is all about ME!

Alex is dead. I'm legend! Zoobies, stick, hail, and dick, I rule. For the next five minutes I'm the fooking future, then the next designer comes along. And ya can bet he's gon screw it more than me and cal on it and it gets bigger and darker and meaner and more used up.

C'mon-c'mon. Render unto Nero. It's fooking cold and I ain't got a century on stage.

That's it. Pull it out.

That's fookin' it? Bog!

Six lousy bucks? That's the sum of it? Six fookin' Uncle Sammies. You dragged me out on a night like this and all yer gonna hand over is six fooking Uncle Sammies?

Fuck. Get outta here before I want more than moloko cutter.

Run, Fooker, run!

❋

Yes, Sir. Yes, Sir.

It's the big bad clock made me do it. Clock's big as the moon. Looks down on ya. Slaps ya and guffs . . . *The big bad clock . . .*

Don't care a fook 'bout us.

Like we're ghosts or ants. *Or cal . . .*

Don't.

All the ashes comin' at'cha—never stops.

Never stops . . .

the ashes . . .

ashes . . . ashes . . . *all fall down.*

[MC5 *"Motor City Is Burning"* and *"Rocket Reducer No. 62 (Rama Lama Fa Fa Fa)"*]

Engravings

Straight rain. Mean and murderous. Its eyes screaming for blood.

Denver faded three hundred miles back. Three hundred miles of wet asphalt back . . . It could have been a thousand . . .

Rain. Mean and murderous—Engraving the world with sheets of thorns. Rain. Screaming like the Old Man on a gin bender. Screaming like the Old Man before the belt and the fists.

Thirty years back . . . Or it could have been yesterday.

This run was supposed to end in the desert, not in a ditch. But the clock pressed. Tick-tock/tick-tock. Like a boss with eyes that only said FASTER.

He needed coffee and a pack of smokes. Maybe some eggs and toast . . . And something other then this Bible-thumping Forever that poured out of the radio. A nice sexy waitress—not some upper-class package with radar eyes searching for money, but earthy—knowing, with blue eyes and a big butt that swayed. Not unkempt and worn, but nice and maybe with a little extra. And she would wink all-sexy-like when she refilled his coffee.

Rain—full throttle, carrying violence with each slap. Like the Old Man crossing the hardwood floor.

For the last fifty miles or every step he'd ever taken.

Broken. The knobs wouldn't work. He couldn't turn the fuckin' radio off or down. The wipers working overtime, fighting off this wallop of darkness.

He should pull over and wait it out. But he needed a smoke and needed to be warm. Wanted . . . Wanted something to look at that didn't hurt his strained eyes. Wanted to hear something—someone other than Rev. James Theodore Ellison's promise to heal you if you sent him money. To be healed by money. That's what got him here. Got him on this road. Got him out this night . . . With The Package in the trunk.

He should pull over and check The Package. When he did that

360 five miles back, almost running off the road, he heard it slam into the side of the trunk. Heard it thud. Jittery balljoints, shitty tires and bad shocks—shitty-ass Pontiac junkbucket, new this thing never purred along Nirvana Road like a hot kiss; a Chevy would, "Ain't nothin' like a fine-ass Chevy glidin', top down in the sun. A fine candy-apple red one, not this black piece of crap." And that timetable. He was screwed if the Package was damaged. That's what Mr. Phoenix said. Promised. Stark as bloody murder with one look and few words.

But that wasn't his fault. Wasn't his fault Mr. Phoenix gave him this car. Made him drive on thin tires. Not in this shit. This was Mr. Phoenix's fault. Not that he could tell him that and live.

Mr. Phoenix and his red tie and his red stickpin and the red cuff-links . . . Red. It stared right into your eyes. Drilling. Burning, hungry venom. Mr. Phoenix and his cats—five of them, four black as midnight, 1 smoke and fog grey. Licking his hands. Staring at you, right into your eyes. Drilling.

He hated cats. His Old Man had moved like a cat, slinky and graceful, even when he was oiled. Then the claws came out. Blood. Red. Red was everywhere.

Then . . . And now. Red.

All his life driving away from it. Fast. And here it was again. Waiting. If he wasn't on time. If The Package was damaged. Red. Waiting to let its claws out.

"Fuck all this rain. Pissin' like someone in Hell drank all the fuckin' beer in every shithole bar this side of the Mississippi."

If he had time he'd pull over and yank the fuse for the radio out. At least he could stop Rev. set-aside-your-sins-and-ask-God-for-forgiveness' moral deluge. But Mr. Phoenix said 11:30 sharp. Said he'd be waiting. Waiting. Red tie, tight and just so. Red stickpin and the red cufflinks. And probably those fuckin' cats. Licking his hands. *Sick-shit lettin' animals lick ya. All those fuckin' germs. Germs from licking their assholes. Might dress like old time money—all uptown, but he was fuckin' nasty. Nasty ass cats lickin' shit.*

"Fuckin' treacherous cats. Yeowlin' like saxophones. Ballin' like that Nigger music set 'em on fire." *Should kill all the cats like they did back in Europe when they was burnin' the fuckin' witches.*

He looks at the clock on the dash. 100 miles and less than an hour to make it there.

Raining. Harder. And Rev. James Theodore Ellison blatherin' like he knew it all.

And the Old Man, tellin' ya he knew it all.

And Mr. Phoenix actin' like he knew it all.

And this rain comin' down like the end of it all.

And those fuckin' cats and their hungry eyes, lookin' at'cha like they wanted it all.

"Fuck-it-all! Gonna take my cash and hit some Mexican beach and score some nice Mexican pussy. Gonna leave all these wounded motherfuckers to their wounded neighbors and just lay there. No more in a hurry to get there. Fuck that." *Outta the flame and into the wine. Bye bye bullshit. I'm spendin' my days and nights in the shade. On my soft cushion—blue or green like the color of the water. Starin' at some sweet shang-a-bang-bang that don't wanna bring me down. Tomorrow there'll be sunrise and I'm gonna hit Sugartown without a problem in sight . . . Might even have a little garden where I can grow some of that sweet Mexican shit.*

Sixteen hours of drivin' rain and barely a moment where it let up so he could pull over and take a piss. Sixteen hours behind the wheel with the clock following him. Pulling. Pushing. Mile after mile. Pushing. Proding. Poking. Mile after mile. Minute by minute. Not even fifty minutes left and the clock wanting it to be over. And him wanting it to be gone. And that bastard Rev. James Theodore Ellison sayin' The End is near—Bet the only thing he ever got near was the pink little backside of an altar boy. And the mean, murderous rain not letting up . . .

The flat 10 hours back really put a dent in his plan, laid out all nice and straight. Fucked plans. Now all banged up and hollow. It seemed like it was last week and it killed any hope of stopping for dinner—some eggs and toast and hot black coffee would be nice, but . . . The rain and the clock and the flat killed at that. Left the day a victim. Roadkill, that got ran over and nicked and flattened and ran over again and again 'til it was pulp. Red. A red mess no one would stop for. No one would miss. Not even the clock.

He had a headache. Starin' through wipers killing themselves to beat off the rain hour after hour with no coffee and something filling in his belly. He had a headache. Wanted to sleep. Wanted to eat. Wanted to wake up beside something warm and nice. And willing. Wanted this shit to be over. Now.

Wanted it to stop fucking raining. Let Mr. Phoenix build an ark and him and his fuckin' cats could sail off to one of those places like Babaluma or Zanzibar. He wanted this chapter closed and he wanted his money. Now.

If it would just let up and he could find a 7-Eleven or a gas station that hadn't dozed off into goodnight. Just one cup of java and a pack of smokes and he could make it 'til The End.

There'd be Mr. Phoenix at the End. Standin' there. With that stone, spider smile turnin' to poison and asking for The Package. Bet if it was still rainin' the rain wouldn't touch him. Bet he had red eyes under those thick black sunglasses. Come to think of it he'd never seen him, day or pitch black, without them. Albinos had reddish eyes, and Mr. Phoenix could—maybe?, even if he was as black as the ace of spades, black as any old Mississippi bluesman with broken eyes filled with sorrow. Yeah. He had red eyes. Just like one of those hellfire demons in those creepy old movies.

And that wasn't all that wasn't right with Mr. Phoenix. Always decked out in that stupid scarlet robe. Did he think he was some pope or old pharaoh? All that Egyptian stuff layin' around his office—The place looked like some creepy assed museum. And that time down by the trains on Hennepin St. when the dogs ran from him bawlin' like he beat them with an ugly stick and he had his back to 'em and was at least twenty feet away. And those clove cigarettes, red tip burnin' like hellfire—smelled like they was rolled in Hell too. And his voice, sounded as if it came from deep in a well and it boomed, those old Bible prophet's must have sounded like that to fill people with doom and damnation. Sounded pitch black and wise. Wise in things That Were.

But he had to get there first. Had to beat this clock ticking, pulling its load into some unknowable future. Had to get outta this rain.

Highbeams trying to read the snake-curve of the road. The rain confusing the context of space and time. Rain. Here now. Here then. Like a plague.

A sign—*The Sign*. The sign said just ahead. On the left. Almost here. All those hours almost free. Almost free to go to Mexico. With all that money. He'd have eggs and toast and smokes and sweet Mexican pussy with that money. He'd have every day on the beach— With no rain. Never a fuckin' drop! And he'd never have to deal with Mr. Phoenix again. Never look at that stone grin that froze yer bones.

Never have to hear the fuckin' cats yeowlin'. He was gonna buy two dogs—wasn't gonna let any cats near his beach house in Mexico. The sign said just ahead.

Fifty thousand dollars. Just ahead. Long afternoons alone with a cold beer—drunk and ready for a nap if he wanted, unless he wanted her around. Everything he wanted, just ahead.

Hours and hours in the dark. No sky, no horizon. Now—wet and repeated endlessly. No shore. Minute by minute. No clouds. Minute after minute. No moon. Hour after hour. Rain. Leviathan.

Out of it. Hot summer complaining. Cactus. Sand. Moon—low and somehow energetic, smiling in satisfaction. Rev. James Theodore Ellison's sermon instantly ended, cut off. Joshua trees, bent old crones, twisted and passing for dead. The yellow spine down the middle of the road, dry, untouched by the merciless storm. Everything here in this exhibition of midnight and the small hours of morning bone-dry.

The hill off to his left. What passes for a road leading to it. Brakes. Left at the big boulder, just where he was told it would be. The tires quieter in the sand. Slow, not wanting to kick up dust. Three minutes late, not wanting to face Mr. Phoenix.

The Pontiac stops in front of three large rocks, sentinels, white as bones. They have no eyes, arms, hands. Still he sees them as dangerous. Something about them pulses. They don't belong here. His finger touches his mother's crucifix under his shirt before passing between them.

He steps from the deep black shadows of the sentinels on to white sand. *Ground from bone,* he thinks. *An ocean of bones.*

Two more steps—ghost steps. He feels he's walking up a long hill toward a great dark house, carrying something obscene and unwanted. He feels slight. Stops. He doesn't know if he should get The Package out of the trunk. Doesn't remember his instructions. Was there a script that disappeared? He'd like to turn back. But he doesn't know the way.

The flash of a match, a scar burning this cell of night. Mr. Phoenix without his dark-brimmed hat, face under it, glowing black edge to black edge. Mr. Phoenix carved out of sharp moonlight. Smiling. Smiling that blasted, open-faced, silent smile that soured his stomach, that could hit you like a shot to the ribs. Mr. Phoenix seated at a table under a canvas pavilion. Saxophones—a pair?—coming from a tape recorder by his feet, playing blind, surging interstellar meditations, the lost music of some vertical invader awakened from slumber, hungry, hunting. Saxophones screeching and yeowlin' like those fuckin' black-souled cats had their tails on fire. And his cats, pushing each other aside to lick his hands. Mr. Phoenix singing, "In the Outer Nothingness, Heavenly things dancing in the sun . . . They Dwell on Other Planes." Empty well-deep voice—thin, stone lips hardly moving—reflecting yesterdays gone with the wind.

Not a drug deal. Not a delivery of some hijacked old shit. Devil worship? He turns his head and looks back at the Pontiac. At the trunk. The trunk he'd never looked in.

"Hello, Johnny."

"Sorry I'm late, but the rain—"

"Rain?"

"It stopped just over there. Freaky. Like there was a barrier it couldn't pass through."

"Rarely does the rain hunt in the Halls of Fire." With a hand, thin wisps of curling smoke rising off it, he removed his sunglasses.

Red eyes leveled at him. Unblinking. Stabbing red eyes, bare of all except contempt.

Fuck, that's . . . Unholy! His mouth open—language flattened out with a bang, the burning air rushing into it.

The dark man has not moved. As cursed shadows tethered to forgotten riddles his cats sit at the edges of the table.

"Heavenly things dancing in the sun . . . They Dwell on Other Planes." Empty well-deep voice. Thin, stone lips hardly moving.

How does he do that? His hand moves to his left for comfort—no gun. He has a gun, but it's on the seat of the car. Forgotten in haste; to get this over and get out of here, to get his money.

The moon falls between cracks in the clouds. The air smells of light-devouring blackness. And the black man has not moved. And the scarring pattern of the swelling music boils on.

All he can do—simple and terrified—is stare. At the loud red eyes. He wants the End. Wants the money—*his money.* Wants to leave, to be on his way to Mexico. Wants Now to be over. But all he can do is stare.

The song the black man sings ends. The red eyes grow cold, the smile widens. "So we have arrived. Dark and light in shadows on this hill. Dark and light, one to take and one to give."

Shit, the package. It's still in the trunk. "Right. Sorry. I'll get the package."

Low laughter dancing. "I've no need for it. I know the way."

"But I have it. It's in the trunk. Right where your man said it was. I've never touched it. Never even looked at it . . . Could I get my money? And go?"

"Money? Oh, yes, that. Calm yourself, my boy, you'll have no need for money—not that there ever was any. Not where you are going."

The stone smile.

Bait. Tricked.

Going? I'm going to get my fuckin' gun. He'll give me my money, then . . . And I'll put two in his head for fuckin' with me. Shoot his fuckin' cats too.

"Johnny, I can see by your face you think to do me violence and leave. That will not happen. I control the opening of every door. I've a few moments to fill, so allow me to amuse you with a detail or two about you and the road traveled.'

"Your dear mother was a drunkard and a whore, not that she took money for her wanton rutting mind you, but for a few cheap drinks she would spread her legs wide. And I had a need, a need that required a vessel to carry a drop of my essence. A need for an act to occur under a star engraved in times ancient. A little song in her ear followed by a several glasses of gin and she . . . How would you put it? She fucked like a rabbit—Climbed on top and took to my lust as if she were a maggot to an apple. I left her sleeping and dripping with my seed."

Black laughter brands him.

"I never saw her again, yet I've kept an eye on you. The night you were born the moon was fire-red—Did she never tell you of The Burning? My pets were there, watching, walking in your first dream. After engraving you they came and reported to me. As the years found themselves whitened by the teeth of time, I've sent one of my servants to check on you from time to time. You'll recall the attorney who suddenly showed up to rid you of your legal entanglements when that girl died. He was a servant I employ on occasion. And Pitt—even the worm fears the scent of what he sends to the soil, did you ever wonder why a cold-blooded monster like that befriended and protected you in jail? Again, my handiwork. Remember the evening your father fell down the stairs to his death, consumed by the spleen of a hard drunk?"

Mr. Phoenix's finger strokes the neck of the cat sitting at his right hand. "*Mesah* was there watching that night and made certain the coarse mite flew to the Labyrinth Where the Damned Howl. I could not, after all, have you damaged. Every time some loose extreme put you at risk I cut it back to nothing."

Assaulted by the life sprawling in his telescope of memory, his skin crawls. He wants out of the bullring, wants the weathervane to turn. Wants something sane. Wants his life to be another life, one not framed in the shipwreck of 100 sabbaths, not washed away by the teeth of 1,000 drinks. He is too stunned to cry. All capacity for speech is stitched shut.

"Though your life has been dark and violent, have you never taken note of the fact that in thirty-two years no scar has been born upon your body?'

His mind weak, beaten down. He is desperate for words. For some key to freedom.

"I see you wish you could trade the empty box in the trunk for your liberty. Yes, Johnny, the box contains *nothing*." The word a grave.

"You see, for this, what shall we call it? Prelude To Windfall, perhaps . . . You needed to come here freely. The package was merely a vehicle for you to do so. I can see you're searching for a reason for all this . . . I'll be plain. I am called by many names. Tonight the verse of stone and wind call me, The Opener of the Way. You and I are here to open a door. A door opened by the harvest."

Harvest? As in dead?

He would run—the keys are still in the Pontiac's ignition, but finds himself bound, held knee-deep in sand.

Mr. Phoenix's hands glow. Tendrils of jet-black smoke curl from his spider-fingers. There is a blade in his hand.

The black man stands. His stone smile widens.

He finds his tongue, hisses, "A door to what?"

"To something you'll never see, nor would you understand."

Lost and overwhelmed. "I don't—"

"The only thing you need understand is there will be blood spilled."

(for ST.tanley-ra! No one does it better!)

The Last Few Nights in a Life of Frost

Dim . . . and slightly damp. A cramped basement, fleabag-of-a-room in something less than a flophouse. It's the best cast-offs blacklisted by fate can find when they're on the run . . . Even from the swords of punishment within . . .

ST puts down his cigarette. Opens the letter he's been staring at for over an hour. In it a key. A note says GO HERE.

There is a map.

No return address.

Looks at the postmark. It's very old. Dead letter old. A decade before he was born old.

Who? And how in the hell . . .

Doesn't pack much; his gun, a few changes of clothes. And the picture.

Envelope left behind, dropped in the middle of the floor for the maid. Forgets to tear something up, or slam the door.

Takes a bus downtown. And another to a trucking hub out near the airport.

In a truck stop diner he steals a car. Twenty miles later in a Prime Inn motel parking lot he abandons it and steals another.

Drives two hours west and abandons that one as well.

Takes a taxi to the airport in this other town. In the long term parking lot he steals the third.

Four and a half hours later as the sky darkens he leaves the car in a supermarket parking lot.

Walks to the Prime Inn motel. Checks in.

#17.

Gun drawn, safety off, he enters the room.

From Illinois to Arkansas to Georgia to Nebraska to Arizona there are 532 Prime Inn budget motels. Exactly 25 rooms in every one.

1330 in all. Seen one you've seen all. Budget, meaning cheap, mattress. Budget, meaning cheap, TV, sometimes they work OK. Budget, meaning cheap, everything else. About half are sorta clean about half the time, if you're lucky. But everyone is cheap. $22.50 a night, or an hour, if that's all that's required. Most of the whores that use the rooms are in and out in less than 60 minutes. Dope deals take a little more time because there's more money to count.

The room is empty.

Sets his small, cheap suitcase on the floor and looks around.

Nothing.

Checks the bathroom.

Nothing.

Lifts the receiver from the cradle. Has dial tone. Sets in back down.

Begins waiting.

Edgy, he wonders what or who he's waiting for.

Three cigarettes and five pulls off the pint of whiskey later he turns on the TV. The strawberry blonde smiles and says, "You made it. That's good. We weren't sure you would come."

ST picks up his gun.

"No need for that. There won't be anyone tapping on your door. While you wait, you might like to read what we've left for you. It's in the drawer." She's stopped smiling. "I'll talk to you again soon."

The TV shuts itself off.

He knows the strawberry blonde. Did a job for her a million years ago. Funny, she doesn't seem to have aged. Not too much.

ST remembers the job. Dirty.

And bloody.

And she didn't pay him. Didn't fuck him either, though she had promised. Whispered it so sweetly. Her fingers on the back of his hand, hot enough to melt steel. Her hips pressing against his, hot enough to forge steel.

Opens the drawer slowly.

An old and worn leather diary. His initials embossed on the cover.

But he never kept or owned a diary. No need to. He remembered *everything*.

Takes it out of the drawer. Looks at the back. Nothing.

Pushed the button to release the clasp.
Hello.
That's the whole of page one.
Sets it down and lights a cigarette.
Sets his gun down beside him on the bed.
Turns to the second page.

He grew up to be a cold fuck. Looked at it
and killed it, or couldn't be bothered and
just walked away.

But when he was young he had a home. Nothing fancy. Simple and clean. His parents died
when he was nine. Fire. Local paper called it
a real inferno. Maybe arson. They sent him to
a home for foundlings.

ZIMMS

Bet you remember Zimms.
A dark place. Even by day.
Cold and hard. The matrons colder than death
. . . and meaner than the pent-up sadistic,
schoolmasters at Ichabod Crane who couldn't
figure out safe ways to fuck those little just-
about-to-blossom schoolgirls you sat beside.

You remember those nights, don't you?

Bet you well recall Mr. Stark too. The
shiny black suit, those unsightly, black horn-
rimmed glasses. That weapon-growl voice, and
its unending, cold questions. Remember, or do
you pretend it's water under the bridge?

His expression doesn't change but his eyes go cold. If there were
any living thing within twenty feet of him at that moment it would
be dead from the killing frost.

He's seen strange. Walked where it walked. Dealt with it. Killed it.

And this is strange. Even to him. And when he finds her and the
them she mentioned he's going to kill them too.

Her last.

She's going to wish she fucked him. She's going to beg. Little miss

Barbara and her honey-alto promises will be on her knees begging to fuck him or anything else he wants and . . .

ST turns to the next page.

`Back with us now? Good.`

`Curious?`

`If you are we'll get to that. For now fol-`
`low the directions. When you get there we'll`
`speak again.`

He reads the directions. The rest of the diary is blank.

He turns on the TV again. No Barbara. Nothing but snow and white noise on every channel. Decides to catch a few Z's before heading out.

Three hours later. Washes his face. Checks the TV, still nothing. Walks out leaving the door open and the diary in the cheap waste can.

Steals another car.

Six hours west under clouds that announce summer's over. In and out of grey open wounds those trying not to die call cities; he's been drunk in a few, spread a rain of death-sleep over dreary orchards that didn't have enough tire for suicide in others. Stops for a meal of eggs and toast and whiskey and to change cars three times.

Finds the next motel.

The directions stated the door would be unlocked and the room paid for. Just go in. Further instructions would be inside the room.

ST steps into the dark room. Gun leveled. Very ready. Flicks the light switch.

There's a woman, young by her look, tucked under the covers. Lying there like she's laid out in a casket in a funeral parlor.

He softly closes the door. Stares. Nothing in the room moves. No rise and fall of her chest. She's not breathing.

Checks the bathroom. Empty.

Doesn't touch the phone.

He didn't expect a warm welcome, but this is . . .

"You want games, Barb. You're going to get my best game."

Standing over the woman. Pulls back the covers. She's naked. A bullet hole in her chest.

Her hands are folded over her chest. A diary is in her hands.

On the night stand beside the bed a cigarette butt, his brand, and half a glass of whiskey. The imprint of blood red lipstick, no ice.

No smell of tobacco or red lipstick on the girl's lips.

Carefully looks her over. Bettie Page cropped black hair, natural. Black lipstick. Black nails and heavy black eye make up. Vampire bat earrings and a ruby nose piercing. One nipple pierced. Arms and shoulders and neck, legs, covered in ornate, expensive tats. Her sex is shaved. She's his type. Would be. If she was alive.

And one in the heart is his method.

ST takes the book from her hands. Covers her back up.

Stares at his initials on the cover before releasing the clasp and opening it.

Some hello, huh?

Wanted you to feel at home. Is it working?

Au, poor little boy, no fucky-fucky for you. Unless you've acquired a taste for cold kisses. And dead pussy.

Maybe next time we'll find something that can stand upright before it lies down.

So our wayward hell's angel is out on the road, moving from yesterday to now in hot cars. Stopped for a quick meal and a pint I wager. Perhaps we've worked our way up to fifths?

Pissed?

Turn on the TV and we'll chat.

Closes the book. Sets it on the bed by the woman's feet.

Lights a smoke and turns on the TV.

Barbara smiles through the exhaled whorls of the blue-grey cloud. Wiggles the fingers of her raised hand in a hello. Coughs. Then frowns. "Must you smoke those damn things? It took you long enough to get here. Are you getting old, or have you just grown more wary? You are quite the piece of shit aren't you. Alive or dead, you just can't seem to make it work."

"Fuck you, Barb."

"God, you're still pissed I didn't spread my legs for you. Well, maybe if you're a good boy this time?"

"I've got something *good* to give you."

She shivers as if excited, sexually. "I'm looking forward to *it*."

"Care to—"

"Not yet, sweetie. Read the instructions. Follow them. Ta-ta."

And the TV goes to white noise and snow again.

Trying to bring depth and focus closer he sits and smokes in the darkened room with the dead girl lying beside him before returning to the dairy.

You and Pamela. Vale Cemetery. Almost half drunk on cheap wine. Annie Green Springs piss, right? By old Doc Johnson's headstone. Moonlight and skunk cabbage, and her shirt and her bra were mostly off . . .

Mr. Stark found your love poems to her in your English notebook. Read them aloud. Critiqued them for the whole class. They laughed, bruised you with their damning crisscross of hushed gossip and scathing looks in the halls after.

He sent a note to the headmistress of Zimms and she took over your instruction.

Did you find Miss Gross's bed of torture inspiring?

Really doesn't matter. Just keep following the directions.

So he does.

This time he's to take the body with him. And go to a graveyard he knows all too well and inter the girl.

X marks the spot, Sweetie.

65 mph on the Interstate in a stolen car. Dead woman in the trunk.

Arrives by moonlight. Parks in the woods at the south end. Carries the body to the grave.

Dr. Byrne Mayer Johnson. Stone hasn't moved an inch in a quarter century.

There's a shovel resting on the headstone.

He digs.

Finds another diary covered in sheer white cloth and plastic. Takes the book. Leaves the girl.

When he's done tossing the dirt back in the hole he sits and opens the diary.

The night you ran away you killed Miss

Gross. Strangled her while you were thrusting, filling her hard loneliness with your fear.

She didn't make a sound.

But her eyes screamed.

Took the money she had in her purse and got on a bus.

You fell in with demons. Stole. Tried to stay away from the insensitivity and menace you saw in the buzzing neon. Looked in windows to find things. Took them. Ran with the blood drinkers until you saw her.

Waif. Little monster girl—blood-dreams on her fingers—dead, but it had yet to lie down. Sweet poison you just had to touch. To taste.

She talked to you. Frail words of darkness, cool and tender. Wrote your name in her book of sand and make-believe fate. Etched it beside the ivy scrawl of her haunted, tar-paper black runes. You gave her your blood and fell for her.

Fell into her hunger.

Kissed the bleeding compass tattooed over her heart.

Killed them so they wouldn't kill her.

And what she wanted you to kill for her you did.

Then you killed her.

Gave her body to the ghouls. But wouldn't dine with them. All night long you sat there as they begged and cajoled. "Come and try," each one whispered.

Tell the truth. You thought about it.

Can you remember her name? Do you remember the timbre of her last breath? "Everything beautiful . . . dies." Was she holding your hand tenderly at the last?

Remember, daredevil, once you step over the line, there's no retreat from oblivion.

ST closed the book. Left.

Drove.

Zoomed east.

The grey, open-grave cities shrieked like things in need of emergency rooms. He didn't turn on the car radio to hear the calls for help. And he was afraid Barbara's voice would come out of it.

He wasn't playing Barbara's malignant game any more. Her madness was her madness. He'd lived it up—almost—sometimes, and watched it go down. All the way down.

Old wounds that hadn't healed and she was ripping them open. Pouring in restless and salt. And old lies dressed in old promises. This time around they weren't seamless and he wasn't an dry idiot locked in a cage hoping for the softest touch.

A small town in the coarse muzzle of rough weather. Robs a closed-up-at-7 liquor store. Smashes more than he takes. Rides across the state line with his whiskey. Finds a place to let it rock him to sleep.

Half a bottle in. On the bed, gently fingering old dreams. Shivers when the nightmares enter his trip back to broken hearts. Wolves and claws, sinister teeth, tear the curves and whispers.

The pretty girls, dark and tender. Lost. Lonely. Velvet and wine, in his arms.

Lays them down softly . . . Comfort.

And they go away . . .

And he's left with the blood.

Drowning in shadows . . . His need a weight . . .

Arms of velvet and wine . . .

He needs another.

Drives, a hellbound fast-train hunting, until he finds one.

Thin. Pale. Cold. No place to go. Sick of the play and its plague of no futures.

He has a bottle. A room away from the stage with no rain. Shows her his heart.

She takes his hand. He sells his soul . . .

Wonder again. The skin on her arm is a thousand miles long. Sweet talk whispered. Desire. Flame. Sweet poison. He lets her rob him blind. From eye and delta she takes faith and spirit. Leaves only flesh and bone. He takes all her pain . . . For a moment, at last . . . tired hearts . . .

One . . . expires.

In the dark, minutes later, no magic in the air, he wonders if it was all just a dream.

. . . Her. He's already forgotten her name, that girl, stashed in the trunk. Back. The road to them. Back. In the city by dead river of muddy water and industrial waste. Back. Through the old iron gates. Home, as close as he ever had. No god, no saints, in this hiding place. Under the lawns of departure, the nightshade Labyrinth of Requiems where angels and other things that have collapsed are laid to rest.

Stands before the dead breed. Offers his offering of summer set.

Watches as the Grave Keepers hold it tightly. No woe in their eyes, no hint of bereavement on their hyena faces. Watches as they, unable to conquer the lunacy of their fever, tear at the throat, at the small pale beast, split the skull, froth . . . Feast.

The tang of crimson joy fills the chamber . . .

And he leaves . . .

"Time to end this."

Drives . . .

A Ford . . . Through the night . . . Could be cactus or a chicken joint or sleeping factories or canyons or hobo camps hunkered down against the frost hidden in the darkness. Steals an Impala, this end of the city to that side and beyond. A V-8 Chevy Silverado. Over small dark hills and out of the thunder-thick weather.

Another town with no name . . . Steals a Dodge . . .

Sees no fools. No kids or chins or shipwrecks or clocks or razz-matazz or outlaws or signals or healers . . . No song or voices come to his ears . . . Moving quickly under the unarmed silence of the stars no dharma tunes come to him . . . Passed the forest of night cluttered with the open dreams of things that feed on weakness and tears . . . over bridges . . . passed unworthy and mythical . . . and function and diversion and take-it-or-leave-it . . . passed irritating misfortunes, now scrambled off to bed . . . Revved-up, he fails to notice current tactics playing cat 'n' mouse with her first dance . . .

Stops in Tillman. Next to a pawn shop and a check-cashing Mom and Pop, both closed, eats. Eggs and toast. No meat.

Gets a room and opens the book for the second time.

```
Always sick and tired. Always running. From
ruin? Why? It's everywhere.
```

And you can never stay away.

It touches you. There is no passage away. You can not hide in trees or behind mountains. No normal street with lawns and childrens' bikes and Sunday barbecues by the pool will hold you. Midnight is everywhere.

The time has come for you to grow up and come in from the cold.

ST turns on the TV.

"Hello." Barbara says.

He lights a smoke.

She doesn't say, must you, but her smile dims a bit.

"News has come to me you've given them another one."

He nods.

"You know I have the cure. The only thing I've ever wanted for you is to share in it. The rest was a mistake. You were young ... *And I didn't understand.*"

His lips part. Says nothing. Takes a drag off the smoke instead.

"This is crazy."

"Finally we agree," he says.

She smiles. Hopeful.

"Reunion?" he asks.

Barbara nods. "The day after tomorrow there will be a moon. A moon is fitting, don't you think?"

A quiet, dry tone: "There was a moon that night. One at the start, one when it comes to its end."

"*End* ... There is a village of ghosts in the desert. On the far end of town is a weathered brothel where hard men shivered in the arms of well-fed women who could strip those who claimed no sin of far more than cash. It, though closed these many years, has a well-stocked bar. I'll be waiting for you there. I'll be the heartbreaker with the bottle of Jameson."

A half laugh. But something different, almost sad, in his eyes.

From her a full smile.

He remembers how she could light up the world.

She sees it in his eyes. Hopes.

"Will you sleep tonight?" she asks.

"I'll try."

"Goodnight, then."

ST turns off the TV.

Lies on the bed and stares at the ceiling. He remembers "Kind of a Drag" playing. Slow dancing with her. Barbara's hips pressed to his. Her lips by his ears . . .

Hears her sing softly . . .

Steals his last car. Heads into the setting sun . . .

Colors he can't recall paint the sky . . .

The road becomes no road . . .

Moon rides high. Clouds herded to its right.

A lone cactus stands sentinel at the crest of the hill.

Perhaps once someplace to be, perhaps once unique, now forgotten by the big sky and all that sits under it, her ghost town. Dead. Not even a ghost. The desert has reclaimed all, even the simple, scarring markers on Boot Hill.

The brothel, out of captivating and Saturday night salvation. Parts of the sagging roof are wind worn, torn, and ready to cave. The front door looks like it wants to lie down in the dust and sleep. All the windows are dusty, but still intact. The merest hints of what might have been red and yellow paint yet to exit the boards of the outer walls look like stains.

Parks in front of the doors.

Stands there and smokes. Takes off his shoulder holster and tosses it and his gun on the front seat.

Worn boot heels on the steps.

Perhaps uncertain of her legs, she does not stand when he comes in.

"They said you had filled out well," she opens with instead of hello. *You have*, she thinks.

"You look the same . . . *Good.*"

Thanks in her eyes, on her lips.

He crosses the room. She finds her legs, stands. Can't decide if she should hug him or not. Pours two drinks. Hands him one.

He takes it.

They sip.

She's dreamed of this meeting a hundred times.

He's thought about this meeting a hundred times.

Her red shoes two steps from him.

His black boots two steps from her.

World's apart.

Closer now.

She sets down her glass.

As does he.

She steps forward.

Almost touching.

Demon. Murderer.

He feels her heat. Her desire.

Almost touching . . .

Mouths open . . .

Almost words.

Almost.

He steps back. Breathes.

Takes out a small, razor-sharp knife . . .

She steps back from its loud clarity.

. . . Cuts along the outer shore of his face . . . Fingers dig under the skin of his brow and pull the flesh down . . . Reveals his true face to her.

Her eyes wide, lips parted . . .

His true face, not a mirror of hers as it has not partaken of flesh.

"The son, in his inmost depths, desires his mother. Flesh of his flesh, to have and to hold . . . You brought me into *this* world. This madness of fever and frost that lies between us . . . I will take you . . ."

The flash of a smile on her face. She steps forward.

"out . . . and by consuming you . . ."

Frozen. The backbone of her conception shattered.

"will enter the world you wished for me."

A hiss of disappointment and disbelief from her as his blade, a barrage of fire and lightning in her bewilderment, slices deep and across her throat.

Shock as she goes limp and is transported . . . Exhausted, about to be null and void.

Tears. He holds her as she bleeds out. Kisses her as her last breath flees her body.

Licks her warm dark blood from a fingertip.

Somehow she has slipped out of her red shoes . . .

On that night so many years ago she was about to offer him her breast. He remembers how the moon shone on it . . .

Carries her outside into the moonlight. Sits in the middle of the street. *Pietà*-like, he cradles her in his arms and lap . . . Strokes her cheek with the blade . . . Sighs . . . Pops the buttons of her blouse off with his knife. The cold fever is hard in him, slices rather than unhooks her bra. Looks at the nipple-rose on the field of pale flesh. Carves his first piece of meat from the breast he never got to kiss . . .

Chews . . .

Swallows.

Baptizing blood on his face. "Too many roads, *Barbara*. The only way I know is alone . . . *If I had known then* . . . But only sight may move backward."

From his pocket he removes a very old picture of her, a picture taken the night they slowly danced. Smiles a regretful smile. A picture of lived here before the hours slumped and were undone. Tears it up. It falls like snow.

Bridge crossed he eats one of her eyes. A corpse eye. Remembers it being blue . . .

Perhaps I'll see what you gazed on.

Strokes her hair . . . The frost of his longstanding no melts completely. His old life trails off. There are new colors in the air. They tease him with possibilities.

His eyes alter. Now red burning things, they gaze at the troubled face of the moon.

It wishes it had eyelids . . . It's seen more than its share of unending, wretched damned dance itself into decay, and despair unraveling until its little better than a moth-eaten corpse, and not nearly enough magic. It would pay—almost anything, to turn off the turmoil and brutality, if only for a night or two.

*(After Jack O'Connell's 2003: in the dark corner
with a drifter named loftus and Neko Case's Blacklisted)*

Epilogue for Two Voices

A gray shore. The gnawing murmurs of small waves. A rock as weathered as the throne some miles away.
Dusk gleams.

	Thale sits upon a rock as grey as the mists of the lake. His hands are open as if he has let questions fly from them. He closes his eyes as his right hand begins to reach toward Carcosa, toward Camilla, but he lets it fall away.
	Enter a masked stranger who stands at Thale's left shoulder.
The Masked Stranger:	Struggle not, Thale. The moon and the suns have set.
Thale:	(*Thale slowly turns a ring resting in the palm of his hand. He looks at it as if it might speak to him.*) For . . . ever?—Are there no more openings in the forest of time? No space in the undergrowth? I remember a bird whispering in the olive tree, the aroma of a harvest . . . I walked winding passages to ivory sheets as glorious as sunlit clouds. After, I stood at a window where sunset spoke . . . Why must dusk come like a blade to dismiss—
The Masked Stranger:	Weary poet, must even the stars and the banquet of the spider be explained?
Thale:	Have I no time? (*Thale slides the ring into a pocket.*)

The Masked Stranger: To waste here like blind hands scraping night's stone hymn?

Thale: (*He turns and looks upon the featureless ivory mask.*) To settle the errors of day ... (*Thale looks down at his hand. His thumb gently rubs a fingertip.*) I remember the whisper of a petticoat on my fingertips ... There was no frost then.

The Masked Stranger: (*The Masked Stranger has not moved. Not even the scalloped tatters of his pallid robe flutter.*) I will not discuss your sensibilities, or innocence, or your sister's lovers. The wings of the End are in view, there is no time for portraits of being.

Thale: Who are you, sir? Are you a poet who knows the all the orbits of the heart?

The Masked Stranger: I am not a chapel. Nor am I the spade. I am merely the ferryman. (He looks away from Thale to the lake. The still surface holds no reflection of sun, moon, or stars. A small boat slowly glides to *shore. It comes to rest before them.*) Nothingness is unnamable ... And immortal. (*Thale opens his mouth, but all his hours, beggars, can not even whisper.*) Come now. (*But neither moves.*) Vision and festivals are over. Nights of flowers and reason are letters memory has forgotten.

Thale: Forgotten? (*Thale places his hands upon his knees. He turns to the Masked Stranger, but does not look upon the ivory mask. He nudges a dull pebble forward a few inches with the toe of his boot until it rests in the shadow of a large, dark rock.*) Over comes and all is forgotten? True, I was only sitting, waiting, perhaps longer than was necessary, but doing was to come. Even the reed rests between breaths of the raw wind ... Sorrow finds a home among the blue flowers of laughter, then dear light arrives and sorrow moves on to the yellow flowers. I was merely waiting for the light to return ... It can return? Can it not bloom again in this country? (*Thale looks directly at the mask.*) Is there to be no more light? Can the wheels that move the clock hands turn no longer?

The Masked Stranger: Leave your line of questions for other pockets. Movement is speechless and still ... Come, the meadow of Eternity blooms upon the lake. There sits the boat of wintertime. (*The arm of the Masked Stranger resembles a weathered fingerpost. His narrow finger etches a somber line colder than death toward the prow of the small boat.*)

Thale: Do the empty rooms of autumn need my soul to fill their gloomy silence? I am leafless, little more than a drifting grain. (*His hands flutter.*) Is there not some wilder bird of radiant silver with feathers woven of honey-kissed psalms and constellations of moon wine to—

The Masked Stranger: Enough, Child.

Thale: (*His tone more than a question.*) Time? I will cast aside uncertain and all my stony islands of sand. (*His hand, palm up, reaching.*) Turn oblivion and I will flash. I could be a cistern of well, a flock overrun with the bonfire verses of dawn—

The Masked Stranger: Off we go. Let your baggage of everyday rest in the ashes of that time. Yesterday is a tired stone that will not. (*Thale stands, shoulders slumped. He looks like a scarecrow beaten by wind & rain & a hundred bitter seasons. With firm, even strides the Masked Stranger walks to the waiting boat. He steps aboard and beckons to Thale. Thale looks back to Cassilda's keep.)*

Thale: *(In a slow whisper.)* Good-bye, Day. *(The wind rises and turns him to the field of parting. In the thickening fog the Masked Stranger holds a lantern filled with winter.)*

. . .   .

To Live and Die in Arkham

Arkham. A nice upscale college town. Just the right shops and bars and restaurants, grills, and cafes, if you have Money—a name helps too. If you don't, there's the other side of town—the side always twitching with things from the inside of Midnight. The city fathers and the police call it, The Downside. Drugs, and cheap street whores workin' the dreamless corners by pool halls and gin joints and open sewers the city fathers call abandoned buildings where the homeless hide and hungry eyes that will take your cigarettes and your wallet and your watch and your life if you can't walk fast enough or if you're a plain John Q. citizen who is not supposed to be roamin' the cold blocks. That's the side Albert Bergin had come to. He needed something done and this was the place to find fixers and doers of just about anything, if you have the money or the juice.

$200 just for the name and directions to the door. Like anyone needs them, you just follow the rot. But Professor Bergin wasn't looking for some tail or blow ... He had a task that needed to be performed, he called it an old score, and for that he needed someone who knew The Game and how it's played on The Bottom.

✦

"You want him tits-up maggot food. What'd he do? Fuck yer wife while you were at some *sin*-posium fucking your secretary in the ass?" Will laughed. His 9 didn't.

"He is in possession of an article of mine and I want it back."

"Can't blame a hound for not returnin' good pussy. Can ya, Fuckhead? She give good head?"

"I'm not married." Professor Albert Bergin sat rail straight. No smile.

"With that face and that gut I'm not surprised. They got this thing called walking nowdays. Ya might try it. Maybe you'll meet some fat bitch who wants a mercy fuck?"

"Could we skip the . . . *bullshit?*"

"Ah. Now yer talkin'. Get yer thing and get it back to you and kill the fuck—Just like that . . . *That's hard cash.* You prepared to soak me in it?"

"I have money."

"I can see that, but are you willing to part with it? Your jones itch that much?"

"If need be."

"It need be."

"How much?"

"Details, then you get the bill. If you can pay, I play. If you can't. You've wasted my expensive time and you pay in *other ways.* Or you can lay a grand on me right this fuckin' minute and blow. Pick a door, fuckhead."

"I will pay 25,000 dollars."

"You'll pay what I tell you . . . If I do it. And I get half upfront. Now, get on with it."

"Professor Daniel Washington . . ."

❁

Will skipped his regular info gathering. Spreading around cash would be a waste with these bookworm types. He'd follow the guy for a day or two and sit outside his house and see what he did at night. Besides, once Professor Washington showed up on a slab and the cops started digging, Will's name would pop up as a person of interest if he inquired about Washington's name or the address. Better to keep this as far under the radar as he could.

All the prim and proper Miskatonic U crowd had their paper reps and little else, he figured. An old boys and ignored pussies clique, who at the end of the day wanted what everyone else wanted, they just took a deep breath and stayed hush-hush about it.

"Sinful Suzie" Jaymes, 5' 6", 109 lbs., Green/Blonde, 38D [so her doctor said after cashing her check for 10 grand]-25-36, she was a favorite of lawyers, investment suits, and bookworms. Will hit the The Treasure Chest looking for Suzie. They'd been on and off half a dozen times in the past few years and the straights really lost it for her. She came on like a librarian turned feral and if you had the cash she had the ass, many of her clients said it could start a revolution, or she had any other part your kink required.

Lap dances in your home. Blow jobs in your car. Bubble baths or spankings in hotel rooms, you pick it she pretty much did it, just so as you paid up before the ride.

Will bought her a drink and asked if either Washington or Bergin were on her dick list. Washington was a no go to both the name and the photo, but Bergin was known. Some of the girls said he was heavy handed. A real Mr. Wham-BAM!. He'd spread around some big money to cover the scars he'd left on a couple of girls.

"He's been in here sniffing around, but never looked at me. Never looked at any of the girls with big tits. Likes 'em skinny and young I hear. Your mark is a hardcore power-tripper. No fuckin', only head. You peel, dance around a little, and give. He gets. You've met the type."

Will had. Fuckin' pussy scumbags. They'd bounce a woman around—fists or whatever else was handy when they popped, but didn't have the balls to even talk hard to other men. Fit his assessment of Bergin.

He left her a C-note and told her he'd call her.

He hit the street. Time to circle the target's nest and see how to play this out.

❧

Will got all the formal paperwork on the S. French Hill St. property of Daniel Washington from the bureaucracy first then cased the house. Two floors, open access from the back and sides, and a botanical garden's worth of trees and deep, tall scrubs all around. Almost the perfect place for a quick and quiet in and out.

1 P.M. Sunny. A model afternoon on a model street. He walked up the steps and rang the doorbell. He had his line ready should need arise. Waited. Played it casual. Looked in windows—bookcases and bookcases and bookcases. Suppressed a laugh examining the lock.

It's a wonder these idiots have indoor plumbing.

Assholes, so deep into their books and lectures and papers they didn't know how to lock up and lock down properly. Not that it really mattered, no one wanted to rob these academic types, their houses were full of books and books and books—like anyone was going to pay good money for Professor Hilary Shitfart's Memoirs of Some Dead Old Fuck From East Boring as Hell or Sir Ralph Fuckface's A Case Study of the Glories of 28 Quiet Sundays in Solitude, and art crap you couldn't pawn easily, not in New England. No expensive TVs, no DVD players, no iPods, bullshit laptops, and next to no jewelry. And tryin' to dump big heavy antiques in this part of the state was a sure fire 3 to 5, the way the Staties were all over the market. Fuck robbin' 'em, they spent their whole lives in their minds.

Tomorrow night. If he was home. If he was alone . . .

✸

Will rang the bell. Daniel Washington answered. Will's gun backed the older man up.

"Sit yer fuckin' ass in that chair and don't say a word. When I ask you a question, you answer, then shut the fuck up. Got it?"

"Yes." Thin, weak, frightened as his eyes. "Good. If you move or talk you die."

Washington nodded.

Will looked around the room . . . He froze. There was a photograph of his mother on the mantle and one on the desk. Expensive frames. Dusted though most of the other things in the room were not.

"Where did you get the pictures?"

"I had them taken nearly thirty years ago."

"Why?"

"I was going to ask Seton to marry me."

His mother's name on the lips of this stranger. The gun was moving right to left. Finger and trigger hungry to talk.

"Keep talking."

"Do you know her?"

"I ask the fucking questions, Asshole."

"I was a student at M. U. Seton worked in the diner on Boundary near St. Mary's. We were in love."

"What happened?"

"Why are you so interested? Did you—"

"I said, *I ask the questions.*"

"There was a terrible— She died."

"I know that."

Daniel Washington looked at the man. He had her eyes. Her coloring. Could this somehow be her child?

How could he be?

"If you want to live you'll tell me everything you can about you and her. Start right fucking now."

"We were young and in love. I was a poor student working my way through my second year at M. U. We dated for almost a year. One night on her way home from work she was savagely attacked near Hangman's Hill. Beaten, raped, and horribly scarred by her attacker. I went to the hospital several times to see her, but she wouldn't see me. A nurse told me her face was horrible to look at."

Will remembered her face, and the black veil she hid it under. He'd been four, maybe five. Remembered coming out of his bedroom in the small flat and seeing her crying before the mirror. He'd screamed. She closed the bathroom door.

"Two weeks after the attack I received a letter from Seton saying telling me to leave her alone. I went to her rooming house but her landlady said she'd moved away. I couldn't find her . . . Back then I had very limited resources. Several years later I heard she died. That's about all I know."

Will knew the back end of her story. She scrubbed floors for a living. Drank gin straight from the bottle. And tried to never touch him. She didn't abuse him, but she couldn't stand to touch him. She didn't like to talk to him either. When he was eight she slit her wrists in the tub with a broken gin bottle and he went to the orphanage. After that he went to jail and back to jail and back to jail . . . From the age of eight until seventeen days after his twenty-fourth birthday he was locked up.

And sitting before him was the only link to his past he'd every met. Ever heard of. He was here for money not to face his past. Will tried to keep his nights full and avoid solitude or any point in time where his mother's ghost would sit across the table or at his elbow and watch him. It was like surf, rising, a great weight pulling him from his mental steeping stones toward . . . Outside. The zone of stark, lonely dunes no drug could cure, no woman could kiss away.

What the fuck is this shit?

"I said everything." The rules are simple the 9 said. "And I meant *everything.*"

A delicate, hollow blind man lost in the echo of a love song frightened to death by evil, Daniel Washington went down in the dark place of cold rain better left undisturbed.

"Back then I had nothing but her smile and my dream. She gave me so much love, made me so very happy, then they told me she was . . . When she wouldn't talk to me, see me, I searched for details. When you take Valentine's Day from a man he seeks redemption. For me it was in facts."

All the horror came out. Fact after fact. The ones carved in stone and the ones his heart knew but could not prove.

"I own a gun, but have never had the guts to shoot him."

"Who?"

"I can prove nothing."

"Give me the fucking name."

Daniel Washington was trying to make sense of this, but couldn't get his mind around it. All these years he'd been faithful to her memory and now this man he thought might be her son was going to kill him. How? Why?

"The fucking name."

"Albert Bergin raped her. Left her for dead."

Will tried to catch his breath. He'd sat in a room face to face with the monster that had killed his mother and sent him into the tombs.

The two men in the room were stone. Outside the world in an episode of cursed sensations. In a distant valley, naked, raped, no roof or sky, only despair . . . And anger. Crawling from the labyrinths of heart and mind. Claws bared. Hate sharpened and raw. Hate and claws becoming the everywhere. The red wind screamed the monster's name.

The gun lowered. Eyes choking back tears.

"I can't be completely certain it was him."

The room the contract was written in was in Will's mind. The face, he studied it and studied it. Took it apart. Something about that face. The set of the jaw. The nose . . . It was like . . . Looking in a mirror.

The gun almost slipped from his hand. Will had never known a single fact about his father until this minute. Now he knew too much.

"Look at me. Can you see him in my face? Do I look like him?"

Daniel Washington strained to see through his tears. And it was there.

"Exactly how old are you?"

Will told him. Washington's expression told him the final fact.

"Your jaw, your nose—he's your father. You're the product of—"

"Rape."

The air was almost too solid to breathe.

"Can I tell you something?"

"Sure."

"Albert Bergin and I were rivals in school. We were both studying the same subject. I was a better student and quicker. Our professors favored me. I know Bergin disliked me and was jealous ... Everyone knew how in love I was. I think he raped your mother to unseat me. If I stumbled in my studies he could catch up, maybe surpass me. He destroyed her because of professional jealousy. I always knew he had a black heart, but ... I can't believe I never saw this before. Guess I've always thought he was drunk or something and lost his temper."

"But why do you think it was him?"

"Once in the library he was a little drunk. He was reading the newspaper. He had this, almost triumphant, grin on his face. I don't know, the cat that ate the canary, maybe? It was pleased with itself, and evil. Cold. *It was very cold.* And I thought I heard him say, 'She should have shut up.' When he got up he left the paper and I went over and looked at the article he had been reading. It was about your mother and the rape. I should have went after him and killed him. I went to the police but they didn't believe me. A friend of his family was the investigator on the case and thought because we were rivals in school I was trying to tarnish him."

Will wanted to be out in the cool night air. Running. Running from the photos, running to someplace where he could get a drink and his bearings.

"I'm not here for the reason you think. Bergin sent me to get something and bring it to him. *And to kill you.*"

"What are you to get for him."

"A book. Faded red leather with a scorpion like emblem on the cover."

"The Navarre. It all makes perfect sense. We both studied philosophy, religion, and metaphysics back then. Do you believe in magic or the supernatural?"

"No."

"I do. And so does Bergin. That's what we pursued in our studies."

"Ghosts and shit?"

"No. More like a little-known religious belief. There is a race of terrible beings who once savaged the universe. Somehow they were imprisoned, awaiting a time when they would be free. We tried to separate myth from fact regarding these entities. As a believer I have always sought to understand as much as I can to keep them imprisoned, if that's possible. Bergin had a jealous nature and was power hungry. His lust led him to dark places and darker studies. The book he wants is said to contain rituals and spells to free these otherworldly beings."

"Like bring the things here? He wants to tear the roof off Hell and let these monsters out?"

"Yes."

"That's fucked up."

"I'm going to kill him."

"No you're not. My mother, he owes me for her. And for *my life*."

"Then let me have some retribution too. Your gun is too merciful. I know a way."

"I'm listening."

Daniel Washington stood, he seemed dry, a faded summertime photograph, and walked to a bookcase. The ghost hand, now off its knees, deliberate, pushed a hidden button and a door opened. There sat a book and what looked like a rusty iron can.

"Take these items to him."

"Is that the book?"

"It's an exact copy. The real one is locked up."

"And that thing."

"Something he will think is one thing, but it is something entirely different."

"What does he think it is?"

"He will think it holds magical vapors which grant vision. A mage who studied the things Bergin and I have studied once said, *'Great Cthulhu sleeps in his house and shapes the dream of what shall be, dead Cthulhu waits dreaming.'* Based on an incorrect translation, Bergin believes with these vapors he'll be able to see into the dreams of this being."

"Shit's poison. Ain't it?"

"Something far worse."

"You sure he'll be dead?"

"Yes. Certain."

"What do I do?"

"Just give him this and leave."

"Huh?"

"Tell him I'm dead and give him this copy of the book—tell him it's the only one you found. Tell him as compensation you picked this up, thinking it might interest him. Tell him you saw the sigil and it being the same as the one on the cover of the book you thought they might be related in some fashion. Then leave. *Do not stay there.* You do not want to be in the house when he opens this."

"Why? Is it going to blow up?"

"Something like that."

"I'll be back."

❦

Will rang the bell. Albert Bergin answered. Will's gun backed the older man up.

"There's your shit. Where's my money?"

The 9 was heat-soaked stone ready for blood. Bergin knew it.

"He's dead?"

"No, Fuckhead. I put him on a plane to Vegas with a blonde. Yes. Dead as yer grandmother's pussy. My money—now!"

"Of course. I just want to see the book first."

"Then look."

Bergin opened the backpack.

"This is not it."

"It's all I could find. The thing on the cover looks like you said it did. You said it was written in French. That looks like fucking French to me. And there's no fucking doubt it's old. The fucking thing's falling apart. The old fuck was crying before I shot him, said it was a copy. Look at that can-thing I grabbed while I was there."

Bergin removed the object from the bag. If a demon could be delighted with an unexpected present, his eyes said he was.

"This is . . . Navarre's. How? Where was this?"

"With the book. It's got the same logo thing on it as the book. Figured they went together or something. Now where's my money."

Bergin began to open the container.

"Fuck that! You ain't openin' that fucking thing while I'm here. I seen shows on TV about when they opened those old tombs in Egypt and I ain't breathin' in any old germs that would lay my ass over in Potter's Field. You can wait 'til I count my money and leave."

Bergin sat the container on his desk.

"It's all there. Count it. And leave."

Will picked up the brown manila envelope and began counting.

"We're square. You have fun with yer fuckin' shit there and forget my name and that you ever saw me." Will leveled the 9 at him. "You understand?"

"Yes."

And Will was gone.

Bergin's hands opened the vessel containing Navarre's Vapors. Coughed. His hands burned. Cold and shadows came into the room . . .

Tentacles of yellow/greenish curling smoke. A burnt odor. The sound of roaring fire in howling wind and a great grinding. Albert Bergin has It in his hands and It has him in its hands . . .

Will had been locked up in labyrinths and abysses for years and years, passed from hand to hand by creatures with demonic faces and demonic hearts of utter blackness. Cast into a life of Hell by the demonic hands of his father. Will heard a scream inside the house. Remembered the first time he'd screamed when the creatures had him in their hands . . .

Will remembered some bookworm in a bar once saying something about the child is the father to the man. He wasn't sure just what the guy meant by it, but he knew his take on it. "Just returning the lesson, Daddy."

The real world in slow motion. Will lit a cigarette. Starting walking away from Back. "Who says that's just the way it is? I've never hit a woman or sold dope to kids." *Never killed anybody that didn't have it coming.* "Maybe I still have options."

He took a drag off his smoke. The sun was out. He started walking toward Daniel Washington's house . . .

The Last Twenty Miles of Wandering Again

for David Crosby

"The people in my songs are all me."—Bob Dylan

1955. Tomorrow somewhere down the line . . .

Me and Dylan (sparrows—from the start never good with floods, goodbyes, and the la-de-da's of mermaids) got older. Got our parts shaded in. We twisted some. Sought a few thrills. The cheap kind, we didn't have much cash back then. Many brains either.

Roared when we crossed time and place.

We shoulda tried a feat with a guarantee.

Didn't.

Wound up letting the rain in . . .

Figured the morning light would dry things.

Didn't.

Pity.

Horses, borrowed cars, leaky boats, or sand & sun smoothed boot leather a bit faster than gentle strides, over the decades we'd poked around some . . . Spent a night with a cactus that cried. Said there was no flash in his pan . . . Spent an afternoon in a church house whose dignity couldn't escape senile, though it had money enough to retain a good lawyer . . . Rode the New Purple Sage in the Madmonths. Neither of us tanned so well . . . Made it through The Echoes without seeing a single bride . . . Took in the portraits of a few hearts in Gone City, as it was the Between Season the bedsprings creaked louder than usual when heartbreak cried . . . Avoided the demon-brewed opiates of the O Z . . . 4th of July 1969 passed as we parked at the Fell Behind & Forgot What's It's Like Bar in Babaluma . . .

Cages, traffic, needles filled with brightlights, butterscotch dinners in Candyland, we spent space-time trying to confuse the cosmos (we called it payback) ... Sometimes, when we were in a good mood, with nonviolent performances ...

The road our chain. Sowing wind, never crying over storms or wishing for gentle bundles of botanical rainbows—not too often anyway. Not bound for heaven or glory, never seemed like it was time for solutions.

There and way the hell over here, looked or took: Old faces happy they weren't alone; Nights dining on bare bones; Lost buttons and keys and words, many, many words to rivers of circumstance; Wasted history on menus that weren't serving Today; Dry days— hustled by blue, we turned our lamps down low, flowed with sin; Hard luck up a hard country tree; Bottle-backing long-neck Thens in a Rattlesnake Gulch juke-joint offered nothing but gone away; Stood on golden sand and filled our pockets with tears; Felt so good when we—in full masquerade, were benched by the future for a beast with a bigger bat; Lost secrets when the wind lifted her reckless skirt ...

Served time—won't say we played it well ... And played tourists broke down at a fork in the road ... time and time again ... From the Sierry Petes clear to the partly cloudy peaks of Mtn. Belzoni ...

Stepped outta night's black light only to find bloodlaw sprawled over a stray sideshow ... Traded business cards with the Heron King's monk at the ancient gates of Bakeblikk, figured they'd be good to patch the holes in our umbrellas when the snow came callin' ... Tore up the islands on our last outta the country. Didn't tilt at the white windmills, sat with a shape-shifting today (first page to third chapter) in a meadow on Mykonos. The sun was a titan. Wind rose up, slammed the door. We didn't stick around to see who'd clean up the mess ...

Never found a virgin angel, or got a glimpse behind the flowing white beard of the great sage, we did however procure a pack of smokes from him—snuck out without paying ... Ate enough style and form for two lifetimes—for all the good it did ... Kept turning over rocks looking for friends only to find just begun.

Just two old boys in a patchwork cowboy movie tryin' to get by or get around. Without getting' took down ...

We met Bloom and his lead monkey at a crossroads that had never seen mercy. He rode up on a grey horse. Had a fistful of bad time in his pocket and the world pinned to sleeve. Asked if we knew if there was a doctor around.

Never had the knack for second sight, we shook our heads no.

He rode away.

Another soul always on the go-go.

Heard he didn't get far.

Just then we couldn't go back. Straight ahead looked cold and way too tight. We turned left.

Maybe shoulda gone back. Not that home was a choice. Maybe shoulda not walked into all that blood.

The streets were grey poured over grey. Worn. Picked over by something hostile, something that stung and turned fields to fire.

Could see it didn't happen in a day. Or a week.

Figured too many were nights killed trying to wring unknown hours out of tongues. Truth didn't come. Darkness did. Came deep and stained in blood.

Lots of stars fell.

Dreams too.

Sky got cold.

Everything got hard.

Some that didn't dare dream passed their prayer beads didn't survive the gunshot wounds.

The phantoms still trapped here call the place Carcosa. Pointed to the palace, said, "Cassilda lives there."

So that's where we headed.

Messrs. Tweedle Dee and Tweedle Dum maybe shoulda turned and run.

Didn't.

We'd been headed this way since that rainy night in '55. Figured we should finish what we started. Didn't figure on coming up a dollar short.

Met two tattered hobos standin' at the rusted gates of the cage. Said they'd come from a life of slavery on the Mississippi when the moon came up and told them their days were numbered. They had a tree staked out, had a rope, but it was too short. Gave 'em ours. Looked long enough.

Before we walked on, we saw them fold up the past and tuck it in their pockets. Dylan said he figured it would fall out of the holes in their pockets when their boots came off. I didn't disagree.

I didn't stop to buy postcards from the pot-bellied vulture with the sugar-coated bleet. Even if I had a stamp to cover the ride, who back in that civil war wanted whispers from a million miles away?

We moved from there to HERE. Looked down and sure enough there we were, standing right on the efficient red X.

Dylan said: "Seems we're expected."

"Seems so."

I took two-bits from my change purse and dropped them in the conveniently positioned coin-slot by the entry bars. They opened and we moved on down the road.

Happened on two crows and a raven singing 'bout frozen summer days on the palace steps. Their pockets were loaded with the choices of the deaf man and the blind. Told us the wedding bells were rusted and wouldn't ring. Just thought we should know. Then they laughed.

So much for sentimental.

Heard dogs barkin', but we never bought information from hounds that couldn't shake the dark clouds from their tails.

We came upon Thale and Uoht sittin' in the foyer picking tedious from their albatross veils.

Dylan looked at me. I looked at him. Expressions said, funny how much they look like the bums we lent our rope too.

Thale asked if one of us was Romeo. Dylan said his middle name was Casanova. Did that count?

Uoht was pretty sure it didn't. But if he had the stomach for it, he might get away with a few misdemeanors. Said: "Just remember to be polite." Asked what we though of the yellow wallpaper.

I mentioned as a wanderer in moonlight I didn't have the imagination to comment on his treasure without the moonlight on.

Dylan said he was sorry but currently blue was his thing and he hadn't attended medical school. He could do red and/or back-stabbing, at least since he crashed his car into this week, but wasn't good on yellow. Not since the teacher broke the No. 2 on the back of his hand.

I asked if Cassilda was in.

Uoht told me since the stranger in the yellow mask stopped in, she'd become so overgrown with stark naked she didn't get out much.

Hankering, Dylan smiled.

Still got a few prurient fantasies our boy. When he's not crying that is.

I thought he was going to laugh. Mostly he does when it comes to spiritual matters.

Holding out my Get-out-of-jail-FREE card, I followed up with, "Do I need an appointment?"

Thale replied, my low profile would be OK, but the tattered sleeves of my war coat would have to go.

I guess the extra miles had let too much of my time runaway, and the humanity of my Sunday-go-to-meeting finery had faded when I tried to open the windows on all those driftwood horizons.

Uoht asked if we'd come to see the movie.

"Are we in time?" Dylan asked.

"You can catch the last show," Thale replied. "Down the hall and to the left. Pick any seat you like," he said, taking my Get-out-of-jail-FREE card as a down payment.

They hadn't turned down the lights yet when we entered the theater.

Dylan's sole comment, "Looks like someone shoulda started a fire and made off with the insurance settlement."

Guinevere was sitting with Anita Berber and her little monkey. They were holding hands. There was something wicked in the way they were singing "Love Is a Crime."

Monsieur Sartre was sitting in the back row on a hardback wooden director's chair. His popcorn was on the empty seat beside him. Asked if we liked Woody Allen pictures.

Told him we'd already done Broadway—the hard way.

He scrunched up his face, turned away in distaste. Waved at the ladies. "Yes. Love is a crime, Dear Ladies."

Guess painting the town is tiring work.

Our gazes rolled over the rows.

The Poe-Eddie, down in the front, in the threadbare seats, was stitching editorial notations in the margins of his worn copy of "Closed on Account of Rabies." We decided we didn't want to sit by him and get feathers stuck in our hair.

On the aisle, slumped, Sisyphus was sleeping. Not snoring, but the candle in his losing hand looked like it needed a serious overhaul.

As we'd been baptized with rocks earlier in our careers we moved along.

"Thought we were supposed to meet Cassilda?"

"She's not in here," the hunchback usher said.

Dylan pointed to a weathervane.

It said EXIT so we did.

Fast.

We cruised around the horn and saw the doors. Big and black. Ornate carvings, all the tell tale signs. The Yellow Sign parked right dead center in the last one on the right.

Kinda said leave yer perception HERE.

We didn't.

Hadn't before. Why start now?

Dylan knocked. Said: "Care to try open Sesame?"

Fresh outta abracadabra since we had words with the bronze-eyed troll on the Bridge of Bane I figured I'd give the door handle a shot.

It opened.

The room didn't blaze with treasure. Little but ghosts and spider webs breathed in the Pale Queen's chamber.

The ill-fated heads of tiny beheaded birds were scattered in corners twisted with ink-black shadows. Slain by assassins of sin, or sorrow, or envy, the cracked faces of several watches out of history no longer offered ever-shifting tales.

This was the room where the levy had broken and all hope had spilled out.

Cassilda turned when she heard our footsteps interrupt her blue weaving.

She sat on a ragged old bed. The once golden bed-sheets, about the size of an elephant or the top sail of a galleon, were torn (faded, and soiled) and thrown on the floor. The only thing she had on was a crown of dead moths and rings of gold on her toes.

Guess when you reside in Paradise you don't need articles of sartorial design, or maybe all the local haberdashers just up and fell from the vine.

Cassilda had three teardrops tattooed on her cheek below her right eye. One on her chin. Several descending the slope of her alabaster breast and a pool of tears on her belly. The last splash creating ripples.

She saw us looking. "These." Her finger moving south from teardrop to teardrop. "Well, I dried up when Dear Orence left—The moon came, whispered, everything is wide open, he followed like desire's migratory bird . . . I had these done to remember days that blossomed where the summer waters flow."

Out of spells to dazzle, my lips were dry. Too much fight, not enough won I guess.

"Oh my. You're not Stanley and Livingstone. I don't believe you're supposed to be in here."

"Sorry I was just following my nose," Dylan said.

"Are you here to feast on myths?"

"Just passin' through, ma'am."

Her tiny mouth formed an O. No word came out.

That's when the school bell rang and she pointed to the curtains.

So much for our date to have soul food.

We followed the direction of her finger. Left her to her hard time lonesome day.

Drifted past thirty-two doors . . . Not a one with an OM or a tortoise, or even a late hare . . . Didn't see one that said OPEN ME . . .

Came to the end of the hall without tongues and the gift of gab.

And the last door. Cold and covered in ghost skin.

"Last piece of the puzzle?"

I shrugged my weak maybe.

Dylan opened the door. Didn't need a key.

The waiting room of the anesthetist. Silent white walls. Stiff white chairs. White carpet crawling with dull melodies.

Sign said: Dr. Archer

A white door opened and there stood the day nurse. Legs like blasphemy and curves that could bend the mind of a squid.

Taking in the hot curves of the nurse with the cold ugly eyes behind unsightly horn-rimmed eyeglasses I skipped the "Helloooo, Nurse."

That met with a stern frown you couldn't cut down with Conan's sword. Dylan and me, we been neck deep in mud before.

Scowling (demons shining in the corners of her eyes): "We are not very prompt, are we?"

Dylan to me: "If you weren't a worn out star, you might get a smile."

Gave him my best does-everything-have-to-be-my-fault look, said: "It's just the price we pay for lost celebrity."

"And who do we have here? Mister Dylan and Mister Black & Blue I take it."

Hands in his pockets, Dylan shrugged.

I nodded. Felt like I was wagging my tail.

She said: "The Doctor will see you now."

I could tell by her rusty-iron-bell tone she gave Dylan the creeps.

"Back from the ends of the earth," I said in my best it's-a-laugh voice.

She just stood there holding the door open. Didn't bother to hide the big horse needle with the vile foaming goo inside. Didn't even smile.

Across the lion's jaw threshold we stepped.

Dr. Archer (his cold ugly eyes behind unsightly horn-rimmed eyeglasses) stood—dressed like a valet in a top-dollar 5 star, said: "Well, you boys are just in time."

We could see the gallows out his window.

Just then I couldn't manage a snappy, so we are.

Dylan said: "Maybe we shoulda just bought the damned post-cards?"

He looked at this hand. I saw the splinters.

I cocked my head to the side and lifted my shoulder in a slow shrug. "Or maybe we should have squandered a few more minutes waiting for Godot?"

"Woulda been hard. Place didn't have a dining room."

"No beds, either."

"And they never turned off the lights. Hard to have happy little dreams with lights blazing plain as day all the time."

Dr. Acher's sweeping hand cast a shadow on the couch. Sounded like Gabriel blowing his horn . . .

We sat.

He sat on his throne, shuffled some official-looking papers and in his best evil-stepfather voice, said: "You can set your hats and boots there. You'll have no need of them in as you stroll My Garden."

Dylan and me chimin' in twin harmony: "And they say the road goes on forever."

(after a series of "modern" Dylan songs and an Easter-nap dream)

Acknowledgments

S. T. Joshi, thanks for being my editor a second time around!

Stan Sargent, thanks for listening and always having just the right comment, prodding, and being my friend!

Bob Price, Then & NOW, The Firestarter!

Robert Bloch, your terrors have never left me! Thanks for Norman, Jack, and Juliette!

Laird Barron, your praise humbles me. A million thanks for the intro!

Bob Dylan, Bohren and Der Club of Gore, Weather Report, Brian Eno, John Lee Hooker, and *David Sylvian*, thanks for the music, it was the best company a voyager could have.

Derrick Hussey, thanks for being crazy enough to do it again.

Clark Howard, thanks for whispering in my ear about "The Other Stuff" at an early age.

Robert W. Chambers, thanks for invading my brain (and heart) with your (still!) beguiling King In Yellow tales!

Frank Zappa, thanks for showing me it was OK to mix them together.

Thomas Ligotti and *Michael Cisco*, thanks for helping unlock the nature of Night for me.

Jack O'Connell, thanks for always blowing my mind with your amazing tales!

a certain Mr. Hopfrog, Esq., thanks again old friend!

Alanna Quinn, thanks for the Yellow Chamber [again!] and for being so inspiring!

a certain Lady L, thanks for going through these so painstakingly and your very kind and thoughtful comments!

David Schultz, thanks for the splendid job building *Blood*, and this one.

And to every musician, band, artist, film, writer, etc. listed in my story endnotes, thanks for the insprations and the *often* astonishing works! Much of this book would not exist without your talents sparking fires in this cauldron I call my brain!

With respect and admiration,

a bEast

JOE PULVER started his publishing career in the 1990s with a number of short stories published in various American small press magazines, foremost among them was Robert M. Price's *Crypt of Cthulhu*. His tales cover subjects ranging from Robert Wiene's *The Cabinet of Dr. Caligari* to H. P. Lovecraft's Cthulhu Mythos and Robert W. Chambers's *King in Yellow*.

His professional debut came with the publication of his Lovecraftian novel, *Nightmare's Disciple*.

In addition to various American small press magazines, Joe's work has been featured in numerous anthologies in the USA, UK, and Japan, including: *Black Wings: New Tales of Lovecraftian Horror, The Tindalos Mythos, Spawn of the Green Abyss, The Book of Eibon, Lin Carter's Anton Zarnak: Supernatural Sleuth,* and *Rehearsals for Oblivion*.

Of Pulver and his latest work (*Blood Will Have Its Season*), published by Hippocampus Press, critically acclaimed author Thomas Ligotti has said, "Some writers one admirers and others make one want to do as they do, or try. For me, Joe Pulver is of the latter type. His imagination is so vile so much of the time that it makes me giggle with amazement. And the prose so deadly visionary. I'm grateful that the pieces in this collection are those of a fellow horror writer who has raised the ante on what it means to be such a creature."

Multiple award-winning Lovecraftian biographer and scholar, S. T. Joshi, has said, "The prose of Joe Pulver can take its place with that of the masters of our genre—E. A. Poe, H. P. Lovecraft, Ramsey Campbell, Thomas Ligotti—while his imaginative reach is something uniquely his own."

Acclaimed Lovecraftian editor, scholar, and writer, Robert M. Price has stated: "From the earlier book (*Nightmare's Disciple*) I already recognized Pulver's genius in his ability to shape-shift stylistically between Raymond Chandler and Thomas Ligotti—without you even noticing! Like the gospel demon, his name ought to be Legion, since he assumes a new voice and persona as every particular chapter or sequence requires. In the new book, Pulver's polyphonic gifts mutate to a new and even more powerful pitch. The short scope of these many works allows him to write less leisurely, more rapid-fire. The author possesses another unique gift. The only way I know to describe it is to say that he combines the headlong, violent pace and savage sensibilities of Robert E. Howard with the refined and baleful mood of Robert W. Chambers and Tom Ligotti, and all this in an intricate, almost blank verse poetic diction. There is nothing like it!"

Joe Pulver has also been the editor of *Midnight Shambler* and *Tales of Lovecraftian Horror,* and edited collections by Ann K. Schwader (*The Worms Remember*) and John B. Ford (*Dark Shadows On the Moon*).

Joe is currently working on a new novel.